THE OTHER SIDE
OF MORNING

Jo Lambert

Published in 2014 by ThornBerry Publishing UK
ISBN 978-1-909734-23-4

Also available as an Ebook

ThornBerry Publishing UK,
South Gloucestershire, England
http://www.thornberrypublishing.com

BOOKS BY JO LAMBERT

When Tomorrow Comes

Love Lies and Promises

The Ghost of You and Me

Between Today and Yesterday

Dedication

With thanks...

To my wonderful editor Kit Domino for all her hard work in ironing out the wrinkles and setting me on the right pathway.

To Jane Dixon Smith for yet another stunning cover... choosing this first was great inspiration for the writing.

To the awesome Cathy Helms for putting together an amazing book trailer.

Enormous thanks to Jane Risdon for all the background knowledge on rock band tours.

And finally to my muses, without whom my characters would never be able to be brought to life.

Disclaimer

All characters, institutions, organisations, events and some locations in this publication, other than those clearly in the public domain, are fictitious and any resemblance to any actual institution, organisation, or person, living or dead, is purely coincidental.

Cover Design

Jane-Dixon Smith

1996

ONE

'Do you know something, Anna? I'd always fantasised about falling in love in paradise,' Lucy Benedict admitted with a dreamy sigh. Stretching out on her sunbed she ran her fingers casually through her thick, dark curly hair.

'And now, Holy Dooley, it's happened.' Her bikini clad companion, Australian Anna Singleton, rolled over to look at her friend. Wrinkling a small, neat turned-up nose dusted with freckles, she giggled. 'He's a bonza bloke, Luce! You're one lucky girl.'

Lying next to Anna on the golden beach fronting the beautiful Balinese resort of Amankila, Lucy closed her eyes, enjoying the warmth of the mid-morning sun. The sea sparkled, the breeze was warm; yes, this really was paradise and yes, she really was blissfully in love. All her dreams had come true in a way she could never have imagined they would.

Lucy loved travelling; the last few years of her life had been an absolute blast. Starting off in Europe, exploring each country in turn, she had gradually worked her way towards South East Asia, where she had spent the last year. Sometimes she stayed in hostels, and sometimes when the whim took her, she spoiled herself with five-star luxury. It was a life of adventure and meeting people, with the occasional relationship thrown in if some special man took her fancy and chose to share her journey for a while.

She had met her pretty red-headed companion in a bar in Bangkok. Anna, who was also travelling around South East Asia, might be the same age as her but as they got talking Lucy began to see their lives were worlds apart. Brought up in a working-class family in Brisbane with a truck driver father and a stay-at-home mother, Anna had told Lucy her parents had put every penny of their savings towards sending her and her older sister to university. Although most of her school friends had decided on a gap year before they settled down to university life, Anna felt she owed it to her parents to get her degree first. It was while she was studying she decided she was going to travel during her year off, and set about finding a part-time job in order to put money away. She did bar work, cleaning, even pizza delivery to save for her holiday of a lifetime. Now, however, her money had run out and she was about to get a flight home. She couldn't wait to see her parents, she said, they were so proud of her success and there would be big celebrations on her return.

Lucy thought about Anna's situation: working hard, achieving her first class honours in English, with plans to become a journalist. She knew how easily it could have been her story too. Instead, as soon as she was twenty-

1

one and inherited her trust fund, she had walked out of Exeter University in the last year of her Business Administration degree course, grabbed her passport and headed straight for Heathrow and a flight to Paris.

Unable to face her parents, she had written them a letter instead, explaining her reasons for leaving, knowing even before she put pen to paper they would never really understand. How could they when they were both work-driven and successful? I'm young, she told them, plenty of time to think about a career. Right now there was a big old world waiting out there and a huge amount of money for her to draw on. It had all been fun, and at first she didn't feel at all guilty. However, recently there had been moments, usually in the early hours of the morning when unable to sleep, she lay alone in her bed staring at the ceiling and wondering whether, once this adventure was over, she would ever be able to go home and face them. Guilt had pricked her conscience to such an extent she had decided to treat her friend to three weeks in Amankila before Anna returned home to Brisbane.

Amankila was a cluster of Balinese beach houses – rooms and suites – nestled in lush hillside vegetation facing the sea. The resort was linked by elegant, raised stone walkways which connected rooms, suites, pools, restaurants and other public areas. It was breath-takingly beautiful bathed with the golden glow of artificial light each evening when darkness fell and so very peaceful. Lucy had booked a suite with its own pool which gave them both the option of privacy if they wanted it. But mostly they took advantage of everything on offer. The whole ethos of the place was relaxation and pampering, every creature comfort taken care of. And then, as she thought things could not get any better, quite unexpectedly Ethan Maddison had walked into her life.

It was on their fifth evening, she remembered, when she had gone down to the restaurant for dinner ahead of Anna, totally refreshed after an afternoon of detox, massage and a relaxing yoga session. She was busy studying the menu and wondering whether to suggest they take one of the guided tours tomorrow when she was aware of someone standing over her. Looking up, expecting to see their usual tall middle-aged waiter hovering, she found instead the arrival was well dressed, young and good-looking with a shock of blond hair.

He indicated one of the chairs opposite. 'May I?' Hearing his accent, Lucy noted that like Anna, he was Australian.

'How do you know I'm not waiting for someone?' she challenged, amusement in her smoky brown eyes as they met his incredible blue ones.

'Because,' his mouth lifted into the most exquisite smile, 'despite your protests I have this feeling you are very much alone. And in my world a beautiful woman should always have company for dinner.'

'Behave yourself, Ethan.'

Anna smiled as she joined them. She was wearing the pale turquoise silk dress and matching Jimmy Choo snakeskin sandals which they had purchased at the Gayson Plaza in Bangkok. The shopping trip to a mall packed with designer names had been another of Lucy's generous treats.

'Do you two know each other?' Lucy asked, feeling sure Anna would have mentioned running into someone as tasty as this.

'Let's say Anna's a new acquaintance.' Ethan gave his fellow Australian a friendly grin. 'I bumped into her in the open-air bar earlier – I'm another antipodean on a great adventure. And you, I gather,' his eyes lingered on her warmly, 'must be the Lucy she has told me all about.'

Lucy glowed under his close appraisal. 'Yes. Lucy Benedict. Please, why don't you join us?'

That had been the start of it all. There was something about Ethan which Lucy found totally irresistible. Not only was he very handsome and had the kind of body most women lusted after, he also seemed to encompass everything she wanted in a man. Looks aside, he was great in bed – something she took less than twenty-four hours to discover in her eager pursuit of him. He was also intelligent, with a degree in geology, was an accomplished pilot and excelled in most sports. And, of course, he was fun to be with.

At first, she had been keen to include Anna in all their trips and activities but as Lucy's relationship with Ethan progressed, Anna began to exclude herself during the day, meeting up with them only at breakfast and in the evenings. Today, however, had been an exception; Ethan was scuba diving, and not wanting to join him Lucy had decided to spend some tanning time with Anna.

'I'm so pleased for you.' Anna was now sitting up and hugging her knees, an affectionate expression on her face as she smiled at Lucy.

'You know, he's not like anyone I've ever met before. But I feel bad about you,' Lucy confided. 'After all, you met him first. I feel like I've muscled in.'

'Oh, Luce, please don't.' Anna shook her head as she got to her feet and waved out to a passing waiter. 'Him and me? That was never going to happen.'

'Oh, rubbish.' Lucy pulled off her sunglasses, frowning up at her friend. 'How can you say that?'

'Guess he hasn't told you who his father is then, has he?' Anna replied, as Lucy sat pushing her fingers through her hair.

'No, I haven't a clue,' she said. 'I know Ethan works in the mining industry and his family is quite wealthy, and that his father's name is Jack.'

'Yes, Jack Maddison.'

'Who?'

'Jack Maddison. He owns the Goorumba Diamond Mines. They're in North Western Australia, near Kimberley. He's mega-rich, Luce; very old

3

Australian money. Ethan's great company but I'm realistic enough to know he'd never get serious with me. But you... you're special; a girl from his world.'

A girl from his world. Lucy turned the phrase over in her mind as the waiter arrived and Anna ordered two more orange honey mojitos. *And soon to be something a little more*, she thought as she looked out across the intense blue water of the Lombok Strait, for there was one thing she had not disclosed yet: Ethan Maddison had asked her to marry him.

TWO

Australia. She was really about to land in Australia. Lucy smiled as she looked down at the cityscape of Sydney below. The plane banked and turned seaward before looping back to make its final approach to Kingsford-Smith Airport. Only yesterday she had been immersed in the exotic atmosphere of Bali and now she was about to land in a completely different country, one which she guessed would be more like home. Ethan, however, had assured her Australia was very far removed from anything she had learned about in geography text books at school.

'Don't be fooled into thinking this is going to be a warmer version of Land of Hope and Glory,' he said with a smile and one of his normal soft digs at most things British. 'We Aussies are a very cosmopolitan lot now.'

The plane was lining up for its final approach when Ethan's hand crept over hers. 'Okay, gorgeous?'

His smile could light a room, he's absolutely perfect, she thought with a sigh as her eyes met his – from his highly toned, beautifully tanned surfer's body, to the shock of golden blond hair which fell in tousled disarray over his forehead. And he had the bluest eyes she had ever seen. In fact, she'd known as soon as she met him he would be special. As the plane touched down Lucy squeezed Ethan's hand and smiled back at him; yes, very special, she smiled to herself, thinking of the day ahead and meeting her father-in-law-to-be.

After they had collected their luggage and cleared customs, she followed Ethan out of the airport to where a silver chauffeur-driven Bentley was parked. The blue-liveried driver tipped his cap to her as he opened the rear door of the limousine.

'Morning, Randall.' Ethan gave him a friendly smile as he handed him the luggage for stowing in the boot.

Randall nodded. 'Morning, Mr Ethan. Miss Benedict. Mr Maddison is expecting you for lunch. He's booked a table at The Waterfront, but I'm to take you to the Park Hyatt first where suites have been reserved for you both and you can unpack and freshen up.'

For the next thirty minutes Lucy watched from the darkened windows of the rear of the vehicle as they drove north from the airport on a flat road system punctuated by intersections. Ethan was quiet, occasionally clasping her hand reassuringly. All at once she felt slightly uneasy; was he nervous about meeting his father, worried he might not approve of such a whirlwind romance? After all, her own parents were rich but nothing like this. What if his father thought she was some kind of gold-digger after his son's money?

Pushing the thought to the back of her mind, she tried to concentrate on the scenery outside. There was so much space and variety – residential one moment, business park the next, and everywhere surprisingly green interspersed with an occasional tantalising glimpse of distant high-rise buildings and blue sea. Eventually, they were back to cityscape, the Sydney Harbour Bridge loomed ahead to the left and the Bentley purred to a stop outside their destination.

Extracting their luggage from the boot, Randall tipped his cap and said to Ethan, 'I'll be back in an hour.'

'Make it an hour and a half would you, Randall?' Ethan grinned at Lucy and winked.

'Ninety minutes it is, sir. I'll let your father know.'

The Park Hyatt was one of Sydney's newer hotels. With its artistically curving entrance, it afforded spectacular views across to the Sydney Opera House from the exclusive suites Ethan's father had booked for them. Wrapped in a bath robe, her mass of curly black hair still damp from the shower, Lucy gazed across the water, fascinated by the beautiful shell formation of the great building. A knock drew her to the door where she found Ethan carrying a bottle of champagne and two glasses.

'I thought we'd have a little pre-lunch drink.' He brandished the bottle with a lazy smile which wavered when he saw her expression change. 'Hey what's all this?' Abandoning the champagne, he immediately pulled her into his arms. 'Hun, I know you're nervous but honestly, Dad will love you. What's not to like about you?' Releasing her with a kiss, he returned his attention to the bottle. Foil and wire dispensed with, the cork came away with a healthy pop and an explosion of pale liquid which he caught effortlessly in one of the glasses, tilting it against the bottle until it was full.

'Oh, I forgot – the ring will be here tomorrow,' he told her as they touched glasses. 'It's a beaut. Maddison diamonds, of course, set in platinum. So here's to you and me, babe, and the fantastic life we're going to have together.'

'To us,' Lucy echoed softly, as she swallowed back the champagne, feeling alcoholic bubbles hit her empty stomach. She studied Ethan thoughtfully, her gaze washing over his handsome face and superb physique. *This man is the one*, she told herself, there is no way I can possibly lose him. For goodness' sake pull yourself together, Lucy Benedict, she scolded herself; you can do this.

'Sorry, I'm being very silly, aren't I?' she said as the effect of the champagne kicked in, boosting her confidence and making her feel slightly light-headed. 'You're right. Your dad's going to love me, isn't he?'

'Exactly!' He put his half-empty glass down and stepped closer, his fingers moving impatiently to the ties of her robe. 'Now, before we go meet the big bad wolf, how about a little pre-lunch bed sport, Red Riding Hood?'

Randall was back at one thirty to take them to the restaurant. Lucy had decided on an emerald silk short-sleeved dress and light green Jimmy Choo heels with a matching clutch bag. Her jewellery was expensive but understated: a Tank Français Cartier watch, a thick gold rope chain and matching stud earrings.

Ethan laced his fingers in hers and gave her one of his stunning smiles as she crossed the lobby with him. 'You look fantastic.'

'You're not so bad yourself,' she teased, stretching up to kiss his cheek, enjoying the smell of his Hermes aftershave as they made their way out of the hotel to the waiting limo.

The Waterfront was only a short drive from the Hyatt. With an external canvas awning for al fresco dining running the whole width of the building it, too, had fabulous views of the Opera House. As Randall opened the door and helped her out of the car, she swept her eyes across the tables fronting the restaurant, with their starched white tablecloths and gleaming cutlery, fully expecting to be seated there. However, the Maître d'hôtel led them inside to the main restaurant area where, at a quiet corner table in the cool interior, a large brown-haired man in a pale suit sat perusing the menu.

'Dad!' Ethan's smile widened with pleasure as they approached the table. The Maitre'd backed away discreetly.

His father set his menu down, his features forming into a matching smile as he got to his feet, moved around the table and caught his son in a bear hug.

Eventually Ethan broke away and turned back, reaching out for Lucy's hand. 'And this is my very special girl – Lucy.' He gave her an encouraging smile, pulling her close to him.

'Lucy!' Jack moved over to where she stood and took both her hands in a strong grip, the same blue eyes as Ethan's scanning her from top to toe. He leaned forward and kissed her cheek. 'We meet at last.'

Lucy smiled; it seemed he liked her. She relaxed – everything was going to be fine.

THREE

Lunch had gone extremely well, Lucy thought as the waiter arrived with a tray of coffee. Jack Maddison had not been at all what she imagined. Welcoming and genial, he had asked her about her life in the UK, about her parents in particular and her family generally. He tended to smile a lot. A warm, sincere smile which made her feel he accepted her, even though, as he had said at first, he was slightly shocked at the speed at which his son had made the all-important decision on the woman he planned to spend the rest of his life with. Lucy's eyes went from Ethan to his father. While they were in Bali, Ethan had told her his mother had died five years ago, a fall from a horse which had broken her neck. Since then his father had become married to his work. However, Jack, as he'd insisted she call him, appeared surprisingly relaxed and laidback, never once touching on the subject of the family business. What she did know was that the Maddisons had a 10,000 acre ranch in Western Australia which she would be flying up to visit in a couple of days' time. They also had large house in the exclusive Point Piper district of Sydney, a luxury home on the banks of the Swan River in Perth and a 60 acre island off the Queensland coast.

Ethan was adding sugar to his coffee when his mobile rang. Pulling it from his pocket he checked it and got to his feet. 'Sorry,' he said, 'I'll take this outside if you don't mind.'

As he disappeared, Jack turned to Lucy. 'It's clear my son is totally besotted with you,' his expression clouded, 'but personally, I have to say you worry me a little, Lucy.'

'Oh!' Lucy felt her heart sink, wondering what he was about to say. 'Well, everything I've told you about myself is true, Mr Maddison... Jack. And I'm not a gold-digger, if that's what you think. I honestly love Ethan.'

'Oh, I know you're not lying.' Jack Maddison surveyed her carefully as he paused to take a mouthful of coffee. 'I had my people check you out before this lunch was arranged.' He returned the cup gently to the saucer. 'I'm aware everything you've told me about yourself and your family is true. And I believe you really do love Ethan, but there's something else which makes me a shade uncomfortable.'

'There is?' Thrust into the spotlight, Lucy tried to sound light hearted, but somehow she knew she wasn't going to like what was coming.

'You came into one hell of a lot of money a little over three years ago, young lady, and what did you do? You walked out of university and have been living the life of Riley travelling the world ever since.' He shook his head and gave a soft sigh. 'Now, if you were in my shoes, wouldn't alarm bells be ringing? After all, your family is relatively wealthy but what we have is far beyond that. I don't want my son settling down with someone whose only interest in life is spending money and having a good time. In this family we're grafters; we work. And Ethan will eventually inherit a pretty impressive business empire. I want him to have a wife he can be proud of, not one whose day consists of trivial activities like beauty salons, lunching and shopping for clothes.'

Lucy swallowed hard as she tried to think what she could do to remedy Jack's disapproving view of her. She felt everything slipping away, aware now that her recent lifestyle had perhaps been a little frivolous. She knew she was probably still in deep trouble with her parents, that was one issue she still needed to address, but this more immediate problem required urgent attention – her future depended on it.

'I guess I was overawed by having so much money,' she replied meekly, carefully choosing her words. 'To be honest with you, Ethan was horrified at my extravagance. He kept telling me there was more to life than simply having fun. And Anna, a girl I met in Bali, made me feel guilty too. Her parents went without so she could go to uni. She told me of the debt she owed them and how proud they were of her first class honours degree. I realised then maybe I should have stayed and finished university before travelling.' Lucy bowed her head. 'And I regret that very much now.' She raised her eyes to Jack. 'But I know I can change... only maybe I could do with a little help.' She fastened her gaze on him and gave one of her most beseeching looks.

Jack's expression softened. 'Well...' He pursed his lips and thought for a moment. 'Have you thought about investing rather than spending?'

'Investing?'

'Yes. Look, why don't you come to my offices in Martin Place tomorrow morning? It's only a few blocks away from here. I'll send the car for you at, say, ten thirty. We can discuss it then. Would that be helpful?'

'Yes, perfect.' Lucy smiled, relieved her problems had been solved with one simple suggestion. She still had access to a substantial amount of money and if Ethan's father had anything to do with it, she might even recoup all she'd spent so far.

'Good!' Jack pressed his palms together and smiled. 'Ah, here's Ethan. Now, not a word, eh? This will be our secret. And don't worry, I'll arrange to get him out of your way tomorrow morning.'

'You've done *what*?'

Returning from lunch, Ethan and Lucy had spent the rest of the afternoon in her suite indulging in more champagne and leisurely sexual exploration. Relaxing in his arms afterwards she had accidentally let slip Jack's suggestion.

'But I want to do it, Ethan,' she protested, leaning over him, wild black hair teasing his chest, her pink mouth pushed into a pout. 'Both you and your father have made me realise I have been selfish and irresponsible in many ways, and I want to change. Your father is helping me by giving me the opportunity to do something for myself.'

Ethan shook his head. 'I deliberately asked him not to talk about business and as soon as my back is turned, he's hitting on you to invest money.' He studied her, his expression serious. 'How much are we talking about, Luce?'

'We hadn't got around to detail. But I was thinking of around fifty thousand. I know given your family's circumstances it's probably small change but—'

'On the contrary, Luce, I think it's an awful lot of money. Can you run to that much?'

'Oh, don't worry, I was never allowed to draw on the bulk. Mum wasn't stupid; she must have had a sixth sense I was likely to fly as soon as the trust fund became available, so the money has been controlled. I get full access on my twenty-fifth birthday but,' she ran a teasing finger along his jawline, 'by then it won't be such an issue, will it? We'll be married.'

'You could set up a trust fund for the kids.'

'What kids?'

'The ones we're going to have.' He pulled her down into his arms and kissed her. 'Two boys and a girl.'

'I see you have it all sorted, Ethan Maddison.' She grinned, wrapping her arms around him tightly. 'But I'm afraid colour choice isn't an option. We might have all blue or all pink.'

'Whatever we have, Luce, I'll love them.' He kissed her again. 'And I love you. Thank you for making me the happiest man on earth.'

FOUR

Charlotte Kendrick slung her leather tote over her linen jacketed shoulder and grabbed the tab from the restaurant table. Beside her, her petite friend Beth Reynolds got to her feet and slipped her pink silk jacket over the short black lace dress she was wearing, a puzzled expression in her green eyes.

'Hey,' Beth protested indignantly, making an unsuccessful grab for the bill. 'I thought we were going to split the cost?'

Charlotte closed her fingers possessively over the small piece of paper. 'Changed my mind. It's going to be my treat instead.'

'Lottie!' Beth reprimanded.

'I insist,' Charlotte argued. 'After all, it was me who invited you back to Warwick today for lunch. And it was good to wander the streets and have all those memories of our student days come flooding back, wasn't it? Some pretty important things happened here.'

'Like losing our virginity, you mean?'

Charlotte gave an amused grin, remembering. 'Well, that was down to you.'

'Was it?'

'Yes. When we first met it was you who told me it was the one thing I had to get rid of PDQ. Remember?'

Beth rolled her eyes. 'Yes, and what did you do? You took absolutely months to do something about it!'

Charlotte shook her head solemnly. 'I wasn't prepared to give it away to anyone, Beth. There had to be some connection; at the very least I had to actually like them. Besides, I wanted a mature man.'

'Mature?' Beth laughed as she ran a hand through her spiky blonde hair. 'Oh yes, Ben Travers was all of twenty, wasn't he? And then there was Gavin Jackson. However...' She paused. 'You saved the best for last; I think you ended up more than liking Jake Harrison, didn't you?'

'I did, actually.' Charlotte's expression was pensive as she pulled her purse from her tote and handed her credit card to the waiter. 'He had serious grey-blue eyes and a wonderful smile. We had a thing going for a while. He was warm and funny and—'

'He fancied you something rotten.'

Charlotte's eyebrows lifted curiously. 'Did he? I can't think why.'

'Oh, rubbish. Look at you!' Beth smiled, thinking as always Charlotte seemed oblivious of what everyone else could see. She had a great figure: long legs, curves in all the right places, a mane of black hair which fell in a loose torrent of waves down her back, and the most incredible blue eyes. Her Achilles heel was her clothes. Her colouring, Beth thought, cried out for dramatic support – vivid red, blue or yellow or green. Instead Lottie wore pastels. Always pastels. It was as if for some reason she didn't want to be noticed, to blend into the background. Something deep and Freudian going on there, she decided. 'Oh yes, I forgot,' she continued with an amused laugh, 'he was after your mind, wasn't he?'

'Well, we were both good at mathematics. Or rather I was good, he was a genius. I mean, he got accepted for Harvard Business School, didn't he?'

'Yes, and with his father being a big corporate name…'

'Yes, I know… He's probably amassing his second million as we speak.'

'You should have hung on in there, girlfriend. Think what your future might have been with him – you could have ended up the glamorous wife doing her bit for charity, owning a fabulous house in the country, and mother to a couple of gorgeous kids.'

'No, I wouldn't, Beth. I'd have been right here talking to you. Thank you,' she said, distracted from their conversation for a moment as the waiter handed her back the card and her copy of the receipt. Slipping them both into her purse and shouldering her tote, she trailed Beth to the door. 'You of all people should know,' she continued. 'I'm a free spirit and I'm lucky enough now to possess the kind of money to support that independence. You want to know something else? If I do decide to settle down and have kids, it's going to take a very exceptional man, and I've still to meet him…' Her blue eyes met Beth's and she laughed. 'If he exists at all.'

They emerged from the restaurant into the balmy summer afternoon. Lingering on the pavement, they drifted into conversation briefly then pulled out and examined diaries, penning in another date to meet in a few months' time, promising to keep in regular touch in the meantime. With a final hug they parted.

Charlotte watched her friend disappear down the road towards the station to catch her connection back to London, thinking how strange fate had been bringing someone like Beth Reynolds into her life. It had been an automatic assumption she would apply for a place at Oxford or Cambridge, but much to everyone's surprise she had chosen Warwick. And it had been a good choice, because not only did she fall in love with the city during the three years she was there, the petite art student she had roomed with had now become her adoptive sister.

Checking her watch, Charlotte headed quickly for the car park and her red Lotus Esprit. She was expected back home by six o'clock and the drive to Little Court, the manor house in West Somerset where her family lived, would take her at least a couple of hours. New arrivals had moved in to Higher Padbury Manor and her uncle and aunt – Matt and Ella Benedict – had invited them over for an informal evening as a welcoming gesture.

Ella was an accomplished social animal. After all, Little Court, which had once been great grandmother Laura Kendrick's home, not only belonged to Ella now, it was also her business. Well, not only her business. Charlotte's mother Jenny and her Aunt Issy, who had grown up with Ella and been friends for years, were now her partners. Lawns at Little Court was an upmarket functions business for weddings and corporate occasions, and business was booming – currently there was a nine-month waiting list for weddings. A new law had recently come in allowing premises other than registry offices to conduct civil weddings. The 'Holy Trinity', as Charlotte's stepfather Rowan Miller referred to her mother and aunts, applied immediately. The licence had now been granted and one of the day rooms on the ground floor with doors opening onto the rear terrace had been earmarked for conversion to the Ceremony Room. All clients who had booked their reception with Lawns but had not yet committed to a venue for their service were contacted immediately and offered a special discount. Oh yes, the Holy Trinity were a bunch of shrewd business women.

Picking up the M5 south of Worcester, Charlotte's thoughts turned to Christian, realising his Australian tour was about to finish and he would be home soon. Of course Beth knew absolutely nothing about her secret relationship with one of rock's leading stars, which had been running for around a year now.

Eight years ago Uncle Matt had discovered Christian Rosetti quite by chance, recognised the potential singer/songwriter talent he had on his hands and immediately signed him to his record label, Evolution UK. Bringing Christian together with a four piece called Oblivion whose lead singer had just quit, they changed their name and Rosetti was born. The band had a successful career for three years, after which they went their separate ways with the exception of Christian and Rosetti's bass guitarist, Jimmie McShea. Christian was now not only a solo star but part of Matt's successful song-writing team, and Jimmie, who now liked to be referred to simply as Jay, had taken over as Evolution UK's Product Development Manager and personally oversaw all Christian's tour arrangements.

Christian had come into her life when she was sixteen years old and she had felt a connection with him from the moment they met. He had been a raw twenty-year-old then and she had been a teenager struggling with family issues, a couple of stone heavier and rarely out of black and Doc Martens. Charlotte cringed as she remembered how the phase had dominated her life, something she had quickly discarded on arrival at Warwick. All through those dark days with her father's illness Christian had been there for her when she needed him; strong and supportive; asking nothing but giving everything.

That it had taken so long for their friendship to move into a more intimate level was something she never understood only accepted without question. However, after their first night together he made it clear for the sake of his solo career it was important fans believed he was not permanently attached to anyone. He was so insistent about this she found herself giving in without argument, simply happy to be with him. At first, having a secret affair with one of the music business's most eligible stars had been quite exciting. Of course, they had been caught eating out in London by the paparazzi on a couple occasions but Matt, mindful of his star's demands for secrecy, made sure his PR machine reported they were no more than good friends. Matt also made sure that at public events or nights out at fashionable London clubs Christian always had some pretty young thing on his arm, boosting his image as someone who very much played the field. Only the immediate family was aware of the real nature of Charlotte's relationship with him.

Lately, however, she had begun to realise things were beginning to change; the last time they had spent any intimate time together was months ago when she visited him in London. Even taking into account the time he was away touring, Christian definitely seemed to be drifting away from her. And it was not merely a falling out of love. Over the last six months his personality had begun to change too; it was as if someone else were living in his skin. He had become not only cool towards her but had developed a confrontational attitude which surfaced every time he came down to Little Court. Everyone there, including herself, was beginning to find his behaviour extremely tiring and no longer looked forward to his visits. Perhaps, she reflected, she should not be too disappointed at being relegated from lover back to friend. In fact, if the truth were known given the Christian they all had to deal with now, she actually welcomed it.

The motorway had been left behind some time ago; she began the transition from A to B roads as her journey brought her closer to home. Traffic was sporadic: a few cars, a horse box, a tractor hauling logs. Finally, she saw the first sign for Meridan Cross and smiled, knowing she was nearing her destination. Turning left off the main road, she decided on a short cut through Foxbarrow Lane which would bring her out at the top of Hundred Acre Wood. From there she would be able to see Little Court's Elizabethan chimneys, the pale stone of Willowbrook Farm facing it across the valley and between them, nestling on the valley floor, the village of Meridan Cross.

Foxbarrow Lane was a single-track road with a mixture of high overgrown banks, dry stone walling and intermittent passing places. As usual, she made her way cautiously, conscious that meeting a tractor or some other vehicle from the village was a distinct possibility. What she did not expect as she rounded a right-hand bend was to find a black Range Rover approaching at high speed on the straight stretch of lane in front of her. Instinctively, she hit the brakes and aimed the Lotus towards a spot bordered by a low dry stone wall where she could see the road was slightly wider, estimating there would be enough room for both cars to pass if they both slowed down. The great dark vehicle reached her still speeding while it greedily hogged most of the narrow space. At the last minute she had no option but to swing the steering wheel hard to the left and brake, bracing herself for any impact. There was a crack and scream of metal as the vehicles passed. The Lotus came to a shuddering halt.

Releasing her seat belt, Charlotte shoved at the driver's door, anger bubbling up inside her. Whoever was behind the wheel either had a death wish or was a complete idiot and she was more than ready to take them to task over it. However, climbing out of the car she found the road empty, and for a moment wondered whether she had dreamed it all. But no, walking around the front of the Lotus she could see the damage where the wall had claimed her wing mirror – now twisted metal and shattered glass – and gouged a pathway down the passenger door. The thought of how close the other vehicle had been and how near she had come to harm made her angrier than ever. Getting back into the car her one thought was to find that driver. At the very least compensation and an apology were in order.

'I saw you come up the driveway; whatever's happened to the car?' Jenny Miller called out as Charlotte walk towards the house. A petite, attractive brunette in her mid-forties, she stepped back to let her much taller daughter in. Today, Jenny was wearing her usual gardener's uniform of a short-sleeved cotton shirt under blue dungarees, her hair scraped back into an untidy pony tail. Anxiety filled her brown eyes as she followed Charlotte into the kitchen, watching as she dumped her tote on the worktop.

'Some maniac in a black Range Rover decided to try to run me off the road in Foxbarrow Lane,' Charlotte answered angrily, turning to face Jenny. 'It was so stupid. They must have been doing at least sixty!'

Jenny stretched a comforting hand. 'Never mind, at least you're not hurt.'

She always tries to pacify, Charlotte thought as her mother gently reached up and stroked her hair in a calming gesture. It must be the years of practice she had with Dad during his illness. Not that it ever did much good from the amount of bruises he managed to cover her in. She forced a smile, blanking out the sad memories of the past.

'No, I'm not. But I will find out who it was, and they're going to pay for the damage after I've given them a piece of my mind.'

'I gather you didn't get the licence plate?'

'Sadly, no, but I'm sure they're local. Probably someone from the barn conversion development over at Morden. You know the sort – townie who wants to embrace country life but drives around as if they're still on the M4, they…' She hesitated, noting her mother's high colour.

'Are you okay, Mum? You look a bit flushed.'

'I'm fine,' Jenny said, her hand shooting to the base of her throat as the colour seeped away from her face.

'You haven't been arguing with Aunt Issy again, have you?'

'If you must know it's the Grande Dame of Higher Padbury Manor – the one we are entertaining this evening.'

'Thérèse D'Alesandro? Why? What has she done?'

'She was extremely rude.' Jenny's ire was evident. 'She called here this morning while Ella was out. Said she needed to see her about oh, I don't know, something or other! As soon as I opened the door I was treated to a most demeaning attitude, even when I introduced myself her eyes were continually fixing themselves on my clothes. She didn't have to utter a word, her expression said everything. Damn the woman, I'm a gardener!'

'It was probably a silly mistake.' Now it was Charlotte's turn to soothe. 'She'll be different tonight, I'm sure. You might even find she apologises.'

Jenny shook her head grimly. 'Don't count on it. I'm glad Ella's dealing with her. The uppity woman's certainly no one I want to have much to do with.'

'Come along,' Charlotte looped her arm in her mother's, 'the best thing you can do is to go upstairs, shower and change into something wonderful that will show her the kind of woman you really are when she arrives.'

Jenny checked her watch and looked at her apologetically. 'Sorry, darling, end of rant. I'm on my way.' She stopped as she reached the kitchen door, her smile returning briefly. 'Oh, by the way, Rowan and I have been busy sorting out the river garden this afternoon. He's got some good ideas about bringing it back to its former glory. I think you'll be impressed.'

'I usually am,' Charlotte conceded. 'He's very gifted, Mum.'

Jenny smiled warmly. 'Yes, he is, isn't he?'

Rowan Miller had been married to her mother for four years now – an extremely happy marriage after the harrowing experience they had all gone through with her father Nick's depression and subsequent fatal accident. Before their marriage, Rowan, landscape gardener and long-term family friend, had managed Little Court's gardens. He had been an absolute rock for her mother following Nick's death and seemed only natural he and Jenny would eventually get together. They were both quiet people and their mutual love of all things growing saw them taking responsibility for Little Court's extensive grounds with a team of highly trained gardeners. The sort of expertise Thérèse D'Alesandro in her world of fashion would know very little about. She was sorry it appeared her mother and Thérèse had got off on the wrong foot; maybe this evening in the relaxed and happy atmosphere of the barbeque things would be different.

'How's the food prep gone today, by the way?' Charlotte asked, pulling her mind back into the present as she retrieved her tote and followed her mother out of the kitchen.

'Like clockwork,' Jenny threw over her shoulder, sounding relieved. 'For once, Ella and Issy seem to be in complete harmony.' She stopped and turned to study her daughter for a moment. 'But that's probably because they have Kieren as referee. The Ryan–Elliott wedding next Saturday,' she raised hands in the air in a gesture of helplessness, 'is, of course, an entirely different matter.'

'Kieren's here?' Charlotte's concern about her car vanished for a moment at the knowledge her stepbrother had arrived.

'Yes, he's out on the terrace, setting up the barbeque.'

'That's such good news, Mum. So does it mean he's made up with Rowan?'

'You'd better ask him yourself.'

'I'll just go and say a quick hi.'

'Make sure it is a quick hi, then.' Jenny tapped her watch as she watched her daughter turn to leave. 'I know what it's like when you two get together. Remember you need to be ready by seven.'

'Mum...?'

'What?'

'Stop worrying and go and have your shower.'

Charlotte found her stepbrother balancing a large bag of charcoal on the ledge next to the huge purpose-built brick barbeque, slowly easing its contents into the pit. Clad in jeans and a faded *Frankie Says Relax* t-shirt, the long lean twenty-four-year-old had the same messy dark hair as his father. Seeing her approach, he dumped the bag onto the floor of the terrace and dusted his hands off down his thighs.

'Hey, little brother,' she called out. 'Long time no see.'

He wrapped his arms around her in an affectionate hug. 'It's good to see you too, Lottie.'

'I can't believe you're back. What's happened? Have you sorted your differences out with your father?'

'Sort of...' He looked at her uncomfortably. 'I'm a single man again. Leon's gone; left the village last week.'

She frowned. 'Really. No one mentioned it.'

'I hardly think splitting up with my partner qualifies as an appropriate topic for discussion over dinner at Little Court, do you?'

'Probably not,' Charlotte agreed, knowing how upset her stepfather Rowan had been. She knew he loved his son desperately, but to discover the nature of his relationship with one of the O'Farrells' farmhands, when it appeared the rest of the village already knew, had been both embarrassing and painful. Added to that, of course, was the fact that as Romany, Rowan found the idea of same-sex relationships totally abhorrent.

After the discovery Kieren had left Little Court straight away, moving into a room at the Somerset Arms, where he worked as cook. His employers, Stuart and Terri Harper, had taken over the pub six months ago from the outgoing publican, and bringing in a cook and turning the lounge into a restaurant had been one of their first projects. Hiring Kieren, who had trained in Bristol, the new venture was doing very well. Charlotte knew Rowan was

17

aware of his son's involvement in turning the tired local around and was extremely proud of him. Maybe splitting from Leon might be the final step needed to bring father and son back together again. She hoped so. Returning her mind to the present she looked at him seriously. 'I'm glad you're back. We've all missed you not being here.'

'Leon leaving won't make any difference.' Kieren shook his head, making her realise her hopes might have been rather premature. 'Dad seems to think my association with him was a moment of juvenile foolishness and I have now turned back into the heterosexual son he thought I was. I haven't, and I hate to think what will happen when I get into another relationship. Because it will happen sure as God made little apples.'

'But the fact he's happy you're back here now is a start.' She squeezed his shoulder gently. 'Try and see it that way: a positive start. Something you can both build on. Don't think of what might happen in the future, make it all about now. Take one day at a time, eh?'

He grinned, pulling her into his arms and giving her a hug. 'Ah, Lottie – always the peacemaker.'

Above them a window opened and her mother leaned out, her head swathed in a white towel. 'Lottie! It was supposed to be a quick hello.'

Lottie waved up at her. 'Sorry!' After giving Kieren a peck on the cheek, she began making her way back up the terrace steps towards the house.

FIVE

'Aidan, are you still in there?' Rachel O'Farrell rapped her knuckles against the pine panelled door. 'We're all waiting and you are going to make us incredibly late!'

The door swung open and she stood back, all of her annoyance dissipating as she took in the vision in front of her. Dressed in Levis and a black t-shirt, Aidan was now taller than his father, and work on the farm during his breaks from Cirencester Agricultural College had been instrumental in turning the young lanky boy into a finely muscled and fit young man. *Fit*. Rachel reflected on the term. It was something his equally attractive mirror-image twin sister Caitlin, or Kayte as she now insisted on being called, always used in relation to men, but she knew it had a completely different meaning in young-speak. To Rachel it meant healthy, to them attractive, desirable. And he was, of course. How could he not be with the combination of golden blond hair and blue eyes which made him so like his father had been at that age? Niall... Her mind drifted back over the years. She had never imagined when he first came to live in the village she would become his wife. He'd been involved with her best friend Ella for a while. Such a long time ago. A funny thing fate...

'Sorry, giving my teeth a final brush.' Aidan stared at her. 'Mum, are you okay?'

'What? Oh, yes. Come on.' Dragging herself out of her daydream, Rachel hurried him down the stairs and out to the waiting car.

'Hurry up, you two,' Niall O'Farrell called from the driver's seat of the family Volvo, watching as his wife closed the front door of the farmhouse and locked it. 'Ella said seven thirty and it's almost that now.'

'We're coming.' Rachel opened the front passenger door and slipped in beside her husband, leaving Aidan to join his sister in the back. Fastening her seatbelt, she shot a quick glance over her shoulder at her sullen-faced daughter. 'Kayte, what's wrong?'

'Nothing in particular.' Kayte gave a bored shrug, avoiding eye contact with her mother. 'Only wondering what all the fuss is about. What's going on tonight anyway? It's like we've got visiting royalty. Who are these people?'

'Thérèse D'Alesandro and her son and daughter have recently moved into Higher Padbury Manor,' Niall replied, as he drove the Volvo down the track towards the main road. 'Ella and Matt have invited them all to a barbeque this evening, a sort of "get to know the neighbours" event.'

'And my question is still what's so special about them?' Kayte wound her finger around a tendril of her blonde hair and heaved her shoulders. 'We've had loads of new people in the village and they've not had this sort of celebrity treatment.'

'Well, for a start,' Rachel replied calmly, hiding the anger she felt at having to deal with her petulant daughter, 'Thérèse used to model in the sixties and Matt knows her from his days with The Attitude.'

'And…'

Rachel frowned. 'What do you mean "and"?'

'Well, there's got to be something else, hasn't there?' replied her daughter. 'You don't make all this fuss over someone because your husband knew them thirty years ago.'

'When she left modelling Thérèse turned designer,' Niall joined in the conversation as the car entered Meridan Cross village. 'She has her own label, Emerald Desert, and she's about to add a bridal range. Satisfied?'

'Ah, so it's all about business and making money,' Kayte said gleefully. 'I should have known; bloody typical of that Little Court lot!'

'Kayte, language!' Rachel skewed around in her seat to reprimand her daughter. 'How dare you speak so rudely about our friends! They've been very good to you over the years – like family. What is the matter with you?'

Aidan grinned. 'You've wrecked her evening; she was on a promise.'

'I was not!' Kayte elbowed him in the ribs. 'Be sensible… there's nothing remotely resembling a real man around here!'

'What is it then, Kayte? Come on, tell us.' Niall's voice indicated his patience was at breaking point with his argumentative daughter. 'Exactly why don't you want to be here this evening?'

'It's boring and I haven't anything in common with any of them. None of them are my blood relatives, thank goodness!' She rolled her eyes. 'I mean, look at them. Ella and Matt are straight off the pages of *OK* magazine, Issy Taylor bullies poor Mick something terrible, and as for those scruffy up-market eco-warriors Jenny and Rowan, well…!' She shook her head disdainfully. 'You forget, I do waitressing there for functions; I know everything about them – believe me, they are so up themselves!'

'Have you quite finished?'

She noticed her father was glaring at her in his rear view mirror. As they reached the High Street he drew the car to an abrupt halt.

'I will not have this rudeness,' he said, unfastening his safety belt and pushing open the car door. 'If you don't want to be part of this family evening, Kayte, that's perfectly fine with me.' He pulled opened her door. 'You're free to go.'

Kayte sat there open-mouthed. This was not what she had expected, not at all. Although she had turned boundary pushing into an art form with her parents, she realised this time she had gone too far. The expression on her mother's face told her not to expect any support. She was well and truly on her own.

'Go on, get out!' Her father waved a hand at her. 'I've no wish to inflict your rudeness on everyone else this evening. I'm sure there are places you would rather be and people you would rather be spending time with.'

Knowing an apology was the only way out of this and reluctant to back down, Kayte slowly slid out of the car, struggling to hold on to her air of cool indifference.

'Have you got your keys?' Niall's disapproving eyes were still on her as he slammed the passenger door. She nodded mutely as he got back in the car. 'Right, then, we'll see you later.'

Kayte stood there in the middle of the road watching the Volvo disappear, and wishing she had not been quite so forthright in her views about Little Court's residents. However, they were the older generation and they were boring, that was the truth of it. Their conversations centred on business, farming and other issues close to their bank balances. Of course, there was the younger generation: CJ and Charlotte – two serious, boring workaholics – and Lucy... the only fun person had escaped to spend her trust fund, she thought bitterly, knowing how much she would love to have gone with her. No, there was nothing that made her feel bad about missing this evening's barbeque, other than the unfortunate state which she now found herself in with her parents.

The blast of a car horn made her realise she was still standing in the road. She turned to see a black Range Rover heading towards her. She stepped aside to let it pass but instead it stopped. There was a low hum as an electric window lowered and the driver leaned out.

'Sorry to bother you, but am I on the right road for Little Court?'

Robbed of speech, Kayte could only stare at the occupant behind the wheel. 'Oh, sorry, yes,' she said, finally finding her voice. 'Yes, you are. In fact, I'm on my way there too,' she added quickly.

'Can we possibly give you a lift?'

She had been so busy concentrating on the driver she had not noticed his passenger, a glamorous older woman, who now leaned forward with a friendly smile as she clutched a small white dog.

'Thank you.' Kayte tore her eyes away from the driver as the rear door opened. 'Thank you so much.'

SIX

'Watching the gathering of the clans, are we?'

A voice interrupted Charlotte's survey of arriving guests as she stood on the galleried landing above the great hall. Turning her head, she found her brother Christopher standing next to her with his usual friendly grin, long tapered fingers splayed across the oak balustrade. Named for both his grandfather Christopher and great grandfather Jonathan, he now answered to the name of CJ – a nickname earned at university through the need to identify him from the two other Christophers on his architects degree course. Dressed for the barbeque in a pink Ralph Lauren shirt and dark blue chinos, his fair hair fell untidily around his ears. Charlotte smiled back; he was so like their dead father in both his height and features and possessed that same aura of golden freshness she had seen in old family photos. She wondered whether her mother ever noticed this striking resemblance. She'd have to be blind not to, she thought, giving him her full attention

'Yes. It's great to see them all together, don't you think?'

'Yes, it is.' CJ nodded and smiled as he watched the warm exchanges between the small group. 'Changing the subject…' He cast a thoughtful eye in her direction. 'Mum told me you had a bit of a run-in with a Range Rover earlier today. Are you okay?'

'Yes, no broken bones, but the Lotus has a wrecked wing mirror, a huge groove down the passenger door and I'm going to kill the idiot responsible when I—' She broke off as her attention was drawn across the void to the window above the main door. A black Range Rover had appeared and was speeding down the driveway towards the house.

CJ followed her gaze then shook his fair head and laughed. 'Oh, sis, no! That is way too coincidental. After all, now we've got half of London making their weekend homes down here Range Rovers are ten a penny.'

The vehicle came to a standstill outside the house, its front and rear doors opening.

'Thérèse and Felica D'Alesandro and if I'm not mistaken, Chi Chi the Bichon Frise,' CJ said, with the sort of expression that indicated he liked what he was looking at as an attractive forty-something carrying a small, fluffy white dog, followed by a pretty, dark blonde haired girl, stepped out from the car. Both were immaculate in pale linen dresses and high heels. 'Italian glamour hits Meridan Cross. Oh, and they've brought Kayte too. I wondered where she'd got to.'

'Thérèse is part Italian; her father was English,' Charlotte corrected. 'Her husband is based in Milan but Thérèse wanted to relocate her business to the UK, hence the purchase of the manor. They also have a house in Kensington, a huge house in Tuscany and a villa on Lake Como.'

'Well-heeled lot, aren't they? Anything else I should know, oh oracle?'

'Well, Felica and her half-brother Gianmarco were both educated in England. Aunt Ella had lunch with Thérèse last week, I got all this from her,' she explained in response to her brother's perplexed expression. 'Did you know she knew Uncle Matt? She used to model with Cordelia Carmichael, that's how she came to buy the manor from her.'

CJ shook his head. 'Cordelia was a complete mad woman. She was lethal behind the wheel of that Mercedes of hers, wasn't she? I hope Thérèse's driving isn't as bad.'

'Hers might not be, but Gianmarco? Well, as he's the one who's driving, he's definitely another matter.'

'Now hold on, Lottie, you're on dangerous ground,' CJ warned. 'You can't run around accusing people simply because the colour of their car happens to be the same as the one which caused your accident. Besides, how do you know it was him driving?'

'Oh, come on! You saw the speed he was doing when he came down the driveway. It is him, I know it is.' She shot her brother an infuriated look. 'Marco bloody D'Alesandro: rich, irresponsible and accelerator happy, causing accidents wherever he goes. A total driving nightmare!'

'Is there nothing I can say to stop you going ahead with this folly?' CJ asked, sensing trouble. 'You can't accuse without proof. You have nothing tangible, and remember, this *is* supposed to be a welcoming party. I can understand that you are angry but please remember Ella is about to go into business with Thérèse. A public confrontation could wreck everything.'

'Oh, don't worry, I'll be very discreet. I know exactly how to deal with the arrogance of the over-privileged; I met enough of them at uni. I'll take him somewhere private and have a quiet word.' She shot her brother a wicked grin. 'A very quiet word.'

Thérèse and Felica were now in the hall where introductions were being made, hands shaken, cheeks brushed. Niall and Rachel both appeared a little taken aback as they were joined by a smiling Kayte.

CJ frowned. 'What's going on there, then?'

'No idea. I saw her in the village last week. She was quite adamant that spending an evening with the Little Court elders was not her idea of a good time. I didn't think she'd be here tonight… and brought by the D'Alesandros. Very strange.'

CJ smiled. 'Our Kayte doesn't mince her words, does she?'

'Oh, she has a lot of her maternal grandmother about her,' Charlotte said thoughtfully, watching Kayte hanging back behind Thérèse. 'As we all know, Margaret Sylvester has a tongue like a Strimmer and doesn't hesitate to use it. Once it was her husband who had to bear the brunt of her venom, now it's the other residents of her care home. Hey, Mum's waving; I think we're needed for introductions.'

Charlotte and CJ made their way down the stairs towards the small gathering where Helen Baxter – Ella and Matt's tall, grey-haired housekeeper – was busy circulating with glasses of Pimms. As they reached the bottom they were met by Jenny, who took them over to be introduced to Thérèse and Felica. Thérèse was very glamorous, every inch the stylish former model with her thick, dark blonde hair cut into an elegant bob. Her steely eyes scanned Charlotte but there was something reflected in them strangely at odds the warm smile.

'So pleased to meet you.' She handed the dog over to Felica. 'It is so lovely of your family to welcome us.' Even her words had a hollow ring, Charlotte thought as Thérèse brushed cheeks with her own.

'Oh, my aunts love these social occasions.' Charlotte smiled brightly, determined to remain upbeat as she accepted a glass of Pimms from Helen. 'I guess it's because they are in the hospitality business.'

'Ah yes, Lawns at Little Court,' Felica said. Slightly smaller and with the same exotic looks and colouring as her mother, she nodded as she sipped her drink. Having been relegated to the floor, Chi Chi was now sitting patiently at her feet like a big ball of white fluff staring up at her with adoring eyes, the occasional whine escaping from his small throat.

'Mother and I are very excited about the boutique. We have been invited to look around next week,' Felica continued, her smile genuinely friendly, her perfect English holding an attractive hint of accent. 'I believe you have a wedding coming up next weekend?'

'Yes, we do.'

'And do you get in involved in these... these events?' Thérèse waved a theatrical hand and cocked her head inquisitively, giving Charlotte's jeans and t-shirt yet more critical assessment.

Finding herself under the same microscopic scrutiny she suspected her mother had been subjected to, Charlotte said, 'Oh, I'm the meet and greet. I get the wedding guests settled in with a drink and canapés before they go through to the main reception.'

'Ah, so a little waiting job,' Thérèse responded with a smile, a glimmer of condescension in her voice. 'Felica, of course, is involved in fashion, like me. She studied at St Martins College in London, graduated last year and is currently designing her own collection.' There was no mistaking the pride in her voice, or the put down. 'And Marco, well—'

Ignoring the woman's efforts to belittle her, Charlotte smiled back, running her eyes over the hall and its occupants. 'Yes, where is he?' she interrupted, realising she would probably face the same type of superior arrogance when she came to deal with him.

'Oh, he's returned to the manor to fetch my shawl; he'll be back shortly. My fault, I'm afraid.' Thérèse gave a syrupy smile. 'All those years in Italy have spoiled me; as soon as the sun goes down here I really feel the English chill.' She gave a mock shiver. 'Don't worry, as soon as he arrives I'm sure he'll... well, be pleased to meet you,' she said with another quick appraisal of her, which told Charlotte it was the last thing he'd probably want to do.

She was about to make excuses to leave when she heard Matt indicating they should all move out into the garden.

'Where is he?' CJ hissed in his sister's ear, catching her up as they made their way out onto the terrace.

'He's had to return to the manor on an errand for Thérèse. He will be back though.' Charlotte gave her brother a calm smile. 'What do you think of them?'

'Felica's very sweet. I find Thérèse a little too gushing maybe. What about you?'

'Felica's okay, but for some reason Thérèse doesn't like me. She made me feel, oh, I don't know... scruffy I suppose is the best way to describe it,' she said, looking down at her white t-shirt and jeans. 'Hell, it is a barbeque, CJ.'

'Don't let it upset you.' He waggled a finger at her. 'You're right, it is a barbeque. The way they are dressed they'd look more at home shopping in Knightsbridge. I doubt the pair of them has any idea what casual means.'

Cheered up by her brother's supportive words, Charlotte drifted over to where Kieren was turning home-made burgers and giving the chicken portions a liberal brush of one of his special marinades. She sniffed approvingly.

'It smells fabulous. Has Rowan caught up with you yet?'

'Yes.' Kieren gave her one of his lopsided grins. 'We're fine. You were right, it's a start.' He glanced across at Thérèse and Felica, who were now talking to Niall and Rachel. 'What are the new neighbours like?'

Charlotte smiled, turning to appraise mother and daughter. 'Felica is fine but I felt Thérèse was incredibly condescending. I don't know, maybe it was...'

She stopped mid-sentence when a figure in an open-neck white shirt and black jeans appeared through the French doors and walked out onto the terrace, a blue silk shawl in his hand. Tall and broad-shouldered, his loose inky-black collar-length hair fell in an untidy curl around a face which looked as if it had been stolen from a Botticelli painting. He paused for a moment as dark brown eyes under a black slash of brows surveyed all those assembled on the lawn. Then they settled on Charlotte, and stayed there with a stare so intense she had to turn away.

Spotting him, Thérèse smiled regally and waved in his direction. 'Ah, Marco! Do come and meet everyone.'

'What's the matter?' Kieren asked, abandoning his supervision of the food, his eyes fixed on Charlotte.

'Nothing.' As she took a gulp of her Pimms she saw CJ heading across the lawn towards her, a gleeful expression on his face.

'Well, sis, still fancy tackling him?'

Kieren's eyes flitted between brother and sister. 'Come on, share the joke.'

'A Range Rover ran me off the road this afternoon and *he* was driving it.' Charlotte nodded towards Marco.

'Lottie *thinks* it was him,' CJ corrected. 'She was planning to sort him out, give him a piece of her mind.'

'I wouldn't mind sorting him out myself.' Kieren raised his eyebrows suggestively as CJ continued to laugh.

'Not funny.' Charlotte gave them a discomfiting frown. 'He was staring at me. He recognises me, I'm sure of it.'

'Oh, but isn't he absolutely gorgeous?' Kieren stared at Marco with undisguised lust. 'So alpha male. Look at those shoulders and as for the face, well... he's got to be a model for some fashion house, hasn't he? Hello, our Kayte's staking a claim already.'

Charlotte followed his focus, watching Kayte as she crossed the lawn towards him, a glass of Pimms in each hand. She handed him one of the tumblers, smiling up into his face as she positioned herself next to him and began to chat.

'Damn!' Lottie muttered under her breath. 'She's going to hang around him all night, isn't she? I need to get him alone. How am I going to get rid of her?'

'Leave it with me,' Kieren said, a mischievous glint in his eye. 'I'm sure I can think of something.'

CJ nudged her. 'Guess we'd better go and introduce ourselves then. With you under the D'Alesandro microscope the last thing we want to appear is rude.'

From the expression on Kayte's face as they reached Marco it was quite obvious she was not at all happy with their arrival. Glaring at them, she edged herself nearer to him, resting her body against his in a blatant display of possession.

Ignoring her, CJ extended his hand in greeting. 'Christopher Kendrick. Everyone calls me CJ. I'm Jenny Miller's son, and this is my sister Charlotte.'

'Pleased to meet you both.' Marco shook hands with CJ and then with Charlotte, his smile warm as his dark eyes lingered on her for a moment. He held onto her hand a fraction longer than she felt comfortable with. 'You are the architect, I think?' he said, eventually releasing her from his grip and turning his attention to CJ. His accent mirrored his half-sister's.

'I am, and I believe my practice is going to be involved with the changes at Higher Padbury Manor.'

'Yes, my mother has some ideas she wants to discuss. And you, Charlotte, what do you do?' He spoke her name in two distinct syllables, the sound sending a strange flicker of heat through her.

'Well…' she replied hesitantly, 'at the moment I'm—'

'Marco, do you think you could get me another Pimms?'

The voice cut rudely through Charlotte's sentence as with a toss of her long blonde hair, Kayte slipped between her and Marco and thrust her empty glass under his nose. With a polite smile he took it from her but remained where he stood, re-fixing his attention on Charlotte.

'You were saying?' He bent his head towards her, ignoring Kayte's sulky expression.

'I—' Charlotte felt his eyes on her again, intense and dark.

'Ladies and Gentlemen…' Kieren's voice saved her as it rang out across the lawn, 'the food is now ready to be served.'

She saw Jenny making a beeline across to where they were standing.

'Marco, do come and help yourself to food,' she said as she reached them. 'I can see you've been monopolised for far too long.' She fixed Kayte with a disapproving stare.

'Thank you, Mrs Miller.' Marco gave her a stunning smile as Jenny tucked her arm in his. 'This is such a beautiful location, and you and your husband are responsible for the gardens, I understand. You have done remarkable things here,' Charlotte heard him say as they walked away, Kayte trailing behind.

'Oh God!' Charlotte watched them go, sheltering her eyes under her fingertips.

CJ looked at his sister curiously. 'What is it?'

'I don't like him. I don't like Thérèse either.'

'You've only just met them, Lottie. How can you make such a sweeping statement? I thought they were both all right.'

'They are both patronising. She thinks we're a load of country hicks and he thinks he's god's gift.' She glared at CJ. 'And whatever you believe about the accident, I know it was him and I intend to do something about it.'

SEVEN

The evening had progressed well. Kieren had prepared a delicious array of tempting food to accompany the meat course. With full plates, the gathering had settled themselves comfortably at a series of circular white tables dotted across the lawn, immersing themselves in feasting and conversation. The hubbub of voices mixed with muted laughter carried on the evening air, and then:

'You stupid idiot, Kieren!'

Eating and conversations were halted as guests turned to see a furious Kayte, who had followed Marco up for a second helping of food, glaring across the buffet table at Kieren. At first it wasn't clear what was wrong until she turned to reveal the front of her blue short-sleeved shirt splattered with tomato ketchup.

'Oh dear!' CJ, who had recently returned with a plate of food and settling himself next to his sister, suppressed a smirk. 'Well, I guess that's one way of getting rid of her. Not sure it's the best way to do it though; she's got a hell of a temper. Let's hope she doesn't punch him.'

'Don't worry.' Charlotte eyed the explosion of crimson which had begun to migrate slowly down Kayte's front. 'If it turns violent remember he's the one holding the ketchup bottle. If she starts anything he'll probably give her another squirt for good measure.'

Kieren whipped around the table to join his victim. As he tried to placate a furious Kayte with a grovelling apology he worked to repair the damage with a clean tea towel.

'Stop it, stop it, you're making it worse!' Kayte slapped his hands away angrily.

Everyone's attention again turned back towards the barbeque. Charlotte watched Niall and Rachel make brief eye contact before she crossed over to where her daughter stood and whispered something into her ear. Moments later Niall joined them, car keys in hand.

'I'll run you home to change,' he said in a tone which said he was not in the least amused with her behaviour.

'Something else that's going to upset her day,' CJ leaned forward and whispered in Charlotte's ear as an irritable Kayte departed for home. 'I stopped for a brief chat with Felica at the buffet table a short while ago. She tells me Kayte is wasting her time; Marco already has a girlfriend in London and her name is Lauren. She works in advertising.'

As Niall and Kayte disappeared into the house, Charlotte took the opportunity to get up from the table and take her empty plate across to where Marco, having stepped back from the argument, was currently helping himself to more salad.

She gave him a friendly smile. 'So... how do you like living in the country?'

'I am not sure I can answer that at the moment,' he responded, his gaze caught between her and the rice salad he was currently spooning onto his plate. 'I do not think I have been here long enough to give an honest opinion.'

'You'll find it very different, I'm sure,' she replied, helping herself to French bread.

'Yes, very. I tend to think of Tuscany as my home, although I was educated in the UK.'

'Oh.' She feigned ignorance. 'Where was that exactly?'

'Scotland. An old castle in the middle of nowhere. Very beautiful countryside when the sun shone but very bleak during the winter months. You want to know the worst thing? It was the porridge – lumpy and grey. Like eating wallpaper paste.' A smile of amusement lit his face, revealing perfect white teeth.

'The weather here can be depressing too,' she said, realising his smile had pushed the handsome needle right off the Richter scale and was giving her a strange fluttery feeling in her stomach. 'But it's still a very beautiful place. Spring and summer are my favourite months,' she continued, willing herself to concentrate on her real reason for talking to him. 'Hundred Acre Wood is at its best then. But I have to say, rain or shine, I've always loved this valley.'

'You grew up here?'

She nodded. 'I went to the local state school here – Kingsford College – my father was headmaster there. He died in an accident six years ago.'

'I am sorry.' His voice was gentle. Conversation halted as he seemed at a loss to know what to say next, choosing instead to concentrate on making choices from the buffet. Eventually he settled his dark eyes on her again. 'And after school you went to university?'

'Yes. Warwick. Got a first class honours in mathematics then trained in accountancy. And you?'

'Milan. A business degree and then a Masters in food management. I work for my father in his leisure business. What do you do?'

Spotting an empty table, Charlotte gestured towards it, conscious Thérèse was watching them intently.

'I help out with weddings here at weekends, and during the week I work part time for Matt,' she told him, as they settled themselves down and began to eat. 'He runs several charities. I joined the Safekeeping team a year ago; it's a homeless charity. Matt believes society should support people who have fallen foul of the system and ended up in nowhere land. Every person, he feels, deserves a square meal, a place to sleep, and somewhere to shower or bathe – basic support to help them get back on their feet. He already has two large night shelters and is planning a third. '

'Are they local?'

'No, London. I work there three days a week, staying in the company flat. It's only a couple of hours' drive.'

'My part of the business is now based in London too. I have an apartment there, but when I'm staying at the manor I often leave my car at the station and take the train. I use the journey time to go through paperwork, prepare for meetings.'

'Do you do much driving?'

'Some.' He trailed the fork around his plate to capture some escaping grains of rice salad. 'I have a Porsche although I do use the Range Rover occasionally. What about you?'

'Oh, a Lotus.'

'Nice.' His expression spoke of interest. 'Are you happy with it?'

'Very. Would you like to see it?' Charlotte smiled; the ease at which entrapment was proceeding both amazed and pleased her.

'Sure. Let's finish our food then you can show me.'

'Ah, I see, one of the stables has been converted to house all your cars?' Having finished their meal, Charlotte now stood watching Marco as he gazed around the huge concrete-floored building.

'Yes, we keep a few horses in the block next door. But if any of our guests fancy a ride we tend to send them up to Willowbrook Farm where they have a trekking centre.'

'Ah, yes. Kayte told me about that. And do you ride?'

Charlotte nodded. Five years ago she had never been near a horse and had no intention of doing so. Now she found it very relaxing; an afternoon's gallop to blow the cobwebs away or a leisurely ride through Hundred Acre Wood above the village – a quiet, peaceful place ideal for times when she wanted to be totally alone with her thoughts.

'So,' he gazed along the line of parked cars, 'where is the Lotus?'

She led him to the far corner and pointed. 'Here.'

'You have had an accident.' He stared at the car and then turned to look at her, concern in his eyes. 'Luckily it seems you were not hurt. When did this happen?'

'Today,' she said calmly, watching him, her hands clasped in front of her. 'I'm surprised you don't remember.'

He looked puzzled. 'Me? Why should I?'

'Because you were the one who caused it.'

'What!'

'Foxbarrow Lane. It links the main road to the top of Hundred Acre Wood.'

'It must have been someone else; I have not been behind the wheel until this evening.'

'Well, it was definitely your Range Rover. You came at me doing at least sixty on a very narrow road. I couldn't believe you wouldn't stop or at the very least slow down. But no, you ploughed through and I had no choice – it was either hit the wall or hit you.'

Walking over to the car, Marco carefully inspected the damage. Charlotte watched him lift the damaged wing mirror and run his long, well-manicured fingers down the deep scratches in the bodywork. The sleeves of his shirt were rolled up to his elbows and her eyes were drawn to the fine dark hair covering his tanned arms.

He walked back to join her, a confused expression on his face. 'I am sorry, but this was definitely nothing to do with me.'

She took a deep breath, trying to keep hold of her temper. Despite his protests she was convinced he was lying, and what made it worse was the way he was standing there doing it so calmly with a look of such innocence on his face.

His hand touched her shoulder gently. 'Charlotte? You are trembling.'

'I am furious!' she snapped, pushing him away and taking a step back. 'Bloody furious you can lie so easily and care so little. I *know* you did that.' She jabbed a finger in the direction of her car. 'Have you no sense of responsibility?'

Marco raised a calming hand. 'Charlotte, you are not listening to me. I said this was nothing—'

She had intended to slap him, so outraged was she at his supercilious manner, but as her right hand whipped towards him, he intercepted it, grabbing her left at the same time.

'What are you playing at? Let me go!' she protested, struggling as he marched her across the stable and pushed her against the wall. Pinning her hands above her head, he blocked her with his body so she had no opportunity to kick out at him. Mesmerising eyes stared down at her, anger flaring in their dark depths.

'What the hell are you doing? Let go of me!' Charlotte scowled up at him, desperately trying to free her wrists from his iron-like grip.

'Not before you promise me you will not try something stupid like that again.'

She glared at him. There was no alternative; he was far too strong and obeying was the only option if she was to get away from him and the disturbing feelings he had begun to arouse within her. She tried to calm her breathing, to take control of herself but he was standing far too close for comfort. That, coupled with the grip of his hand around her wrists and the hardness of his body against hers made it impossible to stop her heart from thudding against her ribs. What the hell was going on here? She hated him; not only was he arrogant, he was a liar as well. How, then, could thoughts of kissing the tantalising mouth now hovering within inches of her face be running through her brain?

'Listen…' He gave a sigh and released her hands, resting his own gently on the edges of her shoulders. 'I have no idea who did this to your car but it was not me. I came down by train this afternoon. As I told you, I have not been behind the wheel of a car until this evening.' He stared at her for a moment, his expression creasing into a worried look. 'You are trembling again. I can feel it.' He sounded troubled. 'What is it? Did I frighten you?'

'Of course not, I simply hate liars. And you are a liar, Marco D'Alesandro!'

'Please stop arguing! Marco is telling the truth.'

Charlotte turned her head to see Felica standing in the doorway.

'He is innocent, he really is. It was me,' Felica said, fixing her gaze on the Lotus with a tearful expression. 'I am the one you should blame. I am so very sorry. I had no idea…'

EIGHT

Lucy was collected by Randall at ten the next morning and driven to Jack Maddison's offices in Martin Place, one of the oldest and most beautiful commercial parts of Sydney. A wide pedestrianized area with modern underpasses and heavy sculptures saw buildings in a mix of post-modern, art deco and neo-classical style facing each other in an effortless mix. Jack's lavish offices were on the tenth floor of one of the more contemporary skyscrapers with a view out towards the harbour. Here she met Sebastian Walker, the family's lawyer; a solid man, expensively suited with a shock of white hair and a firm handshake. Jack told her Sebastian would also act for her. A man he totally trusted, he said, one who had been at university with him in the sixties.

'I hope you don't mind but when I left you after lunch yesterday I phoned Seb. We had quite an in-depth discussion about your investment plan and we think we have come up with a first class deal for you. In fact, we know we have.'

'Well, I'm quite happy to have left it to you experts,' Lucy said, pleased she had not needed to sit through complicated discussion and options.

Acknowledging her words with a smile, Jack cleared his throat and continued. 'Seb has burnt the midnight oil preparing the document. He'll take you through the details, then you can sign and we'll arrange to transfer the money.'

It all sounded very straightforward. Lucy sat listening to Seb as he outlined the plan: her money was to be invested in a new mine which Jack had recently opened. Then Jack produced a small green pouch.

'They started production a few months ago,' he told her. 'These are the first gems to have come out of the mine. They have been cut and polished and were flown in this morning.' He emptied the contents of the pouch onto a black velvet cloth on his desk. Picking up one of the stones between his finger and thumb, he held it out to her. 'See this? We're looking at premier grade. Did you know Australia produced thirty-nine million carats of diamonds last year? That's big business, girlie.' He laughed. 'And a totally safe investment for your money. It's my prediction you'll triple your money in no time. And I've been in the mining business for many years, so I should know.'

Lucy needed no more persuading. She signed and dated the document before being taken through the process of transferring the funds electronically to the Goorumba Corporation, something she had already setup with her bank in London the previous afternoon. Once this was done Jack congratulated her. 'Welcome to the Maddison family,' he said, wrapping his arms around her in a fatherly hug.

Champagne was opened, toasts made and then both men took her out to an alfresco lunch at a smart French restaurant overlooking the Opera House. Later, the limo returned her to the hotel to get ready for a celebratory dinner which Jack had booked in the Park Hyatt's dining room for that evening. As planned, Ethan had pretended to be surprised when they went down for their evening meal to find Jack and Seb already there and more champagne cooling. When told about Lucy's investment, Ethan had hugged her and told the two men he was glad they were there because along with the shipment of diamonds from the new mine, Lucy's engagement ring had arrived. Now they could have a real celebration. Lucy was in seventh heaven as with Jack and Seb watching, Ethan slipped a four carat diamond set in platinum onto her finger. Full of excitement, she promised to call her parents in the morning to tell them the news and make arrangements for them to fly out and visit as soon as possible.

It was agreed that the next day they would all check out after breakfast and take the company jet to the family's ranch for a few days. Then they would head to the Maddison's island. It would be an opportunity, Jack told her, for her and Ethan to decide whether they would like it as a venue for their wedding. Lucy was so excited. Little Court did not even figure in her thoughts as he told her this; Koomara Island sounded far more luxurious and exotic. Despite currently being at odds with her parents she knew they would understand – after all, didn't every parent want the best for their soon-to-be-wed daughter? Especially when she was marrying into family with such huge wealth. With Ethan next to her topping up her glass, and Jack and Seb opposite all smiles, this had to rate as the best evening of her life. Ever!

Lucy came to with a groan and opened one eye. She glanced at the electronic clock on her bedside table. It was a little after eight am. She put her palm to her forehead and groaned again; she felt as if someone was inside her head using a pneumatic drill. Throwing off the sheets she swung her legs out of bed, resting on its edge for a moment, gradually focussing on her surroundings. Beyond the shrouded window she could sense the blinding brilliance of the morning sun. Too much champagne, that had been the problem. But everyone had been in celebratory mood, hadn't they?

Pushing herself off the bed she went to the bathroom and splashed her face with water. Raising her head from the basin she peered painfully into the mirror. Her memories of the night before were patchy. She remembered leaving the dining room and getting the lift up to the suite, and she was sure Ethan had undressed her and put her to bed before taking off his own clothes and climbing in beside her. The warmth of his arms around her came back as a familiar memory. *So where was he now?* she wondered, turning from the basin to stare back into the room. Maybe he'd got up early to go for a run; she remembered him saying he often did when he'd had a heavy night. Clear your head with a shower, she told herself, and then go and find him.

An hour later she left her room, not forgetting the most important thing of all – the ring. She splayed out her fingers and watched how it sparkled under the corridor lights as she walked towards the lift. It was simply beautiful and she felt so lucky to have met someone who would not only be able to give her a dream life here in Australia, but whom she absolutely adored.

Reaching Ethan's suite, she knocked and waited. She heard footfalls beyond the door and saw it begin to open.

'Good morning, darling,' she said, closing her eyes and throwing herself forward into his arms. Her hands connected with a body, but it wasn't Ethan's. Her eyes flew open and she found herself in the embrace of a dark-haired chambermaid. 'What are you doing here?' she demanded.

'I'm servicing the room, madam.'

'But this is my fiancé's suite; he hasn't checked out yet.' She pushed past the young woman and into the room. 'You shouldn't be here.'

'I was definitely told the guest had checked out,' the chambermaid insisted.

'Well, I think you're wrong,' Lucy countered. 'As I said, there's been a mistake.' Annoyed at being contradicted, she walked over to the wardrobes and slid back the doors, finding to her surprise a rail of empty hangers. She turned to face the maid again. 'I don't understand...'

The maid moved towards the phone with an expression caught somewhere between sympathy and embarrassment. 'Shall I call reception, madam? They're bound to know what's happened.'

'Thank you,' Lucy replied sharply, trying to regain her composure as she moved quickly towards the door, 'but I think it would be better if I go down and talk to them myself.'

Moments later, standing in the confines of the lift as it made its descent to the ground floor, her mind was in free fall as she tried to find a reasonable explanation for Ethan's disappearance. Maybe his cases were in reception, ready for Randall to pick up and he'd gone to breakfast alone, not wanting to disturb her. Well, whatever had happened she would soon find out, she thought as the doors parted with a sigh.

After checking the dining room and finding no sign of him, she crossed the pale floored reception area and came face to face with a neat suited woman, her blonde hair swept back in a neat chignon, rimless designer glasses framing her face. Lucy noted her name badge: Stefanie.

She gave Lucy a welcoming smile. 'Good morning, how can I help?'

'Good morning,' Lucy said, smiling back. 'I'm Lucy Benedict. My fiancé and I are in executive suites 422 and 435. It appears he has vacated his room already. Could you tell me whether he's left his luggage here? The name's Ethan Maddison. I seem to have lost him.'

'Of course.' Stefanie consulted her screen, eventually raising her eyes to

Lucy and nodding. 'It appears Mr Maddison checked out early this morning. As there's no indication of luggage being left I assume he took it with him.'

'Are you sure? I was due to fly out with him later today.'

The girl checked her screen again. 'Oh, one moment... there is a note on the system.'

'Thank goodness!' Lucy's hand rested on the base of her throat as the thudding of her heart slowed.

'Actually, it's about the bill.'

'His father is picking up the bill. Jack Maddison.'

'Jack Maddison?' There was a puzzled look. 'I'm sorry, that's not a name I recognise.'

'He's only the fifth richest man in Australia.' Lucy glared with annoyance. 'I'm surprised you don't know who he is. He owns diamond mines.'

The receptionist looked confused then shook her head again. 'Well, I'm sorry, I don't. And from the note here it's not Mr Maddison who is responsible for the bill, it's you.'

'Me?' Lucy glowered at her. 'Are you trying to be funny?'

'No, it says here the booking was made by a Miss Lucy Benedict.'

'That's me, but there must be some mistake.'

'No mistake,' Stefanie insisted. 'The booking was definitely made in your name.'

'Well, how much is the bill?'

Organising a printout, the receptionist handed it to her. Lucy stared at it in disbelief. Not only had the cost of the two suites been charged to her, but also the lavish dinner they had had eaten the previous evening.

'I'm not paying for this,' she insisted loudly.

'Well, I'm afraid if you don't I'm going to have to call the manager.'

'Do what you like.' Lucy's steely stare locked on the girl. 'There's no way I'm liable for this!' She threw the printout at her.

'Problems, Stef?' As if summoned by telepathy, the manager appeared out of nowhere. Sandy-haired and smart-suited, his gaze fell immediately on Lucy before he transferred his attention to his receptionist.

'It's about Miss Benedict's bill, Mr Ward.' The receptionist handed him the printout. 'She tells me she's not responsible for payment. She says a Mr Maddison is paying.'

He checked the sheet of paper before taking over the terminal and checking once more. After a moment he shook his head, his eyes directly on Lucy.

'Well... the suites were booked for you and Mr Ethan Maddison. However, I'm afraid the system says the booking was made in your name, Miss Benedict. In fact your credit card details were given to hold the rooms.'

'What!' Lucy frowned. 'When was this?'

'Five days ago.'

'But I was in Bali then. I didn't use the card while I was there.'

'I'm sorry, Miss Benedict, but as far as this hotel is concerned the reservation was made in your name with your card details.' Gregg Ward regarded her with a kind of expression which told Lucy she wasn't going to win this argument. 'American Express Card ending 4256. And that, I'm afraid, makes you liable,' he continued. 'So I'd be grateful if you'd settle the bill otherwise I'll have no alternative but to call the police.'

Realising something was badly wrong but knowing she would be forced to pay the bill before she could investigate further, Lucy angrily pulled her purse from her shoulder bag. Extracting her credit card, she tossed it across the reception desk.

Stef swiped the card through the terminal. It emitted a buzzing sound. She frowned. The process was repeated again with the same result. The manager took the card and left the reception area, walking back across the foyer towards an office in the far corner.

'What is he doing with my card?' Lucy demanded, as she watched him leave.

'Oh, Mr Ward is probably going to check it. The card may be faulty or...' She hesitated.

'Or what?' Lucy snapped.

'There may be insufficient credit available.'

Lucy shook her head. 'That's impossible. I cleared my account balance two weeks ago and since then I've not used the card. Insufficient credit will not be a problem. Look, I'm going to call my fiancé, he'll put a stop to this nonsense once and for all,' she declared and, dipping once more into her bag, she found her mobile. Keying in Ethan's number, she frowned when the ringtone immediately indicated the number was unobtainable. She tried again with the same result. Her teeth snagged her bottom lip apprehensively. What was going on?

Moments later Gregg Ward returned, an uncomfortable expression on his face as he handed Lucy her card. 'I'm sorry, Miss Benedict.' He cleared his throat. 'It appears you are all spent out on this card. Have you an alternative method of payment?'

'Spent out? Impossible!' Lucy stared at the card then at him. 'And, no, I don't have another card.'

'In that case you give me no alternative.' He grabbed her by the arm. 'You can wait in my office while we call the police. Stef, if you would please.' He signalled to the receptionist, who immediately picked up her phone and began to dial.

'What? No! Let me go!' Lucy tried to pull away but found herself in a grip she was unable to shake off. A uniformed security guard appeared and took her other arm. Flanked by two men who now held her firmly, she had no option but to accompany them across the marble floored foyer and into the manager's office, her embarrassment made worse by the fact the whole scene was now being watched by at least a dozen people.

'Right, missy, sit here please.' The security guard, who she guessed from his colouring and features was part Aborigine, indicated a seat to the left of the door, and stood over her while the manager seated himself behind his desk to wait.

Lucy's mind was in turmoil. Where was Ethan? Surely he couldn't have abandoned her? And Jack, well... he would be furious when he discovered what had befallen his daughter-in-law to be. Rummaging in her bag, she found the card he had given her on the morning she had gone to his offices to discuss the investment.

'I want to call someone,' she demanded frostily.

Gregg Ward nodded and sat back, lacing his fingers.

Clutching the business card and her phone, she got to her feet. 'My future father-in-law will not be happy at the way you've manhandled me or the public spectacle you created,' she muttered, glaring at them both furiously as she punched in the number.

Putting the phone to her ear, she waited for the call to connect. Both men watched her impassively, noticing the confused look which crossed her face as she eventually cancelled it.

'I must have dialled the wrong number.' She grimaced impatiently as her fingers carefully pressed the phone's keypad once more. Again she waited then dialled a third time. 'I don't understand... He has offices in Martin Place. I was there yesterday. He gave me this card, but the line is dead.' She looked up at the manager.

His expression softened slightly and he beckoned for the card. 'May I see?'

Lucy handed it to him and watched as he held it in his hand and stared at the details, then at the security guard.

'Kulan, ever heard of the Goorumba Mining Corporation?'

The guard shook his head before fixing his sympathetic gaze on Lucy. 'No, but I do know what goorumba means, missy. It's the Aborigine word for lies.'

NINE

Lucy stared blankly at both men. 'You mean to say...?'

Gregg Ward nodded. 'I'm afraid you appear to have been the victim of a scam, Miss Benedict.'

She put her hands to her face, thoughts whirling around her head. 'Oh my God!' Her eyes widened as she stared at Gregg. 'Then Anna must have been on it too.'

'Anna? Who's Anna?'

'Anna Singleton. I met her in Bangkok. We really hit it off. I treated her to a three-week break with me in Bali. That's where we met Ethan Maddison, my fiancé. She was the one who told me all about the family, how wealthy they were.' She thought for a moment before raising her eyes to Gregg. 'We shared a suite. She must have been the one who used my card to book the hotel.'

'Miss Benedict, I think perhaps we should leave this...' Gregg began, but his words were lost as a sharp tap on the door saw Stef leaning in to announce the arrival of the police.

Two plain clothes detectives in short-sleeved shirts were ushered into the room. Gregg briefed them on the updated situation. The hotel bill still remained to be paid but Lucy's status had changed dramatically from villain to victim.

'We need to discuss this in more detail down the station.' One of the detectives, a thick-set man with black hair and pale blue eyes who had introduced himself as Ellis Turner, motioned for her to stand. 'We can take a statement and run some of our most wanted past you. Hopefully there's a chance you might recognise someone.'

Lucy hesitated, nervous of being whisked away from a place of relative safety by two complete strangers. She may have seen their IDs but, so far, others she had trusted had turned out to be out-and-out rogues.

'It's okay,' Greg Ward said, as if reading her thoughts. 'You're in safe hands. And you do need to sort all this out. These people are still at large; they need to be caught.'

'What about the hotel bill?'

'Don't worry about that for now. Please go with the officers.'

She nodded and thanking him, followed them out.

Two young men, one dark, one fair, both in faded jeans and t-shirts, emerged from the stage door of the Sydney Entertainment Centre and into the glare of morning sunshine, pausing for a moment as one of them pulled out a mobile to make a call. Christian Rosetti and Jimmie McShea stood together; Jay as everyone called him now, talking into his phone for a few moments before they continued their journey towards the front of the building.

'Right, that's everything sorted then,' Jay remarked, reaching up into his thick shaggy fair hair and angling his sunglasses over his eyes. 'Now, you're sure you're happy with all the changes for this evening?'

'Of course I am, Jay. You seem to forget it was me who suggested them in the first place,' Christian answered with slight irritation. 'What you have to remember is tonight is my last night, so it's important I blow them away.' He pushed his black curly hair back from his face as they reached the road and stood waiting on the edge of the pavement.

'Man, you always blow them away.' Jay smiled at him with blue-eyed admiration. 'You're the ultimate pro.'

'Thanks for the endorsement, mate.' Christian's black eyes glinted and his mouth formed itself into a smile of self-satisfaction. 'But you know as well as I do, I had to bully Matt into letting me have this tour. Therefore, it's important we return home with everything an absolute success so he knows my decision was the right one and he was wrong. I want to make sure he respects that fact.' He shaded his dark eyes against the brightness. 'Now, where's that bloody limo?'

As if on cue, a silver Mercedes with tinted windows drew up in front of them. Their Australian driver, wearing black chinos and a green and gold Rosetti Australian Tour polo shirt, got out and opened the rear door. They climbed in but not before Christian had stopped to lecture the man about being late.

Settling himself into the back of the car next to Christian and stretching out his legs, Jay puffed out his cheeks. His former band mate's self-important attitude on this tour had been breath-taking, and at times totally irritating. What had happened to the old Christian? The guy whose talented song writing and unassuming manner had endeared him to everyone? Where the hell had he gone? Resting his head back and closing his eyes, he was thankful tomorrow they would be on their way home and next week would see him having a respite from Christian's obnoxious behaviour.

The Sydney Entertainment Centre was only minutes away from the hotel and the Mercedes was soon there, stretching itself along the pavement behind a centrally parked green saloon.

'Thought this was a no parking area,' Jay called out to their driver.

'Yeah, it is, unless you're cops,' came the reply. 'Looks to me like an unmarked police car.'

'Wonder what's happened. Someone had too much to drink and punched a waiter?'

The driver shook his head. 'Nah, uniform would sort something like that out. Plain clothes sort out the more serious stuff. Hey,' he gestured towards the hotel entrance, 'this looks like them now.'

Christian and Jay did a double take as they watched the three figures coming out of the hotel.

'Grief, is that who I think it is?' Jay squinted at the young woman in a blue sundress walking between two older men, her head bowed and dark hair partially hiding her face. 'No, surely not?'

'Yep, it's her!' Christian confirmed with an annoyed sigh. 'Matt's little girl Lucy.' He shouldered the car door open. 'Come on. Let's see what she's got herself into this time.'

'Lucy?' Jay began walking towards her while Christian hung back, the expression on his face indicating he was less than pleased.

'Jay, is it really you?' Lucy threw her arms around him as he reached her. 'Something awful has happened.' She burst into tears.

Jay pulled a handkerchief from his pocket and handed it to her. 'What's going on?' He directed the question at the two policemen as she mopped her eyes and blew her nose.

The taller of the two fixed him with a hard stare. 'Who's asking?'

'We're—' Jay began, but was cut off by Christian who had stepped forward, his face etched with irritation.

'Are you honestly saying you don't know who I am?' The tall rock star towered over them with a disbelieving glare. 'For the last three nights I've been appearing to packed audiences at the Sydney Entertainment Centre. There are posters all over the city. Are you blind or something? I—'

Jay raised a hand to silence the tirade. 'I'm Jimmie McShea; I work for Matt Benedict who runs Evolution UK, and this is Christian Rosetti,' he nodded towards him, 'one of Matt's artists. As he's informed you, he's currently appearing at the Sydney Entertainment Centre. And Lucy, believe it or not,' he gestured towards her, 'is Matt Benedict's daughter.'

'You're kidding me!' One of the detectives, who Jay gauged was in his mid-forties, made eye contact with his partner and shook his head. 'I remember Matt Benedict and The Attitude. I saw them here back in the early seventies. Great band.' He turned his attention to Lucy. 'So, you're his daughter, are you?'

Lucy nodded silently.

'Well, gentlemen,' Jay continued, 'now we've identified ourselves perhaps you'd be good enough to let us know why Lucy is under arrest.'

'Oh, she's not under arrest,' the forty-something replied. 'She's helping with enquiries.'

He eyed the man sceptically. 'Isn't that the same thing?'

'Not at all. We're taking her to the Day Street station so she can make a statement and look at some photos in connection with a scam.'

'A scam?' Christian's gaze immediately fixed itself on Lucy. 'What have you been up to now, Lucy?' he asked with a scornful shake of his head. 'Your parents haven't heard from you for God knows how long and here you are up to your neck in trouble.'

Lucy found her voice, tears replaced by indignant outrage. 'Don't you dare speak to me like that. You wait till my father—'

'Enough, both of you.' Jay raised his hand once more. 'We'll come to the station with you, Luce.'

'You go do the nursemaiding if you want to,' Christian said, giving Lucy the benefit of yet another disparaging look. 'Me? I've better ways to spend my time.' And without another word he turned away and walked into the hotel.

'Looks like it's just me, then.' Jay gave her a friendly grin as one of the detectives opened the rear door of the police car for her. 'I'll follow in the limo.'

'So it was Felica all the time?'

Sitting with CJ having breakfast on the terrace the next morning in the sunshine, Charlotte was discussing the events of the day before.

'Yes,' she said. 'Apparently she was on her way to the station in Abbotsbridge to pick Marco up and was running late. She was horrified; she kept apologising and assured me she will pay for all the damage.'

'And did *you* apologise to Marco?' CJ asked, before pushing the last of his toast into his mouth.

Charlotte tossed her brother an indignant look. 'Apologise? What for? He manhandled me and pushed me against the wall.'

'Only because you were going to hit him.'

'He deserved it; he's an arrogant pig! Why is it all you men stick together?'

'I'm not standing up for him, Lottie, I'm—'

'Ah, there you both are.' A smiling Jenny appeared at the French doors. With Helen Baxter on a day off, Jenny had volunteered to cook this morning's breakfast and was still wrapped in her navy and white striped kitchen apron. 'Glad I caught you both,' she said excitedly. 'You'll never guess what's happened – they've found Lucy!'

'Lucy?' CJ stared at his sister in astonishment then back at his mother. 'Where?'

'In Australia, and quite by chance too. She was staying in Sydney, at the same hotel as Christian and Jay.'

At the mention of Christian's name Charlotte realised his tour there must have reached its conclusion, which meant he'd be home soon, and no doubt visiting Little Court. She hoped time away had mellowed him and they weren't in for more of his overbearing rudeness. 'Are they bringing her home?' she asked, turning her mind back to the subject of Lucy.

Jenny nodded as she began the task of clearing breakfast things away. 'Yes. Jay phoned from the airport as they were about to board.'

'How was your evening with the Grande Dame, by the way?' Charlotte asked, helping collect up the remaining breakfast plates.

Jenny's face lit up. 'Oh, she was very gracious and you were right, she did apologise. She even asked Rowan if he could drop over to discuss improvements to the manor's gardens. We got off on the wrong foot, that was all.'

Charlotte nodded thoughtfully as her mother disappeared with a tray of crockery, wondering whether she had been so fired up for a confrontation with Marco that she too may have misinterpreted Thérèse's attitude.

'Major fireworks tomorrow then, or maybe we'll be killing the fatted calf.' CJ contemplated his words for a moment before he turned to look at her. 'What do you think, sis?'

'I think...' She paused for a moment. 'I think Matt and Ella will be very relieved she's been located.' She looked up at him with a thoughtful smile. 'However, my money is on the fireworks. She was totally out of order disappearing like that; they won't let her off lightly this time.'

Lucy relaxed back in the comfort of her white leather seat. The Evolution private jet had taken off an hour ago. Now with the help of several glasses of champagne, Australia and the events which took place there were beginning to fade. Jay had been absolutely wonderful. He'd stayed with her at the station during her interview and her scan through photos of potential suspects, run her back to the hotel in the hired limo and arranged for the enormous hotel bill to be picked up by Evolution. She'd even had a VIP pass to Christian's concert that evening, which had been followed by a glittering end-of-tour party.

Christian, however, had kept his distance and when she had tried to make small talk with him at the party, he had made it clear he wasn't interested, moving on to engage other guests in conversation. The last she saw of him was as the celebrations ended and Jay led her to the waiting limo to return to the hotel. She had stared, unable to believe what she saw happening a few vehicles in front: Christian and a very drunk blonde in a short skirt and extremely high heels were getting into another limo.

'It goes with the territory, Luce,' Jay had told her with an amused smile as he'd opened the car door for her. 'It's part of most rock stars' lifestyles. Part of his, anyway,' he'd added as he'd watched the departing vehicle with a grin. 'Sometimes I don't know where he gets his energy from.'

She closed her eyes, deciding when she returned home Jay's kindness would be top of the list of things to tell her father about, followed by the totally unacceptable behaviour of his so-called star Christian Rosetti.

TEN

'I can't for the life of me understand how you could have been so stupid Lucy!' Matt Benedict said, giving an angry shake of his head as he sat behind his desk watching his daughter intently. For the past hour he had been listening to her account of what she had been doing for the last three years of her life, right up to events of a few days ago and the loss of fifty thousand pounds of her trust fund at the hands of a gang of Australian con artists. 'And not only stupid,' he continued after a moment's silence, 'completely irresponsible! Your great-grandmother would wring her hands in despair if she were still alive thinking her money had been stolen so easily!'

'I'm sorry, Dad,' She chewed her lip. 'So very sorry. They were so plausible. But,' she brightened, 'at least I got to keep the ring.' She fingered the four carat diamond Ethan had given her.

'The ring? You're kidding me! You think that's a *real* diamond?' Matt stared at her hand, his face a picture of disbelief. 'Wake up, Luce. The stone is as phoney as they were!'

'But I thought…'

She watched him as he shook his head, got to his feet and walked over to the window, stopping there for a moment to gaze down into the street below. Running a hand through thick, dark brown hair edged with a light peppering of grey, he turned towards her, his hands pushed into the pockets of his brown cords.

'Right,' he said, his tone indicating he'd made his mind up about something. 'I think it's time we brought you back down to earth, young lady, and got you a job'

'Not Little Court?' She shook her head and raised her hands as if to emphasise her reluctance. 'I don't do catering, Dad, not in any shape or form.'

'No, not Little Court. I want you to come and work for me.' He returned to his seat and considered her thoughtfully. 'So I can keep an eye on you.'

'Here?' Lucy smiled. She had dreaded facing her father, knowing her long-term absence would probably be met with a severe lecture and some sort of punishment. Now it appeared that was not going to happen. Instead, she was coming onto the payroll. 'Fantastic!' she said, her face full of enthusiasm. 'You know I've always wanted to work for you. So what's the job?'

'Tour Cordiality Executive.'

'It sounds great. You'll pay me the going rate, of course?'

'Yes, I don't see why not and if…' he hesitated, 'if you make a success of it, there will be promotion.'

'Wonderful! Of course, I'll need my own staff and an office. Oh yes, and a company car.'

'Let's slow things down, shall we?' He checked his watch. 'I've got a meeting in five minutes. I'd like you to start on Monday when I have more time; we can discuss the whole thing in more detail then and settle you in.'

'Fine.' Lucy gave her father the benefit of one of her radiant smiles. 'Brilliant!'

'Oh, and Lucy…' his face suddenly became serious, 'when we get home this evening I want you to apologise to your mother. I don't think you understand what you put us both through, her more than me.'

'Oh, I will, of course,' Lucy confirmed, damping down her excitement and switching instead to a suitably chastised expression. Yet again her father was a soft touch – she'd not only escaped punishment but been rewarded. She couldn't believe her luck.

Ella Benedict stood watching with some satisfaction as partner Issy Taylor's catering staff went about their business setting tables in the huge purpose-built marquee attached to the house. When her stepfather Liam Carpenter had designed the wedding venue extension six years ago she thought it quite beautiful on the plans. However, when it was finally finished she viewed it as an absolute triumph. Liam never ceased to amaze her. For a man now well into his seventies his talent had in no way diminished and with an exceptional young architect like CJ under his tutelage, she hoped his legacy would continue. Now the whole organisation and execution of weddings could be carried out quite separately from the main house. Part of the design had included a state-of-the-art commercial kitchen, with the whole thing linked to the main house so guests could arrive via the north door. There, the huge entrance hall had been refurbished and was set with comfortable seating where guests could receive a welcoming drink and canapés before being called through to meet the wedding party and take their seats for the reception. Seven guest rooms were also available and since the granting of a licence, there were now plans to extend this to accommodate suites for the bride-to-be and her entourage should they wish to take full advantage of the Lawns' new pre-nuptial beauty package. Liam's cleverly designed changes to the huge old manor house meant it could be used as a business while the family still enjoyed privacy in the south and west wings.

'How are things going?'

'Pretty near perfect,' Ella confirmed with a satisfactory smile as Jenny joined her. 'And…' she nodded towards the sunshine outside, 'I'm hopeful this weather will hold; it will make the photographs in the garden look fantastic. Rowan's guys have done an excellent job. The lawns, the flowerbeds, everything, as usual, is flawless.'

Ella noticed her sister-in-law's quiet smile of pride as she took in her last comment. But it was true. Between them, Rowan and Jenny had turned Little

Court's gardens into a horticultural wonderland; a splendid backdrop for both the house and any wedding which took place there with its sculpted lawns running down to the river, rose arbours and the ornate sixteenth-century Italian fountains.

'And how's Lucy?'

'Oh, you know…' Ella's eyes clouded and she gave a resigned sigh. 'Unrepentant, as usual. She did apologise for ducking out of her degree and for going away and not keeping in regular touch, but I'm afraid deep down Lucy's sorry doesn't really mean a lot. She simply chooses the right words for the right time, and five minutes later has conveniently forgotten there was ever a problem in the first place.'

'And what about the scam?'

'Ah, I think at least that's one area where she has learned a valuable lesson. Thankfully, the Australian police have been in touch and they have a good idea who they're looking for. They say it will only be a matter of time before they're caught.'

'That's good news.' Jenny hesitated for a moment before saying, 'Then I guess you'll have her on your hands for a while now. Maybe we can co-opt her into the Lawns team for the time being, give her something to keep her occupied.'

'Nice thought, but Matt's beaten us to it. He's given her a job with Evolution. She starts on Monday.'

'A job at Evolution?' Jenny raised a curious eyebrow. 'Doing what exactly?'

'Well, it's under wraps at the moment,' Ella responded with a teasing smile. 'I will tell you, but I'm swearing you to silence. If you breathe a word I might have to kill you.'

Jenny laughed at her sister-in-law's humour, sensing Lucy's job was going to have a sting in the tail somewhere. 'Come on then, tell me what Matt has done.'

'Well, you know him, he's always been fair. However, this time he's had enough of Lucy and her antics. He wants to keep an eye on her. So, he decided if he offered her a job within his company and dangled future promotion in front of her if she did well, she'd go for it. And she has in a big way. She's very enthusiastic, in fact.'

'So, what's the job?'

'She's going to be the new Tour Cordiality Executive.'

'And what exactly is that in English?'

'She's looking after the hospitality riders for his stars.'

'Oh!' Jenny gave an amused laugh. 'So he's making her start at the bottom.'

'Precisely. But Lucy thinks it's going to be a breeze. She has it in her mind she'll be managing staff who will be doing all the work and it will all be a big social thing for her. I'm afraid,' Ella supressed a smile, 'when Matt sits down and goes through the detail with her on Monday morning our daughter is going to get the shock of her life.'

Charlotte watched bride and groom posing under the rose-covered gazebo halfway down the main lawn, while a group of women in assorted pastels and large hats, and men in morning suits sipped Bucks Fizz and indulged in small talk on the terrace above. Everything was perfect: the weather, the gardens and, of course, the function suite as always was spectacular. With its layout of circular tables, starched cloths, gleaming cutlery and huge bowls of white roses it looked magnificent.

Ten minutes later she was standing in the entrance of the marquee as bride, groom and their entourage met, shook hands with or embraced guests before she took over and directed them towards the huge lectern showing the seating plan. The event was soon underway, uniformed waitresses moving around the guests, setting down plates under the critical eye of her Aunt Issy who watched from the edge of the room. Corks popped, wine was served and everyone settled down to eat, the hubbub of voices gradually fading. Happy everything seemed to be going well, Charlotte left and began making her way back to her room to change, her duties over for the day. As she reached the stairs she heard someone call her name and turned to see her plump aunt approaching.

'Charlotte, I'm so sorry…' Issy patted her chest, clearly out of breath as she reached her. 'One of the girls has had to go home; a family emergency. I don't suppose you could help out with the waitressing until the evening shift arrives, could you?'

'Yes, no problem.' Charlotte felt quite happy to do this for her aunt. After all, she had no plans for the rest of the day other than having to suffer hearing her recently returned cousin bragging about her important new job.

She made her way to her room to change into the straight, knee-length skirt and gold blouse with its black Lawns at Little Court monogram on the breast pocket as worn by the other female catering staff.

The afternoon flew by. The first course was cleared away, followed by mains and dessert, champagne was uncorked and then it was time for speeches, toasts and finally the cutting of the cake. By the time the village church clock struck six everything had been cleared away and most of the staff were taking a break before their next set of duties – setting up the buffet for the evening disco.

Kayte O'Farrell, a magnet for Issy Taylor's lectures on skirts that were far too short and blouses which revealed altogether too much cleavage, got to her feet, saying she was going outside for some fresh air. As Charlotte watched her head for a spot behind the walled garden down by the river, she noticed one of a group of young male guests standing outside the function suite drinking. He appeared to be watching Kayte's departure. Placing his glass on a nearby table, he began to move away, cutting a straight line across the lawn towards her.

At first, Charlotte thought he intended to intercept her, but his leisurely pace, hands tucked into his suit trouser pockets as he crossed the grass, gave the impression his intention was to follow. She gazed at the departing figure for a moment before realising she was looking at the short stocky frame, red hair and florid complexion of Gavin Edwards. Gavin's father, Henry, owned Windrush Farm a few miles south of Higher Padbury. She wondered whether Kayte was involved with Gavin, although if that was so she doubted Henry would approve. He was what the locals called a gentleman farmer with a very tenuous link to the land, employing others to manage and run his nine hundred acres. Oh yes, flirty good-time girls, even if they were the daughter of one of the area's most successful farmers, would be very much off someone like Henry Edwards' approval list.

Kayte had now disappeared from sight and she saw Gavin hesitate before peering around the corner of the wall and then resuming his journey. Sensing something was not quite right, she decided to follow and slipped from the room. The grass was soft and spongy under her feet as she passed the perimeter of the function suite and headed for the gravel pathway where both Kayte and Gavin had walked only moments before.

When she eventually reached them, Kayte was leaning against the wall, a bored expression on her face as Gavin's stood beside her, his voice angry and emotional. Eventually, Kayte pushed herself away from him with a contemptuous scowl.

'I've had enough of this,' Charlotte heard her say. 'You're beginning to bore me, Gavin. I told you, it's over.' And with a final scornful glare, she pushed past him.

'You can't do this, Kayte,' Gavin snapped, reaching out and grabbing her, one of his large hands encircling her upper arm as he pulled her round to face him. 'I love you.'

'Listen to yourself, you're pathetic!' She wrenched herself from his grip. 'It was fun, Gavin, simply a bit of fun!'

'Ah, there you are, Kayte.' Deciding it was time to diffuse the situation before matters got out of hand, Charlotte stepped out from the shelter of the shrubs to confront the pair. 'You're needed back at the house to help set up the buffet.'

Gavin's eyes narrowed as he saw Charlotte approach. 'She'll come as soon as we've finished here,' he said abruptly, turning his attention back to Kayte.

'Gavin!' Clearly annoyed, Kayte tried to wrench herself away from him. 'You heard what Lottie said. Come on, let me go, eh?'

'You'll go when I say and not before,' he snarled, shoving her against the wall, his hands pinning her there. He pushed his face close to hers. 'You can't leave me, Kayte. I won't let you.'

'Get off me!' Kayte pushed at him with both hands at the same time as her knee connected with his groin.

'You bitch!' Gavin shouted, staggering backwards, his hands automatically going to the tender spot Kayte's knee had found only moments before. By the time he had recovered, she'd fled, leaving Charlotte standing beside him.

'Are you all right?' she asked, her hand on his back as she bent forward to speak to him.

'Leave me alone,' he growled, one hand still nursing his crotch as he pushed himself upright. 'This is your fault. If you hadn't poked your nose in—'

'You'd have probably done something you would have been sorry for,' she interrupted. 'She's trouble, Gavin.'

'But I love her so much,' he said, tears threatening. 'I can't help it.'

She put an arm round him. 'Come on, let's get you back. The others will be wondering where you are.'

He nodded miserably, then quite unexpectedly leaned over her and resting his head on her shoulder, began to sob.

'Oh dear, Gavin...' She gave his back a comforting pat; this was the last thing she had expected.

What happened next was frighteningly fast and quite surreal. One moment she was standing with Gavin leaning against her, his tears creating a damp patch on her shoulder, the next he was shooting backwards, a horrified expression on his face as arms flailing, he was grabbed from behind.

'What the hell are you doing?' Charlotte stared with horror as she watched the new arrival, a good six inches taller than Gavin, holding him by his jacket collar and giving him a good shake before sending him on his way with a kick in the rear for good measure.

'I came to rescue you,' Marco said, watching with satisfaction as Gavin ran off clutching the seat of his trousers. 'I saw Kayte.' He gestured in the direction of the marquee. 'She told me he was here with you and he was dangerous.'

'Oh, for goodness' sake!' Charlotte put her hand to her face and gave a tired sigh. 'She's his ex-girlfriend. She has just dumped him here in front of me. He needed sympathy, not your boot up his backside.'

'She dumped him?' His face creased with confusion. 'Because of you?'

'Me?' Charlotte bristled. 'What? It's none of your business! What are *you* doing here anyway?'

'I... I came to see CJ,' he said, quickly adding, 'about the changes to the manor.'

'Was he expecting you?' She eyed him suspiciously; her brother hadn't mentioned anything about having a meeting with him.

Marco shrugged. 'No. I happened to be in the area. I thought I would call in.'

'What, on a whim?' She frowned irritably. 'CJ doesn't work weekends, it's his only time for relaxation, and I think it's a bit rude you simply turning up like this. What was so urgent it couldn't have waited until Monday?'

'I am in London for most of next week.' His eyes settled on her, making her feel uncomfortably hot. 'Perhaps dressing up at weekends and playing waitress may pass as a job where you are concerned,' he said as annoyance flooded his face, 'but I have a proper business to run – although I doubt you would understand that sort of responsibility.'

'How dare you speak to me like that.' Charlotte glared at him, feeling rage bubble inside her. He was insufferably rude, and even more egotistical than Christian.

'I dare to speak to you the way I do,' he replied, his voice full of slow measured anger, 'because you invite it by your constant offensive manner.'

'Offensive manner? Me? Now wait a minute…' But her words trailed away as he simply turned his back on her and walked away.

Marco returned to his car. Slapping the palm of his hand against the steering wheel, he drew in a heated breath and waited until his anger subsided. What had happened to his determination to steer clear of the opposite sex because they were not worth the effort? In the nine months he had been in London there had been a handful of young women in his life; pretty young women he had naively thought were attracted to him. He had even slept with a few of them but soon realised they had only been interested in two things: the places they could be seen out with him and the amount of money he was willing to spend on them. Tiring of this shallow female company and feeling his looks had become a curse, he had decided to turn his back on all women for the foreseeable future.

That was until the evening he walked out onto the rear terrace of Little Court and saw Charlotte Kendrick. As her brilliant blue gaze met his, the attraction he felt pulse between them was overwhelmingly powerful, and like nothing he had ever experienced before. Chatting as they ate together, he had warmed to her. She was bright, intelligent and he sensed a depth in her none of his London ladies possessed. The more they talked the more he wanted to get to know her. But far from succumbing to his charm, she had challenged him over her damaged car and tried to slap him. Even today's peace-making visit, dressed up as a bogus visit to talk to CJ, had been a total failure with verbal insults being hurled.

Now as he sat weighing up the situation, he was beginning to wonder what the hell he was doing putting so much effort into pursuing a woman who made it very clear she did not like him at all. *Pursuing.* The word

50

echoed around his brain. He had never pursued a woman – without exception they always chased after him. This was new and alien territory, one where an insistent inner voice was telling him to give up before it robbed him of his sanity. However, dented pride would not allow this; he was determined to win this battle of wills. Perhaps, he reflected, he had been a little harsh with her. Maybe a change of tactics was needed to bring her round.

He continued to sit there for a while sifting through his options. After a moment an idea came to him. He started the engine and eased the Targa back down Little Court's driveway towards the road, confident his next move would yield the positive results he was hoping for.

ELEVEN

Lucy sat gazing out of the window across the West London skyline. This was the first day of her new job and she was in absolute heaven. Swivelling her high-backed leather chair round to face the room, she surveyed her new domain with satisfaction. Beautiful pale furniture complimented by thick carpet, state-of-the-art equipment and a first floor location at the front of the building. But then she was the boss's daughter, wasn't she? It was an expectation that he would have sorted out this kind of accommodation for her.

She got to her feet and walked around the room, giving a closer inspection to her surroundings. Some of the wall art would have to go, she thought, staring up at a huge shot of Christian on stage in New York. There was absolutely no way she wanted to stare at that all day, it would be bad enough having to see him here in the flesh on a regular basis. Thank God he's not here, she reminded herself, pleased she did not have to contend with his arrogance and rudeness on her first day. In fact, she thought as she smoothed down the skirt of her beige Armani suit and peered down at her pale tan Jimmy Choos, hopefully there will be no reason for me to have anything to do with him at all. I can easily delegate that to one of my staff. *Staff.* She considered the word. Her father had yet to enlighten her on who they were and how many. Hearing the door open, she turned around to find him standing there smiling.

'Settling in okay?' Matt asked, moving into the room and stopping to gaze around at the expensive furniture he had arranged for her new office.

'It's perfect, thank you. However, there are a few things I still need.' She breezed over to her desk to pick up a piece of paper lying on the blotter. 'Here.'

Matt took it from her and she watched as he scanned down the list, appreciating that not only did she have a glamorous job, she was also the envy of many of her friends. After all, not many girls had mothers who could be mistaken for older sisters. Or fathers who looked the way he did. There might be a little grey in his hair now but he was still very handsome and, from the amount of fan mail he got, fancied by a good portion of the female population.

He nodded. 'Seems fine.' He folded the paper and tucked it in the back pocket of his grey cords. 'Now then,' he perched himself on the edge of her desk, 'I think we need to talk in a little more detail about your role, don't you?'

'Great!' Lucy returned to her chair and sat waiting in enthusiastic anticipation to hear more about her empire.

* * *

Little Court was back to normal. Sunday had been a day of clearing up: crockery, cutlery and glasses washed, table cloths consigned to laundry bags, tables and chairs stacked and floors vacuumed. Now it was Monday morning, and returning from a ride through Hundred Acre on Jet, Charlotte found the Holy Trinity locked in Ella's office having their usual post-event analysis meeting. For the three of them it was an essential part of the business, discussing how well things went, whether there were any problems and what, if anything, could be improved on. It was all part of making sure Lawns at Little Court was *the* place for wedding receptions.

That afternoon, her mother had told her, Thérèse and Felica were coming over for discussions about setting up their in-house wedding boutique. CJ was also involved, joining the meeting to advise on the suitability of converting the old stone armoury attached to the side of the main house to accommodate the new premises.

With her riding crop tucked under her arm and pulling off her gloves as she walked, Charlotte crossed into the hall, heading for her room to shower and change her clothes before joining the others for lunch. She'd taken the day off to see Christian, who was due to arrive at Little Court sometime today, although she was not sure exactly when. As she reached the foot of the stairs, she heard the familiar jangle of the bell pull. She stopped, realising he had arrived. Instantly, she turned towards the door, intercepting Helen making her way to answer it.

'I think this is for me,' Charlotte said, dodging around her.

Swinging the door open ready to give Christian a hug of welcome, she found herself facing Marco D'Alesandro instead. Dressed in an expensive charcoal grey suit, he was holding a large bunch of red roses. The sound of a vehicle coming to a halt in the distance distracted her for a moment before she quickly turned her attention back to him.

'I was on my way to London, but I could not leave before I came to see you to apologise for my behaviour towards you over the weekend.' He bowed slightly, their eyes meeting as he raised his head to look at her. 'And to give you these.' He offered her the bouquet. 'To make up for my rudeness.'

'Thank you, apology accepted.' She took the flowers from him slowly, concentrating hard on the blooms in front of her, not daring to make eye contact with him as she scrabbled around in her brain for something sensible to say as heat gradually seeped into her face.

'What the hell's going on?'

Swiftly raising her head, she saw Christian standing beside Marco, his black eyes filled with fury as he stared first at him then the roses.

'Nothing at all. Marco was about to leave,' she said quickly, realising the car engine she had heard was Christian's Maserati.

'Damned right he is and he can take these bloody things with him,'

Christian growled. He snatched the roses from her hand and shoved them back at Marco with a glare. 'She doesn't want your fancy flowers, mate, or anything else. So do me a favour, eh? Get back in your flash car and bugger off!'

For a moment, seeing both bewilderment and anger fuse in the young Italian's shocked expression, Charlotte thought he was about to hit Christian but instead he simply shook his head. 'It is not what you think,' he said quietly.

'Christian, please! There is no need for this. I can explain...' she said, adding her support, but Christian waved her away, moving to stand between the two of them as if asserting his ownership of her.

'Quiet, Lottie,' he hissed as he continued to glare at Marco. 'Leave,' he demanded through gritted teeth.

Flowers in hand, Marco took one last look at both of them before making his way back to his car. As the Porsche disappeared down the driveway, Charlotte stood there feeling a mixture of anger and dismay welling up inside her.

'Did you have to be so rude?' she snapped at Christian.

'Why, what is he to you?' Ignoring her reprimand, he watched her closely. 'Come on, Lottie, tell me. Something been going on behind my back while I've been away, has there?'

'Of course not. He's a neighbour, that's all.' She shook her head, blinking back the tears which threatened.

'A neighbour? Bringing you red roses? I don't think so...'

'Think what you like, Christian,' she threw back at him defiantly. 'There is absolutely nothing going on. Anyway, why should you care? I had the feeling things between us had cooled off considerably lately.'

'Did you, my sweet?' His smile could in no way hide the belligerence in his voice. He slid his finger under her chin and leaned forward to give her a chaste kiss. 'Well, maybe now I'm back I want things to be different. The point is, I don't want to see him here again. Understand?'

'Perfectly.' Charlotte stepped back with an enraged intake of breath as, overnight bag in hand, he strode past her and into the house. How dare he, she thought as he headed for the stairs. He's all but ignored me for the past few months. Now he wants me again. And why? Because he thinks someone else is trying to muscle in. Poor Marco; in an uncharacteristic moment of rashness she actually found herself feeling sorry for him. The old Christian would never have treated him like that, she thought with a shake of her head as she saw him reach the top of the stairs and disappear along the landing. But then, as everyone knew, the old Christian did not exist any more, did he?

Lucy's day was gradually getting worse. It had started so well, the arrival at Evolution UK's offices in Hammersmith, the familiar reception area of glass and chrome decorated with gold and platinum discs, guitars and posters of its stars. Matt's flame-haired Hungarian receptionist Magda was well-known to her, as were many of the others, so it therefore followed joining her father's company was going to be easy. Only now things had gone badly wrong. When he perched himself on the end of her desk and folded his arms she waited patiently to be told the extent of her 'domain'. Now she realised he had tricked her. True, she had the office, the three series BMW and a great salary, but when she mentioned staff he had simply tilted his head and smiled.

'Do you know what a Tour Cordiality Executive does?' he asked.

'Yes. It's all about making sure the stars have everything they want while they're on tour.'

'Got it in one, Luce.' He sounded suitably impressed. 'And your job—'

'Is to oversee everything.' She nodded animatedly. 'Yes, I know.'

'No, Luce, not oversee. There is no staff – only you.'

'But, I thought—'

'Yes, I know you did, but it's about time we brought a little reality into your life. I want you here in the business working for me, but I'm not prepared to simply hand you the job of your dreams on a plate because you are my daughter. You have to earn it, meaning you start at the bottom. That way, you'll really learn the business too.'

Opening her mouth to protest Lucy found him raising a hand to silence her.

'You know, you come over as a complete airhead sometimes.' He gave her an amused grin. 'But I know you are quite capable of doing a good job if you set your mind to it. So here's my challenge. Do this job for a year, make a success of it and I'll guarantee you promotion in an area of your choice.'

'What kind of promotion?' She eyed him warily, sensing another trap.

'What appeals to you most?'

She thought for a moment. 'Creative media. Promotional videos...'

'Yes, I don't see why not. But,' he waved a finger at her, 'only if you make a success of this job.'

He left her then to think it over, handing her a sheet of paper with a collection of 'must haves' for the first artist she was required to work with. A dark cloud of depression settled itself over her as she took in the list and then read the name at the top of it. She thought about the horrors she faced if she took the job on and the even worse situation she would be in if she didn't. She loved her father and the last thing she wanted was to let him down but...

'Hi! Thought I'd check on you, see how you're doing.'

She raised her eyes from the list to see Jay's smiling face peering round the door at her.

'Oh, I'm fine, I guess. Had a few dreams shattered, that's all.'

'The hospitality thing, you mean?' he asked, coming into the room and leaning his long denim-clad legs against her desk. 'I did it for a time; it was quite good fun actually.'

'What, playing nursemaid? You've got to be joking.'

'Oh, come on. Think of it as a challenge. I'm sure when you get into it you'll enjoy it.'

'Like hell I will! Dad's already left me this.' She shook the paper at him. 'He's winding me up deliberately, isn't he?'

'Who? Matt?'

'No. Christian! This is what has been negotiated for his forthcoming dates in Scotland.'

Pushing himself away from the desk, Jay took the sheet from her and ran his eyes down the list. 'Well, well, fussy sod, isn't he? Oh, and a different single malt in each venue.' He grinned at her. 'And there's me thinking he didn't even like whisky.'

'I told you it's a deliberate wind up.' She gave a painful grimace. 'I want so much to please my father but I'm not sure I can cope with this. Dad's expecting me to go with him. Christian can't stand me and I know he'll be using any excuse to get me into trouble.'

Jay nodded as he handed the sheet of paper back to her. 'I know he can be a complete bastard at times, but you won't be alone. I'll be with you.'

'You will?' Lucy's eyes widened in surprise, wondering why her father had not told her.

'Yes. You see, part of my job is seeing the venues meet the technical rider requirements of Evolution's artists, which means things like health and safety, staff, instruments, lighting, equipment. So you won't be thrown in at the deep end, I'll be there to hold your hand.' His blue eyes gazed into hers. 'And if for any reason his lordship decides to kick off he'll have me to deal with, okay?'

Lucy stared at Jay, unable to believe her luck. He was promising to help her. He was also perhaps a little smitten, she decided, from the way his eyes had seemed to follow her all the time when they were in Australia. She smiled. Now all she had to do was work out how to off-load the lion's share of this hateful job without him even realising.

Friday evening at the Somerset Arms was a busy time in the newly created restaurant area. By eight o'clock all tables were full and the kitchen buzzing. Plump brunette Terri Harper moved among the diners, taking food orders and sorting the drinks for each table while Kieren, an assistant and a full time waitress busied themselves with food preparation and delivery.

Behind the bar, Terri's stocky red-headed husband Stuart served the drinkers and newly arrived diners with the help of their recently acquired barmaid, Kayte O'Farrell. Stuart watched the pretty twenty-year-old in her tight skirt and lacy top pulling pints as if she was born to it. She had only been here a week but she was proving very able and also extremely popular, particularly with the younger male drinkers. He knew, however, her reputation was such that he'd need to keep a strict eye on her. She was a serial flirt, already having broken several hearts among Meridan Cross's young male population. What he wanted to avoid was any of these young bucks crossing swords in his pub with the disastrous consequences pub punch-ups usually left in their wake.

He had just finished serving a group of new arrivals and was handing change to one of them when the door opened and Marco D'Alesandro walked in. Clad in jeans and a black t-shirt topped with a linen jacket, there were appreciative female glances as he crossed to the bar.

'Marco!' Stuart moved along the counter with an easy smile. 'What can I get you?'

'I'll serve Marco,' Kayte said, stepping in front of him. 'Dry white wine, isn't it?' She gave him a dazzling smile before pulling a wineglass down from the rack and setting it on the bar. Then opening the glass fronted fridge she held up a bottle of Frascati to which he nodded in confirmation. 'There,' she said, uncorking it quickly and filling the glass.

Returning the bottle to the fridge, Stuart watched her take the note from Marco's hand, open the till and hand him back his change, her hand lingering slightly longer than necessary over his open palm while her eyes danced wickedly as they gazed across the bar at him. Called away to settle a bill with departing customers, Stuart had no alternative but to leave Kayte to her own devices for a moment. He sensed trouble and hoped Marco was wise enough not to encourage her. However, when he returned he found him still there with Kayte now leaning across the bar, her head nearly touching his in an intimate fashion while at least four customers stood waiting to be served.

'Kayte!' He nodded towards the first of them. 'Customers.'

'Yes, Stuart, I can see them,' she answered tartly, tossing her head with annoyance as she reluctantly drew a pint of draught Guinness for Tom O'Reilly, one of the retired village locals.

A few minutes later she was back, topping up Marco's glass, her laughter resonating above the din of conversation in the room as she shared a joke with him.

'Kayte!' Again Stuart tried to prise her away, indicating there was work to be done. With an irritable sigh and matching expression she reluctantly extracted herself from behind the bar and began clearing and wiping down tables. Stuart watched her, becoming more and more annoyed as she brought used glasses to the counter, depositing them right next to Marco, making sure she either accidentally touched or brushed against him each time. In a packed pub Stuart knew there was little he could do without causing a scene but he promised himself he was going to give her a good talking to about appropriate behaviour once they closed. People were beginning to notice; he could see amusement in most of the male faces there. They all knew what she was like and it was becoming embarrassing.

When Stuart later rang the bell for closing time he gave a sigh of relief. Eventually, everyone finished their drinks and left, apart from Marco. He took himself off to a table in the far corner by the huge open fireplace as if waiting for something or someone. Terri appeared, Nikki the full-time waitress on her heels.

'I could murder a drink,' Terri said, grinning at her husband. She turned to blonde Nikki as she selected a tumbler and pushed it under one of the optics, treating herself to a double brandy. 'What's your poison, Nikki?'

'Thanks, but I've got to drive.' Nikki turned to Kayte, who was hanging glasses up behind the bar. 'You nearly ready, Kayte?'

'Oh, I won't need a lift tonight, thanks.' Kayte shot a triumphant smile across to where Marco sat in the corner. 'Marco's taking me home.'

Stuart and Terri's eyes met in a shared message of unease.

At the mention of his name Marco looked up. 'I am sorry,' he said, looking confused. 'I never agreed to do that, Kayte.'

'You've been chatting me up all evening,' she snapped. 'You said you passed Willowbrook on your way home and I would be welcome to have a lift any time.'

'Yes, but not tonight.'

'Why? Where are you going?'

'Kayte, there's no need to be so rude,' Stuart said sharply.

'I think there's every need to be rude when someone lies to you.'

'I did not lie, Kayte,' Marco insisted.

'Well, what other reason would keep you here?'

'He's been waiting for me, that's why.'

They all turned as Kieren pushed through the curtain which separated the kitchen from the bar. His eyes were fixed on Marco and he was smiling.

'What for?' Kayte demanded, noticing Kieren carried a black holdall.

'Marco's taking me up to London tonight.'

'Why?'

Getting to his feet, Marco crossed to the bar and joined Kieren. 'You ask too many questions, Kayte,' he whispered as he passed her. 'Ready, Kieren?'

Kayte lay in bed, feeling too angry and humiliated to sleep. No one, but no one, made a fool of her. The world existed on her terms; she chose men and she dropped them – those were her rules. Only on this occasion that had not happened. In fact, her ego had been dealt an enormous blow. To be left for another woman was bad enough, not that it had ever happened to her before, but to be passed over for a gay cook was too much. *Was Marco also gay?* she wondered. He was extremely good looking and lots of very handsome men batted for the other side, as her father termed it. She lay there, thinking. No, maybe she shouldn't be so hasty. Her parents were always telling her she overreacted and had a habit of cutting off her nose to spite her face. Hot men like Marco D'Alesandro came around once in a lifetime, she would be crazy to turn her back on him on the strength of what had happened in the pub earlier. After all, for most of the evening he had been attentive and funny and appeared to be enjoying her company. No, she decided, clutching her pillow and trying to imagine he was lying there beside her, it's worth another try. She smiled, a plan already forming in her mind.

TWELVE

'What the fuck do you think this is?'

Lucy pushed her way into Christian's dressing room to find him staring at the bottle of whisky on the table.

He turned his angry eyes to her. 'Well?'

'It's what you asked for. Aberdonia twelve year malt.'

'No, it's bloody well not! I asked for *Abercrombie* twelve year malt. What's the matter with you, can't you get anything right?'

Lucy turned away from his venom. She knew this was going to happen; ever since they left London he had been in a foul mood with her, never missing an opportunity to find fault. The two nights in Edinburgh had gone well; he had played to packed houses at the Playhouse Theatre, although he had griped about the hotel. That was Jay's responsibility and he had merely shrugged off the criticism, telling Christian if he could do better than the five-star Waldorf Caledonian then perhaps he should sort out his own bookings in future. As far as he was concerned that was the only way to deal with Christian. Whether it was because they went back a long way or because he was male, Lucy wasn't sure. One thing she did know was that when it came to her, Christian was snapping at her heels all the time. And so with Jay's help she had made sure all his requirements at the Playhouse had been met. Keeping him on her side helping her get through this nightmare was important, and currently she had him eating out of her hand. Only now, on arrival in Aberdeen, this happened. Abercrombie whisky? It had definitely not been on the list.

'Well?' He glared at her, his arms folded across his chest. 'Haven't you anything to say?'

'I thought I ordered the whisky you specified, Christian.' She raised her hands in a gesture of helplessness. 'I'm sorry, okay?'

'No, not okay, Lucy.' He shook his head as he walked over to the table. 'I want it replaced. Now!'

'But that's impossible...' She picked up the bottle and looked at it. 'This whisky was a special order and my guess is Abercrombie is the same. It's Sunday and I'm not sure I can get the theatre to replace it by this evening.'

Christian checked his watch then gave her an evil grin as he snatched the bottle from her. 'Well, I'm not drinking this rubbish!' To her horror, he opened it and began to pour it down his dressing room sink. 'And I'm not going on tonight unless a bottle of Abercrombie twelve year malt is here within the next hour.'

'But—' Lucy began.

'Get on with it!' he bellowed.

Lucy ran from the room and down the corridor, tears blurring her vision.

As she turned the corner she ran straight into Jay, who caught her gently by the shoulders.

'Hey!' His concerned eyes took in her tear-stained face. 'What is it? What's happened?'

'The whisky in his dressing room, it's wrong,' she blurted out. 'I ordered Aberdonia. It was on the list and he says he wanted Abercrombie, and he refuses to go on tonight unless it's replaced.'

'Oh, for God's sake!' Jay sucked in his breath 'He's taking the piss, isn't he? Leave it with me, I'll sort it. It's far too late to change anything so he'll have to put up with what's there.'

'But he's poured it down the sink.'

'What! Go back to the hotel, Luce,' he said, gentling his tone. 'Freshen up, put on your best dress and wait for me in reception. I'm taking you out to lunch without,' he jerked a thumb in the direction of Christian's dressing room, 'King Kong down the corridor. But first, I need to speak to him. He's gone too far this time.'

Lucy watched him stride off down the corridor, heard raised voices followed by a slamming door. Wiping her eyes, she made her way to the front of the theatre to hail a cab.

Jay had always prided himself on having an even temper and being very much a peacemaker. Heaven knows he'd spent enough time sorting out differences within the band during his time with Rosetti. Now with his back against the door of Christian's dressing room, he faced the surly star with the feeling he wanted to punch him. The tall, muscular, tattooed rock star sat slouched in one of the chairs, looking totally unrepentant.

'What's all this crap about the whisky?' he demanded, eyeing Christian with undisguised irritation.

Christian gave him a smug grin. 'Silly bitch got it wrong, didn't she? She's fucking useless.'

'No, Christian, she's trying incredibly hard to make this job work and you're not helping. Abercrombie whisky – is there such a thing?'

'What do you think?' Christian arched an eyebrow, mischievous spite written all over his handsome features.

'I think it's about as likely as red steam and left handed cups.'

'You got it in one, brother.' The grin, wide and malicious, surfaced again.

'Well, stop it and stop it now, do you hear? I want you to leave her alone.'

Christian laughed.

'What's so funny?'

'Jay, old son, you're so bloody transparent, all this shining white knight stuff. Do you honestly think it's going to get you into her knickers? You're on the payroll, mate, simply another one of Matt's employees. You'll never be anything else so get used to it. Lucy Benedict's not for the likes of you,

61

never has been, never will be.'

Jay gave Christian a long cold stare before pushing himself away from the door and grabbing the handle.

'Back off, Christian,' he said, a deadly chill in his voice. 'I mean it.'

And with a slam of the door he was gone.

Felica D'Alesandro, at the wheel of the black Range Rover, drove slowly down the gravelled driveway towards Little Court Manor. She was near to tears; something dreadful had happened and with her mother away she needed help. Chi Chi had gone missing. One moment he had been on the lawn having his usual early morning wander around inspecting the garden, and the next he was nowhere to be seen. Despite calling and searching the grounds and outbuildings there was no sign of him. She had already been up to Willowbrook to try to enlist help there, where she found Kayte saddling up about to leave with a party of trekkers. Obviously unable to assist, Kayte was very apologetic but promised to give the manor a call this afternoon, pledging all her spare time to help the search if the dog was still missing.

Unfortunately, Kayte's father and his men were busy taken up with the harvesting, and he was unable to spare anyone to assist either. Ever helpful Niall had suggested she try at Little Court because Ella, Jenny, and Charlotte, who was home for the day, all rode and were familiar with the area. He had called ahead to let them know she was coming.

As she rounded the final bend before the house she smiled through her tears. Coming towards her were three women on horseback, one leading a saddled chestnut mare. As they reached her she pulled to a stop, got out and locked the vehicle.

'Thank you, thank you so much,' she said, taking the reins of spare horse Ella was leading and mounting up. 'Mother is in London and I was not sure what to do. Marco's home though and he said he would drive into Morden to ask there.'

'Don't worry,' Ella's confident tone reassured her. 'We've already discussed where to search. You come with me and we'll check the eastern part of the wood and circle back towards the manor. Jenny,' she nodded towards her sister-in-law, 'will go west and come through Sedgewick Woods, and Lottie will do a sweep through Hundred Acre. Between us I'm sure we'll find him.'

After an hour of searching Charlotte emerged from Hundred Acre. Rain, the sort which swept down the valley with little warning, had overtaken her while she was still deep in the wood. The trees were so heavily meshed and the canopy of leaves so thick it was impossible to have noticed the dramatic and rapid change from blue sky to dark cloud. And now here she was, damp and uncomfortable, and there was still no sign of that bloody little dog. She shivered as she came out of the wood and gazed across the valley – Willowbrook to the right and Little Court to the left – both a good twenty-minute ride away. It was just as well, she thought with a smile, Fox Cottage, once owned by Willowbrook but now belonging to her, was only a few minutes away. Since buying it from Niall and Rachel she had used it as a bolt hole; a place where she could come to clear her head or simply chill out when she needed the space and solitude Little Court, with its non-stop activities, was unable to give her. And, of course, she always kept a change of clothes there and the tumble dryer would soon take care of the damp things she was currently wearing. Kicking her heels into Jet, her black hunter, she turned him east along the border of wood and field towards the cottage.

Moments later she was there. After tying Jet to the porch, she punched in the four-digit code for the tiny wall-mounted safe, retrieved the key and opened the front door. Closing it quietly behind her, she pulled off her boots and left them in the inner porch before throwing her riding crop onto a nearby chair and heading for the stairs, peeling off her clothes as she went. She retrieved a large white towel from the bathroom cupboard, pulled off her underwear, and began to dry herself thoroughly. Then wrapping the towel tightly around her body, she gathered up her damp clothes and made her way downstairs.

As she reached the bottom a noise pulled her up sharply. There was an unfamiliar scraping sound coming from the kitchen. Slowly she crept across the sitting room towards the kitchen door. There was an old dog flap in the back door, left from the time Niall's foreman Sam Robinson and his family lived here with their border collie Nelson. She had never bothered to have it blocked up and she knew in the past the odd stray cat had been known to use it. But this did not sound like a cat, it was something far bigger. Chi Chi maybe? Well, there was only one way to find out. Retrieving her riding crop from the chair and clutching the towel tightly, she made her way slowly towards the open kitchen doorway, determined to confront and either capture or eject whatever had managed to get in.

'What the hell are you doing here?' Shock and surprise mingled in her voice when she walked into the kitchen and found no sign of the escaped Bichon Frise. Instead, a wet Marco D'Alesandro was in the process of climbing through the open window, beads of water dripping off his dark untidy hair.

'The window was not shut properly, I managed to lever it open. I came in here to shelter,' he said, easing himself off the draining board, his gaze running over her. 'I got caught in the rain, searching for my sister's damned dog. It seems you did too.'

Instinctively, Charlotte clutched the towel tighter.

He studied the towel and smiled, a mocking glint in his eyes. 'Not afraid of me, are you, Charlotte, now your ill-mannered boyfriend is no longer here to protect you?'

She eyed him disdainfully. 'Gay men don't scare me, Marco.'

'Gay?' he snapped, tugging at the buttons of his shirt. 'Who says I am gay?'

She didn't reply for as the shirt came off, she could only stare at the body beneath it. The well-muscled chest was covered with a fine mat of dark hair trailing into a thin line which travelled downwards, eventually disappearing beneath the waistband of his jodhpurs. If this man is gay, she thought, unable to take her eyes off him, it's enough to make womankind weep.

'Ah, most of the village, actually,' she answered when her senses kicked back in again.

'Why are they saying such things?' He frowned at her as he tossed his boots into the corner and peeled off his socks before beginning to unzip his jodhpurs.

'What are you doing?'

'Getting out of these damp clothes,' he replied, as if it were the most natural thing in the world to be stripping off in front of someone he hardly knew.

'Not in front of me you aren't,' she said, feeling the heat of something more than embarrassment flood into her face

'If I make you feel uncomfortable, leave the room.' He waved an impatient hand at her.

Charlotte did not need to be told twice; she exited immediately. Gay or not, he was still having that same strange effect on her and the sooner she got some clothes on, the better.

'Charlotte, I need a towel,' he called out as she reached the stairs.

'Please!' she shouted back, thinking *rude bastard* as she went into the bathroom, hastily trying to blot out the image of his half naked body.

By the time she returned with a large white bath sheet she had pulled on jeans and a t-shirt. Hovering outside the kitchen doorway she dangled the towel through the open void. He took it without as much as a 'thank you'. Irritated by his continued rudeness, Charlotte returned to the lounge to sort out the damp clothes she had dropped when she had gone to investigate the noise in the kitchen.

'So...' He appeared in the doorway, pushing his hair back off his face. 'What is all this about my being gay?'

'I'm surprised it bothers you,' she said brusquely, annoyed he was unable to let go of the subject. Gathering up her shirt, sweater and jodhpurs, she headed for the kitchen, carefully avoiding him and the white bath towel which, sitting low on his hips, somehow made his state of undress even worse.

'Of course it bothers me!' He frowned as he watched her pass him. 'What are you doing?'

'Drying my clothes.' She hesitated, then turned back to look at him. 'Would you like me to do the same with yours? In the tumble dryer,' she added in response to his blank look.

He nodded, collected them up and handed them to her.

Charlotte rammed the garments into the machine, feeling she was being treated like a lackey. Didn't 'please' and 'thank you' exist in his vocabulary? Still, anger was good, she decided. If she was angry with him then she didn't have to deal with the other more scary emotions caused by having him wearing very little uncomfortably close to her. Closing the tumble dryer door, she set the timer and turned away only to find him standing within feet of her.

'What have I done to make people think I am gay?' he demanded.

She shrugged, wishing she had never raised the issue. 'I have no idea.' Deliberately trying to ignore his closeness, she focussed her gaze on the tumble dryer. 'But I suppose because you've been keeping late nights with Kieren at the pub, and he's stayed over in London with you. You also appear to have rejected Kayte's advances. This is a small community, Marco.' She turned to glance briefly at him. 'What starts as a rumour can quickly escalate, and boy, do they love their gossip here.'

'You believe this gossip too?'

She gave another uncaring shrug, eyes still fixed on the rotating garments. 'All I know is Kieren is gay and despite her efforts, you don't seem to be at all interested in Kayte. To some that would be evidence enough.'

'Well... maybe they don't see what I see. I know now Kayte is a child in a young woman's body; a very dangerous child. It is why I have to keep as far away from her as I can.'

Charlotte took her eyes off the dryer and nodded in agreement. 'Sometimes I don't think she has any understanding of how provocative her behaviour is.'

'You women rarely understand the effect you have on men.' He gave the kind of slow smile she had seen that very first day at the barbeque. It was enough to send her whole body into meltdown.

'Perhaps we don't, but if you're the red-blooded male you claim to be then what's going on between you and Kieren?' she asked quickly, staring back at the tumble dryer again, trying to blot his smile from her mind.

'I have been spending time with Kieren because I want him to come and work for me in London. I run a restaurant chain.'

'Ah, so that's what you do...' She remembered interrupting Thérèse at the barbeque, more interested in finding out where he was than hearing what he did for a living.

'Yes, it is what I do. Kieren has a natural talent not only for cooking but also for presentation. He is wasted here. I want him to work in San

Raffaello's and train under my head chef, Florentine Pagamo. I believe Kieren has a great future.'

'You own San Raffaello's? Florentine Pagamo works for you?' Her eyes widened in astonishment. 'Aunt Issy is a huge fan of his TV programme. She would kill for a—'

'Charlotte, I am not gay,' he interrupted as he closed the gap between them.

'Okay, I believe you.' With a disinterested lift of her shoulders she took a step back from him, his bare chest and the insubstantial white barrier that was the towel too much to cope with. 'Luckily our clothes aren't too wet, the tumbler won't take long,' she murmured, checking the timer and wishing she could make it move faster.

'Charlotte!' He was standing right beside her. 'Look at me. Please.'

She stopped what she was doing and as she reluctantly raised her eyes to his, a tiny trickle of water escaped from the thick tangle of his hair and began to run slowly down his face. She was so lost in the depth of those dark eyes that without thinking, her hand reached up to intercept it, her fingers connecting with the warmth of his cheek.

'I am not gay,' he repeated, and curling his fingers around her wrist, pulled her hand away and bent his head to kiss her.

The shock of his warm touch followed by such an unexpected and intimate action took her totally by surprise. She tried to manoeuvre herself away from him but found herself trapped against the worktop, held not only by the weight of his body but by those mesmerising brown eyes. There was nowhere to go. The thought of aiming a slap at him flashed through her mind, but when his hands came to rest either side of her face and his mouth met hers the thought spiralled down in flames.

The kiss, gentle at first, gradually became more demanding as his tongue invaded her mouth. All resistance left her and her arms snaked around his neck, fingers meshing in the dampness of his hair. His mouth, tasting of mint, was arousing, his insistent tongue spectacularly wonderful and she realised, despite her initial anger, she had wanted him to do this to her from the first moment she had seen him. Then all at once she was aware of his hands leaving her face, moving lower to begin gently coaxing her t-shirt from the waist band of her jeans. His warm fingers worked their way slowly under the material, tracing a path up her rib cage to cup her breasts. At the same time, Charlotte felt the none too subtle reaction underneath the towel of his body against hers.

'Marco, no!' As they teetered on the edge of the abyss an invisible force materialised from nowhere and hauled her back. 'I think you've proved your point, thank you,' she said breathlessly, grabbing his wrists and pushing him away.

He stepped back, uncertainty shrouding his face as he ran a hand through his hair. 'I am sorry,' he said, and turning towards the window, a hand to his face, uttered, 'Forgive me, I should not have touched you.'

She raised a reassuring hand. 'It's... it's okay. It really is.'

They stood silent and embarrassed in the confines of the small kitchen, avoiding each other's eyes. The dryer stopped. Glad of the distraction, she released the door, pulled out the dry clothes and handed him his things. He took them silently, avoiding making eye contact with her, and disappeared into the sitting room. Moments later he was back, fully dressed.

'I hope you find Chi Chi,' she said, watching him pull on his boots. 'And please let everyone know what's going on with you and Kieren, will you. Otherwise all this stupid gossip will only get worse.'

'So, you do not believe the rumours?' He stopped to stare at her for a moment before opening the back door.

'No.' Without thinking, her fingers automatically went to her lips. 'No, I don't.'

'It was well worth the kiss then,' he said, his eyes drawn to her face. He left, closing the door behind him and leaving Charlotte standing alone in the silence of the kitchen.

She watched as he swung himself into the saddle before turning his horse's head up towards the wood. Moments later he was gone, swallowed up by the leafy canopy of the trees. She turned away from the window, knowing she should feel relieved she had managed to stop him before things had got completely out of control. But as she contemplated what had taken place moments ago, little niggle of regret began to seep into her consciousness. She wished for one moment in her life she could have been a different Charlotte; one who threw caution to the wind instead of always treading the middle path of common sense. But even if she had been the other spontaneous self, she knew nothing would have happened between them. The gay thing may have been a baseless rumour, but the girlfriend in London was not, and because of that there was no way she could have let things go any farther.

Emerging from the wood, Marco gave the horse its head, letting it stretch its stride across the open fields back towards the manor. He could still feel Charlotte pressed up against him, the softness of her body, the responsiveness of her mouth and the smell of that exquisite perfume she wore. He must have been mad doing what he did, but she had been so close to him and he simply could not resist her. He closed his eyes for a moment, absorbing the truth about his feelings for her, of what they had nearly done, what had happened before she stopped him. Their encounter had revealed a hidden heat and passion within her, and the thought of such fire within a woman he desired so much both excited and challenged him. He simply could not walk away now from this. Not now. She wanted him, he knew she did. The way she had responded to him told him so. Her hesitancy, he guessed, was probably due to her involvement with Christian – a man who had no idea how to treat a woman. A man almost certainly on borrowed time. He smiled; he had infinite patience, he would wait.

THIRTEEN

By the time Charlotte returned home it was nearly five o'clock. She found Helen in the kitchen getting dinner preparations underway.

'They found the dog,' Helen said.

Charlotte pulled milk from the fridge and poured herself a glassful. 'Oh, good. Where?'

'Hiding in one of the outbuildings at Willowbrook. Rachel phoned about half an hour ago.'

'How did it manage get itself in there?' Charlotte took a mouthful of milk.

Helen gave a meaningful smile as she finished peeling a potato and dropped it into the large saucepan in front of her. 'I think it had a little help from you-know-who. She was the one who discovered it, apparently. Felica is, of course, very relieved her dog has been found and she's gone with Marco to pick it up. He's the reason she stole the dog, isn't he?'

Charlotte nodded. 'Crazy, isn't it? Hasn't she heard? Half of the village have him down as gay.'

Helen pointed the peeler at her and laughed. 'Oh, Charlotte! Marco D'Alesandro is definitely not gay. If you ask me, for some reason he's hiding behind some sort of smoke and mirrors thing, exactly like Christian.'

'Christian's not pretending to be gay.' Charlotte gave an amused smile.

'No, but he's pretending to be in love with you,' Helen said firmly, as she attacked another potato. 'He's used you to get a foot in the door here, hasn't he? Look at him – he's already flexing his muscles, treading all over this family. I can cope with his bullying ways but I don't approve of what he does to everyone else, especially your mother.'

Charlotte nodded, knowing she was only hearing from Helen, usually one of the calmest people she knew, what other members of the family had begun to voice. However, her uncle was insistent he could control him and get him to keep the aggressive arrogance, which had begun to tip over into his Little Court visits, for his stage performances. Not that it appeared to have worked so far.

'I agree, Christian is totally out of order.' Charlotte finished her milk and consigned the empty glass to the dishwasher. 'And I would like you to know, despite what happened the other day on the doorstep with Marco, I am not romantically involved with Christian in any way whatsoever, even though he seems to have decided to reclaim me. As far as I'm concerned it's just a friendship thing.'

'I'm glad to hear it.' Helen stopped peeling for a moment and smiled. 'Oh, and talking of friends... you had a call from Beth.'

'Beth?' Charlotte's curiosity was piqued. 'But I thought she was on holiday in France?'

'No, she's back. Said she had some exciting news to tell you.'

'Right, I'd better call her, then.' With a parting smile Charlotte turned to leave the kitchen.

'Oh, Lottie?'

She stopped as she reached the door and turned back to Helen, who was now lifting the heavy saucepan onto the Aga.

'I'm sorry,' Helen said. 'I tend to be a little too outspoken for my own good sometimes.'

'About Marco?'

'No, Christian. I should learn to keep my thoughts to myself.'

'On the contrary.' Charlotte gave her a wry smile. 'I'm glad you were concerned, but as I said, you need not worry. Christian and I are no longer together nor are we ever likely to be.'

Returning to her room, Charlotte retrieved her mobile and dialled Beth's number.

'Hi there,' she said as the call connected and she heard Beth's familiar voice.

'Hi! How are things?'

'Oh, buzzing. The bridal boutique opening is imminent and Christian is coming down to perform. Everyone is very thrilled of course, having a famous star endorse the new business. So what's this exciting news? Ah, let me guess... You've met the man of your dreams and you're getting married.'

Beth laughed. 'Not yet, it's still very much on the back burner. No, I've been given an art gallery.'

'Honestly? Beth, that's fantastic. Who by?'

'My Great Uncle Hector. He owned a small gallery in Dartmouth for years, Water's Edge. Remember? I told you ages ago.'

'Yes, he was the one who never married, wasn't he? Used to teach art at one time?'

'That's right. And he painted too. He was very gifted, particularly with watercolours. Well, he had to close a little under a year ago because of ill health. He's recently gone into residential care and I got a call asking if I would visit. And to cut a long story short, as he has no children of his own and wanted the gallery to remain in the Reynolds family, he's given it to me. He said as I'm now the artist in the family it was quite appropriate.'

'Beth, that's great news. When are you going down to look at it?'

'I'm already here, Lottie. In fact I've been here for a few days now, sorting out the shop. There's a first-floor storeroom with excellent light. It would make an ideal studio. At the moment I'm renting a house close by.' There was a pause. 'You must come and visit, you must.'

'Of course I will.' She thought for a moment. 'Things are currently a little hectic at this end but I'll give you a call when I'm free. Maybe sometime next month?'

'Yes, yes, please do. It would be great for us to spend some time together.'

As she ended the call, Charlotte sat and thought for a moment. Dartmouth... It would be a chance to get away for a few days; what had happened with Marco at the cottage had unsettled her. She needed to confide in someone outside the family, and if anyone could give her sound advice it would be Beth. Her mind still on men, she remembered Christian would be here soon performing at the opening – another good reason to have a change of scenery and see Beth again.

Closing her phone, she walked over to the small desk in the corner of her room and flipped open her diary to today's date. 'IMPORTANT,' she wrote in large letters in the right-hand notes page. 'Make arrangements to visit Beth, Water's Edge Gallery, Dartmouth.'

Marco was not in a good mood. On arriving home and stabling his horse, he was met at the top of the stairs by his excited sister.

'Chi Chi has been found,' Felica exclaimed, her face radiant. 'Would you come with me to collect him?'

'Yes, of course,' he replied, unbuttoning his shirt as he walked along the corridor to his room, eager to be out of his riding clothes. 'Where is he?'

'Willowbrook.' Felica kept pace with his long strides. 'He was found in one of the outbuildings.'

Marco came to a halt and pivoted round, eyeing his sister suspiciously. 'And how did he manage to get in there?'

'I do not know.' Her eyes widened innocently. 'But it is where Kayte found him.'

'Kayte O'Farrell?' He nodded thoughtfully. 'Why am I not surprised?'

'I do not understand.'

'It is probably better you do not.' He pushed the door to his room open. 'Give me five minutes to change and I will be with you.'

Now, turning up the track towards Willowbrook Farm, his mind took him through the route the dog would have taken to reach the farm. The distance he would have needed to travel was impossible in the time he had been missing. Chi Chi had been deliberately stolen, and he knew why.

As soon as the Range Rover pulled to a halt, Felica rushed up the garden path, carrier in hand, and knocked on the front door, eager to be reunited with their beloved pet. As Marco joined his sister, the door swung open and Kayte stood there smiling. Wearing jeans and a low cut top, her bra-less state left nothing to the imagination.

'Marco!' Her greeting was for him and him alone. Ignoring Felica, she pushed herself invitingly against him.

'I believe you have our dog,' he said, his hands on her shoulders,

71

thrusting her away.

'Yes, would you believe he was in one of our outbuildings?' Kayte giggled. 'I was so surprised when I found him. I couldn't wait to call Felica.' She turned to give Marco's sister a fleeting smile before turning back to him.

'Well, as you can see we are both here now.' He waited for Kayte to make a move.

She smiled up at him again and moving deftly, snatched the carrier from the floor where Felica had placed it.

'No need for you to come,' she said as Felica made to follow her. 'Although I could probably use a little help from Marco.'

As his sister opened her mouth to protest Marco raised a firm hand. 'Do not worry, I will deal with this. Here,' he handed her the keys to the Range Rover, 'I will not be long.'

'Are you sure?' Her eyes rested uncomfortably on Kayte before moving back to her brother.

Marco squeezed her shoulder. 'Trust me.'

As Felica returned to the vehicle Kayte gave Marco a small smile of triumph as she crooked a beckoning finger at him. 'This way.'

He followed her around the back of the farmhouse to where a clutch of low dark buildings clustered around a square yard. In one corner, a large brown bull leaned his chin over the top of the heavy iron gate of his pen, regarding them with a silent bovine stare. Apart from this the place was deserted; everywhere deathly quiet.

'No one about today?'

'No.' She gave him a teasing grin. 'Dad and Aidan are out harvesting and Mum's gone to visit Granny in the care home. We're quite alone. It's over here.' She indicated a long, low, creosoted wooden building in the far corner.

Once there, she grabbed the large metal handle set in the door and swung it open. Inside was a strong aroma of warm hay. Chi Chi, his collar secured by a length of rope, was tied to one of the stalls. On seeing Marco, he got to his feet and started to bark, pulling against the restraining cord, eager to be reunited with his master. Kneeling down, Kayte slid back the lock on the pet carrier, untied the rope from Chi Chi's collar and coaxed the dog inside. Securing the lock, she stood up and smiled at Marco.

'There we are, safe and sound,' she said, edging towards the door.

'Thank you.' Marco stepped forward to pick up the carrier but as he did, Kayte snatched it out of his way, blocking the door.

'Not so fast.' She eyed him with a predatory smile. 'Aren't you forgetting something?'

'And what something would that be?'

'My reward for finding Chi Chi.'

'Your reward?'

'God, I love your accent.' She stepped towards him. 'But then, I love everything about you, Marco.'

'Do you?' He watched as she lifted her hands and ran her fingers through her blonde hair, letting it spill all over her shoulders as her breasts heaved against the thin material of her top.

'Yes, yes I do. And do you know what I want as my reward?'

'I cannot begin to guess.'

'A kiss.' She smiled, his sarcasm totally lost on her. 'I want you to kiss me.'

She closed the gap between them, stretching out her arms to capture her prize. But as she reached him, he sidestepped and gave her a firm shove, sending her sprawling out of the barn and straight into a nearby pile of manure.

She rolled over, glaring up at him, straw and horse dung sticking to her hair and clothing. 'What the hell are you doing?'

He scowled down at her. 'How dare you! Do you think we are idiots? I may not have lived here long but I know there is no way my sister's dog could have got here by himself from the manor.' He jabbed an accusing finger at her. 'How could you? Can you even begin to imagine what my sister has been through today? The worry. The upset. And then there are the people who gave up valuable time to search for him. Time wasted, was it not, when you had him shut in this barn? And for what reason? So you could play some stupid game with me.' He walked over to where the carrier lay. 'Save yourself for someone who does want you, Caitlin, for certainly I do not.'

'You are gay, then?' she threw at his departing back.

'Believe what you like, I honestly do not care.' Marco turned with a careless shrug. 'Now if you will excuse me, my sister is waiting to be reunited with her dog.'

It was Tuesday, the seventeenth of September and Little Court was full of activity. Today was the opening of Bridal Dreams, Thérèse's in-house wedding boutique. Several weeks of work by Taylor-Macayne, Issy's husband's company, had seen the armoury turned into an impressive glass-fronted shop. The actual opening ceremony at two thirty was to be preceded by champagne and a light lunch followed by a fashion show set up in the function suite. Thérèse and Felica had liaised with Ella, who took charge of the project, with Issy responsible for the catering, and Jenny the flower arrangements.

Charlotte and Lucy, having both taken the day off work, watched with interest as lorry after lorry arrived and unloaded the component parts for the day. One ground floor section of the east wing had been given over to the event – brides, bridesmaids and pages outfits hung on rails and wrapped in protective polythene. Over in the function suite a catwalk, or runway as Felica referred to it, was being erected surrounded by tables of six where invited guests would enjoy their pre-show refreshments.

Hairdressers and make-up artists had arrived shortly after the lorries and then a couple of coaches with the models – from young women built like thoroughbred racehorses to small angelic children, all ready to play their roles in Thérèse's big day. Issy had arrived early too, chivvying up her staff, anxious to make sure the preparation of food was on schedule while at the same time making sure the champagne was chilling at exactly the right temperature. Jenny had co-opted Helen into helping out with the positioning of flower arrangements throughout the house and in the function suite.

Charlotte smiled; as always everything looked absolutely perfect. She hoped Thérèse would appreciate the hard work the Little Court ladies had put in to create this perfection. Thérèse's attitude towards her appeared to have mellowed since the barbeque, but Charlotte was not fooled; the warm politeness she now experienced each time they met was very much at odds with the judgemental expression which still hung in those steely eyes. In total contrast, Felica had become close friends with her and Lucy and today had offered them the use of the hair and beauty team. Lucy needed little persuading and demanded to be first. Charlotte watched as her cousin's long, black curly hair was pinned up in her favourite style with little corkscrew curls falling prettily around her face. Watching Lucy leave to change, hairdresser Tasha, a willowy girl with black spiky hair, ran her hands through Charlotte's long wavy curls and made a suggestion. Hair straighteners were produced and although reluctant at first, eventually Charlotte decided to step out of her comfort zone and surprise everyone.

'My God, Lottie, what have you done?' Lucy gaped in disbelief as she opened the door to her room and found her cousin standing outside, her hair falling in a straight black glossy waterfall down her back. 'I know Tasha wanted to make you look completely different but I had no idea it would be—'

'Don't you like it?'

'I think it's absolutely fabulous,' Lucy replied, ushering her in and closing the door. 'But I hope you've not gone to all that trouble for Christian because, believe me, he won't even notice.'

'Lucy, will you shut up about Christian!' Charlotte rounded on her cousin, annoyed she was spoiling things by being her usual irritating self and poking her nose in where it wasn't wanted.

'I wish you'd stop protecting him. You know, I can't imagine why you got involved with him in the first place. I was horrified when I got back and found out you two were an item,' Lucy yelled back. 'A whole year, Lottie! I'm amazed you could waste your life on someone so... so not worthy of you. You should work with him – he treats staff like dirt and he disrespects Dad and Baz. If you want my advice, I think the best thing you could do is dump him.'

'Well, thank you for tramping all over my life with your expert advice, Lucy, but I keep telling you we're not together any more. He's a friend. Understand? A friend.'

'So what was all the Tarzan stuff going on when Marco turned up with the roses?'

'How do you know about that?' Charlotte bristled, feeling her cheeks fire with embarrassment.

'Helen told Mum and Mum told me. Two men fighting over you, Lottie. Exciting, don't you think?'

'Oh, stop exaggerating,' Charlotte snapped. 'There wasn't a fight. Just shut up, will you.'

Lucy was about to respond when the bedroom door opened and her mother appeared. Dressed in a long-sleeved cream lace suit, her dark curly hair skimming her shoulders, Ella looked at them both and frowned.

'What's going on? I heard raised voices.' Her gaze fell on Charlotte's hair and she smiled. 'Heavens, Lottie, it's fantastic. Makes you look completely different. Jenny!' she called, leaning back out into the corridor. 'Come and see your daughter's hair, it's beautiful. Don't you like it, Lucy? Is that what you were arguing about?'

'Yes, I do and no, it wasn't.'

'So what was it, then?'

'Oh, the usual cousin wars,' Charlotte cut in before Lucy could elaborate. 'Nothing serious.'

The arrival of both older women thankfully calmed things as Charlotte's hair became the subject of much discussion. Eventually, she made excuses and returned to her own room to change. Lucy had always been difficult, she thought as she slipped on a knee-length, short-sleeved pale blue dress and zipped it up. She was always grabbing centre stage; spoiled, ungrateful and unapologetic. Arriving home from a total fiasco on the other side of the world, which had seen her losing fifty thousand from her inheritance, she thought at first lessons had been learned. But they hadn't. In fact, the job Matt had given Lucy seemed to have made her worse. She was a troublemaker, always trying to stir things up in one way or another. But she's not going to succeed with me, Charlotte decided, as she slipped her feet into cream suede stilettos. Christian and I are not together so her efforts are totally wasted, and as for Marco... well, there was absolutely no way she was going to breathe a word to Lucy about what he had done. The thought of what her cousin would do with that sort of knowledge did not bear thinking about.

FOURTEEN

There was a flurry of excitement as local fans, gathered outside the house behind a specially erected barrier leading up to the main door, waited the arrival of Christian Rosetti. Flanked by security guards, they all hoped for a glimpse of the star and maybe an autograph. Eventually a long black vehicle arrived outside the house, a huge minder emerging from the front passenger seat and opening the rear door. Christian got out, straightened his jacket, ran a hand through his hair and quickly made his way up the steps, oblivious of those standing there in hopeful anticipation with their proffered pens and autograph books. Two blonde women followed him, each with long hair scooped tightly back. Both wore identical black dresses and bright red high heels, their mouths covered in matching crimson as they marched behind him carrying a small case each.

As Christian came swaggering into the hall, the girls on either side of him, he was met by Charlotte.

'Hey, babe!' He gave her a warm smile, putting his arm around her as he briefly pressed his lips to her cheek. 'You smell good.' He stood back, tilting his head. 'Something different about you?'

'My hair, maybe?' Charlotte said as she made eye contact with the two blondes then stared back at him, wondering if given his slightly spaced-out stance he'd been dipping into the bar in the back of the limo on his way here.

'Ah, yeah, yeah it's good,' he decided with a grin. Snaking an arm around the waist of each girl, he moved off. 'Sorry, gotta go, things to do. Catch you later,' he called over his shoulder.

Charlotte glared after them, Lucy's words echoing in her ears as she frowned at the two girls. *Whatever was Matt doing employing women like that?* she wondered. Where were Ginny – Christian's PA – and his personal hairdresser Heidi? She understood they were to accompany him, so who were these two replacement blonde clones?

'Fabulous! Absolutely fabulous.' Issy Taylor clapped her hands together in admiration as the models paraded down the catwalk to the sound of Billy Idol's 'White Wedding'. Although the brides' dresses were in traditional colours of white or ivory, the materials and styles varied to suit every wedding style, conventional or modern. Each bride was accompanied by supporting bridesmaids, pageboys or a mix of both, giving the guests a real flavour of what Bridal Dreams was capable of delivering. Off to the left of the runway Thérèse, in an elegant plum coloured satin dress and jacket with matching shoes, stood with microphone in hand, giving a full description and price of each item. Seated beside Issy, Ella and Jenny watched, totally engrossed.

'This is going to be such a success,' Ella whispered to Jenny. 'These dresses are a world apart from what is on offer locally. So many different styles too and the prices are very competitive.'

'Isn't there a shoe boutique as well?' Charlotte, sitting between the two older women, asked curiously.

'Yes, and Thérèse has plans to offer a range for brides mothers soon,' her aunt responded.

'It's brilliant, Ella.' Issy smiled her approval. 'Absolutely brilliant. This will really put Lawns on the map.'

Across the aisle, Lucy watched as the show came to its conclusion. The last two models were the two blondes she had seen arrive with Christian, both were wearing short tight dresses, one in red, the other in blue. As they had not been on the running list and they weren't in wedding dresses, she guessed he had brought them along to support his performance. When they got to the end of the catwalk, the two models paused for a few seconds before turning and walking back, disappearing through the blue velvet curtains at the rear of the main stage. Moments later they re-appeared arm-in-arm with Christian. In a dark suit with a red and blue waistcoat which exactly matched the girls' dresses, his dark curly hair bounced energetically against his cheeks as he blew a kiss to the audience. They responded by enthusiastic applause and there were whistles and cat calls as, microphone in hand, he began to sing.

Lucy knew most of his songs by heart. The one chosen for this afternoon, 'White Lace Woman', was a track from his last album *Prophecies*. As she watched him, his hips swaying suggestively as he moved between the two girls, she wondered what his fans would think if they knew what the man behind the façade was actually like.

The song came to an end and applause broke out all around, disturbing her thoughts. Christian was bowing to the appreciative audience while either side of him the two models smiled and posed, hands on hips. Then all three turned and walked back towards the end of the catwalk and with a last bow from Christian, headed off stage. From where she was sitting Lucy saw his left hand caress the buttock of one of the models. The girl turned her head and smiled at him. The kind of inviting smile Lucy had seen on so many other occasions after shows. A smile which she saw him return as his hand moved up to caress her shoulder. Lucy shook her head in dismay. Oh God! He can't be serious. Not here, not today. But she knew with certainty it was exactly what he was planning.

'Ladies and gentlemen…' Thérèse was on stage again. 'We have now come to the most important part of the afternoon: the opening of Bridal Visions. If you would be good enough to follow Felica back into the main house.' She gestured towards the end of the vast conservatory where her daughter stood waiting.

Chairs were pushed back, tables vacated. Lucy sighed thankfully as Charlotte left the room with the three older women. Soon the room was empty. She remained, staring at the balloons, bunting and general disorder left behind, then made to move but stopped when she heard giggling coming from behind the curtains. The sound of Christian's laughter followed, then more giggling. So she had been right about his intentions but, boy, was he taking a chance at being discovered. Frustrated that she was unable to challenge his activities without ruining the D'Alesandros' day, Lucy left the room, threading a slow path through the tables. She had better catch everyone else up before she was missed and someone sent to find her. Stopping briefly to chat to Helen, she continued her journey.

Entering the main hall, she was surprised to see Christian emerge through the side door of the function suite. He was pulling off his tie. She stopped to watch him as he raced up the stairs, and was wondering whether her suspicions had been a little too hasty when, moments later, both blondes appeared through the same door. Now in short black dresses and high red heels, they marched confidently towards the stairs, one of them clutching a bottle of champagne.

'Excuse me!' Lucy called out, intercepting them. 'Upstairs is off limits to visitors.'

'And you are?' One of them gave her a haughty stare, clearly annoyed at being challenged.

'Lucy Benedict. My parents own this house. The bridal boutique is that way.' She emphasised the point by indicating the arrowed sign on the wall.

'We're looking for Christian,' the taller of the two said, her mascaraed eyes fixed on Lucy.

'We're his assistants,' the second girl announced to a nod from her friend. 'He hired us a few weeks ago and we need to see him.'

'Christian doesn't hire and fire, my father does,' Lucy replied frostily. As the taller blonde opened her mouth to argue Lucy stepped in front of them to block the stairs. 'I'd like you both to leave please.' Neither girl budged; they stood there with ferocious expressions on their well made-up faces. 'Now!' Lucy reinforced her request. 'Or I'll have to call security.'

'But the limo isn't due for ages, how will we get back to London?' one of them bleated, as they reluctantly moved off in the direction of the front door.

'Once you reach the main gates, turn left and the station is about half a mile. Shouldn't take you more than,' Lucy took in their high heels as she accompanied them, 'half an hour. Trains to Taunton for your connection to London run every two hours. Lucky for you it reopened last year.'

'But our things?' the shorter of the two protested. 'We need—'

'Don't worry, I'll sort it. And I'll take that, thank you.' She snatched the bottle from the taller girl before shoving them both out of the door and closing it.

* * *

Christian's room was situated down a small flight of stairs towards the end of the west corridor. At the oak panelled door, Lucy drew a deep breath, gripped the handle and pushed it slowly open.

'Thought you girls had got lost,' came the amused voice from within, and as the door opened fully Lucy found herself face to face with Christian resting comfortably against the pillows of the four poster wearing nothing but a grin.

'What the fuck are you doing here?' he bellowed as he rolled over, his hands going to his groin to cover himself.

'Are you sure you need two hands to cover something so small?' Lucy was enjoying his discomfort.

'Why are you here?' he snapped. 'What do you want?'

'Oh, I came to tell you room service has been cancelled. They're heading for the station as we speak,' she said matter-of-factly, determined to suppress the outrage she really felt. 'Don't you dare try something like that again in my father's house!'

'Your *father's* house?' He stared at her, dark eyed and contemptuous. 'Sorry, did I hear you right? And there's me thinking it belonged to your mother. After all, she's the one with the balls as well as the money, isn't she? She calls the shots. And your father? Well... he simply does as he's told, doesn't he?'

She shook her head. 'That is so not true.' She glared at him. Her parents had an exceptional relationship. They loved each other. Yes, her mother was a strong woman but when she was with her father, he was definitely the one in charge. There was no way she called the shots, as Christian had put it.

'Oh, yes, it is. You know it is.' Still holding himself, he slid off the bed and walked over to where his clothes lay. Turning his back to her, he grabbed his boxers and pulled them on.

'No, I don't.' Lucy watched him, her smile fixed. Jay had warned her he played serious mind games to get at people. He knew exactly where her vulnerable spot was – her father –and he was trying to wind her up big time. Well, it wouldn't work. 'If he knew what you'd planned up here this afternoon he'd have fired you,' she said confidently.

He shrugged as he tugged on a pair of Levis and zipped them up. 'I doubt it. I'm his star act. He couldn't afford to let me go even if he wanted to. The court costs would cripple him.'

'You've got an inflated idea of your own importance,' she hit back. 'You wouldn't be so arrogant if I told Lottie what goes on when you are on tour.'

'You leave Lottie out of this; she's nothing to do with this.'

'She has everything to do with this, Christian. How do you think she'd feel if she knew about your after show activities?'

'She wouldn't believe you,' he said, slipping into a sweater and tugging it

79

down over the top of his jeans. 'Lottie's very trusting.'

'Then you don't know her very well. She'd believe me over you.'

'Don't talk rubbish! Everyone knows you have no time for Lottie.'

'Maybe, maybe not,' she acknowledged, watching as he sat on the edge of the bed pulling on socks and slipping his feet into Timberland boots. 'But I do know she deserves someone far better than you.'

'Like the Italian, you mean?'

'Who?'

'Marco D'Alesandro, or whatever his bloody name is. I caught him here sometime back on the doorstep about to hand her a bunch of fucking red roses!'

'Yes, I know.' Lucy laughed.

'What's so funny?'

'Don't be silly; there's nothing going on there. He's gay.'

'Gay?'

'Yep, gay. Oh dear!' She put her hand to her mouth. 'Now what made me say that? Maybe if he's been showing an interest in Lottie, he's not. I could be mistaken, you know. After all, it's merely village gossip. Probably half-truths,' she added with a shrug.

'Your humour sucks,' Christian threw back with a heavy-lidded scowl.

She gave him a satisfied smirk. 'I try my best.'

He pushed past her and opened the door. 'I think it's time you left. You're beginning to bore me.'

'Be careful, Christian. I'm watching you...' she said with a hint of menace. 'Hurt any of my family and you'll have me to deal with, I promise you.'

'Yeah, I'm so scared, Lucy.' He gave her a shove in the back to help her out of the room.

'Bloody airhead!' he said, slamming the door. He walked to the window, taking in the view down towards the river and stood for a moment trying to ease his building temper. Something in Lucy's words still niggled. If he split with Matt he knew other record companies would be queuing up to sign him; that was not a problem. What was, was what she had said about Marco. The memory of the red roses caused vicious jealousy to flood through him as he stood clenching and unclenching his fists, trying to decide how best to deal with it. Lottie was his property and he needed to send a clear message to the Italian that would make sure he kept well away.

Today, on the way down in the limo, he had given the problem a lot of thought and the only solution he could come up with, other than sending in a few hard men to give D'Alesandro a good going over, was not truly a path he wanted to go down. If he did, once it was public knowledge it would ensure he lost all credibility with his fans. He made such an issue of his playing the field image and while they might forgive him for having a change of heart, they would never accept he had chosen someone as ordinary as Lottie. They would feel betrayed, expecting nothing less than someone beautiful with celebrity status. And so he had left the whole situation in limbo, deciding to come back to it when the need arose. The conversation with Lucy now reactivated those thoughts.

He gripped the window ledge, frowning deeply. Should he go ahead with this or not? Was it committing commercial suicide? He had no idea and it was making his head ache. He needed a fix. Only with the help of his little helpers would he be able to come to the right decision. Unzipping his overnight bag, he located the small plastic wallet of pills and swallowed two with a swig of bottled water from his bedside table. Closing his eyes, he took several deep breaths – in a few minutes they would take effect and he'd be cruising again, his current problem a straightforward, solvable matter. As his thought processes eventually cleared he suddenly remembered there was a more immediate issue to sort out: the girls. Quickly, he left his room.

From the landing above the great hall he saw Jenny Miller talking to a couple of guests who were about to leave. The gods were with him; she of all people would be least likely to ask questions. He waited until she had shown the couple out of the front door before making his way down the stairs.

'Hi, Jenny,' he greeted her warmly.

She returned his smile. 'Christian, there you are. It's been a great afternoon, hasn't it?'

'It certainly has. I was glad to help out.'

'You were fabulous – as usual.'

'Thank you.' He accepted the compliment graciously. 'I... ah... need to borrow a car.'

'Oh, right, well... I guess you can use the Mercedes estate. The keys are hanging in the kitchen, red key fob. There's plenty of diesel in it. Where are you—?'

'Thanks, I'll see you later,' he interrupted, eager to nip any questions, even harmless ones of the type someone like Jenny Miller would ask, in the bud. Moments later he was driving out of the main gates and heading for the station. On those heels Talia and Leyna couldn't have got far. Once he caught them up there were plenty of isolated places around here where he could tuck the car out of sight for a pleasurable half hour before he eventually put them onto the Taunton train for their connection to London.

'So where did you go this afternoon?' Ella asked later that evening, directing her gaze across the dining table towards Christian as the family were having dinner.

'Taunton, I had some business,' he replied, concentrating on helping himself to vegetables as he spoke. 'Jenny said it was all right if I borrowed

81

the car.' He raised his eyes and looked around the table for any dissent. 'Was there a problem?'

'No, not at all.' Ella gave him a cool shake of her head. For the last twenty minutes she, like the others, had been treated to Christian butting in to their conversations with various views of his own. Matt wasn't due back from London until late, making Rowan and CJ the only other men at the table. So far, Christian had managed to upset CJ with his 'I know best' opinions on architecture. Charlotte's face was beginning to heat with embarrassment, she barely raised her eyes from her plate, while Lucy, across the table from Ella, looked as if she wanted to throw her food at him. They ate silently for a while and then Christian decided to start on Rowan. After having to listen to Christian comparing the quality of Little Court's gardens against those of his own fifty-acre estate in Hertfordshire, Rowan put down his knife and fork.

'Dinner is a time for relaxation, not antagonism,' he said evenly, taking his gaze around the table and seeing agreeing nods. 'There's a gym in the west wing, Christian. Go and take whatever's eating you out on the punch bag there and stop trying to find someone to scrap with here, if you don't mind.'

'Sorry.' Christian backed off with a careless shrug, knowing he was on a hiding to nothing. It did not diminish the intense irritation he felt. He needed a couple more pills to calm him down, he could feel his temper building again; a sure sign he needed a top up. He resumed eating, trying his best to ignore them all, to finish his meal as soon as possible and get back to his room and his little plastic bag.

Another conversation had started up around the table, one he had only vaguely been aware of, but now it had his full attention.

'The D'Alesandros are coming over for a drink later on,' Ella said as she set her knife and fork tidily on her empty plate. 'They have an announcement to make.'

Her words made Christian want to punch the air, his spirits immediately rising as he realised how this might assist in the scheme he had reluctantly decided upon to get rid of Marco.

'What about?' CJ wanted to know, frowning curiously. 'More plans for the boutique?'

'No, it's business, but something completely different.' Jenny smiled and fixed her gaze on her husband. He returned the gesture, indicating they shared some secret knowledge.

'Mum, what is it? Is there something you're not telling us?'

'All in good time, CJ, all in good time,' said Rowan, smiling.

Perfect, thought Christian. They will all be here. I could not have arranged things better myself.

FIFTEEN

The D'Alesandros arrived at nine thirty, an hour after Matt arrived home from London. The ladies were still in high spirits after the show while Marco, as always, shadowed them quietly. As soon as she walked into the lounge where all the family including Matt were now gathered, Thérèse made a beeline for Christian.

'Thank you so much for what you did this afternoon, Christian. You were fabulous,' she said, taking his hands and squeezing them tightly as she smiled up into his handsome face. 'And so were your two assistants. What were their names...? Ah yes, Talia and Leyna.'

'Thank you,' he gushed, 'but it's the least we could do for you, and I enjoyed every single minute of it.'

Lucy watched him, irritated by his blatant overacting.

'So why are you all here tonight, Felica?' CJ asked as he joined them. 'Come on, what's the big secret?'

'This is Marco's evening,' she replied with a teasing smile, seating herself next to Lucy. 'It is for him to announce, but I think you are all going to be very pleased.'

Checking around the room to make sure everyone was present, Matt disappeared, returning moments later with bottles of champagne, Helen Baxter in his wake carrying a tray of glasses. Matt uncorked the bottles and poured, leaving Helen to hand round elegant flutes of pale effervescent liquid to everyone.

'Champagne? This must be something very special,' CJ said, moving over to sit next to Charlotte on one of the brown Chesterfields. They watched as Marco left the room.

'I wonder where he's going?' CJ said, curious.

'Felica's told you nothing, then?'

'Nope, only that it is something we will be very pleased about.'

Charlotte nodded, holding onto her secret. Kieren had texted her earlier telling her what was about to happen. She was glad Marco had taken her advice in deciding to announce his news to the family and in doing so, killing mischievous village gossip once and for all.

'You know something, don't you?' CJ said, catching her expression.

'Me? Of course not!' She shook her head and laughed.

'Don't lie, Lottie, I know you do.' CJ was about to pressure her for an answer when Marco re-entered the room with Kieren, in his usual uniform of jeans and t-shirt.

'Oh my God,' CJ said in a low voice. 'He's abducted him from the pub. Are the rumours buzzing around the village true, Lottie?'

Charlotte sighed and rolled her eyes. 'Don't be silly.'

CJ followed the direction her gaze took across the room towards Marco. He noticed the way he smiled at her as his hand rested gently on Kieren's shoulder.

'Tonight is very special,' Marco began, 'for Kieren and for me. I am pleased to announce that my London restaurant, San Raffaello's, is about to employ him. He will train under my head chef Florentine Pagamo.' He patted Kieren on the shoulder. 'I believe he has a brilliant future ahead of him.'

Matt's mouth opened in amazement. 'You own San Raffaello's? Do you know how difficult it is to get a table there?'

Marco shrugged, as if owning one of the capital's top restaurants was nothing. 'I do. But if you ever need a reservation, please let me know. I will be pleased to organise it for you.'

'And you employ Florentine Pagamo?' Jenny added in awe. 'Issy would absolutely kill to meet him; she adores everything about him, including his TV show.'

'I can arrange for her to come to London and meet him any time. She has only to ask. But, please, we are wandering away from the real reason we are here.' He raised his glass. 'To Kieren and a great future in food.'

'To Kieren,' everyone echoed, and drank back their champagne, while the subject of their toast smiled, took a sip of his and coloured with embarrassment.

Christian, on his own in the corner, viewed the little gathering with his usual disdain. Listening to Marco, another privileged bastard talking about owning restaurants when he probably couldn't even boil an egg, made the pleasure of what he was about to do even more gratifying. He'd seen the smile pass between Marco and Charlotte, and he didn't like it. Ah well, he won't be smiling in a few moments' time, he thought with relish.

The toast finished, Charlotte crossed over to congratulate Kieren and give him a hug.

'Well done,' she said. 'I'm so happy for you.'

'I'm going to miss you,' he said, pulling back and brushing away the glint of moisture appearing in his hazel eyes.

'Hey, what's with the tears?' Charlotte reached out and stroked his face in a sisterly gesture. 'I work in London three days a week, remember? I can always drop in, see how you are. We can do lunch.'

'Yeah, I'd like that,' he said with sincerity. His eyes drifted to where Marco stood engrossed in conversation with Matt. 'It looks as if Matt is trying to wangle a table already.'

'Kieren, can I ask you something?' Charlotte hesitated before continuing. 'What is your honest opinion of Marco?'

Kieren gazed admiringly at his new boss then, seeing Charlotte's enquiring expression, said, 'He's a great guy. And despite all the gossip I can tell you there's nothing going on between him and me. He's one hundred per cent heterosexual – unfortunately.'

Charlotte smiled at Kieren's reddening face. 'I'm told he has a girlfriend in London. Have you met her yet?'

'No, but I guess she's bound to come into the restaurant some time.' His eyes drifted across to Marco again. 'She's one lucky woman to have such a kind and caring guy in her life. He's been awesomely generous getting me this break, you know. And staff at San Raffaello's think he's amazing. Would you believe sometimes he turns up out of the blue and works alongside the team waiting tables?'

'Yes, I think I would,' she said smiling, her eyes still fixed on the young Italian. She realised during their first abrasive encounters both her anger and Thérèse's attitude towards her had coloured her judgement. Now through his actions she was beginning to learn she might have been wrong. It appeared he was kind and fair and generous and, of course, he had a delicious mouth. Memories of that morning at Fox Cottage made her whole body tingle but she damped down the feeling. He was with Lauren, he wasn't for her and besides, she had her own issues to deal with.

As Kieren left her to join his father and Jenny her gaze drifted across to where Christian sat in the corner, champagne glass in hand, a sullen expression on his face. She knew then if she had felt anything for him beyond friendship it was now over. She didn't recognise him any more. The way he had waded in that morning, throwing the flowers back at Marco and demanding he leave – it was totally unacceptable, as was thrusting himself between them like some testosterone-fuelled Neanderthal. And then today when he arrived he'd been so rude. Well, she had had enough. Staring thoughtfully into her glass she decided it no longer mattered if Christian wanted their relationship back or not, she didn't; it was time to take control of her life again.

'Lottie?'

She was still deep in thought when a hand grabbed her wrist. Startled, she looked up to find Christian standing beside her, leaning in, his dark eyes smiling into hers. She flinched, startled by his sudden close proximity.

'What? What is it?'

'Come with me,' he said.

'Where? What are you doing?'

He snatched the glass from her hand and thrust it back at Helen before pulling Charlotte into the centre of the room. Still holding onto her wrist, Christian raised his hand to silence the conversations going on around them.

'May I have your attention, everyone. It's great we're celebrating this evening. Celebrations are very infectious, so infectious, in fact, I have decided now might be the right time for me to make a very special announcement too.' He turned to smile at her. 'As many of you know, Charlotte and I have been good friends for a long time. That friendship changed a little over a year ago and we became much closer. When I was on tour in Australia I missed her very much, so much, in fact, that I made a decision. A decision which sees me about to ask this wonderful girl a very important question.' Dropping down on one knee, he gazed up into her face and smiled. 'Lottie, will you marry me?'

'What...?' As the situation dawned on her, she tried to extract her hand from his. 'Christian, what are you doing? Get up, for heaven's sake!' she hissed, desperately trying to free herself from his iron grasp.

'Lottie, I'm asking you to marry me.' As he fought to keep his smile in place his fingers tightened, his grip becoming painful.

'And my answer is no,' she replied forcefully, shaking her head, confusion swiftly replaced by anger. 'No, Christian.'

As her words suddenly sunk in he stared at her open-mouthed. His grasp loosened and Charlotte took the opportunity to wrench her hand free and escape.

Jenny glanced across at Christian who was still on one knee, staring at nothing in particular and seemingly unaware the object of his proposal had now fled the room.

'I'd better go to her,' she said to Ella, standing beside her.

Matt walked over and hauled Christian to his feet. 'Are you okay?'

'I guess I shouldn't have sprung it on her quite like that,' Christian replied, as if he was not even aware of Matt's presence. He put his hand to his head, and swayed dizzily.

'Let's say it wasn't one of your better ideas,' Matt said quietly. 'You seem unsteady; come and sit down. You look pale.'

'I'm fine, stop fussing!' Angrily, he shook off Matt's concerned hand and turned to everyone in the room, pulling himself up straight and making brief eye contact with them all, including Marco. 'Sorry, bad timing. I guess this wasn't the best place to do it.'

'Oh my God!' Lucy put her hands to her face as she watched Matt follow him out of the room. 'Did you see that coming? I certainly didn't.'

'Nor I'm convinced did Lottie,' CJ answered, shaking his head.

'He's lying about her expecting it, though.' Lucy eyes met CJ's. 'She told me that side of their relationship is over, said all they were now is friends.'

'So why did he do it?' CJ asked. 'And why so publicly?'

'Well...' she hesitated, glancing across at Marco. 'I think—'

'You think what?

'I think it might have something to do with Marco.'

'Marco?'

'Yes. He turned up with a bunch of red roses the other day. Unfortunately, it coincided with Christian's arrival. There was a bit of a confrontation and

Christian sent him packing. Helen was there at the time, she saw the whole thing. I think this is all about Christian staking his claim on Lottie. You know,' she said, laughing, 'proving he's the alpha male.'

'Don't be so damned dramatic, Luce! This isn't the African jungle and Christian's not a bloody silverback gorilla,' CJ hissed in disbelief. 'And what was Marco doing bringing Lottie flowers when he already has a girlfriend in London?'

'I have no idea but whatever the reason, it certainly appears to have rattled Christian's cage,' Lucy answered with more than a little pleasure in her voice, and wondering whether there was anything she could organise to give the bars another hefty shake.

The next morning, Christian left his room to join the family for breakfast, his mind fixed on a definite plan of action for the day. This morning he would take Charlotte out riding – get her alone, talk to her properly and convince her he loved her and wanted to spend the rest of his life with her. He'd talk about buying the ring, get down on one knee again and ask her in the most romantic way possible, preferably in some quiet wooded glade. He realised doing what he had last night in a room full of people had been a total disaster; his need to send a clear message to Marco had overridden everything else and he had ended up looking totally stupid. But that was definitely not going to happen this morning. As he wandered into the breakfast room he noticed her chair was empty.

'No Lottie?' His eyes scanned the remaining members of the family sitting around the table.

Ella gave him an acknowledging smile. 'Morning, Christian. Charlotte's having breakfast in her room. She'll be down later.'

'I thought we'd go riding this morning,' he said cheerfully, as he helped himself to scrambled egg and bacon at the breakfast counter and poured himself a glass of fruit juice.

'You're supposed to be back in London with me this morning,' Matt reminded him, peering over the top of his newspaper. 'A ten thirty meeting with Baz to talk about the new album?'

Christian seated himself at the table. 'Get Magda to reschedule.' He waved a dismissive hand across the table at Matt. 'I've got more important things to deal with here today.'

Matt folded his paper, laid it on the table and took a deep breath. 'Right,' he said calmly. 'I appreciate what happened last night was upsetting and you need time with Lottie to sort it out, but I want you back in London by tomorrow morning, is that understood?'

Christian gave a grudging nod and continued to concentrate on his breakfast as Matt, Ella and Lucy left the room. Helen arrived with coffee, depositing the small tray silently beside him before beginning to clear away.

87

He ignored her and the clatter of plates and cutlery as his mind wandered back to Charlotte and what he had planned. However, before he attempted anything he'd need another couple of his little pink pills to give him the lift he required.

In the hall, Ella was saying her usual goodbyes to her husband and daughter.

'You're too tolerant with Christian,' she protested, her eyes full of disapproval. 'He was so rude, Matt. And that wasn't an isolated incident; he's like it all the time. He treats the whole family with total contempt. He's changed so much.'

'He's under a lot of pressure at the moment,' Matt said, full of his usual understanding and compassion for his star act. 'With the Australian tour only recently finished, he's now due back in the studio to record the new album. Last night's little fiasco didn't help. Leave it with me.' He patted his wife's shoulder. 'I'll have a word tomorrow when he's back. I'm sure he'll be easier to handle then, once Lottie has accepted.'

Pulling on her coat, Lucy gave a little snort of amusement.

Matt frowned at his daughter. 'What's so funny?'

'Dad, do you honestly think that's going to happen?'

'Well, what would stop her? I mean, I can understand her reaction last night. It wasn't very clever of him to propose in front of everyone, including the D'Alesandros.'

'But don't you see, Dad? That's why he did it.'

Matt's amused gaze fell on his wife then returned to Lucy. 'Sorry, am I missing something here?'

'He was worried about Marco.'

Matt laughed. 'Don't be ridiculous. There's nothing going on between Lottie and Marco.' Picking up his briefcase he stopped for a moment, catching the expression which passed between his wife and daughter. 'Is there?'

'You saw it too then, Mum?'

'I did,' Ella confirmed.

'Saw what?'

'The expression on Marco's face when Christian hauled Lottie out into the centre of the room and got down on one knee. He looked very distraught.'

'Distraught? You women and your over-active imaginations! He was probably as shocked as we all were. Besides, he already has a girlfriend, doesn't he?' Matt shook his head and laughed again. 'Come on, Luce, time we were off.' Stretching over to kiss Ella goodbye, he ushered his daughter out of the house and across the gravelled driveway towards the waiting car.

'We women and our over-active imaginations, eh, Mr Benedict?' Ella said to his departing back. 'Believe me, I know what I saw…'

'So did I.' Jenny joined her at the open door and watched Matt and Lucy climb into the Mercedes. 'I don't know whether anything has been going on, Ella. I decided not to ask Charlotte last night, she was too upset. And to be quite honest, I'm not sure she'll tell me anyway. One thing I do know is she'll never marry Christian, and considering his dreadful behaviour lately, I have to say I'm quite relieved.'

'He's in a foul mood this morning, Jen. If what you're saying is true, I wouldn't like to predict what he'll do if she refuses him again.'

'I don't think it will come to that, but if it does, Rowan's more than capable of handling him,' Jenny countered confidently. 'Now then, let's get down to the serious stuff, shall we? We need to discuss the new booking for the Brooks–Leyton wedding. And don't forget Thérèse is due here at ten with some sample dresses.'

From her bedroom window, Charlotte watched Matt's car leave. Today was one of her days off, time when she enjoyed being home and doing the things she wanted to. After seeing only Matt and Lucy get into the car, however, she now wished she was on her way to London too because Christian was still here. Her mind drifted back to the events of last evening. She hated the way he had put her on display in the centre of the room like the successful bidder at an auction exhibiting his prize. What kind of madness was going on in his mind? How could he contemplate proposing marriage after the off-hand way he had treated her on his arrival yesterday afternoon?

She turned away from the window, trying to work out the best way to deal with the situation she currently found herself in. Unable to stand the feeling that everything was closing in around her, she had fled, not stopping to see his reaction. She knew from her mother, who had followed her up to her bedroom afterwards, he had been extremely upset. Well, maybe a good night's sleep would have brought him to his senses. She hoped so because if not, he was going to have a battle on his hands. There was absolutely no way she was marrying him. Or anyone else for that matter.

Having eaten, Christian emerged from the back corridor into the great hall and spotted Jenny walking towards the Lawns at Little Court office, carrying a sheaf of files.

'Is Lottie still in her room?' he called out, intercepting her.

'Yes, as far as I'm aware,' Jenny replied calmly, watching him approach and realising by his general demeanour breakfast hadn't much improved his temper.

'Well, get her out of there. I want her to go riding with me.'

Jenny didn't respond; she merely waited for him to reach her, his hands in his pockets, a surly expression on his face.

'Why are you still standing here?' He scanned her from her face to her feet, frowning. 'I asked you to go and get her.'

She eyed him levelly. 'Perhaps if you had asked instead of shouting out your demands I might have done something about it.'

'Jenny, I really do need to speak to Lottie. Please. There... better?' He eyed her unrepentantly, a hint of mockery in his black eyes.

'I'm here.'

Above them, Charlotte leaned over the balustrade on the first floor landing.

'Hey there!' His aggressive stance with her mother melted into a warm smile. 'How are you feeling this morning?'

'I'm fine, Christian,' she replied, tossing back shoulder-length hair which had returned to its normal cascade of curl since her morning shower. 'It's okay, Mum.' She gave Jenny a reassuring nod as she reached the bottom of the stairs and walked over to where they stood.

'You know where I am if you need me,' came Jenny's calm response to her daughter's confident attitude. Files in hand, she left to join Ella for their meeting.

'I thought we'd go riding,' Christian said cheerfully, his fingers playing with the round top of the newel post. 'Maybe take a picnic up to Hundred Acre?'

'Actually, I need to be at Willowbrook this morning. I did promise Niall I'd drop in—'

'Niall can wait,' he said forcefully. 'I want to marry you, Lottie, and I want you to accept.'

'No, Christian.'

'What!'

'I said no, I can't marry you,' she reaffirmed with a slow shake of her head. 'In fact, I don't want to marry anyone.'

'Why not?' He couldn't understand her response. 'We're an item. Isn't marriage the next step?'

'Christian, for the last year we've had to pretend you're single; I've had to fit in with what you wanted because of your career. And I've slept with you no more than six times in what I can only loosely call a relationship. Up until you arrived here yesterday you'd shown no interest in me for months. So why the proposal and why now?'

'Because...' he hesitated, 'because I did a lot of thinking while I was away on tour and I decided it's what I want. Isn't that a good enough reason?'

'It may be what *you* want, but this isn't all about you, is it? What about me? You've not even stopped to ask me what I want.'

Impatience filled his face. 'Charlotte, you'd be *Mrs* Christian Rosetti – some women would kill to be in your place.'

'Well, of all the—' Her words were interrupted when a familiar figure walked in through one of the open French doors at the far end of the hall.

Thérèse D'Alesandro, briefcase in hand, strode confidently towards them.

'Good morning, Lottie. Morning, Christian. Sorry for sneaking in, I thought it would save Helen opening the main door.' She tilted her head inquisitively. 'Well, are congratulations in order? Should we be looking at dresses for you, Lottie? I've brought a couple of beautiful new samples with me today to show Ella and Jenny for their next wedding client. One in particular would, I think, suit your colouring. Ah, there are you are, Marco.' She raised her hand, watching as he approached from the same direction she had come. He was carrying two large white suitcase-style boxes. 'Can you bring those dresses over here a moment please?'

Christian watched Charlotte carefully, hoping for some reaction, however small, to the new arrival's presence. Noticing her face was set in an impassive mask as she watched Marco approach, he wondered for a moment whether his suspicions might have been wrong.

Smartly suited and obviously bound for London and work, Marco placed the boxes gently down onto the floor beside his stepmother then nodded a good morning to Christian and Charlotte as he turned to walk away.

'Aren't you going to congratulate us then, Marco?' Christian called after him, unable to resist the urge to taunt him.

Marco hesitated then spun round, his calm gaze resting first on Charlotte and then him. 'I am sorry.'

'You *are* engaged, then!' Thérèse clapped her hands. 'Wonderful news.'

'Yes, we're engaged,' Christian confirmed smugly, buoyed up by Thérèse's eager acceptance of his words. Casting a triumphant smirk at Marco, his arm snaked around Charlotte's waist, eager to reinforce his claim over her. Two birds with one stone, he thought. I've nipped her refusal in the bud, and if *he* did have any ideas, he knows to keep his distance now.

'So, when will you be choosing the ring?' Thérèse rapt expression focussed on Charlotte.

'There is no ring, because there is no engagement, Mrs D'Alesandro,' Charlotte uttered firmly. 'I said no last night, and nothing has changed.' Bristling with anger, she swung around to confront Christian. 'Your insufferable arrogance takes my breath away. How dare you tell such lies. How dare you!'

Ella and Jenny emerged from their office, drawn by the sound of Charlotte's voice.

'Are you all right, Lottie?' Taking in the tableau at the foot of the stairs, Jenny walked over and put a calming hand on her daughter's shoulder.

'No, I'm bloody well not!' Charlotte shouted and pushing her mother away, gave Christian a final withering glance before disappearing quickly up the stairs.

He attempted to follow her but had only reached the fourth stair when

Jenny grabbed his arm. 'Leave her, please,' she insisted, shaking her head as she tried to deter him from following.

'Don't tell me what to do!' He turned aggressively, knocking her off balance.

Marco, standing at the foot of the stairs, caught Jenny in his strong grip.

'Thank you,' she said to him, one hand going to her face as if she was about to burst into tears, watching helplessly as Christian continued to make his way upstairs.

'Christian, I think it would be best if you packed and left.' It was Ella who spoke, her voice calm and authoritative. Everyone watched as she began to follow him up the stairs. 'I have had quite enough of this dreadful behaviour and so has everyone else. If Charlotte has said no then you should respect her wishes.'

He had reached the lower landing now and stood watching her approach. 'Or what?'

'Or risk losing her friendship altogether because, believe me, that's probably all you have left now after the way you behaved.'

'Ah, you would like that to happen, wouldn't you? But it's not going to… Charlotte makes up her own mind about what goes on in her life; she doesn't take orders from you Little Court women.'

'It's precisely because she has a mind of her own she has said no to you,' came Ella's reply as she reached the landing and faced him. 'As I said before, you should respect her wishes. Now, please return to your room and pack. I'll phone for a taxi to the station and let Matt know you are on your way back to London.'

Christian was about to tell her he wasn't going anywhere when he noticed movement below. Someone had fetched Rowan together with a couple of men, who from their build looked more like minders than gardeners. He was on a hiding to nothing here; he might as well go back to London and face Matt. Not that he would do much, of course. All it would amount to would be the usual wrist slap. No, Charlotte would keep. He'd get her back but now was not the time. Grudgingly, he had to admit Ella was right. His behaviour had not won him sympathetic friends here. Time to lie low for a while and maybe try a different approach in a few days' time.

'Okay, you win,' he said, giving a compliant nod. 'I'll go.' He eyed the small group as he walked back down, noticing Marco was no longer there. God, he winced inwardly as he reached the foot of the stairs and they parted to let him through, he'd made a complete and utter fool of himself again. He only hoped his actions had not left the door open for the Italian. The sudden need for a boost from his precious amphetamines saw him practically running across the hall to his room in the west wing.

* * *

In her room, Charlotte sat on the bed and tried to clear her thoughts. She had to get away from this madness. She knew Christian would not let go of this issue, he would bully her relentlessly. So wherever she went it had to be a place he didn't know about. Hand to her head, she tried to think. And then in an instant it came to her. Picking up her mobile, she punched in Beth's number.

SIXTEEN

Christian arrived at Evolution UK's head office a little after three, entering reception with his usual self-assured swagger, his face full of dark-eyed confrontation. Matt's Hungarian-born receptionist Magda announced his arrival in her usual husky manner before showing him into the boardroom, where Matt and his heavy-set bearded partner Baz Young were waiting. He slid himself into the chair opposite them, staring from one to the other with a smug grin on his face waiting to see what they had to say.

'You are totally out of order this time,' Matt began, with a despairing shake of his head. 'I'm a pretty tolerant guy and I cut you a lot of slack. You're my best act but what happened this morning back at Little Court was totally unacceptable.'

'I'm sorry.' Christian bowed his head and then raised his eyes with an expression full of self-reproach. 'I am extremely sorry.'

Matt frowned at him then at his partner. He wasn't fooled; Christian didn't do humility – he was up to something.

'Look, I love Lottie and I want to marry her,' Christian continued, catching Baz's sceptical expression. 'I guess I was so wrapped up with the act of proposal I didn't stop to consider what a special moment it was. What I should have done is taken her out to dinner or somewhere more intimate to ask such a very special question. I blew it last night and as you've heard, again this morning. If it's any consolation, I've arranged for flowers to be sent to Ella and Jenny by way of an apology.'

Matt sat back and steepled his fingers as he watched Christian closely. 'Well, thank you for that,' he said, his gaze drifting across to Baz, who looked equally surprised, 'but I have to tell you Ella does not want you anywhere near Little Court for the foreseeable future.'

'Oh!' Christian's expression turned to one of surprise. 'But I thought—'

'I'm afraid it's going to take more than a bunch of flowers to cut it with my wife. You were totally out of control. They felt threatened. In fact, if Rowan and the gardeners hadn't been there I think Ella would have called the police.'

'The police? What the hell for? All I wanted to do was to talk to Lottie.'

'You were extremely aggressive.' Matt leaned across the table. 'I won't have that sort of behaviour inflicted on my family.'

'All right, all right!' Christian ran an agitated hand through his hair. 'I'll keep away for a few days.'

Leaning back in his chair, Baz calmly stroked his beard and fixed him with a hard stare. 'I'm afraid it will be longer than a few days. You'll be tied up in the studios for at least three months with this album.'

'Sorry, I don't see a problem.' Christian gave a conceited shrug. 'My weekends are my own. I can arrange to see Lottie in London if I'm not welcome at Little Court.'

Baz gave him a slow shake of his head. 'But you won't be here, Christian. You'll be in the Caribbean.'

'The Caribbean? But I thought—'

'I need to have you somewhere where you are concentrating one hundred per cent on your work,' Matt took over the conversation. 'I don't want any distractions. So I've called in a favour. The Evolution jet leaves Heathrow tomorrow morning for the Cayman Islands. I'll arrange for the limo to pick you up at eight.'

'Well, at least I'll be able to give her a call before I go, I guess. That's if you don't object, of course.' Christian eyed them both, his face white with anger.

Matt regarded him coolly. 'She might not be answering her phone. Ella tells me she left Little Court early this afternoon.'

Christian glared at them suspiciously. 'Who with?'

'No one. Why? Did you think she'd gone with Marco?'

'Why would she go with him?' Christian knew Matt was being deliberately provocative, aware the whole of Little Court must have heard about the incident with the roses.

'You tell me.'

'Does Jenny know where she is?' Christian purposely turned the conversation in a different direction; there was no way he was going to admit Marco had anything to do with his behaviour.

Matt shook his head. 'She said she wanted some time away from everyone. But...' he paused for a moment, 'I can see you are concerned about Marco. There's absolutely no need to be. There's definitely nothing going on between him and Lottie.' His eyes locked on Christian's. 'He already has a girlfriend here in London.'

'Well, thank you for that piece of information. Anything else you wish to enlighten me with?' Christian asked with the kind of amused superiority he knew would annoy them. 'No? Well, gentlemen, if you'll excuse me. I guess I'd better go home and start packing.' He eased himself out of the chair and left the room, slamming the door behind him.

It was early evening when Ella answered the front door to find Marco standing there.

'I came to see how Charlotte is,' he said, his tone mirroring the concerned expression on his face. 'She was very upset this morning.'

'Charlotte is fine but I'm afraid she's not here,' Ella replied, studying his anxious face.

His dark brows rose in surprise. 'Gone? With Christian?'

'No, she won't be seeing Christian for a while. Matt's flying out to the

Caymans with him to record the new album. He feels the distance will calm things down.'

Marco gave an understanding nod. 'When did Charlotte leave?'

'Around twelve thirty.'

'Did she say where she was going?'

Ella shook her head. 'None of us know, I'm afraid. She only indicated she planned to be away for a few days. She wanted to be somewhere...' she gave a soft sigh, 'somewhere totally private where no one could reach her. She didn't know about the Caymans then, you see. She phoned to say she had arrived at her destination and has promised to keep in regular touch, but that's all we know. I'm so sorry, I wish I could be more helpful.'

'When she calls again please would you let her know I am thinking of her?'

Ella gave him a sympathetic smile. 'I will.'

As he was about to leave Lucy appeared, dressed in beige jodhpurs and a navy sweater with her hair tied back off her face, a riding hat sat in the crook of her arm.

'Hello, Marco.' She gave him the benefit of one of her most dazzling smiles.

'Marco came to see if Lottie was all right,' Ella explained. 'I told him she's gone away for a few days and that we haven't a clue where she is.'

Lucy gave a nod. 'Yes. To be honest, I can't say I blame her after what Christian did...' She rolled her eyes, her attention distracted by the hall clock chiming seven o'clock.

'Heavens, is that the time?' Ella looked questioningly at her daughter, who nodded. 'Sorry, I must go. I'm due up at Willowbrook in twenty minutes. I'll leave Lucy to show you out, Marco. Oh, and if we hear anything we will definitely let you know.'

'Thank you, Mrs Benedict,' he called, as she walked away.

As the click of her mother's heels faded into the distance, Lucy gave Marco a sideways glance and whispered, 'What would you say if I told you I think I know where Lottie's gone?'

'You do?'

She nodded. 'I'm sure she's gone to stay with Beth.'

'Beth?'

'Beth Reynolds. She's Lottie's best friend. They were room-mates at uni in Warwick. She has a small gallery in Dartmouth called Water's Edge. Lottie was planning to visit her soon, and I do know Beth is probably the one person she would want to be with at a time like this.'

'Thank you, Lucy. Thank you so much.' He leaned forward and kissed her forehead. Then he was gone, hurrying down the steps towards his car.

Lucy watched the red Porsche leave, hoping now Marco had this information Christian Rosetti would soon be out of her cousin's life for good.

* * *

Charlotte arrived in Dartmouth as Beth was closing the gallery for the day. Water's Edge was a small double-fronted shop facing the estuary. Its shiny new coat of navy blue paint on the door and window frames indicated Beth had already been at work. A mixture of colour prints, original oils and some charcoal sketches featured in both windows; a smattering of coastal and country scenes with some still life. After finding a suitable place to park her car for the night, it had only been a short walk to her friend's rented terraced house in Newcomen Road. As Beth slotted the key in the door, each felt the first spits of rain against their face.

Once inside, Beth showed Charlotte upstairs to the light, comfortable bedroom where she would be staying: a bay windowed room which faced the front of the house. The view across the water – a pastiche of terraced houses cloaking the hillside in a swathe of pastel colours – she told her, was Kingswear.

'I hope you don't find the gulls too much of a pain,' Beth added, as Charlotte dumped her case onto the bed. 'They roost on the roof and sometimes it takes ages to get to sleep with all their chattering and thumping about.'

'Thumping?'

'Believe me, webbed feet and hobnail boots sound about the same on my roof.'

'Don't worry, something tells me tonight I'll sleep like a baby.' Charlotte gave an amused smile as the door closed and she was left alone to unpack. She took a deep breath; with all the distance she had put between Little Court and herself, the world suddenly looked a different place. She walked over to the window, watching as a returning trawler chugged slowly through the thin veil of rain which had crept up the estuary. Moments later, the ferry carrying its cargo of vehicles across from the other side of the river broke through the same watery curtain. There was an atmosphere already; an easy pace coupled with a feeling of peace. This was a place where she could, with the help of her best friend and a little time, make sense of all the crazy things that had taken place over the last few days.

Charlotte unpacked and freshened up before joining Beth in the cosy lounge. The fire had been lit and curtains pulled to shut out the dismal evening.

'Dinner will be another half hour,' Beth announced, watching Charlotte curl herself into one of the big comfortable chairs and pick up her glass of wine. 'So that gives us plenty of time.'

Charlotte frowned innocently. 'Plenty of time for what?'

'To tell me the reason why you've suddenly found time to drop everything and arrive on my doorstep.'

* * *

Charlotte awoke around seven o'clock. The night's rain had cleared away to leave a fresh, mid-September morning, the sun sparkling on the water. Below, the town was already awake, fishing boats heading out to sea and the ferry busy with the cross-water transfer of its first vehicles. Once showered and dressed, she joined Beth for breakfast in the tiny kitchen at the back of the house.

'You look better this morning,' Beth said, munching on a piece of toast as she poured their coffee. 'The gulls obviously didn't keep you awake.'

'I am and they didn't.' Charlotte smiled and stretched her shoulders. 'In fact, I had a great night's sleep.'

'Good.' Beth handed her a steaming mug of coffee and pushed milk and the sugar bowl towards her. 'Toast?'

'Please. I'm glad we talked, and thanks for listening.' Charlotte gave her friend an appreciative hug. 'I hope you don't think I'm too much of a burden.'

'A burden!' Beth laughed as she dropped two pieces of bread into the toaster. 'That's crazy talk, Lottie. It's what friends are for. I'm only glad my life isn't as complicated as yours.'

'I did ring Mum again this morning. I was still concerned Christian might try to find me but...' she hesitated. 'But apparently my uncle has switched the location for recording the album to the Caribbean –a friend of his has a studio out there – so Christian will be out of the UK for at least three months.'

'Well, that's one piece of good news. You know, you really surprised me. I had no idea about you and him – you managed to keep that quiet.' She laughed. 'I only got to meet him once, when he came up to Warwick with Rosetti to do a gig for the students' union. Remember?'

Charlotte nodded, then seeing her friend's perplexed expression said, 'What is it?'

'Well, last night it seemed you were talking about a completely different guy. The Christian I remember meeting was kind and funny and caring. He was almost embarrassed about his talent. I mean, he was famous then but he didn't even ask a fee for the band's appearance. The one you told me about sounds like a complete arsehole, if you don't mind my saying. He's controlling and completely selfish. Are you sure we're talking about the same person?'

Charlotte nodded as the toaster ejected two pieces of hot, well browned toast. 'Oh yes, it's the same Christian.'

'So what happened?' Beth pulled out a plate from the rack, juggled the toast onto it and handed it to Charlotte.

'About six months ago, overnight he seemed to change.'

'Was he the special one you thought you'd settle down with?'

'I don't think so. As you know we'd been close friends for years.' She reached for the butter and a knife. 'Then, about a year ago, I was staying over in the company flat in London and he called me up, said he was in town and suggested we go out for a meal. We both had rather a lot to drink and ended up sleeping together. The weird thing was he was good in bed, but for some reason it wasn't how I expected it to be. I didn't feel the emotion or the passion with him I thought I would. I guess he was better as a rock god fantasy. I should have ended it there but because of who he was, somehow I couldn't. Even after the ground rules I—'

'Ground rules! What ground rules?' Beth tilted her head, eyeing her friend curiously.

'He wanted to preserve his single status for the fans. That's why no one except close family knew we were together. Because of that I couldn't be seen out with him. Of course, we were caught by paparazzi on a couple of occasions, but Matt saw to it that Evolution's PR covered it with plausible excuses. As far as everyone was concerned he was footloose and fancy free and having a great time with the ladies.'

'What! Now I know he's a complete arsehole.' Beth fixed her eyes on Charlotte with a frown. 'How could you have accepted that?'

'I guess because at the time I was crazy enough to think he needed someone like me in his life, someone normal he could escape to in a secret world completely separate from the one he lived in. A romantic notion, I know.' Charlotte sighed as she bit into the first piece of toast. 'All part of me putting someone else first. It's what I do. It's one of my weaknesses. Being sensible is another.' She gave a thoughtful sigh. 'But I'm determined by the time I go back home things will be different. *I'm* going to be different.'

'That's my girl! See, you've been here one night and you've made progress already.' Beth beamed at her then, catching sight of the clock, her eyes widened. 'Heavens, it's nearly nine. I must go. I've got someone coming to collect a painting for framing first thing. I've found this wonderful local guy, Jules Mason, he's very reasonable.'

'A hot framer, eh?' Charlotte gave Beth a meaningful grin. 'Is he single?'

'Sadly, no, on both counts. He's a balding fifty-something with a paunch and he has a wife. She's a landscape artist. I'm planning to exhibit some of her paintings soon. She's very good,' she said, pulling her jacket from the back of her chair. 'What are your plans for today?'

'Oh, I'm going to have a wander around, get my bearings and do a bit of browsing. It's wonderful – nothing to do but relax,' Charlotte enthused, as Beth hauled her bag off the worktop and searched for the shop keys. 'And when I've finished browsing, I'll drop in and see you at the gallery. You can show me around.'

'I'm good with that. If you drop in around twelve we can have some lunch. There's a brilliant new bistro in the High Street. I'll book a table, my shout.'

'Certainly not, I'm a non-paying guest, remember? I should be footing the bill.'

'Nonsense, you picked up the last tab in Warwick. It's my turn and so no more arguments.' Beth waved a warning finger and was out of the door before Charlotte could protest.

Left alone, she turned on the radio and finished her toast before clearing away the breakfast things ready to wash up. Back at Little Court this is exactly what Helen would be doing, she thought. In some ways she missed the buzz of home, her mother and aunts with their daily work in organising weddings, milestone birthday bashes and corporate events. But there, she would not have this peace and quiet, somewhere to think, to work out what happens next.

As she pulled on rubber gloves and ran water into the plastic bowl, she stared out into the small paved area at the rear of the house. In the conversation last night with Beth she had omitted to tell her anything about the incident at Fox Cottage. But what was there to tell? That Marco had stolen a kiss in an attempt to prove he wasn't gay? She sighed. If only it had not felt so incredibly wonderful... Closing her eyes, she could still taste the mint freshness of his mouth. I must forget it, she reprimanded herself. I must remember he already has someone. He means nothing, nothing at all.

Lucy was reading through the rider for Sherrilyn Carr, one of Matt's new protégés, when Jay poked his head around her door.

'Heard anything from His Majesty yet?' he asked, his eyes dancing with mischief.

'Having withdrawal symptoms already?' Lucy shot back with a grin. 'Ah, there, you should have gone with him.'

'Like hell I should,' came the reply as Jay lodged himself on the end of her desk and folded his arms. 'I'm only glad we've got three months' peace. Aren't you?'

'Absolutely. I bet Dad's going through hell with him now he can't get to Lottie.'

'It would have been worse if he'd been here. Your cousin is one lucky lady.'

'In more ways than one.' Lucy gave him a knowing smile.

'Oh!' Jay cocked a blond eyebrow at her, curious.

'Well,' she began, 'these new people have moved into Higher Padbury Manor and there's a son, Marco, he's in his mid-twenties. He's extremely good-looking. In fact, he's absolutely to die for. Not my kind of to die for, of course,' she added, seeing what looked like a glint of disapproval in his eyes. 'I don't go for dark Mediterranean types but my cousin definitely does, and so I've sort of given them a nudge.'

'What sort of nudge, Lucy?'

They had not heard Baz enter the room. He stood staring at them before directing his stern gaze on Lucy. 'Tell me, what exactly have you done?'

'Marco came to the house looking for Lottie,' she answered. 'Aunt Ella told him we had no idea where she was but said she'd let him know if we did find out.' Swallowing hard as she saw Baz's less than happy expression, she continued. 'Earlier, we'd all been searching her room for clues as to where she'd gone and, well, I found a note in her diary. I think she's gone to visit her friend Beth, in Dartmouth.'

'And you told Marco this?'

Lucy nodded.

'But not your aunt or your mother?' She sensed the disapproval in his voice.

'No, I didn't.' She dropped her eyes. 'In fact, I hid the diary in my room afterwards so they wouldn't find it.'

'So why tell Marco?'

'Because, well… I think he loves her.'

Baz put his hand to his face and shook his head. 'Oh Lucy!'

'What? What have I done?'

'I thought the whole thing was about letting Lottie get away to sort herself out. Don't you think Marco going down there is only going to make things worse?'

'Worse for whom? Christian? He doesn't deserve her,' Lucy snapped. 'All this getting engaged rubbish… Doesn't anyone but me see what he's really up to? He doesn't love her; he's trying to stop anything happening between her and Marco, that's all.'

Baz eyed her suspiciously. 'So you decided to play cupid?'

'Well, yes, I suppose I did.'

'Or maybe you simply wanted to get even with Christian? After all, he's not exactly been pleasant to you since you joined Evolution, has he?'

'No, he hasn't. He's been a complete bastard.'

'So you decided to wreck his relationship with Lottie while he's out of the country. What a totally childish and spiteful thing to do. Do you realise if Christian gets to hear what you've done it could completely wreck the album, because he'll walk. He won't be able to stop himself coming back here to find her.' Baz levelled a finger at her. 'I'm going to have to let your father know what's happened. He needs to be warned.'

'But why does he need to know? Christian won't have a clue; he's thousands of miles away.'

'And he has people around him who will find out anything he wants. And they can contact him by mobile.' He gave a harsh laugh. 'You didn't think your father would stop him communicating with the outside world while he was away, did you?'

'Baz is right,' Jay agreed. 'I'm sorry, Luce, but despite your father trying to convince Christian nothing is going on, he is so paranoid about the situation he may have already paid someone to keep him informed about what's—'

'Lucy, I suggest you give your cousin a call straight away,' Baz interrupted irritably. 'If Christian finds out Marco and Lottie are together,' Baz shook his head slowly, 'then God help you, because your father has a fortune riding on this album.'

SEVENTEEN

Charlotte had had a relaxing morning wandering the streets of Dartmouth, taking in the small independent shops and many restaurants there. She could see Beth had some stiff competition there as she had come across at least four other galleries on her travels. She now found herself gazing at the properties displayed in the window of a local estate agents. One in particular had caught her eye: a white double-fronted house with a grey slate roof. Inset below it was a gallery of smaller photos, one of which showed a glorious view from the rear garden along the river Dart towards Totnes. She checked her watch; there was still plenty of time before she was due to meet Beth. Moments later she was inside the agents. After a brief discussion with an eager young man in a brown suit, she left with a smile on her face and an appointment to view that afternoon.

Making her way to the gallery, she knew the five-bedroom property, called Gulls' Rest and currently empty, was exactly what she wanted. She did very little with her money beyond investment and a property project appealed. It was lovely here, within easy reach of Meridan Cross, and less than twenty-four hours after her arrival, she was already enjoying the slower pace of life and the easiness of people in shops and on the street. Even a friendly smile from a passing stranger had the strange ability to make her feel welcome. Buying and renovating a property to use as a holiday home, something all the family could share, felt exactly the right thing to do.

Arriving at noon as agreed, she pushed open the door of Water's Edge and walked in. Beth was in the rear of the gallery with a customer, discussing a group of paintings in bright oils. As Charlotte approached them she frowned; there was something familiar about the casually dressed man who stood with his back to her. Beth saw her and raised a hand in greeting. The visitor turned round and smiled. As Charlotte's eyes widened in surprise the house details accidentally slipped from her fingers and fell to the floor.

Stepping towards her, Marco D'Alesandro bent down and retrieved the estate agent's details.

'Charlotte, it's good to see you,' he said gently, his dark eyes staring down into hers as he handed the sheet back to her. 'I was so worried.'

'I'm... I'm fine.' She felt the heat creeping into her face. 'How did you find me?'

'Oh, I have my spies.' He smiled as he turned back to Beth. 'Beth and I have been having quite a conversation.'

Charlotte glared at her friend over Marco's shoulder.

'About art and the best places to eat around here,' Beth interjected.

He studied Charlotte again. 'I gather you two are about to go for lunch.'

She nodded, praying Beth had not asked him to join them. Appreciating the distance he had travelled and remembering the relief in his face when he saw her, she immediately reprimanded herself for being so mean.

'I will not intrude.'

His words brought a silent sigh of relief.

'I have a reservation at the Royal Castle Hotel,' he continued. 'I will check in and would be very pleased if you both could join me there for dinner tonight. Would eight be suitable?'

Beth was nodding vigorously and Charlotte found herself reluctantly agreeing.

'Thank you,' she said, not wanting to appear unfriendly, 'that would be lovely.'

'I will see you both later.' Smiling, he raised a hand in farewell and then was gone.

'Oh my God, Lottie, where did you find *him*?' Beth stood there shaking her head. 'He hasn't got anything to do with what's happened between you and Christian by any chance, has he?'

'No! Definitely not. Really, don't you think I've enough problems with what's going on in my life at the moment? The last thing I want is to be involved with anyone else.' And especially not him, her inner voice added, realising with his arrival the promises she had made to herself over the morning's washing-up were now in pieces.

'Methinks the lady protests too much.' Beth laughed, amused. 'This is me you're talking to, lady. You never mentioned him, not one word. Yet he has cared enough to come and find you.'

'But no one knows where I am, unless...' She paused, frowning as she thought. 'I wrote a note in my diary as a reminder to give you a call. My mother must have found it, but I know she would not have made it public beyond the family, unless... But surely she didn't know...' She stopped; she had let her tongue run away with her.

'Didn't know what, Lottie?' Beth looked at her, her eyes full of curiosity.

'Nothing. Forget it.'

Beth waved a warning finger. 'You will tell me, you know.'

Charlotte gave an unconcerned shrug. 'There's nothing to tell.'

'I saw the way he looked at you when you came in and I saw your reaction. Even a blind man would have sensed what passed between the two of you. You can't lie to me; he is involved in all this somewhere, isn't he? Have you slept with him?'

'Of course not!' Charlotte protested, her face colouring again.

'No, silly me.' Beth clasped a hand to her chest theatrically. 'Of course you haven't. Not yet. But you will, I know you will.'

'Not if his girlfriend has anything to do with it.'

'A girlfriend? He didn't mention anyone while we were talking. Are you sure? Have you met her?'

'Not yet. Her name is Lauren and I'm sure he'll be bringing her down to the manor soon. They live together in his apartment during the week.' Charlotte smiled at Beth's disbelieving face. 'It's true,' she said crossly. 'His sister told us.'

When from Beth's expression it appeared she still didn't believe what she was being told, Charlotte simply shook her head, walked over to the door and turned the Open sign to Closed. 'Come on,' she said, 'let's get some lunch. Oh, and by the way, the M word is banned.'

Christian sat in the shade, drinking beer and watching the world pass by. He had to admit, despite his original anger and outrage at being dragged out here to record, the turquoise sea and white sands he now gazed out on were having a most calming effect, helped by the fact he was now on his third can and a recent intake of pills.

Matt had rented a six-bedroomed villa situated on a small promontory at one end of the island's famous Seven Mile Beach for Christian, himself and the small technical team who had flown out with them. Set in a lush garden of palms and other tropical vegetation, the villa was long and low with a huge front loggia, sun deck and pool. From the shaded balcony Christian could comfortably watch the beach below, its occupants and their activities. There was a huge selection to choose from: windsurfing, water skiing, scuba diving and snorkelling, plus jet skis or powerboats for hire.

It was the first morning after their arrival and Matt and the team had decided to drive out to the studio to check out the facilities. Wanting to avoid any more of the unwanted high spirits he had been subjected to from the technical team on the long flight over, he made it clear he would not be accompanying them. He did, however, flex his VIP muscles, insisting they leave the hired jeep in case he decided he did want to go out, making them ring for a taxi instead. Matt was concerned leaving him alone might mean he would brood about Charlotte, but Christian had assured him he was adult enough to realise she'd have to be put on hold for three months, that there was nothing he could do about it. And, after all, this album was important. It was going to be *so* good, in fact, when he did finally walk out of Evolution there would be a bidding war for him.

Charlotte had occupied his thoughts for most of the flight, his mind see-sawing with confusion. He wanted to believe that Marco was either gay or had a girlfriend, but he still was not convinced. He had, therefore, spent the flight anaesthetising his anxiety with cold beer. When he arrived, he had checked his mobile again, only to find the messages sent prior to leaving the UK still remained unanswered. He had grovelled, saying he was sorry and that he had made a complete fool of himself and wanted desperately – had he actually used the word *desperate?* – to be forgiven. He hoped she would eventually return his call so they could come to some form of long-distance truce. As he extracted another can of beer from the fridge he hoped his newly hired PI was keeping an eye on her every move and would come back to him soon if there was any news.

He cracked open the can. As he took a long swig from it, the doorbell rang. He stood still for a moment, wondering whether he should answer it or not. If he did, it meant he had to deal with someone and did not feel that was his job. He was, after all, the star – people usually ran around after him – but as he was alone in the villa, he realised he did not have much alternative.

'Shit,' he cursed under his breath when he heard it ring again. Leaving the can on the table, he headed for the door.

'Yes!' he snapped irritably, swinging the door open, expecting to see the gardener or some other local on the doorstep. Instead, his eyes widened in surprise. His dark eyebrows arched and a roguish grin stole across his face as he found himself staring at his two blonde goddesses, Leyna and Talia, both dressed in tight shorts and bikini tops.

'Girls! How the hell did you find me?'

'Easily,' Leyna squealed, and threw herself into his arms. 'We missed you. Wow! This is some place you have,' she said, gazing over his shoulder.

Talia smiled as she pushed past them and stood admiring the spacious luxury of the villa. 'Looks like plenty of room for us too.'

'Ah, no.' Christian quickly disentangled himself from Leyna's embrace. 'No, you can't stay. Matt and the boys are here with me. He'll go ape if he finds you both. I'm already in deep shit for bringing you down to the wedding boutique opening.'

'Oh!' Leyna turned to her friend with a frown of disappointment. 'Now that is a shame, isn't it, Talia? We would love it here.'

Talia nodded and shot him a moody pout. 'Yes, I really would love to stay here, Christian…'

'Girls…' he began, 'I—'

'Just as well we're booked into the Marriott Beach Resort, isn't it?' Talia interrupted, laughing at the panic in Christian's face. 'That got you going, didn't it?' They both shrieked with laughter.

'Well, it's great to see you both. Perhaps we can catch up at the Marriott for a drink later.' He checked his watch. 'I'm not being rude but Matt and the boys are due back within the next half an hour and I'd hate him to find you both here.'

'Maybe they are,' Talia teased, her blue eyes flashing with mischief, 'or maybe they aren't…'

'What have you done?'

'Oh, nothing. We've simply organised a little delay. Don't worry, they'll be back in a couple of hours.'

'Talia!'

'We were here earlier and caught the driver of the taxi before they came out,' Leyna explained, her long fingers stroking his cheek. 'With a little financial persuasion we suggested he take them on an island tour with a stop-off somewhere for lunch.' She reached out and smoothed Christian's bare chest with a teasing hand before running a fingertip over his nipple. 'We wanted to give you a proper welcome, didn't we, Talia?'

'Oh yes.' Talia joined her, coiling herself around Christian's torso like an exotic serpent. 'And we didn't want to rush.'

Leyna shook her head. 'No. One thing we never do is rush…'

Christian eyed both of them with a salacious smile. 'And how long do you two plan staying on the island?'

'As long as you want us.' Talia's fingers played along the waistband of his shorts. 'You do want us here, don't you?'

'Oh yes!' He closed his eyes as he felt her reach for the zip. 'Definitely.'

'And we bought you some new supplies.' Leyna waved a small plastic packet of pills in front of him. 'So we can keep the fun going.'

'Ladies, the bedroom is this way.' Christian indicated the direction with a mock bow.

Moments later, he and Leyna lay naked on the bed watching Talia cut a line of coke on the glass top of the dressing table. As he closed his eyes with a smile, anticipating what was to come, concerns about Charlotte vanished like melting snow.

Despite the M word ban lunch had gone well, Charlotte thought as they left the restaurant. Beth had a sunny disposition, rarely lost her temper and was probably one of the most tidy and practical people she knew; traits which ran at odds to the well-known mood swings, passion and general chaos of those with artistic inclinations. They parted outside Water's Edge with a hug, Charlotte heading for the estate agents and her viewing. However, as soon as she walked in through the door she knew something was wrong; the expression on the young estate agent's face was full of discomfort. He came towards her, clearly upset.

'I'm so sorry, Miss Kendrick. It appears another couple saw Gulls' Rest earlier this morning. My colleague took them out first thing. They returned during the lunch hour and made an offer, the full asking price. Of course, it goes without saying our client has accepted.'

Charlotte shook her head in bitter disappointment. In her mind everything had been planned: CJ to look after the structural changes, her Uncle Mick's company to carry them out and redecorate, and her stepfather Rowan to organise the landscaping of the gardens. It was her dream and now sadly that is all it would ever be.

'I'm so sorry…' she heard him say again, then with a more upbeat voice, 'but I've several other equally superb properties in that area, all with fabulous river views.'

'No, I'd set my heart on Gulls' Rest. Sadly, I don't believe anything else would be quite the same. Thank you anyway,' she said, shaking his hand before turning to leave.

Downhearted at the loss of such a coveted property, Charlotte decided on a walk, not only to take her mind off her disappointment but also feeling the need for some fresh air and to stretch her legs after what had turned out to be quite a heavy lunch. She considered her options, wondering where she could go, and then spied the stone silhouette of Dartmouth Castle in the distance where the river met the sea. She estimated it was far enough out of the town to guarantee her the walk she needed. From the estate agents she made her way along the embankment, intending to drop in to see Beth on her way to give her the bad news and let her know she was planning to walk off her blues with a trip to the castle.

However, as she reached the gallery she noticed Marco was back, this time sitting with Beth on one of the comfortable settees to the right of the counter. They were drinking coffee and Beth was laughing at whatever he was saying to her, a rapt expression on her face. Gazing at them from behind the safe cover of one of the large paintings exhibited in the window, Charlotte noticed his hair was shorter than when she had last seen him at Little Court. It now lay heavy and dark against the nape of his neck, the shortness making it curlier than usual. A strange sensation overcame her as she found herself back at Fox Cottage once more... her fingers weaving into its silky thickness, finding their way to the soft skin beneath... Her hand went to her face as the memory made her shiver. Then she noticed the way he was smiling at Beth and the relaxed and intimate way they interacted together. The emotional tremor died, replaced by something else – anger. Anger at the way Beth appeared to be seizing the opportunity to cosy up and make a play for Marco even though she had been told he already had someone in his life. And what about Marco and the way he seemed to have no problem flirting with Beth? *Am I the only one with any moral scruples*, she wondered crossly, *or maybe I'm... jealous?* She wiped the thought away. *No, definitely not!*

With a huff of annoyance she turned away from the gallery and continued her journey along the road, stopping to enjoy the glorious views across to Kingswear bathed in warm afternoon autumn sunshine. Soon she had passed the Southtown area of Dartmouth, where houses with panoramic views across the estuary clung to the side of the hill, one above the other. She upped her pace into Warfleet Road then past the high grey walls of the old pottery building and on into the wooded shade of Castle Road. Ten minutes later she was standing on the battlements of the castle, gazing out to sea. A warm afternoon breeze teased her hair, blowing it across her face. As she brushed it from her eyes she took a deep breath, her thoughts turning to Christian.

Since leaving Little Court he had texted her on ten separate occasions, each message sounding more frantic than the one before. She had deleted each one without responding and now, thankfully, they seemed to have stopped. She expected his arrival in Grand Cayman meant jet lag and a long sleep. Wanting to be rid of his pestering, she had switched off her mobile and refused to look at it. Her mind pulled her back once more to the awful evening and his embarrassing behaviour. At the time she felt cornered and unsettled by his controlling actions, but not any longer. She had only been away from Little Court for one day but already she knew she would never go back to being the accommodating person she had once been. When she faced him again she knew she would have absolutely no qualms about ending their relationship for good. The only stumbling block at the moment was exactly how to achieve that but, she reflected positively, no doubt a solution would eventually come to her. After all, she had three whole months to work out a suitable strategy.

Gazing around, she noticed a balding, middle-aged man in dark cargo trousers and a pale polo shirt standing nearby. He was talking and gesturing around the battlements to a cheerful group of older people who wore comfortable-looking trainers and carried back packs.

'This incredible complex of defences was begun in 1388 by John Hawley,' she heard him say. Curious, she walked over and joined the group, listening with interest as the guide began to reveal the history of the castle.

Arriving back at the house in Newcomen Road a little after five, Charlotte found Beth uncorking a bottle of red wine in the kitchen.

'You're starting early,' she said, eyeing the generous measure her friend was pouring.

Beth raised the bottle in greeting 'Celebration time. Marco has bought three paintings for his London apartment. Would you like to join me?'

Charlotte dumped her tote onto the kitchen table and pulled out a chair. 'Yes, why not?'

'Oh, look at that expression; I know exactly what you're thinking.' Beth laughed as she grabbed another glass from the cupboard.

'No you don't.' Charlotte shook her head slowly. 'You haven't got a clue.'

Beth waved a finger at her. 'Oh, but I have, Lottie Kendrick. And if you must know, the simple truth is we seem to have hit it off. I do like him.' She eyed her seriously. 'And I did say *like*. He's unlike any other man I've ever met. He's funny and interesting to talk to and very old fashioned in some of his ways. And I absolutely love that accent – a sort of melodic fusing of English and Italian. Other than that,' she said with a serene smile, 'there is absolutely nothing else going on between us. Honestly.'

Beth's statement was met with a careless shrug from Charlotte. 'It wouldn't make any difference to me if there was.'

'Lottie Kendrick, you little liar!' Beth countered with a grin as she handed her one of the glasses. 'I think he's perfect.'

'No such thing as the perfect man,' she argued, taking the proffered glass. 'They're all flawed. You start out thinking they're wonderful and then they go and do something crazy that makes you want to sever all contact with the opposite sex for ever.'

'I mean, he's perfect for you.'

'No, Beth, he is not.' Charlotte's tone was challenging, wondering why her friend seemed so keen to hold on to this topic, fussing over it like a dog with a bone. 'Firstly, before I even begin to think of another relationship, if I want one at all, I have to sort out things with Christian. And secondly, as I have already told you, Marco already has someone in his life.'

Beth raised a puzzled eyebrow. 'You do surprise me. We talked about his apartment in London in some detail and he didn't once mention a girlfriend.'

'Well, you know what men are like. When they're chatting up the opposite sex they conveniently forget they have significant others.'

'Lottie, Marco is not Christian. He is the kind of guy who couldn't hide the truth if his life depended on it. Every emotion he feels is in his face. His eyes will always give him away.'

'It seems to me all looking in his eyes has done is put you under some sort of hypnotic spell,' Charlotte hit back. 'Come on, can you honestly believe someone like him lives like a monk in his apartment all week? Surely you're not that naïve?'

'Lottie, please. No more arguing, okay? Let's agree to agree to differ, shall we? It's time for celebration. I've made three great sales today.' Beth raised her glass. 'Here's to more like them in the future.'

Lottie gave a sigh of surrender and they touched glasses.

Beth's hand shot to her mouth. 'Oh! I totally forgot. How did the viewing go?'

'It didn't. Someone beat me to it while we were having lunch.'

'No, really? I'm so sorry.' She stretched out a comforting hand.

'It's okay, I'm over it now. So disappointed though.' Charlotte shook her head. 'Still, as you know, life doesn't always go to plan.'

'True.' Beth stared into her wine. 'Although I've always felt things happen for a purpose. Don't you?'

'Yes, I think you're right. Christian's idiotic proposal tipped the balance for me. Before he did it, I was only thinking of finishing with him. Now it's definitely going to happen.'

'Well, as long as you stay true to that; don't let him brow beat you into changing your mind.'

Charlotte tilted her chin determinedly. 'That definitely will not happen.'

'Good girl.' Beth leant over to top up Charlotte's glass. 'Now then, Miss

Kendrick, changing the subject completely, what are you planning to wear this evening?'

Lucy snapped her mobile shut and gave an impatient sigh. She could not believe her cousin still had her phone switched off.

'Problems?' CJ appeared at her shoulder. He had crossed the drawing room silently and came to sit beside her, brushing back the fair hair which, as always, fell in an untidy curtain over his light blue eyes.

'It's Lottie. Her phone is turned off and I *do* need to speak to her.'

'It's off permanently at the moment because Christian has been hassling her.'

'But she's been in regular touch with Aunt Jenny, hasn't she?'

'Yes, but she's been calling from a public phone box.'

'Damn!' Lucy screwed up her face peevishly. 'What am I going to do?'

'Leave a message,' CJ suggested, wondering why his cousin never seemed to think of the obvious. 'I'm sure she'll check her mobile soon, even if it's only to get rid of Christian's pathetically whingeing messages.'

'You think so?'

'I know so.' He got to his feet, a reassuring hand on her shoulder. 'Urgent, is it?'

'Very. Oh, CJ…' she called after him, 'if you should hear from her—'

'Don't worry, Luce,' he interrupted, 'I'll make sure she phones you, I promise.'

Lucy watched him go, feeling even more frustrated. She was no nearer getting hold of Lottie. And get hold of her she must. Opening her phone again she began to dial.

'Well, what do you think?' Charlotte emerged from her room onto the landing and spread her arms.

Beth considered the question, hand on her chin, her expression thoughtful. 'Actually,' she said after a moment, 'I think you look quite lovely.'

'Lovely – are you serious?'

'Lottie!' Beth gave her a playful swipe. 'What's with the put down?'

'Because I don't do *quite lovely*. If people are being positive about me, the word is usually *nice*.'

'Ugh! Nice is such a boring word but hey, if you're happy with it then okay, I think you look nice.' Beth supressed a smile, gazing at the pale turquoise dress which wrapped itself around Charlotte's enviable curves. 'For what it's worth, although you'll probably hate me for saying so, you've got great skin which doesn't need a lot of make-up, a fabulous figure, and pinned up like that your hair is absolutely fantastic. In fact, I would kill to have hair like yours.'

'You wouldn't if you knew how long it takes to dry.'

'Oh, for goodness' sake.'

'Well, look at you,' Charlotte gestured towards her friend, 'you seem to know exactly what to wear with so little effort. You always seem to have that edge, you're always trendy. I guess it's the artist in you whereas I spend hours only to end up achieving ordinary.'

Beth smiled and gave her a hug. 'Believe me, honey, you are far from ordinary. Now, come on,' she manoeuvred her towards the stairs, 'or we're going to be late.'

Marco was waiting for them upstairs in the restaurant bar with a glass of white wine in front of him. He got to his feet as they arrived, casual in his chinos and open neck shirt, his dark eyes settling on them, his smile welcoming. Charlotte felt her breath catch in her throat. Looking at him, all she could feel was envy for the faceless Lauren; a woman who despite Beth's doubts, did exist and had full claim to this breath-taking man. Reality drew her back from her thoughts as she heard him asking what they would like to drink. Two glasses of red were ordered and they joined him at one of the low tables.

The conversation did the rounds of general chat of Charlotte and Beth's university days and their friendship, and of Marco's family and his father's hotel and leisure empire. Charlotte was about to ask him about his life in London and his restaurant chain, hoping to find out more about the elusive girlfriend, when the waiter arrived to call them into dinner. With Beth leading the way, as they walked Charlotte became suddenly aware of Marco's hand in the small of her back, a firm but gentle pressure, guiding her towards the open doors of the dining room. Beth had termed gestures like this as old-fashioned good manners, but to her it was something completely different; something more personal. So intimate, in fact, it felt like a caress. She was still tingling from his touch as they seated themselves at the window table he had reserved for them. She realised with the feelings he had aroused by one simple gesture, getting through this dinner was not going to be quite as easy as she had first thought. For her, coffee and the bill could not come soon enough.

EIGHTEEN

The meal was over at last. Charlotte had no idea how she had survived but guessed it was probably down to the numbing properties of the plentiful supply of red wine on the table. That and Beth's animated chat appeared to have carried the whole evening, with a mixture of more reminiscences about their uni days together and stories about her oddball family.

As Marco signalled for the bill, Charlotte excused herself and went to find the ladies' cloakroom. She had felt hot and uncomfortable all evening, noticing his gaze constantly switching its attention away from Beth to fix itself on her. Only another few minutes now, she thought, looking in the mirror and taking a deep breath, then she would be out in the fresh air and on her way back to Newcomen Road.

After refreshing her make-up she slipped her bag over her shoulder and left the cloakroom, making her way back to the restaurant. As she reached the open archway leading back into the dining area, she saw Marco signing the tab. He pulled a note from his wallet and tipped the waiter, then returned it to the back pocket of his chinos before turning his attention back to Beth. He said something and smiled, his hands reaching out to clasp hers across the table. Charlotte recognised something way beyond mere affection in his smile. A stab of ferocious anger lodged itself in the pit of her stomach. She walked back towards the table, trying to keep her cool. Acknowledging there was a faceless other in London she could cope with, but the fact he was once more flirting with her best friend who was responding was something she was having great difficulty with. Beth's words earlier about not being interested in him suddenly rang hollow.

She smiled at Beth as she reached the table, noticing he had hastily withdrawn his hands the moment he became aware she was there.

'Are you ready?' she asked.

Beth nodded and got to her feet. 'Thank you for a wonderful dinner, Marco, it was kind of you.' She leaned over and kissed his cheek.

'The pleasure was mine.' He smiled at her before rising from the table, his eyes resting on Charlotte. 'It was a most enjoyable evening.'

'Don't forget the paintings will be ready for collection tomorrow morning,' Beth reminded him, running an affectionate hand down his arm.

'I'll call in and pick them up after breakfast,' he assured her. 'I would love to have stayed longer but I must get back to London; business calls.'

'Yes, I'll be going home tomorrow too,' Charlotte informed them with a forced smile.

Beth's eyebrows rose in surprise. 'Really? But I thought you said—'

'I've changed my mind. I need to get back. I've missed the family and I too need to get back to work.' She turned to Marco, her distance giving him a clear signal she was not about to kiss his cheek like Beth had done. 'Thank you for dinner. I hope your girlfriend likes the paintings,' she added, shooting Beth a meaningful glance.

Marco frowned and opened his mouth to say something but before he could, Charlotte looped her arm in Beth's and with a parting smile, hurried her down the stairs and out of the hotel.

Beth pulled away angrily once they were out on the pavement. 'What the hell are you doing?'

'Stopping you from making a complete fool of yourself.'

'Me? I'm not making a fool of myself; I rather thought you were making a pretty good job of that.'

'I was not! I saw you both.'

'Saw us both what?'

'Holding hands and making sheep's eyes at each other across the table!'

'Don't be ridiculous, Lottie. Italians are very tactile. He was saying thank you for a pleasant evening, that's all.'

Charlotte gave a disbelieving snort. 'Was he? Well, he didn't thank me.'

'Hah! Probably because you spent most of the time in total silence staring out of the window. It was left to me to keep the bloody conversation going. You were rude, Lottie, very rude. He not only took the trouble to travel all the way here to see whether you were all right, he picked up a considerable bill for food and wine this evening. Just remember that!'

Their argument continued up through the High Street and beyond, Charlotte accusing and Beth defending herself. By the time they reached Newcomen Road and the key was inserted in the front door, tempers were still heated.

'I'll make some coffee,' Beth said as they pulled off their jackets.

'I don't want any, I'm going to bed. I'm tired and I'm upset,' Charlotte said stubbornly, and made her way upstairs.

'I realise that, but honestly, Lottie, there is nothing going on between me and Marco,' Beth called to her. She was hoping Charlotte would turn around and come back down so they could resolve this awful argument before they went to bed. The final closing of the bedroom door above, however, told her that was not going to happen.

Next morning, Charlotte awoke to the sound of rain, and a dull ache in her head. Slipping out of bed with a groan, she padded over to the window and pulled back the curtains to be greeted by grey skies and wet splashes against the glass. As she watched a trawler head out to sea there was a knock at the door and Beth appeared with a mug of coffee in one hand and a small packet in the other.

'I've brought coffee and painkillers,' she said, placing them on the bedside table.

Holding a hand to her temple as she felt tears gathering in her eyes, Charlotte turned to face her friend. 'Thanks. Beth... about last night, I'm so sorry.'

'Oh, Lottie!' Beth was there in an instant, her arms around her, hugging tightly. 'What's troubling you? Is it Christian?'

'No.' Charlotte's response was muffled as she pushed her face into her friend's shoulder. 'He's not the problem, it's—'

'Marco. You thought I was hitting on Marco, didn't you?'

Pulling back from the embrace, she nodded uncomfortably.

Beth shook her head sadly. 'I told you the truth last night. There is nothing going on between us. I'm very fond of him, that's all, and I know exactly who his heart belongs to.'

'Yes, it's Lauren,' Charlotte reminded her.

Beth smiled. 'You're still convinced about her, aren't you?'

'Of course I am. It's not a rumour. I told you, it came from his sister and she has no reason to lie.'

Beth did not reply. Releasing Charlotte, she stroked her friend's cheek then nodded towards the coffee. 'Don't let that get cold.' She turned to go. 'And get a couple of paracetamol down you.'

Breaking out two tablets, Charlotte swallowed them back with a mouthful of coffee. 'I was planning to leave after breakfast,' she said, cradling the warmth of the pottery mug in her hands, 'but if you like, I could stop and have lunch with you. Same place as yesterday?'

At the door, Beth turned and smiled. 'Sure, I'm good with that.'

'My shout too, to say sorry.' She gave an embarrassed shake of her head. 'And I am, Beth, honestly I am. I don't know what came over me.'

'Maybe too much firewater, Tonto?' Beth gave an understanding grin. 'You were well away with the red wine, you know. However, I think if you're in sorry mode you should be looking to apologise to Marco the next time you see him. As I said last night, he came all this way to see if you were okay while you behaved as if you loathed him.'

'Oh God!' Charlotte closed her eyes as the memory of last evening came crashing back.

'Don't worry, I'm sure he understands this thing with Christian has unsettled you.' Beth tilted her wrist to check her watch. 'Heavens, must go! I'll catch you in O'Reilly's at twelve thirty, and if you're still suffering we'll have a hair of the dog.'

Unsettled. Well, Beth had got the right word there, Charlotte acknowledged as the door closed. The problem was she had attached it to the wrong man.

An hour later Charlotte was showered, dressed and in the kitchen drinking coffee, anticipating the moment the toaster launched its offering of hot, well browned bread. Taking her coffee to the window while she waited, she gazed out onto the small rear garden. The rain had stopped and the sun had begun to break through, drying up the puddles on the patio and spilling its warmth into the kitchen. On a morning like this she knew she should be looking forward to going home, but part of her was now wishing she could stay on with Beth instead. Here, she could forget all her problems. Start afresh. Settle into a completely different skin and take on a new identity.

The sound of the toaster brought her back to reality. In her life she had learned to understand there were no safe havens; there was responsibility and unpleasant things which sometimes needed facing up to not run away from. Currently she was facing one of the latter.

Something else which occurred to her as she buttered her toast was that apart from the public phone box, her mobile was her only source of communication down here. She might not want to hear from Christian but other people might have been trying to contact her, so she really ought to check it. After cutting each round of buttered toast in half, she reached across for her tote to find her phone. Checking her incoming calls, it appeared Lucy had left several messages. She wondered whatever her cousin could want which warranted leaving so many. A crazy notion entered her mind. What if Christian had done something stupid, like try to kill himself? According to her mother, he had been extremely wound up the morning Ella insisted he leave. That had been reflected in those frantic pleas from him on her mobile afterwards and now everything had gone strangely quiet. Stupid woman, she reprimanded herself, dismissing the idea as quickly as she had thought of it; he only had to sneeze and some paper reported it, so anything like that would have been all over the tabloids and the TV news by now. No, she reflected as she approached the situation from a more logical perspective, this probably has nothing to do with Christian at all; it's more likely to be all about Lucy wanting one of her airhead girl chats.

As it was, each of the four messages revealed absolutely nothing, only a request for her to call back urgently. In the end, Charlotte found herself reluctantly dialling her cousin, convinced Lucy's pressing need to talk to her was, as usual, about something totally frivolous.

'Luce?'

'Lottie, thank goodness!' Charlotte heard a huge sigh of relief at the other end of the phone.

'What's the matter, Lucy? What's happened?'

'I was going to ask you that.'

'Me? I don't understand.'

'What's the latest on you and Marco?'

'So you're the culprit who told him where I was, are you?'

'Yes. I felt so sorry for him; he was desperate to find you. And I was sure you'd be with Beth. I had to tell him, I really had to.'

'No, you didn't. All you wanted to do was to stir things up between Christian and myself, didn't you?'

'I hope there is no more you and Christian. As I told you before, you deserve better.'

'I think I'm adult enough to make my own decisions about the men in my life without your help, thank you.'

'You have seen Marco though, haven't you?' Lucy questioned, ignoring Charlotte's scolding tone.

'Yes, he took Beth and me out to dinner last night.'

'How far have things got?' Lucy's voice was wary. 'Has he asked you to go out with him yet? Because if he has, please, I need you to put him off.'

'What business is it of yours if he has?' Lucy was beginning to irritate her. 'What is the matter with you? You deliberately push him in my direction and now it sounds as if you're telling me to back off. Why?'

'Well, the thing is,' Lucy began, 'Baz accidentally heard me talking to Jay about what I'd done, and he's worried that if Christian gets to hear you've been with Marco it might jeopardise the album. He thinks he might walk out on Matt and come back to find you. If he does that, it will mean not only will the work on the album be ruined, my father will take a huge financial hit. And if that happens… well, he'll kill me, Lottie!'

'And how would Christian know?' Charlotte demanded. 'What are you up to?'

'What do you mean?'

'Well, it seems to me you've been trying to set me up with Marco in order to get at Christian and the whole thing has rebounded on you.'

'Yes, I admit I wanted to pay him back for the way he's treated me, but it's not me you should be worried about. Baz seems to think he may have a private detective following you.'

'He what?'

'I'm so sorry, I didn't think.'

'You never do, Lucy,' Charlotte hit out angrily, 'that's half your trouble.'

'Please don't be angry with me, Lottie.' Lucy's voice sounded tearful and anxious. 'There's something far more serious you need to know about Christian.'

Charlotte felt her patience slipping away. 'Is this more tittle-tattle? Lucy, this has to stop,' she snapped, before curiosity got the better of her. 'Well, what is it?'

Lucy took a deep breath. 'He's had other women.'

'Other women?'

'Yes, on tour, in his dressing room after the show. And they all seem to be blonde.'

'They're called fans, Lucy.' Charlotte rolled her eyes, thinking how stupid her cousin could be sometimes. 'He's probably signing autographs.'

'He's doing a lot more than that,' Lucy insisted. 'Then there are the two girls who were with him at the boutique opening.'

'They were models, weren't they?' she asked, remembering the two self-important females who had arrived with him that day.

'I thought so too, but no. I made some discreet enquiries and discovered they are from a high-class escort agency.'

'They're what?'

'They are up-market tarts, and not only that, I caught them trying to sneak up to his room when he went up to change after the boutique opening. When I challenged them they said he'd hired them. Anyway, I redirected them back down the corridor but they refused to go. One of them had a bottle of champagne with her. They only left when I threatened to call security. I told Dad about it; he was furious.'

'You did what? Why, for goodness' sake?'

'I had no choice, Lottie. Think about it. If the press got hold of the fact Dad was employing escorts they would have a field day.'

Charlotte stared at her toast. It was cold, much like the way she was feeling at the moment. Eventually she said, 'I'm sorry, Lucy, but I'm having real problems with what I'm hearing. Christian may be many things, but involved with call girls? He would never do that. I am sick of you dragging me into this damned vendetta you have going on with him.'

'But Lottie—'

'And another thing,' Charlotte launched into her again. 'I cannot believe you have involved an innocent party like Marco in all your scheming.'

'I didn't drag Marco into anything.' Now it was Lucy's turn to be angry. 'He feels something for you, I know he does.'

'Rubbish! You know he has a girlfriend. Even if he didn't, absolutely nothing is going to happen, do you hear me? After Christian and his stupid proposal I've had quite enough of men. All they bring is heartache. You of all people should know that after what happened to you in Australia.' She snapped her phone shut and threw it back into her bag.

Charlotte frowned at her plate; breakfast was ruined. Cold toast and tepid coffee held absolutely no appeal. Yesterday, she had all the answers. She had cleared her head and knew exactly what she had to do in respect of both Christian and Marco. Now, with his arrival and Lucy's call everything had been sent into a confusing spin. Damn Lucy's meddling, she thought. The stupid creature never seems able to understand the damage she causes in other people's lives, although she certainly would if Christian walked out of the studio. She was right, Matt would kill her. And what was all that rubbish about call girls and PIs stalking her? She gave an enormous sigh and shook her head. Lucy was a nightmare! The sound of the doorbell broke into her thoughts. With a huff of irritation she left the kitchen to answer it.

* * *

Umbrella in hand, Marco took his finger away from the brass button set in the white painted render of the house and stood gazing at the heavy wooden front door. The rain had started again, thin and light, drawing a mist across the estuary, muting the pastel colours of the whitewashed houses clinging to the hill across the water. What he was doing was madness and he knew if he had any sense, he should have been heading for the M5 by now, putting as much distance as he could between Charlotte Kendrick and himself. Instead, he had yielded to Beth's persuasive tongue asking him to drop by for a quick farewell as a favour to her before he left.

Of course, he knew exactly what was going to happen if and when she opened this door. There would be the usual pinched expression followed by a few sharp words before the door was slammed in his face, leaving him standing in the rain. Last evening, he felt she had totally abused his hospitality as she sat there with a bored expression on her face, not even bothering to join in the conversation, continually helping herself to wine and getting slowly drunk. Why was he here wasting so much effort on this woman? The kiss in the cottage all those weeks ago made him feel he had made some headway with her. But now it appeared she was back to being her usual miserable self. Well, he decided, this was definitely going be his final attempt at finding some common ground with her. If he failed he would cut his losses and abandon her completely. Eyes closed, he braced himself for what was to come as the door slowly opened.

'Marco?'

He was greeted not by anger but surprise when he opened his eyes and saw Charlotte staring at him with a perplexed frown.

'Are you all right?' she asked.

'I'm fine,' he replied, noticing the way she now leaned around the door jamb to peer anxiously up and down the street.

'Come in.' She stepped back to let him into the hallway.

'What is it?' he asked, as she closed the door and made her way past him to the rear of the house.

'Oh, nothing... just checking for the postman,' she said.

He deposited the umbrella in the hall and followed her, finding himself in a small tidy kitchen where the remains of breakfast littered the table.

'So what brings you here, Marco?' he heard her ask as she began to busy herself with clearing items from the table and depositing crockery onto the draining board.

'I... I wanted to say goodbye before I left,' he replied, deciding it best not to mention it was Beth's suggestion.

'To me?' She raised her eyes to him briefly and gave a disbelieving shake of her head. 'After the way I behaved last night? I can't think why.' Turning away from him, she opened a cupboard door and returned a jar of marmalade to its shelf.

'Charlotte, are you afraid of me?' he asked as he watched her.

She stopped and turned back towards the table, her brow creasing as if she did not understand the question. 'Of course not. If I had been afraid of you, would I have asked you in?'

Once everything was cleared away she seemed at odds with what to do with herself. He watched her reach for one of the chairs, sliding her hands along the back of it, gripping the wood, the tension showing in her fingers.

'But you tremble, I can see it,' he said softly, observing her closely. 'You have always been this way with me, ever since our very first meeting.'

She shrugged, her eyes meeting his fleetingly. 'I was angry then, maybe I'm still angry now.'

'No, this is not anger, it is a totally different emotion, is it not?'

'If you must know...' she raised her eyes to him and he noticed a flush creep into her cheeks, 'it's because...'

He could see she was struggling with her words so he finished the sentence for her. 'Because you are attracted to me in the same way I am attracted to you?'

'What!' Her eyes widened in astonishment.

He could tell his words had come as a complete shock. For a moment he hesitated, wondering whether opening his heart to her was a sensible thing to do, and then dismissing the thought. 'Yes, ever since the day we were introduced I have thought of no one but you.'

She eyed him warily. 'That's impossible... You already live with someone in London. Felica—'

'Told you that, did she?' he interrupted, with a smile and a shake of his head.

'She told CJ, the day of the barbeque... you know, about Lauren.'

'Lauren.' He gave an amused laugh. 'Is that her name?'

'Yes, and she works in advertising.'

He laughed out loud. 'Does she now? Charlotte, my baby sister is very protective. She created the lie to defend me from unwanted interest; she could see Kayte was throwing herself at me. The truth is I live alone in London; very much alone. Until I met you it was the way I preferred my life to be. In fact, I have been without female company for many months. I have not been very lucky with women. The only true mistress I have now is my work. But things have changed, and the truth of the matter is I want to be with you,' he said calmly, 'and I think although you deny it, you share this feeling.'

'No, Marco, you're wrong.' She eyed him defiantly under her long lashes. 'A man like you would be a real complication in my life, and that is something I honestly do not need.'

His mouth curved into a soft smile. 'I think your kiss told me an entirely different story—'

'That should not have happened,' she cut him off, folding her arms protectively across her chest, eyes rebellious and angry. 'Anyway, you're forgetting Christian.'

'You are planning to go back to him?' He heard the disbelief in his own voice. 'To accept his proposal when he returns?' He continued to probe, ignoring her reprimand, noting the annoyance flare in those stunning blue eyes as they met his.

'Of course not! I plan to end our relationship.' She drew in an audible deep breathe. 'Will you stop, please. This is none of your business.'

'Do you think he will accept your decision?'

'He will have to.' Her voice became calmer but lost none of its determined quality, her gaze wandering once more from his face and fixing itself somewhere on the wall behind him. 'We have no future together.'

'And afterwards?'

She shook her head, her eyes moving from him once more to follow some unseen pattern on the ceiling. 'Who knows? I can't see that far into the future. No one can. At the moment I am tired of relationships. I need time to myself. I—'

'Then can we at least be friends?'

'Friends?' She frowned, as if considering his suggestion. 'Well... yes... I guess so.' She gave one of her indifferent shrugs, her expression indecipherable as they stood in a room which had become eerily quiet.

He could not begin to imagine what she was thinking; he dared not. Despite his calm words and accompanying smile, Marco felt bitter disappointment. He had told her the truth about how he felt because he was sure of what he had seen in her eyes. Could he have been wrong? But no, even as he stared at her now he could see how her off-hand attitude was the way she protected herself. A shield to hold the outside world at bay while she concentrated on ending her relationship with Christian. And afterwards? She claimed she could not see that far ahead, but he could. Once she was free they would be together, of that he was sure.

He glanced up at the kitchen clock. 'Charlotte, I am afraid I must go. I need to be in London by early afternoon. No doubt we will see each other back in the village.'

She looked up at him and the ghost of a smile crossed her face. 'Yes, I expect we will.'

For a moment he felt a burning need to pull her into his arms and kiss her, but he knew if he did make such a bold move he risked losing the one very important concession he had just gained.

In the hall, she retrieved the umbrella he had discarded when she had hurriedly ushered him into the house. 'I think it's still raining,' she said, handing it to him as she reached for the front door catch.

'Thank you.' He took it from her and moved towards the door she held open. 'Have a safe journey home.'

'And you.' Her expression softened slightly. 'Oh, and Marco...' she said hesitantly. 'I... I owe you an apology. You've been very kind and I've been incredibly rude.'

He shook his head, his eyes capturing hers briefly. 'Charlotte, yesterday does not matter. It is today that is important. We are now friends; to me that is a very significant step. Ciao.' With a last lingering look at her, he opened his umbrella and stepped out into the rain.

Charlotte watched him reach the red Targa and climb in. Moments later the engine fired and she saw the car pull away from the kerb and disappear down the road. At first, listening to his confession in the kitchen only moments ago, she had been unable to believe what she was hearing. In fact, she had been stunned at his admission he wanted to have a relationship with her, telling her he had no one in his life, that he was free. She didn't believe him, not for one moment. A man who looked like him having bad luck with women? Only an idiot would believe such a preposterous statement. He knew what she had with Christian was over, and he was simply trying to capitalise on the situation. Beautiful or not, Marco D'Alesandro was simply a more subtle version of Christian, looking to manipulate her into a situation to suit himself. There was no way she was about to let that happen. She had accepted his request to be friends merely to keep him at bay; she only hoped it was enough. Suddenly she felt sorry for Lauren. At the end of the day men were all bastards, weren't they?

Over lunch at O'Reilly's, Charlotte told Beth of Lucy's call and also touched upon Marco's visit, keeping the details as straightforward as possible. To let Beth know the truth would be a very rash thing to do bearing in mind the fact she suspected, despite her protests, her friend was secretly smitten.

Two hours later she was on her way back to Meridan Cross, leaving the calm shelter from the emotional storm her life had turned into far behind.

NINETEEN

Matt sat back in his chair and watched as Christian launched into yet another take of 'Another Dimension', the current track they were working on. He frowned, turning to his senior technician Callum French and asking, 'What the hell's the matter with him this morning?'

The red-headed Scot gave a loud groan. 'He's making a complete pig's arse of it, isn't he? It's a well-named track, look at him – he *is* in another bloody dimension.'

Callum's sarcasm was not lost on Matt. None of team liked Christian, and having spent the last six weeks here in Grand Cayman, the singer was now beginning to grate on his nerves too. The album had been coming together well despite Christian's tendency to have an opinion on anything and everything – one which in his view was always right. The team had been surprisingly tolerant of his behaviour, taking their lead from Matt and leaving it to him to rein in the wilful star when he became too difficult. Matt took it all in his stride; he was a past master at getting the best out of difficult people. The shame of it all, he felt, was when Christian did concentrate on what he was there for, the outcome was totally brilliant.

On the whole he was pleased with progress. Everything was going well, so well, in fact, he was confident they could wrap up this album a little ahead of schedule. From the start of their stay, Christian had set himself apart from the rest of the team during the evenings. On a few occasions Matt had persuaded him out for a meal, but on other evenings he seemed to prefer his own company. Matt didn't push him for any explanation; allowing him this freedom out of the studio appeared to be the right balance to get the best out of him. Up until now he had let things ride, never asking Christian where he went at night, but he knew lately there were occasions when his bed had not been slept in.

And now, this morning, there had been a distinct lack of concentration. Watching him openly arguing with a couple of the session musicians, Matt shook his head. These guys came highly recommended, having worked with some of the biggest names around. However, like the technical team, it appeared they were now to blame for everything from missing intros, hitting duff notes and currently for the arrival of a headache. Checking his watch, Matt made a decision and leaned into the mic.

'Okay, guys,' he said, his eyes on Christian. 'Break for lunch. Back at two thirty please.'

He watched as Christian left the studio, his mobile to his ear. Moments later a taxi pulled up. Christian had not even bothered to stay for the buffet lunch, but then when had he eaten regularly in any normal quantities since arriving? It seemed lately he lived simply on fresh air and alcohol. Matt thought about this morning's behaviour and wondered about the booze for some moments before his mind did a three-sixty degree turn. Maybe booze wasn't the problem – what if it was drugs? He hoped not. Watching the taxi pull away, he decided maybe his star's activities out of the recording studio warranted a little closer inspection. Pulling his phone from his pocket he punched in a number, knowing exactly whom he needed to talk to.

In the back of the cab, Christian fought to clear his head as he checked for messages on his mobile. He'd felt as if he'd had an out-of-body experience this morning. He could not believe he had been so awful; he doubted he could have even sung the alphabet in the right order. He was going to have to put the brakes on with the girls. After a day in the recording studio he found he needed to increase the number of pills he was taking each time to keep himself high for his evening activities. Because of this he was now in danger of Matt finding out his guilty little secret and if he did, he knew he'd abandon the album and have him clinic-bound before he could blink! Compounding all this was his strict ruling about drugs, which meant he would probably sack him too. Once the reason behind him parting company with Evolution was public knowledge, he could forget about taking up with another record company, he doubted anyone would touch him.

His gaze fell to the screen of his mobile and the latest report on Charlotte. Originally, his contact had traced her to Devon, staying with Beth Reynolds, a friend from her university days. Nothing untoward appeared to have happened during the time she was there. Since then things appeared to have gone back to normal. Working in London had not thrown up any evidence of meetings, although on a couple of occasions she had lunched with Kieren Miller, at some pub near Evolution's offices. The fact she had not visited the Italian's restaurant to meet Kieren was a positive sign, he felt. His contact had also reported Marco had gone away with his stepmother and sister to Italy a couple of days ago and had yet to return. Well, at least he was out of the way for a while, he thought with a satisfied grin.

Reading today's message, he gave a relieved sigh and texted a 'thanks and stay on the case' message back. They were halfway through their time out here and although things seemed okay at home, he was well aware a day could change everything. So the surveillance would go on and the fortune he was paying out for this service would continue.

In a small smoky pub less than a mile from Evolution UK's offices, Jay moved away from the bar. He had just paid for a lunch order and two opened bottles of lager which he now carried back to the window table where his companion, a thin faced thirty-something with a shock of thick brown hair curling over the collar of his expensive suit jacket sat watching his approach.

'So, Mickey, how's our Golden Boy?' Jay asked.

Mickey Flynn smiled, his teeth white and straight. He might have been called handsome had it not been for the cold, pale blue eyes which he now fixed on the bottle set down in front of him. Jay knew Mickey from way back; he had been a roadie when Rosetti was a chart topping act. Now he had a thriving security company which included among other things a PI service.

Mickey picked up his bottle and took a swig. 'The bastard's fine,' came his reply accompanied by a rare grin. 'Not a care in the world.'

'That's what I like to hear.' Jay grinned back; Matt knew exactly who Christian would contact to keep an eye on Charlotte while he was away. Only Matt had got to Mickey first, and the man was now the lucky recipient of two lots of fees. However, as Mickey's loyalties always lay firmly with the highest bidder, Matt had made sure that was him and he was now in control of all the information being passed to Christian. Matt had also managed to bring about a dramatic change in his daughter. Full of remorse after receiving an irate call from him, she now feared her stupidity might have cost her the coveted job she thought was hers. Matt not only had his star where he wanted him, but his daughter as well.

Answering the door, Matt Benedict found himself staring down at a young black boy in dusty, red knee-length shorts and a white vest. Huge dark eyes in a solemn face stared up at him as a small hand stretched out offering him a brown envelope. Matt took it with a puzzled frown.

'From Mr Sam,' the boy said with a nervous lift of his shoulders before Matt could speak.

Matt nodded, understanding, and pulled his wallet from his pocket, giving the child a generous five-dollar tip for his troubles. The boy's eyes widened as he pocketed the money, and with an enormous grin as he said thank you, scurried off down through the gardens towards the main gates. He closed the door and made his way back into the airy interior of the villa.

It was mid-November and they were only a couple of weeks away from wrapping this album up. For Matt and the team it could not come soon enough. Everyone without exception was looking forward to going home to their families for Christmas. Seating himself on one of the soft couches, he picked up his cool drink and took a mouthful before easing his thumb under the fold of the envelope. As he opened the piece of paper contained within and read its contents he gave a concerned frown. Getting to his feet again, he pulled his jacket from the back of one of the chairs and walked out onto the loggia.

'I'm going out,' he said to two of the team technicians who were sitting together in the gathering dusk discussing the schedule for tomorrow. 'I'll be back in a couple of hours.'

Both looked up, amusement in their faces.

'Out on the pull then, boss?' Callum gave a mischievous grin as he lifted his can of beer to his lips.

'Something like that,' Matt acknowledged with a humorous smile.

The Jeep followed the coastal road south and Matt soon reached West Bay Road where he continued his journey past bright bars busy with customers and hotels ablaze with light, their lush exteriors bathed in the much subtler glow of garden lights. Eventually, he glimpsed his destination up ahead and swung off the road and into the Marriott's car park.

Sam Hedley, the owner of Sunray Studios, walked towards the vehicle as Matt pulled it to a halt. The blond haired, blue eyed South African was dressed casually in designer jeans and a pale linen shirt with sleeves rolled up to his elbows. Slightly younger than Matt, Sam had worked in various recording studios during his career, including a two-year stint with Matt at Evolution in London back in the late eighties. Five years ago he had come into family money and decided to build his own facility. Many bands chose to record in the West Indies, where the climate was good and the location relaxing. Grand Cayman was a rich man's playground, which was another enticement, but it was also a busy island, and it was with that in mind Sam had decided to search inland to locate a suitable spot to build what was now Sunray Studios, reasoning stars wanted somewhere tranquil and isolated to concentrate on their work. At the end of the day, however, they wanted to relax, have a good time and let their hair down a little maybe, and his exclusive Sunrise Beach Complex was somewhere they could do just that. It was also where, after a phone call from Matt a few weeks ago requesting help, his enquiries had taken him and where he had discovered exactly what Christian Rosetti had been doing.

Matt climbed out of the Jeep. 'Evening, Sam. I gather you have news for me?'

Sam nodded. 'We need to talk.'

'Why didn't you phone?'

'I did, there was no response.'

Matt reached into his jacket. The mobile wasn't there. 'Damn!' He thought for moment. 'I remember now... I took a call at the studio this afternoon. I must have left it in the live room. So what's he been up to?'

'Let's discuss it over a drink, shall we?' Sam jerked a thumb towards the hotel entrance.

From the expression on Sam's face Matt had the feeling he was not going to like what he was about to hear.

'Charlotte, get down at once, you'll break your neck!'

Charlotte stopped what she was doing and gazed down from the top of the stepladder. She had been busy decorating the enormous Christmas tree which stood in Little Court's hall. Cut from Willowbrook Farm's small commercial forest, the tree was now covered in gold, red and green decorations and masses of tinsel.

'I'm fine, Mum, only two more items to hang.' She leaned over to attach them. 'Right, coming down.'

'You know I hate you going anywhere near ladders,' Jenny grumbled, as Charlotte reached the bottom. 'Why didn't you get CJ or Rowan to help you?'

'CJ's not here and Rowan is busy. I told you, it's not a problem.'

'Come and have coffee with me.' Jenny's tone softened as she looped her arm in her daughter's. 'We need to talk.'

'About what?'

'Christian, among other things. He's due back in a week, isn't he?'

'I know.'

'And you'll need to see him.'

'Yes I will.'

They reached the Orangery, where Helen had laid out a small tray of coffee and biscuits on one of the tables amongst the lush vegetation by the window. Seating herself comfortably, Charlotte watched as Jenny poured. Handing her a cup, Jenny then pushed milk and biscuits towards her.

'I'll pass on the biscuits, thanks,' Charlotte said as she poured milk into her cup.

Jenny smiled, mindful her daughter danced around sweet things, convinced even straying with one biscuit had the potential to pile on the pounds. All totally unfounded, she thought with an appreciative glance, there's not an ounce of fat on her, merely enviable curves. She's spent far too long comparing herself with Lucy, and what is she? Someone who lives on celery, carrot juice and fresh air so she can squeeze into a size eight.

'Right,' Jenny moved back to the topic she wanted to discuss. 'The reason I've dragged you in here is because I thought we ought to have a bit of a mother and daughter chat. As I mentioned, Christian will be back soon and as you haven't said anything, I wondered what you were planning?'

Charlotte took a sip of her coffee and studied her thoughtfully before speaking. 'Well, I'm simply going to tell him our relationship is over.'

'Just like that?' Jenny stared at her daughter as if she had lost her mind.

'Yes, just like that,' Charlotte confirmed with a nod as she raised her cup to her lips.

'Oh, Charlotte, do be careful. He was so angry the last morning he was here. If Rowan hadn't brought in those two gardeners I dread to think what would have happened.'

'I'll be fine, Mum.' Charlotte reached across and gave her hand an affectionate pat. 'There's no need to worry about a thing.'

Jenny shook her head, a concerned frown creasing her face. 'Lottie, you mustn't see him alone. Promise me you won't. Take someone with you. Take CJ.'

'I don't need CJ.'

'Of course you do!' Jenny's dark eyes widened in alarm as her cup hovered not far from her lips. 'You can't possibly face a man like him alone.'

'But I won't be on my own, Mum.'

'Oh.' Jenny's eyebrows shot up, her cup clattering back into the saucer. 'Well, who will be with you?'

'Uncle Matt.'

'But he's planning to break his return journey with a stop-off in New York for a few days, isn't he? How can he possibly be there and here with you at the same time?'

'Because I'm not seeing Christian here... I'm flying out to Grand Cayman on Thursday. I'm going to see him out there.'

TWENTY

Charlotte sat with a glass of chilled white wine in the bar of the Ritz Carlton, waiting for the arrival of her uncle. Another warm day in Grand Cayman was drawing to a close, the sun had disappeared over the edge of the sea and the velvet blue of night was beginning to settle all around. In the hotel's well-manicured gardens lights had come on, giving the trees, lawns and plant life an exotic glow. England seemed a world away and yet it was only yesterday she had boarded the plane from a rain-lashed Heathrow. Her late evening arrival at Owen Roberts International, the airport serving Grand Cayman, saw her met by a smiling Matt, his tan clearly indicating he had not been spending all of his time in the recording studio.

Since her father's death her uncle had taken on the role of surrogate father. Although she was close to Rowan, it was always Matt she turned to for advice and help. When Rowan, a man she had known since she was a small child, married her mother, Matt stepped back. He made it clear he was happy to remain in the background, only becoming involved in her life if invited in. However, forty-eight hours ago he had broken that rule.

She had been sitting in her first-floor office, watching sleet sliding down the outside of the window when Hayley, Safekeeping Trust's receptionist, buzzed through saying Matt was on the phone, calling from Grand Cayman and would like a word with her. Probably wanting an update on Safekeeping's run up to Christmas, Charlotte expected.

'Charlotte, it's good to hear your voice.' The line had been so clear it were as if he stood in the next room. As always, he sounded upbeat and optimistic.

'It's good to hear you too,' she replied. 'How's the album coming along?'

'Very well, we're nearly there. In fact, I can't believe it's gone so smoothly.'

'I'm guessing you're calling for an update.' She leaned back in her chair, noticing the sleet had begun to gather in soft icy ridges at the bottom of each of the small panes of glass in her window. 'I've had a meeting with Olivia this morning to discuss extra funding for the night shelters over Christmas. I—'

'Actually, Charlotte, that isn't the reason I'm calling. I need to ask you something. We'll all be returning home soon and I wondered... well...what are your plans for the future?'

'With Christian, you mean?'

'Yes.'

'I...' she hesitated. 'Well...'

'Not planning to kiss and make up, are you?'

'Of course not. Why?'

'You sounded, I don't know... reluctant to say anything. I thought you might have had a change of heart and you didn't want me to know about it.'

'Far from it. It really is over,' she said. 'He left a message last week asking how I was. I told him I would see him when he got back. I don't have any fear of facing him now, but what does worry me is the way I go about ending our relationship because no matter what I do or say, there will be massive fireworks.'

'Fireworks indeed.' His voice took on a serious tone. 'Although maybe not quite in the way you think.'

'Why? What's happened?'

'Charlotte, I need you to fly out here.' He had deliberately ignored her question, choosing instead to issue instructions. 'The jet will be fuelled and ready to leave Heathrow on Thursday morning. I'll get Magda to arrange a car to pick you up; she'll email you through all the details.'

'Matt, what is it? What's wrong? Has something happened to Christian?'

'We'll discuss it when I see you on Thursday.'

'But—'

'I'll be at the airport to meet you when you arrive.'

He'd said a quick goodbye and had hung up without giving her the chance to argue. She knew this had been done intentionally, to ensure she would be on the plane.

Now here she was, sitting enjoying her wine as she waited for him to join her for dinner, keen to find out why she was here. She knew it had something to do with freeing herself from Christian, but exactly what was still a complete mystery.

She looked up after a sip of wine to see her uncle approaching. He was dressed in a black t-shirt and a pale-beige linen suit; square jawed and very handsome, his collar-length dark brown hair showed only a light dusting of grey at the temples. A group of attractive, well-dressed older women crossing the lounge paused to watch him. Charlotte smiled; at nearly fifty he still had the power to turn female heads. He raised a hand to her in greeting. She waved back and watched while he stopped briefly at the bar to order a drink before coming across. She rose as he reached her table, giving him a hug and planting a kiss on a recently shaved cheek smelling of expensive cologne.

'Happy with the hotel and your room?' His eyes met hers and he smiled in that familiar, relaxing way of his as they sat down.

'It's perfect. I slept like a log. And thank you for booking me such a beautiful suite.'

'I thought you'd appreciate the sea view. The beach is quite spectacular, isn't it?' He nodded his thanks to the barman arriving with his whisky.

'Yes, it is,' she replied, as the barman walked away. 'I spent the day around the pool, had a drink and lunch down at the beach bar, met a few fellow Brits. Thought I might try the spa before I leave.'

'Fine, feel free to stay on for a while.' Matt took a mouthful of his drink.

Charlotte took another sip of wine and gave him a thoughtful smile. 'Thank you, but I think once we've done whatever it is you've brought me all this way for, it would be best if I fly home. Olivia and I have to sort out the Christmas arrangements. I've also volunteered to do some hands-on stuff at one of the shelters.'

'Hands-on stuff?'

'Yes. You know, help serve food. I thought it would be good to be a real part of the team for once.'

'Are you sure you want to do that?'

She nodded. 'Of course. Everyone else at Safekeeping takes a turn, why not me?'

'Because you're my niece.'

'Oh, don't be so protective, I'm not—'

'Lucy?'

'That's not what I was going to say.' She shook her head, horrified he could think she would voice such a thing.

'I know you weren't; but I did.' He exhaled an accepting sigh. 'I know exactly what my daughter is like. Although I have to say she's working very hard in the new job I've given her. And it hasn't all been plain sailing.'

'No. I gather Christian was rather difficult when he was in Scotland.'

'He was. A complete bastard, according to Jay, but she didn't let him beat her, or let me know anything about it. She handled it all on her own.'

'Well, if she can face up to Christian without running to you it shows she wants to be a success, doesn't it?'

'Yes, I guess it does.' He gave her a cheerful grin before taking another mouthful of whisky then set the glass down onto the table. 'Now then, let's get down to the reason I asked you here, shall we?' He leaned forward, his elbows on his knees. 'I have discovered a way you can part company from Christian without so much as a whisper of protest from him.'

Christian lounged on one of the couches in the bar of the Sunrise Beach Complex, enjoying yet another cold beer. With the help of the alcohol and a top-up of pills a few hours ago, he had been feeling quite euphoric. Tonight would be his very last night on the island; the album was finished and he intended to go out in style. He knew if the three months he'd spent here had been without the girls he would have gone crazy. Matt irritated him, and the technicians – geeks every one of them without any sense of creativity – had driven him mad. His emotions had see-sawed from mild irritation to storm force anger, especially with that red-headed bastard Callum, who had turned baiting him into an art form. But none of it mattered any more. By tomorrow he would be back home and concentrating all his efforts on pursuing Charlotte once more, taking up where he left off.

131

Thoughts of her stilled the buoyant mood he was in. If he were honest with himself, he still had no idea where he was with her. Yet again his thoughts turned to Marco. According to his PI, Mickey Flynn, she had been nowhere near the Italian in all the time he'd been carrying out surveillance on her. But how accurate was Mickey? What if she'd found out she was being followed and had been taking steps to cover her tracks? He wouldn't put it past that bitch Lucy aiding and abetting either. If the reports were to be believed, she seemed to stick to Charlotte like a second shadow. Anxiety twisted in his gut as the aggressive possessiveness which plagued him whenever he thought of Charlotte and Marco together resurfaced once more. She belonged to him alone, and the thought of someone else in her bed made him break out in an angry sweat.

He recognised he was coming down early from his high and needed a top-up. Reaching into his jeans, he pulled out the small plastic wallet and quickly dropped two tablets into his palm. Shoving the packet back into his pocket, he pushed the pills into his mouth and helped them down with a large gulp of beer, then relaxed back, gazing across the bar to where Talia and Leyna were sitting on the far terrace together chatting and drinking. Quelling his fears about Charlotte, he let his thoughts wash over these two beautiful women instead, observing with interest as two young men approached. The girls flirted with them for a while before the men seemed to lose interest and moved off, probably to some club or other, he guessed. As he watched the men disappear along the beach he felt the pills begin to lift his mood. One thing he could rely on was the girls being faithful, he thought as he continued to watch them – while he was here anyway. But then, he'd been picking up all their bills via his Evolution credit card, including some expensive shopping trips to Georgetown, so maybe, he reconsidered, his belief in their loyalty might be a little flawed.

He noticed Talia getting up, tugging at the skirt of her very short, blue halter-neck dress. Leyna got to her feet too, shooting a glance over towards him, giving him one of her sultry smiles. It was a signal they were about to go back to the bungalow. He had moved them here from the Marriott as it gave them more privacy. He grinned; the credit card bill would be phenomenal and he knew Matt would be furious, but he'd soon calm down. After all, the new album was going to make him a bloody fortune, wasn't it? He ran a hand through his wild dark hair as he checked his watch. Yep, five minutes then he'd join them. An early night, they'd told him, and he knew exactly what that meant.

Keeping pace with a waiter pushing a small trolley containing two ice buckets of chilled champagne, Charlotte followed slowly behind Matt. Set back from the beach, the Sunrise Beach Complex with its ten large luxury bungalows sat among well-tended lawns dotted with palms and other colourful lush vegetation. Last night when Matt had revealed his plan she was hesitant, wondering whether this was such a good idea, but she had learnt this was not all about her; her uncle had his own reasons for wanting to confront his star. Christian, he had discovered after a little investigation, had booked two women into one of the luxury bungalows and it appeared Evolution was picking up the tab, including a hefty drinks bill. Also, a check on the company credit card showed a huge amount of money had been spent on clothes and jewellery in Georgetown. Matt was absolutely furious.

Bruno, the waiter, a handsome young man with ebony skin and very white teeth, was negotiating the trolley off the main pathway and up to the veranda of one of the pale blue wooden bungalows. Rapping on the door, he called out: 'Room Service,' then waited. Matt and Charlotte kept out of sight, not wanting to be seen by the occupants of the room. After a muffled response, Bruno opened the door and wheeled the trolley in.

'Ooh, champagne,' a female voice announced. Giggles and shrieks of laughter followed.

'Behave yourself, girls,' a male voice reprimanded, silencing their hilarity. It was Christian.

Bruno was now well inside the room, the door still open. Charlotte and Matt waited for him to set out the champagne and glasses. Reappearing with the empty trolley a few moments later, Bruno gave them a discreet nod and went on his way. Charlotte noticed he had left the front door slightly ajar for them. Matt put his finger to his lips and they waited. More laughter came from within then gradually faded, as did the voices.

Matt pushed the door open a fraction and peered in. 'Looks as if they've gone into the bedroom,' he said.

After a few minutes more he motioned for her to follow and they quietly entered the bungalow. The pale tiled hallway lit by muted wall lights opened out into a large expensively furnished lounge and dining room. Off of this, through an elegant archway, was a small but equally luxurious kitchen area. Moving slowly through the living area, they eventually reached a small rear corridor leading to the bedrooms. A light was showing under the second of the two doors which hadn't been fully closed. Matt's fingers gripped the handle, he stared back at Charlotte for a moment and then pushed open the door a fraction wider. They peeked in.

In the dimly lit room, the three naked bodies on the huge bed were totally unaware they were being observed. Christian was kneeling with his back to them, trickling champagne over the breasts and stomach of one of the girls lying there. Dumping the bottle on the floor, he leaned over her, lapping up the liquid. She squealed and giggled, Christian laughed and when he had finished, made a grab for the second girl amid shrieks and screams of laughter.

'Right, now you've had your fun, it's our turn,' one of the girls said, pushing herself up and sliding across the bed. She grabbed another bottle from the floor. After a short tussle, both girls managed to pin him down and shook the bottle, spraying champagne all over him like a couple of celebratory drivers after a successful Grand Prix.

'Get off me!' he laughed, playfully fighting them off as they soaked his hair and body. He sat up, cursing them both, grabbing at the sheet to wipe the wetness from his eyes. Brushing his hair back as he dropped it, his eyes widened with shock as he focussed on the doorway.

'Holy shit!' he murmured, seeing Matt and Charlotte standing there.

Leaping from the bed, the girls gathered up their clothes, leaving Christian to quickly pull himself into his jeans while Matt began a verbal pounding, his voice filled with controlled wrath. The abuse of Evolution's money in order to fund his activities was the main issue. Then he noticed the dressing table, where a line of coke had been cut ready for use.

'And what the hell are you doing with that?' he thundered, pointing at the offending white powder. 'You bloody well know the rules!'

'It's not mine!' Christian's face filled with panic as he stared at the dressing table and then back at Matt. 'The girls brought it, it was for their use!'

'Don't make things worse by lying, please...' Matt's eyes narrowed. 'You've been taking drugs ever since we arrived, haven't you? The highs and lows – everyone has noticed.'

'Okay, okay, yes I have,' Christian admitted, his voice wavering. 'But it was pills.' He darted across the room to the dressing table and pulled open one of the drawers. 'Amphetamines,' he said, waving a small plastic wallet at Matt. 'I was pill popping but I'd never do hard drugs. Never!'

Everything went quiet for a few moments while Christian stood there rubbing his eyes, frowning as if he was in a complete haze.

Matt then launched into him again, his outrage now directed at the damage Christian had done to Charlotte. Words such as *unforgiveable*, *disgusting* and *lack of personal integrity* were used.

When he had finished speaking there was an eerie silence in the room broken only by the distant pulse of music from the complex's beach bar. Since entering the bedroom, Charlotte had let her uncle do all the talking while her eyes wandered around the room, imagining what had been going on here for nearly three months. She recognised the two blondes from the opening day of the bridal boutique at Little Court. So, Lucy had been telling the truth, she had not been stirring things up, as she had first thought. It seemed she owed her cousin an apology. Seeing Christian here like this made her realise Lucy had also been telling the truth about his after-show activities with other women. She knew if she had truly loved him she would have been deeply hurt, her world shattered. In pieces. Instead, she felt strangely distanced from what was going on, as if this whole thing had nothing to do with her. She knew then it was because she no longer loved him. In fact, she found herself pitying what he had become. But there were still questions she needed to have answered.

Christian's gaze switched from Matt to her. 'Lottie,' he began, his voice cracking as tears began gathering in the corners of his eyes. 'Please... I know what you must be thinking but—'

'Enough!' Matt raised a hand to stop him, his eyes still full of anger. 'I suggest you get your sorry backside back to the villa and pack. We'll be leaving early tomorrow. If Charlotte decides she wants to see you when we're back, then it will be up to her. However, after what she has just witnessed, I doubt that will be happening.'

'No! I want her to tell me what she will or will not do; I don't want to hear it from you,' Christian shouted. He took a cautious step towards her, extending his hand. 'Please...' he pleaded gently. 'Talk to me. We can sort this out, I know we can.'

'No,' she said, avoiding his touch and moving back to stand by her uncle. 'It's finished, Christian. Over! All this,' she indicated the room and the rumpled bed, 'was going on behind my back yet you still felt the need to get down on one knee and make a great public display of wanting to marry me. Was that the drugs or were you just playing some spiteful game with me?'

Christian bit his lip and studied her a moment before answering. 'It was...' He ran a hand through his hair. 'I guess I wanted to discourage unwanted interest. I know you can see how totally selfish I am. I love my freedom but you are special to me and I need you. I was prepared to do absolutely anything to make sure I didn't have to share you with anyone else. Especially *him*.'

'I hardly know Marco, if that's whom you're referring to.' Charlotte's tone was dismissive. 'Anyway, he already has a girlfriend.'

'That's what Matt said; I thought he was lying.' Christian wiped away the wetness pooling in his eyes. 'When I saw those roses—'

'You swung into action like the overbearing bully you've become. I don't know you any more, Christian, and I don't think I want to.' She realised her voice had gone up several octaves, and quickly indicated with a nod of her head to Matt that it was time to leave. Pausing at the door, she stopped to take a last look at Christian. 'And don't for one moment think you can persuade me out of this on the flight home, because I won't be returning on the Evolution jet. I don't wish to see you again. Ever! Is that understood?'

'No! Please...' She heard his distressing cry and saw him slump onto the bed, cradling his head in his hands. If he thought the action would pull her back into the room, it didn't. She simply closed the door, leaving him to his misery. Outside, she stopped for a moment to draw a deep breath of relief before following her uncle back through the hotel grounds towards the waiting jeep.

135

TWENTY-ONE

Charlotte pushed a strand of her wayward hair out of her eyes and concentrated on pouring custard over the dishes of Christmas pudding Olivia Manning was laying out on the servery table. A former social work team leader, Olivia had more than twenty years' experience in the poorest areas of London. Behind those calm grey eyes and her compassionate nature lurked a strong, committed woman eager to fulfil Matt's mission statement, and Charlotte could understand why Matt had employed her to head up Safekeeping.

The dining area of the night shelter, with its long runs of tables and chairs, was decorated for Christmas with red, green and gold garlands looped around its walls. Matt had arranged for a tree to be delivered from Willowbrook, and the staff had decorated it earlier in the week. It gave the room a welcoming and festive appearance. Tonight, two days before Christmas, was the second evening of Christmas dinners and the dining room at Argent House was yet again full. The main meal was now finished, plates cleared away and a queue had formed for pudding. Olivia smiled as the last plateful was taken by a thin young man in a green anorak.

'Right, Charlotte, that's you finished for the evening,' Olivia said, reaching for the huge ceramic custard jug with the intention of repatriating it to the kitchen.

Charlotte shook her head. 'Not quite.' She indicated the men eating at the tables. 'There's still washing-up to be done – well, emptying and refilling the dishwasher.'

'Ah, but I'm not keeping a girl who's got a hot date,' Olivia argued, standing back to regard Charlotte with a grin.

'But I haven't got a hot date.'

'Oh no?' She nodded towards the doorway. Charlotte followed her gaze and spotted Marco standing by the dining room entrance. He was talking to Max Farr, the House Manager.

'He's not my hot date,' Charlotte snapped. Feeling the heat rise in her face, she wheeled round to face the older woman. 'Whatever gave you that impression?'

'Because he was here at lunchtime asking for you.'

'Asking for me? And you told him I'd be here this evening? Why? He could be a stalker.'

'Don't be silly, Charlotte. You know who he is.'

'Yes, but... well... you don't!'

'Ah, but I do, as a matter of fact,' Olivia challenged. 'He's Marco D'Alesandro. Matt brought him here a few weeks ago to meet us. And you may be interested to know he was the one who donated all the food for the

Christmas dinners.'

'He did?'

'Ah, he's coming over.'

'Marco!' Charlotte cleared her throat nervously as he greeted Olivia with a kiss on the cheek. 'What are you doing here?'

'I wanted to catch you before I left,' he said, as Olivia quickly disappeared into the kitchen with the jug. 'I am flying out to Tuscany tomorrow for family Christmas celebrations. I wanted to know whether you were staying in London tonight?'

'Yes, I am. Why?' Charlotte wondered where this was going.

'Because I would like you to join me for dinner.'

'Look at me, Marco.' She swept a hand down her clothes. 'I'm not dressed for dinner.'

'My car is outside, I can run you back to the Evolution flat. I am guessing it is where you are staying?'

'Yes, it is but—'

'No arguments, please. This way.' He indicated the door with a commanding sweep of his hand.

Shooting a forbidding frown at Olivia, who stood smirking in the kitchen doorway, Charlotte followed him out of the building.

Half an hour later, outside the West London headquarters of Matt's company Charlotte climbed out of the Porsche.

'I may be some time,' she said tersely. 'I need a bath; I reek of food.' Punching the code into the ground floor access door to the penthouse flat, she let herself in only to find he was directly behind her. She turned in the doorway, blocking his path. 'Marco, no. Sorry, I can't have you with me while I'm getting ready. You'll have to wait in the car.'

'Ah, you think I am this stalker you were telling Olivia about?' He raised a questioning eyebrow.

Embarrassed, she put her hand to her mouth. 'You heard?'

Arms folded across his chest he stood there smiling.

Charlotte groaned inwardly. Oh God! This was not going at all well. But he'd caught her off guard, damn him! Since Dartmouth, she had hardly seen him. True, he had been at Little Court with Thérèse on many occasions dropping off dresses, but he had never stopped to speak, always seeming to be in a hurry to be somewhere else. There had also been occasions when she had seen him in the village, but again they had been like ships passing in the night with a sociable wave out and an accompanying 'Hello!' before each disappeared in a different direction. Stupid Charlotte, she reprimanded herself, you thought he'd gone away, didn't you? You thought you were safe.

'Charlotte, I promise I will behave myself.' His tone was reassuring.

Well, that's you sorted, but it doesn't help me, Charlotte thought. He had no idea of the effect he had on her. Even sitting in the car, watching his beautifully manicured hands change gear, sent a prickle of arousing heat through her. This feeling was unlike anything she had ever experienced before with any other man and it scared her. With Jake and her previous uni boyfriends it had been youthful sexual exploration, with Christian a close platonic friendship which had unexpectedly developed into a physical relationship. But this was something earthier and far more primitive which she knew, bearing in mind the existence of Lauren, had the potential to bring an emotional avalanche into her life if she didn't take control of her feelings.

'Charlotte, please?'

The sound of his voice brought her back from her daydream. It was no use, her request for him to stay in the car must seem totally irrational, even rude. Reluctantly, she stepped back and let him in; after all, they had already been together in a state of undress once. Quickly, she damped down the memory of broad, naked tanned shoulders and, of course, that towel.

Opening the door to the flat, she reached for the light switch.

'Amazing!' Following behind her, Marco stopped, his gaze taking in the décor and the muted colours of the expensive furnishings. 'Who did Matt get to do the interior design?'

'Ella. She has quite a gift, don't you think?'

'She certainly has.' He nodded, and pulling off his suit jacket, settled himself on one of the couches then leaned over to pick up a magazine from the coffee table. Opening it up, he raised his eyes to find her still standing there watching him.

'I do not think you had better stand there for too long,' he said, turning his concentration back to the magazine as he flicked through the pages. 'The table is booked for eight thirty.'

'What? Oh hell!' She checked her watch and fled.

Charlotte was ready by eight. With her arms at her sides she stood outside the lounge door, bracing herself for both his gaze and comments. She had agonised about what to wear – nothing too short, too tight, or revealing too much cleavage. Oh God, how she hated this indecision. Had it been anyone else she was eating out with there would have been no way she would have been thinking any of these thoughts. But it was *him*, and she did not want to do anything to give the wrong signals. In the end, she chose black trousers topped with a pale green silk shirt. Matched with a short, black check jacket, some plain jewellery and black patent stilettos she felt it gave a 'dinner date' statement without being too ostentatious.

As she entered the lounge she felt his eyes on her and saw warm approval in their brown depths. Hotness filled her cheeks as she fought to keep her mind on the fact he had agreed to friendship, nothing more. It's what she wanted and she hoped he was not going to use this evening as an opportunity to try to bend the rules. In her mind she had now definitely decided he'd been lying when she saw him in Dartmouth, and that he had a girlfriend who had probably gone back to her own family for Christmas. Yes, that was it, so there was absolutely no way she was going to let anything happen between them tonight, or on any other occasions they might be together.

'You look... fabulous,' he said, throwing the magazine back onto the coffee table. Getting to his feet, he drew on his jacket and fished in his pocket for his car keys. 'Come along, I am starving.'

Of course, it had to be San Raffaello's. And Charlotte realised as she gazed around the packed restaurant full of well-heeled diners it was somewhere she had never eaten before. All her lunch meets with Kieren had been arranged elsewhere in London. She supposed she had done this deliberately to avoid running into Marco. But now there was no avoiding him, for here he was sitting opposite her in one of the private dining booths and pouring her an elegant flute of chilled champagne. Filling his own glass, he raised it to hers.

'A toast, Charlotte.'

Charlotte stretched her glass to his, wondering what was coming next; she hoped it had nothing to do with her – or them.

'Merry Christmas,' he said, touching her glass lightly.

'Merry Christmas,' she echoed, avoiding looking directly into his eyes, knowing there was no way she was going to end up robbed of her senses, as Beth had been.

As they ate, he had told her about his childhood, about losing his mother when he was an infant and then being raised by Thérèse when she married his father. He had a great fondness for her he said; something which Charlotte thought was clear proof of his kindness for Thérèse was a cold fish; she doubted she held much affection for her own daughter, let alone another woman's child. He told her of his life growing up in Italy and finally, of course, about his businesses.

By ten thirty they had finished their dessert and she waited for him to call for coffee. Instead, he left the table, returning with their coats and a thin black-haired man in his forties, whom she recognised as Florentine Pagamo.

Florentine bowed and taking her hand, pressed her knuckles to his lips. 'I am honoured. I trust the food was to your satisfaction?'

'It was wonderful, thank you.'

'You are Kieren's friend, I think?'

She nodded. 'He's my stepbrother. He's not here tonight, I gather?'

'Indeed not, it is his evening off.' Florentine released her hand with a smile. 'I understand you are very dear to him, *cara mia*, as you are to—' He shot a brief glance at Marco.

'We must be going,' Marco interrupted, fixing his eyes on his chef. 'Thank you, Florentine, a superb meal as always.'

'Thank you, Marco.' Florentine gave another gracious bow, his eyes on his boss with a fragment of a smile as if he were in possession of some shared secret.

Charlotte frowned as Marco held her coat open for her. She slipped her arms into the sleeves. 'I thought we were staying here for coffee?'

'No, I have a much more special place in mind.'

'Oh, where?'

'Wait and see.'

His car was already waiting at the front of the restaurant, a uniformed doorman slipping the keys into Marco's hand and tipping his cap to her in a goodnight gesture. Moments later, they were speeding through London past a blur of neon, wet streets and well-lit festively decorated shop fronts. Eventually, he crossed the river and turned left, following the embankment until he reached a long two-storey glass-fronted building with garaging beneath. He turned left into the large paved driveway bounded by a low wall and stopped. As he pressed a button on the car's dashboard, Charlotte saw one of the garage doors lift open with a low electric hum. He drove in, the door automatically closing behind them.

'Where are we?'

'Home.'

'I thought you said you were taking me somewhere special for coffee?' She tried to moderate the unease in her voice.

'And I am,' he said matter-of-factly, as he pushed open his door. 'I am going to make you the most delicious cup of Italian coffee. I am one of the best baristas around.'

She hesitated; this wasn't right. 'Marco, I think you had better take me back to the flat.'

He leaned back into the car. 'Charlotte, I am offering you a cup of coffee, nothing more. Don't be so suspicious. You are quite safe with me. I have never made a woman do anything she did not want to.'

Charlotte sighed heavily before getting out of the car, feeling it was useless arguing, so she simply shouldered her bag and followed him into the lift.

They stood in silence for the short time it took to reach his apartment. Stopping with a gentle shudder, the polished metal lift doors parted, opening into a tiny lobby with pale ash double doors set in the wall opposite. Unlocking these, he ushered her in. Charlotte's eyes flew open in surprise; it was beautiful.

Highly polished floors were scattered with pale rugs and together with a black and white decor and matching furnishings it was style which firmly stated this was a man's home. At the far end of the room was a panorama to die for so she wandered over to the full-length window to look out at the river, the bridges and a city blazing with lights. She turned and noticed he had discarded his jacket over one of the couches and was standing some distance away, hands in his trouser pockets, watching her.

'I've never seen anything like this. It's breath-taking.'

'The view sealed the deal for me,' he said, smiling warmly. 'Do you think my interior designer is as good as Ella?'

'There's no contest, but it probably cost you a fortune. Matt got his done on the cheap,' Charlotte replied with a wry grin, trying to avoid having to look at the way his mouth lifted at the corners, an expression which she knew held the key to a whole lot of trouble.

She spotted the three prints he had bought from Water's Edge. 'Ah, Beth's pictures. They look absolutely perfect.'

'As soon as I saw them I knew they were what I had been looking for. Now, are you ready for that coffee?'

She nodded. 'Actually, I'd like to use the bathroom, if I could?'

'Sure.' He indicated the large elegant sweep of wide wooden stairs by the main doors. 'First on the left.'

Emerging moments later from the pristine white cave of a bathroom with the most enormous bath she had ever seen, she observed Marco fussing with his shirt cuffs as he walked up the stairs towards her.

He grinned sheepishly when he saw her. 'This not so expert barista had a slight disagreement with the Gaggia. And as you can see, the machine won.' He indicated the splashes of brown across the whiteness of his shirt. The cuffs now undone, he opened the first three buttons, tugged the garment out of his trousers, and whipped it off over his head.

The movement so close and unexpected caught Charlotte completely by surprise. She stepped back quickly, conscious in that blind moment when the shirt covered his head he might stumble into her. As she did, her shoe connected with one of the rugs which were spread along the landing and she lost her balance. In a split second, the shirt hurled through the air and he closed the gap between them, grabbing her upper arms and pulling her towards him.

'I am so sorry, I did not think,' he said, looking down into her face, concerned dark eyes settling on hers.

Charlotte could feel his fingers burning into her skin as the heat from his body radiated through the softness of her silk shirt, sending emotional shockwaves through her.

'Marco, I... I think I should go. I...' was as far as she got before he pulled her against his chest and slanted his mouth across hers, silencing her words and driving any sensible thought from her mind.

His hands moved to rest on her hips as he plundered her mouth with his expert tongue. Just like the morning in Fox Cottage, his touch and the feel of his warm bare skin caused her resistance to crumble as her arms snaked around his neck, meshing her fingers in his thick dark hair, enjoying the feel of him against her. With their mouths locked together and a tidal wave building, Charlotte was aware his hands were moving upwards to unbutton the top of her shirt. Easing it open, his mouth left hers to trail soft kisses along her exposed shoulder, making her shiver. All of a sudden reality broke through the seductive spell he had cast, bringing Charlotte swiftly to her senses.

'Marco stop! We can't do this,' she said, pressing her hands to his chest, pushing him away as she tried to untangle herself from his embrace. 'You're with Lauren.'

His dark brows arched in surprise. 'You still think I am with someone else?'

She nodded dumbly, watching as he studied her.

'Then I think you are a very honourable woman indeed.' He ran a gentle finger down her cheek. 'Many women standing where you are now would not care about spending the night with someone else's lover. But your principles are totally misplaced. As I have told you before, there is no one in my life; there is only work.' He took one of her hands and placed it against his heart. 'It is the truth,' he said solemnly. 'I would never lie to you.'

Charlotte felt the steady pulse beneath her fingers as they rested warmly against the dark hair covering his chest. Remembering Beth's remark that Marco's eyes would always give him away, she raised her face to look at him, searching their brown depths to seek the truth of what he was telling her. Eventually, she lowered her gaze and smiled. Her words came in a hushed whisper.

'I believe you.'

Marco gave an audible sigh as he gently brushed an unruly wisp of hair from her face and then dipping his head, brought his lips to hers once more. Without breaking the kiss, she felt him lift her effortlessly into his arms and in one smooth motion, he shouldered the door open and carried her into the bedroom.

'I'm back. No peeking. Open your mouth and poke out your tongue.'

Sandy haired Scott Elliott, one of Niall's three newly recruited farmhands, made a face on hearing Kayte O'Farrell's voice come from behind the living room door.

'Kayte, what are you playing at now?'

'Go on, do it!'

With a heavy sigh he complied with the request. He heard soft footfalls pad across the carpet, and then something metal accompanied by a cold, wet, sweet taste settled in his mouth.

'What the f...?' he spluttered, opening his eyes and grabbing the spoon.

'It's our latest flavour, peach and strawberry.' Leaning over him, Kayte pouted. 'Willowbrook ice cream is very popular, I'll have you know.'

'Maybe it is, but not in the middle of bloody December,' Scott protested, levering himself upright and handing the spoon back to her.

Knowing everyone but Kayte would be out that evening Scott had deliberately turned up at the farm. Ever since he had started working for Niall she had been giving him the eye. This morning, when he called in at the farm shop to deliver bottled milk from the dairy, she'd been there as usual. She couldn't take her eyes off him and from all the hints she'd been dropping about being home alone this evening, he knew she might as well have handed him a gold edged invitation. All too aware of the weedy specimens in this village, he expected his rugged looks and muscular frame were a breath of fresh air and she appeared to be gagging for it. His guess was right – as soon as she opened the door she was standing back to let him in with that expression on her face and wearing something which revealed far too much cleavage. God, she was gorgeous: baby blue eyes, long legs, a great body and blonde hair falling in torrents down her back. Of course, being the boss's daughter he'd have to tread a wary path, but of one thing he was certain: eventually she would be his. Tonight, he realised, she had been doing all the controlling. They had watched some TV, listened to music and ended up together in a heavy petting session on one of the soft settees in front of a roaring fire in the farmhouse's living room.

Wiping the residue of melting ice cream from his face with the back of his hand, Scott watched Kayte flounce into the kitchen to place the ice cream back in the freezer. Moments later she returned, settling herself back in his arms. He kissed her. She responded, thrusting her tongue into his mouth.

She pulled back, and smiling said, 'Mmm you taste sweet.'

'And you are so gorgeous.' He reached out to stroke her hair. 'How about I take you out sometime? We could go into Abbotsbridge for a meal maybe.'

She shook her head. 'I can't.'

'Why not?'

'Because I'm saving myself.'

He threw back his head and laughed. 'Saving yourself? Are you serious?'

'Totally.'

'So what's this then, you and me, here tonight?'

'This is *fun*, Scott. Don't you like fun?'

'Yeah, I do, but I don't understand. Exactly what are you saving yourself for?'

'It's a who, Scott. Marco D'Alesandro,' she said as if he ought to know.

'The Italian? He's years older than you are, and he's gay.'

'Maybe, maybe not. All I know is we're destined to be together,' she said with total conviction, a dreamy expression on her face. 'However, in the meantime,' she brushed her lips against his, 'I believe in having fun.'

Scott's mouth met hers as he pulled her into his arms. D'Alesandro be damned, he thought. Kayte was going to be his and absolutely nothing was going to get in his way.

TWENTY-TWO

Charlotte woke to sunlight streaming through the huge glass panes of the bedroom window. She lay on her back in a large circular bed. For a moment she was totally disorientated until she turned her head, her gaze falling on the figure beside her. Asleep, Marco had the face of a fallen angel: long dark lashes fanning his cheeks, his hair a riot of untidy black curl around his face. She stretched out her hand but resisted the temptation to trace her fingers over the flawless sculpted lines of his face. Instead, she slipped from the bed, reaching for his robe hanging on the back of the door. Wrapping herself in its warmth she crossed over to the window, eager to take a look at the new morning. Beyond the floor-to-ceiling glass London lay covered in a layer of thick frost, the sky above a brilliant blue.

After a moment's contemplation her attention was drawn back into the room, to the bed and the sleeping figure lying there, and the thought of the night they had just spent together. A night of precious little sleep; a night like no other. The power of his touch and his kiss were such that the very thought of what had taken place between them caused a shudder of pleasure to course through her. His talents were such they indicated he was an experienced lover used to having women in his bed but somehow this seemed to be at odds with the quiet, self-effacing young Italian who had wined and dined her last evening. She felt totally perplexed; one night with him had raised more questions than she had answers for.

Returning to the bed and slipping beneath the sheets again, she turned on her side to watch him sleeping. He was so gloriously beautiful she felt like pinching herself to make sure she was not dreaming.

'Why are you staring at me, Charlotte?' he said, his eyes still closed. 'Is something wrong?'

'No, not at all.' The corners of her mouth lifted in a soft smile. She watched as he stretched himself like a sleek muscular cat. Opening his eyes, the last traces of sleep left his face as he smiled tenderly at her. Leaning over, she kissed him lightly on the lips, fingers splaying out to stroke the dark hair covering his chest. Taking her hand, he lifted it and brought his lips to her open palm.

'You have a wonderfully soft body,' he whispered, reaching up to nuzzle her neck.

'And you have…' she hesitated, puzzling over what to say.

His eyebrows rose. 'Yes?'

'Marco, where did you learn to touch a woman the way you do?'

'Ah, Charlotte…' He twisted a stray corkscrew of her hair around his finger and gazed up at her. 'You ask very personal questions.'

'I know I do, and…?' She looked at him expectantly, determined she wasn't about to let him wriggle out of answering.

He gazed at her for a moment then said, 'For my sixteenth birthday my father hired the services of one of the best whores in Italy. It was something that was done for him at the same age.' He ran a finger down her arm, his eyes fixed on hers as he continued. 'I was told she would teach me skills, that I would learn everything a man should know about pleasuring a woman. It is important, is it not, for a man to be a good lover? Especially,' he added with a wry grin, 'if he is Italian. So my experience comes from what I have learnt, not from the number of women I have bedded. Although I have to confess I am by no means an innocent.' The corners of his mouth tugged up again, this time in an amused smile. 'And how many men have you slept with?'

She could see both humour and challenge in his face. Holding his gaze and trying hard to keep a straight face, she answered, 'Oh, I've lost count, there have been so many.'

Marco threw back his head and laughed. 'So many, eh?'

'Stop it.' She punched him playfully on the arm. 'Four actually, including Christian.'

'Ah yes, the Rock God. No doubt he was outstanding?'

'I hope you don't expect me to answer that.'

'No? Such a pity. Would you like to know the woman I have enjoyed the most?'

'Not particularly. Your ex-loves don't interest me.'

'It is not an ex-love. It is you.'

She raised her hands. 'Don't. I know exactly what you are up to. You're trying flattery because you want to know about Christian.'

'I am not. I am telling the truth,' he insisted, as he pulled her towards him. 'Last night I slept with a woman who makes love, not one who has sex. There is a subtle difference.'

'There is?'

'Definitely.' He stroked her shoulder, sending shivers through her body. 'And do you know something?'

'What?'

'I think I would like to experience this again.'

'You would? When?'

Rolling her over onto her back he leaned over, planting soft kisses on her face. 'I think maybe… right now.'

Leaving the apartment later that morning, Marco drove her to the Safekeeping offices, pulling up outside.

'I guess this is it, then.' She forced a smile as he abandoned the driver's seat and walked around to the passenger door to help her out. 'Thank you for a wonderful meal. And for an unforgettable night.' She reached up to kiss him, wanting to take the wonderful mixture of cologne and man with her as a memory of the one very special night he had given her. 'Have a great Christmas with your family and I'll see you in the New Year. You'll be coming back to the manor some time, I hope?'

His face became serious. 'Remember when I told you I wanted to be with you? I meant what I said. This is not the end, it is the beginning.'

She stared at him. 'The beginning?'

'Yes. I will be returning on the fourth of January. I want you to meet me at Heathrow and for us to spend some more time together here in London. Would you like to do that?'

'Yes! Yes, of course I would.'

'Good. Then it is not goodbye, it is *a presto*, as we Italians say. Oh, and I have this for you.' He pulled a brown envelope from his coat pocket. 'Merry Christmas, Charlotte.'

'What is it?'

'Something you will like.' He waved a serious finger at her. 'Not to be opened until Christmas Day.'

'Thank you.' She kissed him again, wishing he didn't have to leave, still not fully believing the changes the last twenty-four hours had brought her. He was perfect; not only beautiful outside but inside as well. Beth had been right: he was very old fashioned in many of his ways but his manners and grace added to the attraction.

Standing on the pavement outside the offices she watched as the Porsche disappeared into London's busy traffic. For her, the fourth of January could not come quickly enough.

Charlotte finished helping her aunt load the dishwasher and then returned to the dining room. Christmas lunch was over and looking around the table, she knew the next thing to happen would be someone suggesting a walk. Sure enough, it was CJ who got to his feet first and hauled Lucy out of her chair.

'Me? No, please... Dad will go with you,' Lucy protested, shooting a pleading look towards Matt. 'You will, won't you, Dad? You'd love a walk.'

Matt Benedict pushed back his chair, stood up and gazed around the table. 'I suggest we all go.'

'Yes, it's a dry day,' Ella nodded in agreement, 'and it will do us all good to walk off Helen's enormous lunch. I'm sure Rowan's dogs would like to stretch their legs too.'

Twenty minutes later, wrapped in a heavy coats, scarves and gloves to protect against the cold grey day, Charlotte and her family trekked down the driveway, Rowan's two black Labradors racing ahead. The walk took them into Meridan Cross and the High Street; a lonely little group in the quiet, deserted village. Above to the right, Hundred Acre Wood sat in all its winter glory sprawling over Sedgewick Hill, low cloud threading through the bare brown branches of its trees. Charlotte could hear CJ talking with Rowan.

Walking ahead of her, they were discussing not only the planned alterations to Higher Padbury Manor, but also the fact Thérèse had now decided the gardens required the benefit of his stepfather's magic touch. Mention of the manor made Charlotte think of Marco and wonder how his Christmas far away in Italy was going. He had already texted to say he had arrived safely and was missing her. She missed him too, she had told him in her return text. It had also been an opportunity to thank him for his incredible Christmas gift.

He had managed to secure Gulls' Rest for her. The note in the envelope explained how he had seen the house details when she had dropped them on the floor and Beth had told him how she had lost the sale. He had been in touch with the agents to have first refusal if the deal fell through. It had, and now it was hers. His company solicitors had arranged everything and he had paid the deposit on it. All she had to do was go down to Dartmouth and sign contracts and pay the final balance. The house would then be hers.

Of course, there was no way she could accept such a costly gift; even from family she would have felt it extravagant. But she wanted the house badly, and when he returned she planned to insist on paying the deposit money back to him.

Marco's return to the UK seemed an absolute age away. The length of his visit home wasn't merely to do with the festive season; it was about business as well, because his father owned a huge leisure empire and rarely switched off. She knew for Marco it would be a mixture of work and relaxation. Patience, Charlotte, her inner self reprimanded, he'll be back soon enough and you'll both have all the time in the world.

'Glad I've got you on your own.' Lucy dragged her out of her daydream as she caught up with her, slapping her gloved hands together in an attempt to warm herself up. 'I've not seen you properly for ages. Have you been avoiding me? I mean, I'd understand if you were.'

'Me? No. Why?'

'I thought you were still cross with me about what happened at Dartmouth.'

'That was weeks ago, Lucy.'

'I know, but I still feel bad about it.'

'Well, don't.' Charlotte turned and gave her a cousin a hug. 'You've already apologised. If anyone should feel bad it's me for ignoring your warnings about what Christian was up to. If you want to know the truth, Safekeeping has been very busy, that's all. I've hardly had time to breathe in the run up to Christmas.'

'I'm glad it's all over with Christian.'

'So am I. I'm also grateful Matt found the means for me to finish it peacefully and I haven't seen or heard from him since. Has Matt sacked him?'

'I don't know; no one knows where he is. He's simply disappeared.'

147

'Oh! Well, let's not waste good conversation on ex-boyfriends,' Charlotte said, looping her arm in Lucy's as they resumed their walk. 'Tell me, how's it going with your lovely McShea?'

'Fine, he's good to me. Better than I deserve actually,' she admitted with an embarrassed shake of her head. 'When we first started working together he seemed keen to support me. I thought: that's great, I can take advantage of this and sit back while he does all the work. But... well, when you work with Jay there is something about him which makes you want to take responsibility – and I have. In fact, Dad says if I continue the way I'm going the job he promised me in creative media is mine. I'm not going to lose such a great opportunity, Lottie. And when I get my promotion I'm going to make sure Jay is aware of the part he's played in getting me there.'

'That's good, Luce.' Charlotte put an affectionate arm around her cousin. She was tempted to tell her about Marco, but decided against it; it was too soon. If and when they settled into a steady relationship, she wanted to be able to bring him home and break the news in front of the whole of the family.

TWENTY-THREE

Marco stood, hands pushed deep into his trouser pockets, taking in the view across the valley. It was a dry day with little wind and the afternoon sun had given up its attempts to break through hazy grey cloud. Lunch had been over several hours ago, and pulling a jacket over his cashmere polo neck sweater, he had ventured out onto the terrace of his father's grandiose castello to lose himself in thought.

The whole estate dominated the hillside a few kilometres from Castelnouvo di Garfagnana in the north-west of Tuscany. The ten-bedroomed mansion with its pale yellow walls and brown shutters was set in elegant landscaped gardens and had stabling for half a dozen horses. Gianlucca D'Alesandro spent very little time here; the house was used mostly as a holiday retreat and for family get-togethers such as this. His business was based farther north in Milan, where he lived in a large house in the exclusive Viale Luigi Majno area of the city.

Although Gianlucca kept a good portion of the locals employed, the staff here seemed far more formal and reserved, almost like silent shadows as they went about their work. How different he found this to the manor or Little Court, where staff appeared to have a far more relaxed relationship with their employers. Thoughts of the UK triggered memories of Charlotte. England was where his future, and his heart, lay. He longed to be back in London, in his apartment, feeling her soft body wrapped around his, his mouth capturing the warm pulse at the base of her throat. For the last two mornings he had woken feeling adrift, as if part of him were missing. How a woman could have that effect on him after only one night in his bed, he had no idea. But she had felt so different from all the others, meeting him with her own warmth and passion – a far cry from the predatory self-seeking females he had experienced before her.

Turning, he noticed his father walking out to join him.

Gianlucca, dressed in a tailored wool half-belted jacket and expensive slacks, was a tall, broad shouldered man in his mid-fifties. His hair was laced with grey and he possessed the same handsome brown eyed features as his son.

'Marco! We need to talk.' Indicating the wide sweep of lawn, he said, 'Walk with me, I have something important to discuss with you.'

Marco nodded and fell in by his father's side, knowing this meant a discussion about business, and wondered what new project he was about to become involved with.

'You have no doubt heard of the Caravello Vineyards?' Gianlucca said.

'Yes, they produce some of the best Chianti Superior in Italy,' Marco replied with a nod. 'We serve it in San Raffaello's. Why?'

'You may not be aware but the owners, Abramio and Daria Caravello, were killed in a helicopter accident some eight years ago as they returned from their ski lodge in Cormayeur. Since then their only daughter, Rossana, has been in the care of her mother's brother Edoardo Carrera and his wife Monica, who sadly passed away some months ago.'

'Yes, I had heard. Poor Edoardo,' Marco said, placing a gentle hand on his father's shoulder.

'Edoardo is in his seventies now, and as you know, he and I go back a long way. He has been a faithful friend both in and out of business. Lately, both his wealth and his health have taken turns for the worse. Edoardo is not well. He has recently developed heart problems and looking after Rossana has become difficult for him. I feel it is time to repay all those years of support by helping him out.' He paused for a moment to gaze into the distance before turning to look back at Marco. 'I have agreed Rossana will come to us as a house guest for a while until he has had the heart surgery he urgently needs and has recovered sufficiently to have her back. I have met her. She is a sweet, shy girl, seventeen years old and quite unworldly. This has arisen as a result of Edoardo and Monica's rather protective regime concerning her upbringing. Coming to live with us would – how do you say? – bring her out of her shell. In fact, I am sure living with a younger family can only be of benefit. The reason I am talking to you now is because she will be arriving this afternoon and I need you to…'

Marco realised it was his stepmother who had halted his father's words as she joined them.

'Marco,' she purred, her fingers splaying gently across his back. 'What your father is trying to say is that Rossana is in great need of some male company. Someone to take her out, to spend time with her. To have fun,' she added with a light-hearted laugh. 'You have been without a woman in your life for far too long, and I fear you risk becoming a sad workaholic. I am sure you will find her company quite refreshing.' Moving her hand up to his shoulder, she walked around to face him.

'Do I detect an attempt to match make yet again, Thérèse?' Gianlucca eyed her coolly, knowing this was not the first time she had tried to steer the course of his son's life in the direction she wanted with some female of her choice.

'You are twenty-six, Marco; you should be married.' She looked across to her husband for support but saw only irritation in his eyes as he stood there hands deep in his jacket pockets.

Marco gave her a chilly smile. 'An unworldly seventeen-year-old? Hardly a good choice.'

'Eighteen in September,' Thérèse corrected. 'Marco, don't you realise there are benefits to be made from such matches?'

'Thérèse!' Gianlucca waved a finger and shook his head reproachfully.

'I mean, a chaste bride from an impeccable background is something of an expectation in families such as ours.' Her eyes settled on her husband with a pleasant smile. 'We must not forget tradition, must we, Gianni?'

'I am sorry but you are wasting your time.' Marco's tone was dismissive. 'I am happy to keep her company, as no doubt Felica will be, but anything more...'

Thérèse eyed him with a look of mild reproach. 'Why so reluctant? You have always enjoyed the company of women; your father tells me Rossana is very beautiful.'

'I do not doubt that,' Marco acknowledged, 'but besides the fact she is far too young, I am already in a relationship.'

'What!' Gianlucca and Thérèse chorused simultaneously, surprise in his face, annoyance on hers.

'Why am I not aware of this?' Thérèse tilted her head with an expression of displeasure. 'Who is she?' she demanded. 'Where did you meet her?'

'It is Charlotte.'

'Charlotte Kendrick?' Her eyes widened in surprise when she laughed.

Gianlucca frowned at them. 'Who is Charlotte?'

'Charlotte is a simple country girl whose parents manage the gardens for my business associate Ella Benedict.' She waved a disdainful hand. 'Totally inappropriate.'

Marco bristled at the way she had deliberately twisted the truth, no doubt in order to try to influence his father.

'Charlotte is no simple country girl, Mother. You know as well as I do she is an accountant with a first class honours degree in mathematics and is wealthy in her own right. Her great-grandmother left her a multi-million pound trust fund,' he added, noting his father's interested expression. 'Not only that, Jenny is Ella's sister-in-law. They are family, so stop making her sound like the hired help!'

'She is a silly little woman who likes gardening,' Thérèse declared with contempt. 'Ella and Issy are the driving forces behind Lawns; they are the people I do business with. And,' she shook a finger at him, 'there is mental illness in the family. Don't forget the circumstances surrounding Charlotte's father's death. Cordelia Carmichael told me he was quite violent towards the end.' She sniffed. 'Which is what probably drove the silly little woman into the arms of the gypsy she's now married to. Knowing her father's history, do you honestly want to take the chance of becoming involved with his daughter? You saw the kind of temper she showed on the morning she refused Christian's proposal. And what in heaven's name has made you decide to become involved with a rock star's cast offs when with your looks, you could have any woman you want?'

'Thérèse, enough!' Gianlucca waved a warning finger at his wife. 'This conversation has got completely out of hand.' He gave his son a sympathetic smile. 'Marco, I am sorry. Thérèse tends to get a little carried away. I am not trying to find you a wife. In fact, I would not dream of interfering in your life. Who you spend time with is your business. All I ask is that you and Felica take Rossana under your wing and make her feel at home. I want her to enjoy her stay with us, become an extended part of our family.'

Marco nodded acceptance of his father's request, his eyes resting on his stepmother's back as she strode away, shoulders taut with vexation. He thought there would be automatic acceptance from her of his news about seeing Charlotte. Resistance from his father he would have expected, but Thérèse! She knew Charlotte, even claimed to like her. But, of course, the opportunity to continue her match-making activities for the D'Alesandro heir, as she often referred to him, with a chaste little virgin like Rossana Caravello was too good an opportunity to miss. It was some time before he had realised she was beginning to take a little too much interest in his life, constantly dropping hints about the fact he should be thinking about marriage and producing another layer of D'Alesandros to work in the business. A series of totally unsuitable young women had been suggested and quickly dismissed by him. But this one was different: the girl would be living with them, which meant more opportunity for Thérèse's mischief. Marco knew he would need to be on his guard.

Agitated by her husband's harsh tone, Thérèse hurried towards the house, not stopping until she reached the upper terrace; she was still shaking. How dare Gianlucca mock her! Could he not see this golden opportunity? He was skilled in business, a powerful man who let no one stand in the way of what he wanted. How could he not see she was trying to help him? Why was he unable to see the benefits of Marco marrying Rossana? Knowing the way her husband operated, she was convinced inviting the girl to stay with them must have an ulterior motive after what he had divulged about his recent dinner with Edoardo. Or had he gone soft all of a sudden? It was time Marco was married and making a separate life for himself. Even though he had been very small when she had married his father, she had never been able to accept him.

How could Gianni ever be hers? Marco was always there – a constant reminder of his beautiful mother Isabetta, who had died so tragically and so young. Over the years her resentment had not diminished, if anything it had grown, and even today she still perceived him as a barrier to her happiness. Gianlucca always put him first. As his wife, Thérèse knew she was relegated to second place in everything her husband did or felt, and she hated it. It was the cause of constant disagreements. Well, I am not done here, she thought, turning back to look at the two men who still stood talking on the lawn below. Marco, your days are numbered for I will have you for Rossana. And when I do, Gianlucca, you will not only be mine, you will thank me.

'Signora D'Alesandro!' Martina, the housekeeper, appeared through the huge terrace doors. 'Signorina Rossana Caravello has arrived.'

Thérèse followed Martina through the house to the pale walled hallway with its wide sweep of staircase and heavy, black rustic chandelier. There in the hall, wrapped in a heavy overcoat and standing among several large suitcases, stood a young woman with shoulder-length hair. Hearing their approaching footsteps, she turned.

Thérèse smiled warmly and wrapped her arms about her guest, kissing her cheek. 'Welcome, Rossana. Welcome.' She stepped back to assess her.

At five foot six inches tall, Rossana was slim, full breasted with high cheekbones, large green eyes, a straight neat nose and thick tawny hair. Her face had a fresh well-scrubbed look with not a trace of make-up. Her clothes added to this lacklustre image: a high necked, navy winter coat over a dark green sweater and grey trousers, black pumps on her feet. Everything was expensive but old fashioned, and totally lacking in sophistication. Far from being disappointed at the vision in front of her, however, Thérèse regarded it as a challenge – an empty canvas on which to fashion her masterpiece.

'Thank you, Signora D'Alesandro,' Rossana replied meekly. 'I am very pleased to be here.'

We'll need to do something with that voice though, thought Thérèse, but her smile has definite potential. Oh yes, once I'm finished there is no way Marco will be able to resist her. She turned to the housekeeper.

'Martina, would you please find Leno and ask him to take Signorina Caravello's suitcases up to the main guest suite?'

Martina nodded and left immediately.

Giving her charge an encouraging smile, Thérèse took Rossana by the arm, guiding her down the hall towards the rear of the house. 'Come with me,' she said. 'I have someone who is dying to meet you.'

As they descended the steps from the terrace, Gianlucca came striding across the lawn towards them, his arms open wide. '*Cara mia*,' he exclaimed warmly, as he reached her and gave her a fatherly hug. 'How was your journey?'

'It was fine,' she said with a nod, looking up at him with an adoring smile. 'I had no idea you owned anywhere as beautiful as this.'

'We love it too,' Thérèse stated, 'and, of course, we have a summer house on Lake Como. But enough of this boring talk of property. I want you to meet our son Marco, he has been looking forward to your arrival. Marco!' she called, noticing he had decided to take himself over to the far edge of the lawn. On hearing her voice, he turned and began slowly making his way back to where they all stood.

Rossana stood spellbound; she had never seen such a beautiful man and it was not only the flawless features which drew her. He was tall, broad shouldered and muscular; she felt her knees tremble slightly. Her perfect man, the one she had read and daydreamed about in the romance novels she regularly read was here in the flesh, a member of the family she was about to become part of. She could not believe it. She looked up shyly from under her dark lashes, feeling herself quiver under his gaze.

'I am very pleased to meet you, Marco. Your father has told me all about you.'

Hands still pushed deep into his pockets, Marco nodded pleasantly. 'Welcome, we are glad to have you here. I hope your stay will be a happy one.'

Rossana felt her flesh tingle all over; his eyes were deep brown and his voice soft and incredibly sexy but his attitude towards her bordered on polite disinterest. There was not a shred of warmth in those eyes, but then what had she expected? That he would take one look at her, sweep her into his arms and promise her his undying love? Those things, she reflected with disappointment, only happened in books.

'Marco is to be one of your shadows while you are with us,' Gianlucca informed her with a benevolent smile. 'My daughter Felica too. She is out riding at the moment, you will meet her at dinner.'

Marco nodded again before excusing himself and wandering off into the house.

Rossana couldn't help but notice the glare Thérèse gave his retreating back before her host wrapped a protective arm around her shoulder and said, 'Well, now the introductions are over, let us go inside, shall we? I will show you to your room and introduce you to your maid. I am sure you would like to freshen up after your journey. Felica will be back soon. No doubt you girls will have much to talk about.'

'So, you were educated in Switzerland but you did not go to university?' Marco asked, attempting light conversation with Rossana, trying to show some interest if only to stop the way Thérèse kept giving him disapproving looks down the length of dining table.

'Oh, there was no need.' Rossana lifted her glass for yet another refill from one of the maids. 'For me education is merely a formality. Why bother with it when your intention is to marry a man who is not only wealthy but good-looking too.' She fixed him with a covert stare from under a fan of long lashes. 'One who will love, cherish and keep me,' she added melodramatically. 'Who will put me on a pedestal and adore me.'

'And I am sure you will find him, *cara mia*.' Thérèse gave her an indulgent smile.

Marco noticed his father's eyes widen in bewilderment before shaking his head and turning his attention back to the food on his plate. Seated next to Rossana, his sister Felica was full of light-hearted chat and suggesting things they could do while she was staying at the castello.

He closed his eyes; the wine was making Rossana sound silly and immature. Which is what she is considering the sheltered existence she'd had since the age of ten, he thought. An unworldly young woman with an obvious crush, given the way she kept batting her eyelashes at him. With no choice but to continue tolerating her childish prattle until dessert had been cleared away, it had been an absolute trial sitting opposite her throughout the meal.

Relieved dinner was finally over, Marco excused himself and went to his room to retrieve his mobile. Checking it, he smiled as he read Charlotte's message. The weather in England was still cold and damp; she had been out riding with Lucy, had dinner with her aunt and uncle in Abbotsbridge, and she was counting the days until they were together in London. He sighed, wishing he was at Little Court with her instead of here with this empty-headed child-woman and his scheming stepmother. He sent back a text saying he was already bored, missing her like crazy and couldn't wait to be with her again either.

After, he stood at the window of his room for a while looking out on the gardens now lit by torches, streaks of light and shadow playing across the lawn. In view of his growing suspicions about his stepmother's intentions he needed a plan and an ally. With this in mind he went in search of his sister.

An overnight frost had spread itself across the landscape and mist hung along the valley beyond the mansion. Marco had risen early and after a light breakfast, walked out to the stables to instruct Vincenzo to saddle his horse. He wanted to be away from the house for a while, alone with his thoughts. As he emerged into the yard leading his mount he saw Rossana, also dressed for riding, making her way towards him. He cursed silently under his breath.

'Marco, good morning,' she greeted him in her usual breathless way. 'I don't suppose...' She cocked her head enquiringly. 'Would you mind... may I ride with you?'

He gave the politest of smiles. 'Maybe another time, Rossana. I would prefer to be alone this morning. If you ask Vincenzo, the head groom, I'm sure he will take you out. He is currently in one of the stalls, grooming Felica's mare.' He nodded towards the open door of the stables.

'Oh!' She frowned up at him, obviously disappointed with his answer. 'Do I gather you are riding to meet someone?'

'I beg your pardon.'

'You have a lover,' she said, widening her eyes dramatically. 'I suppose I should have known; don't all handsome Italian men have lovers?'

Amused, Marco swung himself into the saddle. 'I think you have been filling your head with too many romantic tales. I merely wish to be on my own.'

'Then you have no one?' He thought he caught a glimpse of hopefulness in her voice.

'Actually, I do,' he replied, realising now was the time to put a stop to what he suspected he had seen lurking behind those great green eyes. 'She lives in England.'

'And she was not invited here for Christmas?' Rossana tilted her head curiously.

'No, she is spending the holiday with her own family. We will be together when I return in the New Year,' he answered, adjusting his reins. 'Now, are there any more questions before I leave?'

She backed away. 'Sorry, no.'

'Good. I will see you later. As I said, Vincenzo will be more than willing to accompany you for a short ride. Maybe Felica and I can take you out later in the week.'

Teeth gnawing nervously on her bottom lip, Rossana tried to hide her disappointment as she watched him turn his mount's head and canter out of the yard. She didn't want Felica along; she wanted to be alone with Marco to get to know him better. But, of course, if there was someone else in his life that wasn't going to happen, was it? *Had he been telling the truth?* she wondered. Or had it been a ploy to get rid of her because he did not wish to delay any longer by answering her questions? Whatever the reason, she knew she needed to find out more about him before she made a complete fool of herself again. Turning back to the house, she decided to look for Felica and get some answers.

As she entered the house she met Thérèse coming down the stairs.

'Rossana! Out riding before breakfast?'

'Actually, no. I got as far as the stables and then...' She hesitated, seeing the compassionate look on the older woman's face. 'Marco was there. I asked to go with him but he said he would prefer to be alone.'

'Oh, Rossana, that is quite unacceptable,' Thérèse said crossly. 'I will speak to him as soon as he returns.'

'He has promised to take me out later in the week,' she added quickly, not wanting to get him into trouble. 'We are going with Felica.'

Thérèse shook her head. 'This is very bad. He agreed to spend time with you and here he is shirking his responsibilities.'

'I think maybe he does not want to because his girlfriend will be jealous.'

'His girlfriend?' Thérèse gave a short laugh. 'Oh, my dear, you worry over nothing. Charlotte is a very ordinary young woman, quite plain. In fact, she has chased him unmercifully. I am sure he will tire of her soon, it cannot possibly last.' She fixed Rossana with a calculating stare. 'I gather you are quite taken with him, then?'

'Oh, yes.' Rossana lowered her head, knowing she blushed. 'He is very handsome. The sort of man girls dream of.'

'I think you should do more than dream, Rossana. If you feel that way you should do something about it.'

'Oh, but Signorina D'Alesandro, he is much older than me. Besides, I am not his type.'

Thérèse waved her argument away. 'Forget about age. And as for type, what you need is a little help. Come and see me after breakfast.' She leaned closer, her voice a hushed whisper. 'You and I have some planning to do.'

'Planning?'

'To make you irresistible, of course.'

TWENTY-FOUR

'Happy New Year, Luce.'

Lucy had been so absorbed in her thoughts she had not heard the door open. Jay leaned in, his thick blond hair falling untidily around his face, his eyes holding their usual warmth as they met hers. 'Magda said you wanted to see me?'

'Yes, come in.' She returned to her desk and settled herself behind it waiting while he took up his regular perch on its edge. 'I need a favour but you may think it's a bit of a cheek.'

Jay smiled at her thoughtfully. 'Well, you won't know until you ask me, will you. What is it?'

'The Australian police have been working with the Indonesian authorities. They set up a sting and they've caught a gang trying to dupe a woman out of a large amount of money. Only they're not quite sure they are the same people who robbed me. So they need me to identify them. Of course, I could do it from over here. They have told me they are willing to send through photos to the Met. However, I've decided it would be better if I went over there and saw them in the flesh. I want you to come with me, Jay.'

'What? Why, Luce? Are you having another of your crazy moments?'

'No, I'm not. It's personal, Jay.' Her tone indicated that was all the information she was going to give him.

He shook his head stubbornly. 'Sorry, not good enough. If you are asking me to take time out to travel twelve thousand miles with you then I have to know the reason why.' He levelled a finger at her. 'And no bullshit.'

'I... well...' She shifted uncomfortably before raising her eyes to his. 'I actually need to be there, to see Ethan, if that is his real name, in custody and have the satisfaction of knowing what's going to happen to him, that he will be put away for a long, long time. Identifying a photograph is not enough. If I'm to have closure this is the only way.'

Seeing the shimmer of tears in her eyes, Jay moved round to where she sat and laid a gentle hand on her shoulder. 'Okay, Luce, I'll do it. I'll come with you, although—'

'What?'

'Are you sure it's me you want? I mean, if it's going to be a quick turnaround then maybe Matt—'

'No,' she cut across him. 'It's you, Jay. I need *you* to be there with me.'

Her admission stunned him for a moment. Of all the people she could have chosen it had been him; and then he realised how foolish he was to read anything more into it. She had chosen him because he was her mentor and supporter – someone who was always there for her, who never let her down. Christian was right; she was destined for some rich banker or neighbouring landowner's son, not him.

'Fine.' He hid his torment behind an agreeing smile. 'You want me, you got me. When were you planning to go?'

'I'm tied up at the moment. I thought maybe the beginning of next week?'

'Next week? I thought they'd expect you there sooner than that.'

'It's not a problem as they've already been charged with this latest offence and are currently cooling their heels on remand awaiting trial.'

He nodded. 'Okay, next week it is.'

'Thank you so much! I'll get Magda to organise the hotel and flights,' she said, getting to her feet and giving him a tight hug. She rested her head against his shoulder. 'You're the best, Jay,' she whispered. 'I don't know what I'd do without you.'

Jay's hands hovered around Lucy's shoulders, wanting more than anything to wrap his arms around her delightful body and kiss her. But he couldn't, it was too dangerous. A wrong move could ruin the relationship he'd spent so much time building with her and he knew there was no way he could sacrifice that. So he remained where he was, deciding it was better to be disappointed than rejected.

Charlotte waited in the arrivals hall at Heathrow, scanning the multitude of incoming airline passengers carrying or trailing suitcases in their wake. Around her, people rushed forward to claim their relatives and loved ones with warm embraces and exclamations of delight. As the flood dwindled to a trickle, she checked her watch again and pulled out her mobile to make sure she had not misread the late afternoon flight details Marco had sent her in his earlier text. She found the message and frowned; it appeared the flight had landed half an hour ago.

'Ah, Charlotte! I am sorry for keeping you waiting, there was a backlog in passport control.'

At the sudden sound of his voice she looked up to find him standing in front of her, amusement dancing in his warm brown eyes. Shoving her phone into her coat pocket, she threw her arms around his neck and hugged him tightly, burying her face in the warmth of his coat collar, taking her time, enjoying the smell of his expensive aftershave and the strength of his arms around her. When she eventually lifted her head, their eyes met and he bent his head towards her, his mouth finding hers. The softness of his lips in contrast to the slight abrasiveness of the newly acquired designer stubble covering his lower jaw made him feel deliciously sexy.

'I have missed you so much,' she said. 'So very, very much.'

'I have missed you too, more than you will know.' He ran his finger gently down her cheek and then his smile faded as he noticed she was staring at the floor. 'What is the matter?'

'Where's your luggage? Surely you haven't existed for nearly two weeks

159

with what's in that bag?' she said, indicating the holdall he was carrying.

He laughed at her mystified expression. 'Of course not. I have many sets of clothes. Clothes for London, clothes for Italy and clothes for the manor.'

'My God, you really are rich, aren't you?' It was something she had never considered before.

He shrugged. 'I try not to think about it too much. Coming to live in England has made me feel… quite normal.'

'Well, normal boy, let's get you home.' Charlotte brushed her torrent of dark hair back from her face, and arm-in-arm they headed towards the exit.

It was as they left Heathrow and joined the M4 into London she decided to raise the issue of her Christmas present.

'I'm sorry, Marco, I was so pleased to see you I completely forgot. About Gulls' Rest—'

'It is what you wanted?' he interrupted, a smile appearing as she shot a quick look in his direction.

'It's my dream house,' she said, nodding as they pulled up at traffic lights. 'Thank you so much.' She reached across to squeeze his hand, her expression becoming serious. 'But I cannot accept the money you paid for the deposit; it is far too much.'

'No, it is my gift to you,' he insisted. 'I want you to have it.'

'If you won't let me repay all the money then at least take some of it. You are far too generous and, as you realise, I am far too independent.'

'Well, my independent Charlotte, let us not spoil the day. Let us leave the subject of Gulls' Rest for now, we can argue about it later.'

'Okay,' she agreed with a reluctant sigh, turning her concentration back to the road as the lights changed to green. 'But tomorrow we set some ground rules – this is not what I want or expect from you.'

Afterwards he was very quiet. On stealing a glance across at him Charlotte saw he was staring out of the car window, lost deep in thought as if he had something on his mind. Oh well, if he wanted to share with her then she would listen, if not then his thoughts were his own, she would never dream of intruding.

She tried to concentrate on the positives as she manoeuvred the car through the traffic. Tonight was his first night home, followed by three whole days together. She wondered what he had planned. Whatever they did she would be happy; being with him was the only thing that really mattered.

Once inside Marco's apartment, he disappeared up to his bedroom to change out of his travel clothes. He had hardly said a word. Charlotte sat in the lounge waiting, thinking something was troubling him for this was not like him at all. Seeing him coming down the stairs, she got to her feet and was about to ask when he walked over to her and put his arms around her.

'Come with me,' he said gently, guiding her back towards the stairs.

On the landing he opened the door of one of the spare rooms and ushered her in.

'Why have you brought me in here?' She gave him a puzzled frown as he stepped over to the wardrobe.

'Because of this.' He drew back the door. Inside, on a single hanger, was a beautiful midnight blue and silver dress, below it a pair of matching high heels and a square box topped with tissue paper.

'I am taking you out tonight and I would like you to wear this. My PA arranged it all while I was away, and as you can see there are shoes and underwear too. I thought... it is a beautiful strong colour and you are a woman who suits such a colour palate. But,' he gave an embarrassed shrug, 'after our conversation in the car I feel you may be angry with me for doing this.'

Charlotte studied him for a moment; the last thing she wanted was him showering her with presents. From the amount her Christmas gift had cost she realised he was extremely generous, and she had no doubt his girlfriends in the past had walked away with wardrobes full of clothes and God knows what else. But she was not one of them. She was different and he would have to get used to the fact if they were destined for any sort of relationship. Tonight, however, she didn't have the heart to upset him.

'I'm not cross,' she said with a gentle smile. 'If it pleases you then I will wear it. But what I want money can't buy.'

'I do not understand.' He frowned, as if trying to figure out what she wanted that was beyond his purchasing power.

'I want you, Marco,' she said tenderly, cupping his face in her hands. 'I want the man, not his money.'

While Charlotte was in the shower, Marco heard the muffled tones of a mobile phone. Recognising his ringtone, he pulled the phone from the inside pocket of his coat. It was his father.

'Thérèse has suggested Rossana flies to England for a visit,' Gianlucca said amiably.

Up until then, he had forgotten about Rossana Caravello and the events over Christmas; Tuscany was another world away. The request from his father to chaperone the young woman had faded; it was something for the future, but now, hearing his father's words, it appeared this was about to change. He glowered into the phone.

'Already? When?'

'She has not specified, but I think probably the end of next week.'

'Father, I am so busy at the moment,' he protested irritably, feeling his stepmother was wasting no time in flexing her match-making muscles. 'I have only just returned from our Christmas break. I had planned to fly to Manchester to check on the refurbishment of The Flemish Weaver.'

'If she is there you could take Rossana with you.'

'Absolutely not. It is a day trip and I will be busy with the architect and contractors. It would not be fair to leave her on her own in a strange foreign city. I doubt Edoardo would be happy.'

'Maybe you should delay your trip until Thérèse has advised us of the date.' His father was beginning to sound a little impatient. 'She is keen to have her down at the manor for a few days; she wants to show off her business. Indulge her, Marco, for my sake, eh?'

'Manchester is quite urgent, Father, I can probably fit it in this Friday. As far as everything else is concerned I will reschedule, but tell Thérèse she needs to give me notice. I cannot make time for Rossana's visit at the drop of a hat. I have a business to run.' He sighed irritably. Although he knew his father was attempting to mend bridges with Thérèse following his hard stance with her at Christmas, it was not helping *him* at all. Damn her! He really didn't need this.

'Thank you, Marco.' His father's voice held a warm, genial quality. 'Once I know the dates I'll get my PA to email you all the details. Oh, and please don't sound so worried. I have spoken to Thérèse and made it clear you are happy with Charlotte, and that she is to leave things alone. How is Charlotte, by the way?'

'She is fine,' he said, his tone mellowing. 'We are spending a few days together in London.'

'Good. Maybe I will get to meet her one day?'

'I hope so. I think you would like her.'

'After all you told me about her, I think so too.'

As he ended the call, Marco hoped his father was right about Thérèse. For now, he had some explaining to do to Charlotte about the situation. He hoped she would understand.

The evening had been wonderful. They had eaten at San Raffaello's, and at the end of their meal Florentine had joined them in their booth to chat. His rags to riches story starting in the back streets of Naples touched Charlotte and she knew it was only his great passion for cooking and a determination to be the best which had got him where he was today.

Afterwards, when she thought they were destined to return to the apartment, Marco took her instead to a small cellar club south of the river. The South Bank Blues Club was dark and atmospheric with low lighting, small tables and a central dance floor; she had only seen places like this in the movies. On a raised dais at one end of the dome-roofed room a jazz quartet supplied the music, an exotic coffee-skinned singer in a tight gold dress the vocals. Her dark hair was scraped back from her face and woven into a thick plait which hung over her left shoulder. This exposed sharp angular features with feline eyes which complimented the long, red-tipped fingers caressing the microphone as her body swayed to the rhythm. Her voice, smoky and sultry, seemed to make the atmosphere within the club feel even more intimate.

Marco drew Charlotte to her feet to join other couples who were out on the floor, drawn by the sensuality of the singer's version of Billie Holliday's 'You Go to My Head'. They came together slowly, arms around each other, moving to the rhythm as they circled the small dance floor. The music took over and Charlotte went with it, lost in the moment as she felt the hardness of his body against hers. Marco looked down into her eyes and smiled before lowering his head and taking her lips in a hard, raw demanding kiss, his tongue invading her mouth. Surprised for a moment by the intensity of his action, her hands clutched the strong muscles of his upper arms as if to compose herself before meeting his hunger with her own, her hands moving to the nape of his neck as her mouth responded and the world caught fire.

He was the first to pull away and stood there studying her for a moment before raising her chin with the tip of his finger. He drew in a ragged breath.

'I think it is time to leave before we get arrested,' he whispered.

With all passion on hold as they drove back home, conversation was light and humorous. Occasionally, Charlotte would sneak a glance at him, watching his striking profile as he concentrated on the road, finally arriving at his apartment block.

In the lift up from the underground car park, he watched her with amusement as she regaled the events of the Boxing Day hunt. A pompous London banker spending the festive season with his family in his barn conversion at Moredon had joined them, she told him, on a hired horse which had bolted and thrown him into the village pond. A whispered hiss and parting of metal halted the tale, and stepping out, Marco entered in the four-digit code and opened the apartment door. Charlotte followed him into the apartment, stifling her amusement with her hand, noting that he had suddenly become silent.

'I'm sorry, it wasn't that funny, was it?' she said, wincing as she slipped out of her coat and draped it over a nearby chair.

'Actually, it was.' He crossed the room and took her in his arms, kissing her forehead. 'My mood has nothing to do with your story. It is just that I need to talk to you about something important. It has been on my mind since before we left for dinner. I avoided discussing it earlier as I did not want to spoil our evening.'

'So, it's something serious, Marco...'

Ignoring her comment, he led her into the living room where they made themselves comfortable on one of the couches. Taking her hand, he squeezed it gently.

'Charlotte, when I was in Tuscany for Christmas,' he began, 'we had a house guest. A young woman called Rossana Caravello. Rossana was orphaned when she was ten years old and now lives with her uncle Edoardo

Carrera – an old friend of my father's. Edoardo is awaiting heart surgery and is currently unable to care for her. He and my father go back a long way and because of this, my father has agreed she can stay with us until her uncle is fully recovered.'

'I see,' Charlotte said quietly. 'And exactly why are you telling me this?'

'Because while she is with us I am expected to give up time to entertain her.'

'Entertain her? Forgive me, but this rather sounds like some sort of pre-betrothal thing. Are you trying to tell me your father has rather underhandedly chosen someone for you? Is that it?'

'No, of course not! I am with you, no one else.' He gave a vigorous shake of his head. 'This is merely a task which my father has asked me to undertake. A task, Charlotte, nothing more, and Felica is to help as well. As for Rossana... she is a homely, pleasant girl but has led a very sheltered life. She is quite immature and I have to say a little dull. I promise you there is nothing to worry about.'

'Have you told your father about me?'

'Yes, he knows.'

'But from your tone I gather he's not exactly overjoyed at the fact I'm now dating you?' Her innocent query belied the uneasiness she felt. 'But then, of course, Thérèse has made it very clear she does not like me, so I suppose—'

'She has nothing to do with this,' he cut her off. 'And as for my father, he has told me my relationships are my business and that he would like to meet you one day. Oh, Charlotte,' his eyes took on a saddened expression, 'what would you have me do? Keep secrets from you? Thérèse is going to invite Rossana to spend some time at the manor. I needed to get this all out into the open before she arrives so there would be no misunderstanding when you saw her. I did not want you thinking I was using you like Christian.'

'You could never be like Christian, Marco. You are two totally different men and I am glad I have found you.' She reached up and touched his face. 'Thank you for being so honest with me.'

Marco returned her smile, capturing her hand and placing a kiss on its palm before drawing her into his arms. 'I will always be honest with you. If we do not have trust between us then everything else is pointless.'

Charlotte relaxed as his lips gently brushed hers. Had she found the perfect man at last? It was too early to make such judgements but what she had experienced with him so far led her to believe she was perhaps on the right path.

Marco stretched and opened his eyes. He reached out, his fingers seeking soft flesh, finding instead a warm empty place next to him. Frowning, he pushed himself up on one elbow. Outside, a grey January day was spreading itself across the London skyline. He smelled coffee, smiled and lay back, his mind going over the night they had just spent together. The first time he saw her there was something which drew him; an invisible tug marking her as something special. They had got off to a bad start but he had been patient, and his patience had paid off. She was now his, and even after this short time together he knew beyond doubt he was experiencing an intensity of feeling for her like no other woman he had ever known. He should be the happiest man on earth, but remembering his father's phone call he realised achieving that happiness was not going to be easy. Despite Gianlucca's claims, he knew what Thérèse was like when she got an idea in her head. One thing in his favour, however, was the fact Rossana was quite the terrified rabbit with her large eyes and intense stare, no doubt finding him a little intimidating after all the polite rebuffs he had given her. No, it was all about dealing with Thérèse, about sending her a clear message and nipping her silly ambitions in the bud.

His deliberations were interrupted as Charlotte came through the bedroom door carrying two steaming mugs of coffee.

'I'm no barista, I'm afraid,' she said. 'It's instant. Hope you don't mind?'

'Of course not.' He hid his thoughts behind a smile, deciding next Friday was an eternity away. He had three more days with her and he was going to make the most of them. For him, it was *now* that mattered – he would deal with Thérèse at the end of the week. It was going to be a challenge, but he would not be bullied.

'I meant to tell you,' Charlotte was saying, as she settled herself next to him in bed, her hands clasped around the coffee mug. 'I thought I'd go down to Dartmouth on Thursday to look at Gulls' Rest. I tied up the paperwork while you were away. It's mine now and I need CJ to come with me so I can...'

His mind drifting off with thoughts of Thérèse again was brought back to the present by a tug on his arm.

'Marco?'

He looked up to find Charlotte laughing at him.

'Marco, you haven't listened to a word, have you? I said: will you join us at the weekend in Devon?'

'Ah, Charlotte, I would love to but I cannot. Because of these precious days with you I have much catching up to do.' He took a mouthful of coffee. 'Maybe another time and...?'

'Yes?'

'No more talk about payment for Gulls' Rest, eh? What you have given me is far more valuable than any Christmas present.'

Charlotte shook her head. 'I'm sorry, you've completely lost me.'

'Well, I will tell you.' He eyed her seriously as he relieved her of her mug and wrapped his arms around her. 'It is your gentleness, your openness, the warmth of your smile,' he said, stroking her face, 'but most of all it is the incredible feeling I get when we lie together. I have never felt this with any woman before. And for me these are gifts far beyond anything money can buy. So no more arguments, eh?' He kissed the tip of her nose, his serious moment evaporating as his smile emerged once more. 'Now then, let us finish our coffee and I will organise breakfast, then we can plan what we are going to do on our first day together.'

TWENTY-FIVE

Wednesday dawned cold and bright and it was time for her to leave. Her stay in London had flown by; magical days spent hand-in-hand, wrapped against the winter elements exploring the city and nights of passionate lovemaking in his big circular bed. If she had wondered about her feelings for him before, now she was certain. She loved him; for his modesty, his gentleness and the way his touch made her come alive. Beth had been right about never seeing this kind of man before; he was totally unique and she felt incredibly fortunate to have met someone like him.

As she entered the kitchen to join him for breakfast Marco's mobile rang. He took himself off into the lounge from where she could hear the even sound of his voice. He came back with an amused shrug.

'That was my head waiter Vittorio calling from the restaurant to make sure I was back. He is always checking up on me, like a mother hen,' he said.

Coffee percolated and toast ejected, conversation minimal as she stepped back allowing him the space he needed to concentrate on the day ahead. When she was pulling on her coat he reached for her, imprisoning her in his arms and holding very tightly as if he couldn't bear to let her go.

'I will miss you and I am sorry I cannot come down to Devon,' he said, kissing her forehead. 'I have much catching up to do and I thought Friday might be a good opportunity to fly up to Manchester to check on the restaurant project there. But I will take you out to dinner on Tuesday to make up for the disappointment.'

'That would be wonderful,' she whispered, tilting her head and offering him her mouth.

He brushed her lips with his own in a gentle kiss which gradually deepened. The sound of her mobile pulled them reluctantly apart. Locating her tote, she retrieved the phone and answered the call.

'CJ?' She frowned at the floor then raised her eyes to Marco, concentrating on what her brother was saying. 'She's what? When? Okay, I'll come straight away.'

She pocketed her phone and turned to Marco. 'I'm so sorry, I have to go; family emergency. My mother has been rushed to hospital.' She kissed him lingeringly on the lips. 'I'll keep in touch by phone; let you know what's going on. Thank you for the most incredible few days. I'll see you when I get back from Devon.'

'I hope it is nothing too serious.'

'We'll catch up this evening. I'll call you,' she promised.

Marco gave her a mute nod, watching as she grabbed her tote and overnight case and left. Moments later, as he watched her car disappear from sight around the corner of a nearby building his mobile rang again. He took the call, pacing, listening, his mood growing more angry by the minute. Ending the call, he snapped the phone shut and swore. Rossana was arriving tomorrow. Damn Thérèse to hell!

'Mum? Are you all right?'

Jenny opened her eyes and gazed up into the anxious face of her daughter.

'Of course I am,' she said, waving Charlotte away. 'It was nothing. I tripped and banged my head.' She raised a hand to her forehead and held it against the gauze pad on her left temple. 'Please stop treating me like an invalid.'

'Now, that's not the full story, is it? It happened because you fell down the stairs.'

At the sound of his voice, Jenny turned towards CJ standing by the other side of her bed, his eyes full of worry. She pushed herself into a sitting position and viewed the room.

'I want to go home,' she said stubbornly. 'We're extremely busy and I'm needed. This is silly.'

CJ's strong hand pressed on her shoulder. 'The doctor said you need to stay for twenty-four hours for observation purposes. You've had concussion, they need to be sure you're okay,' he said, his tone reassuring, 'And after all, what is twenty-four hours in the great scheme of things?'

'A lot when there's work to do,' she argued, visibly annoyed at her son giving her orders. 'I can't leave it all to Ella.'

'Ella doesn't mind,' Charlotte assured her. 'Besides, she can cope for one day.'

'But...' Jenny protested.

'No buts. Rest.' CJ was firm.

Jenny frowned up at him. 'You sound remarkably like your father. Oh, all right...' Reluctantly, she lay back on the pillows. 'But I warn you, tomorrow I'm out of here.'

Once out of the hospital, Charlotte pulled out her phone and dialled Marco's number. It tripped into answerphone and she left him a message updating him on the situation. By evening there had been no reply but she was not unduly worried. She figured he was probably busy or had flown up to Manchester early, and so busied herself packing for the trip to Devon.

Beth Reynolds opened the door and stood waiting. Watching from the bay window of her front room she had seen them coming along the road from quite a distance away, CJ carrying their luggage, Charlotte keeping pace with him, her tan tote slung over her shoulder. They were chatting animatedly, no doubt discussing Gulls' Rest and the plans she knew Lottie would have for it. Beth had heard the sale had fallen through and that the house had been resold within twenty-four hours. A mystery buyer she was told. Strange Charlotte had never mentioned buying it. It was all very odd, and she was determined to get to the bottom of it. There were questions to ask.

Regardless, it was great to have Charlotte back again to stay. She enjoyed her company and the bonus was she was going to be introduced to CJ, the brother she had spent years hearing so much about. A brother who appeared to look nothing like her friend at all. He dwarfed Charlotte, well over six feet she guessed, his straight fair hair bouncing off his forehead as he walked. A loose limbed and relaxed walk, the luggage appearing to give him little trouble as he carried it. Charlotte had told her he favoured her father in both colouring and facial features. Well, if this was true then Nick Kendrick must have been quite something to behold as a young man, she decided as he got closer.

Charlotte reached her first, throwing her arms around her in a close embrace. 'Beth! Oh, it is so good to see you,' she said, then stepped back to introduce her brother.

CJ smiled, a friendly open smile. He dropped the cases and held out his hand. 'Beth, I've heard so much about you.' His eyes met hers, a beautiful blue but not quite as striking as those of his sister. 'All good, of course,' he added.

Half an hour later, having settled in their rooms, Charlotte and CJ came downstairs to find Beth opening a bottle of red wine in the kitchen. Capturing three glasses from a nearby rack, she led them into the front room where the brightness of a cloudless January afternoon spilled over the carpet. When they were seated comfortably, Beth poured them each a generous measure of Merlot.

'So where did you manage to park?' she asked, as she handed the first glass to Charlotte.

'The Mayor's car park,' CJ replied, 'It's quite a hike but it seems the parking here is—'

'Diabolical, I know,' she finished the sentence for him with a grin as she offered him his wine. 'Even in winter months street parking is a bit of a no-no.' She turned to Charlotte. 'Did you pick up the keys to Gulls' Rest on your way here?'

Charlotte nodded. 'I can't wait to see it.'

'You've not been to look at it yet?'

Charlotte took a sip of wine and smiled at CJ. 'No, not yet.'

Beth gazed at her curiously. 'What's been going on, Lottie? It was sold subject to contract well before Christmas, yet you only told me you had it when you called to wish me a Happy New Year.'

Charlotte studied her wine for a moment then gazed across at her friend. 'Marco arranged it all. It was his Christmas gift to me.'

'*What!*' Beth's eyebrows lifted in surprise. 'You mean you and Marco

169

are…?'

'Together? Yes.'

Beth punched the air. 'Wow, that's the best news ever. I knew it would happen the moment I saw the two of you together, even though you were so keen to deny it and made it very obvious you didn't like him very much. Oh my God, Lottie, if he did that, he must think a hell of a lot of you.'

'We're taking things slowly at the moment,' Charlotte said, staring into her wine again. 'I've only been with him a short while. And apart from CJ no one else knows. I need to do this in my own time, Beth; no one knows what the future holds.'

Beth grinned. 'Oh, you needn't worry. I know a loved up man when I see one. Believe me, he's there for the long haul.' She eyed CJ curiously. 'And what do you make of all this?'

'I don't know much about romantic relationships but I have to say I do like the guy.' CJ nodded amicably as he smiled across at his sister. 'He seems very straightforward and honest, and if he makes Lottie happy, I'm happy too.'

'I like him too. Very much,' Beth agreed, putting down her glass. 'Now then, when are you going out to see the house?'

'Tomorrow morning,' CJ said, seeing Charlotte's nod of confirmation. He tilted his head enquiringly at Beth. 'Would you like to join us?'

'Oh yes, I'd love to. Would you mind, Lottie?'

'Of course she wouldn't,' her brother spoke for her, 'would you?'

Charlotte studied them for a moment then smiled and shook her head.

'No, I'd love you to come.'

The next morning, after breakfast at Alf Resco's, they headed for the car park to pick up CJ's black BMW. Twenty minutes later they turned into the driveway of Gulls' Rest. Charlotte was first out of the car, eager to unlock the door and explore this wonderful house which was hers now thanks to a man who Beth was convinced must be in love with her. She so wanted this to be, to have this warmth and contentment in her life. He seemed to embody everything good. He was rich but not self-important, he moved through life in a gentle but purposeful way, with impeccable manners and a grace that was almost other-worldly. As she had said to Beth, they had not known each other long, their journey had only just begun but if this did work out, it would be the most glorious thing to have ever happened to her.

Gulls' Rest was in urgent need of TLC. She had discovered the previous owner, an elderly man, had lived there for many years after his wife died. The house had become neglected and needed to be stripped back to the bare bones; a fresh canvas she could work her own creative imagination on with help from Beth and CJ and, of course, Marco. She reached the French doors. Trying each of the keys the estate agent had given her, she eventually found the one which opened them. Stepping out onto a large paved patio area, she gave a soft cry of amazement. The property was situated on a slight bend in the River Dart, the vista before her was even more breath-taking than the photo in the agent's window.

'Good grief, Lottie.'

She heard CJ behind her and knew he was appreciating what she was seeing. This was followed by, 'Oh, good heavens!' from Beth.

All three stood for a moment taking in the view: from the slow meander of glistening water making its way towards Totnes to the deep treeline sprawling down to the river's edge on the far bank. A handful of houses were just visible amongst the foliage, their windows lit with the golden fire of mid-morning sunlight, while hanging in the air above gulls called raucously.

'Ready?' Charlotte broke the silence as she turned to look at her brother.

'I am if you are.' He gazed down at her with a curious smile.

'Oh yes. I know exactly what I want done here,' she said, looking back into the house. 'Shall we begin?'

Lucy was sitting at her desk, going through the latest rider which had arrived. This time she was looking after Urban Fox, a new four-piece girl group Matt had recently signed. Having completed their debut album, he was about to launch their first UK tour. Jelly babies, she smiled to herself as she checked the list. Why amongst all the other requests did everyone seem to want jelly babies?

She had initially hated the thought of having to do this job – seeing to the needs of his stars had, at first, been demeaning for her, the boss's daughter. Her father had tricked her, appealing to her vanity by veiling a basic job with a fancy title, her own office and a car. She realised how easily she had fallen into his trap, so shallow and superficial was she in those days. Of course, today things were different; she had learnt how to be responsible, how to work as part of a team. And she had found friendship. Without exception, all her father's stars when they were in the building dropped in to see her for a chat or sometimes to coax her out for lunch. Jay had also been a big part of bringing about the change in her. At the start, she had thought she could wrap him around her little finger like all the other men she had known before him, and persuade him into dancing to her tune. But Jay was no pushover; instead he encouraged her to work with him. And work she did. Currently, she was in overdrive, still feeling an urgent need to make things up to her father after her foolish behaviour with Christian. To prove she deserved her promotion.

Christian. Well, what had happened there? She had no idea what exactly had gone on in the Caymans, but when he returned he had simply disappeared. No one, not even Jay, had any idea where he had gone. It was as if he had vanished from the face of the earth. All her father would say was that Christian was taking some well-deserved time off. Six weeks had passed and then this morning, out of the blue in he walked as large as life. She had braced herself for the salvo of sarcasm he normally shot in her direction every time they met. Instead, he greeted her with a smile and a compliment on what she was wearing. She had stood there robbed of speech as he walked past her in the corridor, knocked and entered her father's office. Knock? He never knocked; he simply shouldered doors open. It was a shame Jay was currently in Europe checking out tour venues, otherwise he might have been able to tell her what was going on.

She was stirred from her thoughts by the sound of a tap on her door. 'Come in,' she called, her eyes still scanning the rider. When she looked up she saw Christian standing in front of her desk.

'Are you busy or have you got time for a quick chat?' he asked.

She was stunned by the change; she couldn't believe he'd actually knocked and asked if she had time to see him. What a far cry from his usual barging-in bristling with bad temper and a string of complaints. But the Christian who was settling himself opposite didn't look like the man she remembered. This one seemed relaxed and friendly, his smile genuine.

'Sure, take a seat. What can I do for you?' she asked, finding her voice and a returning smile to go with it. 'Is it about the European tour?'

'No,' he said, leaning forward and resting his elbows on the desk. 'It's about lunch? Are you free today?'

Lucy stifled a laugh. 'Are you for real? Me and you – lunch?'

'That's the idea.'

She shook her head and laughed again. 'But you hate me, Christian. Why would you want to take me to lunch?'

His dark eyes met hers. 'Among other things, to apologise.'

'Has my father put you up to this?'

'No, of course not.' He sucked in a huge breath. 'I've been in rehab.'

Her eyes widened disbelievingly.

He nodded. 'Booze and pills! Your father has been incredible; I don't deserve it. But I'm back now and determined to put it all behind me, get back to being the person I used to be. And to kick it all off, I'm inviting you to lunch by way of an apology for the dreadful way I behaved towards you.'

His confession left her speechless, but it all made sense now. The mood swings, his overbearing and defiant stance with everyone. She remembered the evening at Little Court when he tried to propose to Charlotte.

'Okay, you have a deal,' she eventually acquiesced, then paused before asking, 'Are you going to apologise to Lottie too, or was what you did the real deal?'

'How do you mean?'

'Do you still want to marry her?'

'No,' he said, giving a firm shake of his head. 'I was in a really weird place then. God knows what she must think of me. Your mother has invited me down to Little Court in a few weeks' time. I'm hoping she'll see me then so I can try to make things right between us, but I don't hold out much hope.'

'You underestimate my cousin; she's a very compassionate person.' Lucy tried to inject some confidence into her tone. 'Once you've told her what you've told me I'm sure she'll understand. She'll forgive you, I know she will.'

'We shall see,' he said quietly. 'Now then,' he slapped his knees, seeming eager to move on from the topic. 'Getting back to lunch... the limo will be outside at twelve fifteen.'

'And where are you taking me?'

He grinned as he pushed himself from the chair. 'It's a surprise.'

'Will I like it?' she asked, watching him reach the door.

'Oh yes. I can guarantee you'll love it.'

TWENTY-SIX

'San Raffaello's,' Lucy said in surprise when the Evolution limo pulled up outside the restaurant. 'Have you been speaking to Marco?'

'I think he's the last person who would want to speak to me, don't you?' Christian answered, helping her step out of the vehicle.

'So how did you get a table so easily?'

'Matt, of course, he's the one with all the connections.'

Once inside, she surveyed the brick walls with their inlaid glass shelving full of pasta and different types of olive oil, the contrasting block prints and massive inlaid wine racks. Chrome, glass and mirrors had also been used to advantage, while polished wooden flooring beautifully complimented the mixture of light and dark seating, the suspended lighting illuminating each table on this dull January day.

'It's beautiful. You know, I've never eaten here before,' she commented, as they were shown to a private dining booth towards the back of the restaurant. She watched white-shirted waiters buzzing around the tables amid the delicious aroma of cooked food and chatter of diners filling the place. 'Slick, sophisticated and very Marco, don't you think?'

'Yeah,' Christian agreed, as his eyes panned around the restaurant. 'The guy's got great flair. The food's not bad either.' He gave a wicked grin.

Lucy laughed and settled down to inspect the menu, hoping she might be lucky enough to glimpse the famous Florentine Pagamo.

Lunch over, Christian called for the bill.

'Thank you.' Lucy folded her napkin with a smile. 'I've had a fabulous time.'

'And thank you for being such a good listener,' he countered, as the bill arrived. 'You must get Jay to bring you here.' He grinned. 'On second thoughts, I'll get him to bring you here once I get the padlock off his wallet.'

'Oh, come on!' Lucy gave an amused laugh. 'Jay's not mean, he's careful. There is a difference.'

Her comment made Christian laugh. Lucy observed him closely, remembering the raw twenty-year-old who had stolen a kiss from her in the corridor at Little Court all those years ago. She understood the fans' adulation – on stage he looked like some sleek tattooed panther, the lift of dark eyebrows over those mesmerising black eyes making him totally irresistible to women. As she watched, however, she saw his smile morph into a curious stare.

'What's the matter?' She swung around to see what had commanded his attention. Coming into the restaurant she saw Marco D'Alesandro accompanied by a young woman, a very beautiful young woman. They stood just inside the door for a moment while he introduced her to the head waiter, who bowed and smiled. Dressed in royal blue with a short black coat and very high heels, the woman tilted her head and gave him a deferential smile.

'Wow,' Christian exclaimed, watching as they were shown to a booth to one side of the restaurant. 'She is absolutely gorgeous! Great face, well stacked and the most amazing legs.'

Lucy frowned, watching as menus arrived and were handed to the couple. 'Do you think she's the mysterious Lauren?'

'The girlfriend? Could be...' Christian said, tucking a sheaf of notes into the embossed payment wallet. 'Whoever she is, he's one lucky bastard. Hey, I spy!'

The rear door of the restaurant opened and the head waiter appeared followed by a thin, dark-haired man in chef's whites.

'God, it's Florentine Pagamo!' Lucy gasped. 'She must be important if he's coming out to meet her.'

Florentine reached the table and Lucy watched as Marco introduced them, noticing the way the chef's face broke into a smile as he nodded. Again, the girl wheeled out a generous smile and stretched a hand coyly towards him. Florentine took her hand and kissed it graciously, obviously captivated.

'Oh, look,' Christian crowed. 'That little peach can wrap anyone around her finger if she chooses to. Whether she's Lauren or not, my bet is Marco's already had her in the sack.'

'Do you think so?' Lucy studied the girl curiously, still trying to make up her mind as Florentine returned to the kitchen.

'Definitely. Look at the way she's slipped her hand over Marco's arm. And, yes, he's bending his head towards her, helping her with the menu. Ah, she's touching him again. Now that sort of behaviour goes way beyond good friends, Luce, believe me.' He gave a roguish grin. 'She may look like a beautiful innocent but she is seriously hot totty. He is one lucky bastard.'

'And, of course, you're the expert.'

'Where women are concerned, you're looking at the master.' He gave a confident smirk as he checked his watch. 'And much as I'd love to stay and look at her all day, I'm afraid we have to go. You've a meeting with Matt at three, remember?'

As Christian pulled out his mobile to call the limo, Lucy eased out of the booth. Slipping her bag over her shoulder, she stood by him, waiting.

'Louis is on his way,' he said as he pocketed his phone.

'I guess we'd better pay our respects before we go.' Lucy tugged on his arm. 'Come on, I'm dying to find out who this mystery woman is.'

Marco watched Rossana across the table as she perused the menu, running a long red nail down each item one by one. She had arrived a little before noon at Heathrow, expensively dressed, her face made up and looking as if she'd stepped off the pages of *Vogue* – it was such a change he had to admit he hardly recognised her. He suspected, no knew, Thérèse was key to this dramatic makeover. This is what his stepmother had been up to since returning after the Christmas break. More disturbing was that ever since getting into the car with him, Rossana had become extremely demonstrative; she never seemed to stop trying to reach for his hand or stroke his arm. It was nearly as bad as her chatter. For the moment, in this public place he was tolerating her behaviour; later he would gently remind her of how he expected her to behave around him. There was no way he wanted to give Charlotte any unnecessary concerns.

Distracted by a sudden movement at the rear of the restaurant, he raised his eyes and froze. Christian Rosetti was standing by one of the booths talking into his mobile while waiting by his side with her back to the main restaurant stood a woman in a red suit. A woman with a mass of dark hair spilling down her back. Charlotte! For a moment his heart stopped – what was she doing here with *him*? She was supposed to be in Devon. When the woman turned he saw it was Lucy, and quickly chastised himself for even thinking it could have been her. Christian pocketed his phone and as they began walking towards the door, Marco realised they had seen him and were detouring towards his table.

'Marco!' Lucy greeted as they reached him. 'How delightful to see you. We've had a wonderful lunch. You must thank Florentine for us.'

'I will.' He smiled, his eyes resting on Christian, wondering what he was doing here lunching with Lucy. He'd been banned from Little Court and although Charlotte hadn't gone into detail, he knew there had been problems in Grand Cayman. But here he was looking fit and relaxed, his arm around Lucy's waist.

'Good to see you again,' Christian said.

Marco noticed Christian's normal disparaging glare was missing, instead his smile was warm and relaxed; there wasn't a hint of the usual hostility he had come to expect when they were in each other's company.

'Marco, you haven't introduced us,' said Christian, switching interest to his tawny haired companion who although holding on to Marco's wrist, had her eyes firmly fixed on him.

'Forgive me. This is Rossana Caravello. Rossana, this is Lucy Benedict and Christian Rosetti. Lucy is a neighbour and Christian Rosetti is... well...' He looked at her star-struck face. 'It's obvious you know who he is.'

'Yes, of course I do.' The girl's pink mouth parted with a breathy sigh, her wide eyes dancing in admiration. 'My godmother took me to see you in Munich last year. She's a huge fan of yours. I am too, of course, and you were brilliant. It was such an exciting night. I loved all the candles—'

'Thank you,' Christian interrupted with a mock bow, his eyes clashing with hers.

'Rossana is my stepmother's house guest,' Marco explained. 'She has flown in from Milan and will be staying with us at the manor for a week.'

Rossana took her eyes off Christian for a moment and nodded in agreement then flew back to him like iron filings to a magnet.

'Pleased to meet you,' Lucy said. 'I'm sure our paths will cross during your stay.'

Rossana's attention flitted to Lucy. 'Oh yes, I am sure they will. I think Signora D'Alesandro plans to have you all over for dinner while I am there. Am I not right, Marco? It will be so exciting. I never get invitations to dinner parties. It will be good to be able to get to know everyone. I...'

This was the first Marco knew of this. Irritated Rossana had managed to learn of such family arrangements first, he simply nodded in agreement, not wishing to appear the fool. This was not good, Rossana was beginning to become an embarrassment with her silly waffling; he could already see amusement hiding behind Christian's friendly gaze. He gave her a reproachful look which immediately halted her chatter mid flow.

'Well, it's great to see you both,' he said as Vittorio materialised at the table with his pad ready to take his order. 'You must both come again; have a meal on the house.' Heaving a sigh of relief, Marco picked up his menu and gave a nod to his head waiter to indicate he was ready.

'Thank you, Marco.' Lucy touched his shoulder in appreciation and gave Rossana the benefit of one of her gracious smiles. 'And I look forward to dinner at the manor. I am sure my mother will be anxious to invite you all back.'

With a hand raised in farewell to Marco, Christian followed Lucy out to the waiting Mercedes.

Watching them go, Marco knew without doubt Lucy would be on the phone to Charlotte immediately to tell her about their meeting; the girl was an avid gossip. But picking the bones out of what had taken place, he decided it had all been quite harmless: Rossana had been introduced as his stepmother's guest, something Charlotte already knew. The fact he had not been in touch with her since they parted on Wednesday morning was, if anything, going to be the main issue. The truth was, with Rossana's unexpected arrival and an instruction from Thérèse to show her around London, plus his backlog of post-Christmas work, he had not had a moment to himself. As Vittorio walked off to the kitchens with their order, he promised himself once he had dropped Rossana off at the Dorchester later, he would make his call to Charlotte a priority.

Lucy was out of her meeting by four thirty. Returning to her office, she fished out her mobile from her bag and dialled. On the fourth ring Charlotte answered.

'Lottie, it's me – Lucy.'

'Hi, how are you?' Charlotte sounded unusually bubbly and upbeat.

'I'm fine. How are things going down there?'

'Wonderfully well.' The exuberance in her voice surfaced fully. 'CJ loves the place and he's got everything in hand. I think he's looking forward to the challenge. Oh, Lucy, you must come down and see it. I'm sure Beth would like to meet you too.'

Lucy was taken aback. Charlotte had always kept Beth to herself; she had been someone who occupied the other, more personal side of her cousin's life. In a funny way she felt honoured; for the first time in her life Charlotte seemed to be opening up and coming out of that private shell of hers.

'Thank you, Lottie, I'd love to,' she said pleasantly. After a moment's hesitation she launched into the real reason for her call. 'Actually, I've something important to tell you. It's about Christian.'

'Christian?' She heard the hesitancy in her cousin's voice. 'What now?'

'He's coming down to Little Court to spend the weekend.'

'Matt and Ella have allowed him back? Are you serious?'

'Totally. Listen, he wants to see you.'

'Why? What have you been up to now?'

'Me? Nothing. You'll never believe where he's been during the past six weeks? In rehab.'

'So your father hasn't—'

'Sacked him? No. Dad thought he needed help. Lottie, he's an exceptional talent and now he's back to the way he was. He's straightened himself out.'

Charlotte gave a derisory snort. 'Well, there's a first, Lucy Benedict. What's got in to you after all the damage he's done you? How can you be so easily taken in by his lies?'

'Lottie! He wasn't lying. I had a meet with Dad this afternoon and when I asked him, he confirmed everything Christian told me. He even sorted out the rehab for him at Lakeside. Anyway, if you want proof he's changed, wait for it... he took me out to lunch today.'

'He did what?'

'Yes, and he apologised. We spent such a lot of time talking. He told me everything, even what happened in Grand Cayman. He's full of remorse about the engagement thing too. All he wants now is for you both to be friends again.'

Charlotte walked over to the window, her mobile pressed against her ear. Outside, dusk was gathering over the estuary, the wide sweep of grey gleaming water contrasting with the dark silhouette of trees on its far bank. A few seabirds were still visible in the darkening sky. If this house had captured her imagination on paper, it had delivered far more in the flesh. She felt at peace here; but now part of her old life and unfinished business had intruded.

'Well, okay,' she agreed, knowing if Christian was coming to Little Court she would not be able to avoid him. 'If everyone else is happy then I guess I'll have to see him. But there is no way I'm back to how things were. Please make him understand that, will you.'

'I don't think he expects that, Lottie. In fact, he wasn't even sure you'd agree to see him.'

'Do you know when he's planning to visit?' Charlotte asked, not fooled by Lucy's last comment and wanting to be able to prepare herself.

'Some time in February. Currently he's doing some promo stuff for the new album. I told him you were away in Devon this weekend. Oh, and before I forget...' Lucy's voice rose excitedly.

'What?'

'He took me to San Raffaello's for lunch and Marco was there.'

'He was? I thought he was in Manchester.'

'Manchester? Who told you that?'

'CJ.' She covered herself with a lie. 'Thérèse mentioned it when he was over at the manor earlier in the week.'

'Listen, Lottie, he had a young woman with him.'

'Yes, Thérèse mentioned that too; they've got some house guest staying,' Charlotte replied, realising Rossana must have arrived early and wondering whether that was the reason Marco had not contacted her. Since they parted on Wednesday morning his phone seemed to be permanently switched off.

'Yes, Rossana Caravello,' came Lucy's reply. 'Lottie, she's absolutely gorgeous. Christian couldn't take his eyes off her.' She giggled. 'He thinks Marco has already slept with her. We were watching them and she couldn't keep her hands off him.'

Charlotte closed her eyes and leaned her head against the window as she digested Lucy's words. She drew a deep breath, remembering what Marco had said: *If they did not have trust between them everything else was pointless.* And Lucy was prone to exaggeration; it was best to ignore her.

'Lottie, are you there?' came Lucy's anxious voice.

'Yes, sorry. CJ's waving at me. I've locked him out and he's making faces through the French doors. I'd better go and let him in, it's started to rain.' Charlotte eyed the wet slashes against the window, balancing her lie with an element of truth.

'When will you be back?'

'We have finished all we came to do so CJ will be coming home tomorrow. I'm planning stay on with Beth, make a girls' weekend of it.'

'I'll see you Monday then.'

Charlotte closed her mobile and wandered back to the window, staring out into the darkness which had now descended over the landscape, her thoughts running in circles. So Christian was off the hook and if Lucy was to be believed, a much reformed character. But the thing which gnawed at her most, although she was anxiously trying to control it, was Lucy's words about Marco. It was no good; she could not let this rest she had to find out. Opening the phone again, she punched in Marco's number. He answered on the third ring.

'Marco, hello! Got you at last.' She greeted him in her normal light and friendly way. 'How are you?'

'I am fine. How are things at the house?'

'Going very well', she replied brightly. 'CJ is on the case. I am so pleased with his ideas. Marco, I was concerned, you haven't called or responded to any of my messages. Is everything okay?'

'Yes, it is. Charlotte, I am so very sorry. I should have kept in touch but it has been so difficult.' She heard him draw in a sharp breath. 'Thérèse called moments after you left to say Rossana was arriving. Neither my father nor I were aware it would be so soon. Please forgive me. With her and work I have not had a moment to myself, but I will make it up to you when I see you again, I promise.'

'Apology accepted. I'm sure I can wait until Tuesday.'

'Tuesday?'

'Yes, you are taking me out to dinner, remember? So if you're looking to make things up to me I insist on champagne,' she teased.

'I am sorry I cannot see you on Tuesday.' He sounded strange, panic-stricken. 'In fact, I will not be able to see you before Rossana returns to Italy on the eighteenth. My time is completely taken up with her at the manor next week. I am driving her down there tomorrow.'

'Oh, Marco, no. Surely you can spare one evening?'

'Unfortunately not. Thérèse has organised a schedule. It appears Felica will look after her during the day and I will take over for the evenings. She is insisting I drive back from London every night. It is a complete nightmare and I am not happy but I as have agreed to help my father, I cannot refuse.'

There was a pause; she heard muffled conversation as he went off the line for a moment then he was back.

'I am sorry, I will have to go,' he said with an unusual abruptness. 'Someone is here to see me.'

'I'll wait to hear from you, then,' Charlotte said, hiding her annoyance behind her patient tone.

'Enjoy your weekend and give Beth my love.'

'I will. Goodbye, Marco, I…'

The line went dead. He had cut her off.

Charlotte closed her phone and returned it to the tote. Something about all this made her feel uneasy. Although she had been looking forward to a weekend with Beth, she knew home was where she really needed to be. Staying here, the uncertainty would only eat away at her and make her a miserable weekend companion.

* * *

She made her apologies as they sat in Alf Resco's eating dinner that evening.

'Oh, don't tell me... Marco's back early from Manchester?' Beth looked at CJ and grinned.

'No, no, it's something I need to sort out for work. Something I forgot,' she lied, wanting to avoid any awkward questions.

CJ smiled widely. 'Excellent! You'll be able to join us for dinner at the manor tomorrow night.'

'Dinner at the manor?' Charlotte looked at her brother in surprise, trying not to show her unease. 'When was this arranged? Lucy didn't mention anything when I spoke to her earlier.'

He pursed his lips and shrugged. 'I've no idea. All I know is the office contacted me this morning with a message from Thérèse asking me to phone her urgently. When I called back she invited me to dinner, said the rest of the family would be attending. Apparently, it's to welcome their house guest from Italy. When I said I would let you know, she said she understood from Lucy you were staying with Beth and thought it kinder not to disturb your arrangements.'

'So she told you not to tell me?' Charlotte queried, anger bubbling.

'In not so many words. I'm sorry, I didn't think. I knew you and Beth had plans and, well, she said the last thing she wanted to do was to spoil your weekend.' He frowned across the table at her. 'Lottie, are you all right?'

'Yes, yes I'm fine.' Charlotte painted on her best smile as she picked up her wine glass. She wanted so much to believe in Marco's honesty, that somehow, like her, he was an innocent party caught up in all this intrigue surrounding Rossana. However, the last forty-eight hours had left many worrying questions which required answers. Tomorrow night when they joined the D'Alesandros for dinner, one way or another she would know exactly what was going on.

TWENTY-SEVEN

Charlotte and CJ were nearly home. They had left Dartmouth at seven, Beth insisting they at least get some coffee and toast into their digestive systems before they left.

The previous evening, after they had finished their meal they had returned to Beth's. While CJ decided on having an early night, the two women had sat curled up in comfortable armchairs in front of a log fire, drinking more red wine. It had given Charlotte the opportunity to tell Beth about Rossana. They had sat for well over an hour pulling the whole thing to pieces, trying to make sense of what was going on.

'You know, I've come to the conclusion we can talk about this all night,' Beth had said. 'It won't make any difference. Until you actually get home and see the situation for yourself you can't possibly know what is going on. Lottie, I can't believe he'd trick you, especially not after doing what he did for you with Gulls' Rest; it doesn't make any sense. '

Of course Beth was right, as she usually was about everything, Charlotte thought as CJ's car approached the top of Hundred Acre and dropped down the hill under a brown winter canopy of interlocking tree branches. It was best to reserve judgement but despite the advice, after her experiences with Christian the worry would not go away.

The village lay peaceful in the valley, smoke from the cottage chimneys floating out towards the contours of the hills to the south. Moments later, the vehicle was slipping through the gates of Little Court. As the house came into sight she focussed on what she planned to do next. Jet needed to stretch his legs; her time away meant her horse had been either cooped up in his stable or let loose in the paddock for nearly a week. And afterwards, she would take a relaxing bath followed by lunch with the family. Everyone would no doubt be eager for details of the Dartmouth trip. CJ pulled up at the front door, deposited her there with her suitcase and left to garage the car. As she walked into the hall and climbed the stairs to her room the clock on All Hallows' church tower chimed the half hour. She checked her watch: ten thirty.

Leaving her case to be unpacked later, she quickly changed into jodhpurs, shirt and a thick sweater. On the way out of her room, she collided with Lucy.

'Lottie!' Her cousin's eyes were wide with surprise. 'I thought you were spending the weekend in Dartmouth with Beth?'

'Changed my mind. I decided to come back for the meal,' Charlotte said airily. 'After all, it is a family invite to welcome Rossana. I thought it might look rude if I wasn't there.' She observed Lucy's riding clothes. 'Are you going out or coming back?

'Going. Want to join me?'

'Why not?'

'Talking about Rossana,' Lucy took up the conversation as they descended the stairs, 'I saw her last night. I happened to drop into the Arms on an errand for Mum and they were all there having a drink.'

Charlotte looked at her with surprise. 'Really? Why would they drive all this way for a drink? The Dog and Fox is Higher Padbury's local.'

'Maybe it's because Marco is friendly with Stuart. Oh, but do you know what?' Lucy's face creased into wicked amusement. 'Kayte O'Farrell was behind the bar and, well, if looks could kill. Rossana was all over Marco again and Kayte was watching them like a hawk.'

This was the second occasion Lucy had reported the girl's over-familiar behaviour around Marco; Charlotte began to feel distinctly uncomfortable. She stopped and turned to face her cousin.

'Lucy, can I ask you something?'

'Of course?'

'About dinner this evening... Why didn't you mention it when we spoke on the phone?'

Lucy shrugged. 'Because at the time I didn't know. Thérèse phoned Mum yesterday afternoon, it was all very last minute.'

'Oh.' Charlotte gave a thoughtful nod. So everyone had been given a last minute invitation except her. Who wanted her out of the way? Thérèse or Marco? Well, one thing was certain – this evening's dinner would most certainly give her the answers she was looking for.

Jed Marks, the groom, had their horses saddled for them in no time. Soon they were trotting down the High Street in brilliant sunshine with a clear blue sky above, and out towards open countryside where they turned up towards Fox Cottage and galloped along the edge of the barley field towards Hundred Acre. The wood, its trees painted with frost, soon welcomed them into its depths. In parts it was carpeted with the deep bronze of fallen leaves and in more sheltered areas huge clumps of snowdrops had begun to make an appearance.

Charlotte took a deep breath of crisp, clean air as she emerged through a gap between two large beech trees and reined Jet in. This was the view she loved, a place where she could sit and watch the whole of the valley. The village nestled below, the red brick majesty of Little Court to the left, and to the right, pale and golden, Willowbrook Farm, livestock grazing in its surrounding fields. She watched as a train clattered through on its way to Taunton, and in the distance the bleating of sheep carried across the valley in the morning's stillness.

'Brilliant, isn't it?' She turned to her cousin who nodded in agreement.

'Yes, there's nowhere on earth like this, is there? I've been trying to persuade Jay to come down for the weekend but he always seems to be busy.'

'Does he ride?'

The question seemed to amuse Lucy. 'I think Jay's only riding experience has been restricted to the occasional seaside donkey as a child.' She giggled.

'You and I could teach him, you know,' Charlotte added with a smile. 'Who knows, he might be a natural.'

'You're on…' Lucy grinned after giving the matter her consideration. 'I'll mention it when I next…'

From deep in the wood a woman's scream rang out, followed moments later by shrieks of laughter.

'Whatever was that?' Lucy swung around in her saddle, staring back into the trees where sunlight dappled against bare trunks. 'Do you think someone's in trouble?'

'I'm not sure. Let's find out, shall we?' Charlotte turned Jet back into the wood, Lucy following.

Marco stood impatiently over the girl sprawled face down on a pile of damp grass at the foot of a large oak tree. Her insistence in staying where she was and giggling hysterically was beginning to annoy him.

'For goodness' sake get up, Rossana.'

For the thousandth time he cursed his stepmother. Felica was supposed to have been taking her riding today but for some reason Thérèse had decided to send her on an errand into Abbotsbridge instead. To have had to put up with half an hour of Rossana's ceaseless twittering was bad enough, but now she had fallen off her horse. It was a deliberate move done, he guessed, in order to get herself in close proximity to him. He grimaced as he remembered yesterday evening in the Somerset Arms.

Thérèse and Felica had been sitting on the opposite side of the table unable to see what the rest of the pub could: Rossana's sly little hand constantly trying to capture his. To get away from her he had made excuses to go to the bar to speak to Stuart, only to find himself under the hostile glower of Kayte. Everything, it appeared, had gone from bad to worse since his arrival home.

There was to be a dinner this evening in Rossana's honour and all at Little Court had been invited. He had reminded Thérèse that CJ and Charlotte were in Devon and although Charlotte had intended to spend the weekend with Beth, he knew after the disappointment of their cancelled Tuesday evening, she would welcome the chance to return to be with him. It appeared, however, she did not, for over breakfast this morning Thérèse had informed him of her decision to stay in Devon. He had shrugged off the information, not wanting his stepmother to see the disappointment in his face. He hoped Charlotte had not done this deliberately, angry with him because he had cancelled their dinner date. Upon returning to his room, he had called her.

Finding her mobile switched off, he was about to leave a message when Thérèse had appeared and asked him to take Rossana riding.

'Please get up, Rossana.' He leaned forward, offering his arm as he tried to hang on to the last shreds of his patience.

She rolled over and grasped his hand. Hauling her to her feet, he tried to release her but he found himself immediately ensnared as she leapt at him and locked her hands behind his neck.

'Thank you, Marco, you are a true gentleman, and I think you should have a reward for such gallantry.' She pulled him enthusiastically into her embrace.

He pushed her away immediately but as he did their bodies shifted and they toppled against the oak's thick trunk. With his back against the tree he found himself trapped again as she placed her hands on his chest and tried to bring her mouth to his. Clasping her hips, he shoved her away but not before he glimpsed a rider a few yards off to his right, partially hidden by undergrowth.

'Damn!' he hissed under his breath as he watched the shadowy rider depart, wondering who it could have been. Had Kayte been following him? He would not put it past her.

'Get back on your horse, Rossana,' he ordered, bending down to retrieve his crop. 'We are going back to the manor. I am fed up with your improper behaviour.'

'Please do not be angry with me,' she pleaded, turning innocent green eyes up to him.

He thought she might be about to burst into tears. 'You have to stop this,' he said, lowering his tone. 'It is not appropriate, I hardly know you. I am trying to be pleasant, to make your stay enjoyable, as is Felica, but I cannot have this constant pawing. Now come along, get back on your horse, please.'

Rossana did as she was told and followed him silently down through the wood.

'Rossana's behaviour is absolutely dreadful, throwing herself at Marco like that,' Lucy commented, as they cantered out of the wood and down the track towards Fox Cottage.

'Why are you defending him? He wasn't exactly resisting, was he?' Charlotte remarked cuttingly. 'Did you see the way his hands were resting on her hips? He was enjoying every bloody minute of it, the bastard.'

The wretchedness in her cousin's voice caused Lucy to pull up suddenly. She twisted around in the saddle to look at her, taking in her distraught expression. 'Lottie, what's wrong?'

Charlotte took a deep breath and used her gloved hand to stem the wetness gathering in her eyes.

'Oh no, have you been seeing him?'

'Yes,' Charlotte answered dully, staring down at her hands, absently adjusting the reins through her fingers. 'I thought he was different. I trusted him. But now I see he is no better than Christian. Bloody men!'

'Oh hell!' Lucy said loudly. Spotting Fox Cottage in the distance, she grabbed her cousin's reins and dug her heels into her own mount. 'Come on,' she said, coaxing Jet forward, 'the cottage is up ahead. You and I need to have a talk.'

Returning to the manor, Rossana watched Marco hand over his horse to the groom and stride off towards the house. She felt totally downhearted. Thérèse had helped her with her appearance, even provided a maid who travelled with her, and had also told her Marco would respond to warmth and affection but she had been wrong; all it seemed to do was make him angry.

She needed to find Thérèse as soon as soon as possible – she would know what to do. She followed Marco into house, relieved to find her host in the hall.

'Is something the matter, Rossana?' Thérèse asked. 'Marco does not seem very happy.'

Rossana made a face. 'He does not like the way I keep touching him. I am trying to be warm and affectionate as you advised, but he says it is inappropriate. I have a feeling... I think maybe he is thinking of his girlfriend too.' She shook her head miserably. 'It is all so difficult. I think perhaps I should give the whole idea up. It is not working.'

'Do not even think of it, *cara mia*.' Thérèse thought for a moment. She had heard Charlotte was back from Devon and intended joining them for dinner. Although unexpected, this might well work in her favour, she decided, as the beginning of a plan formed in her mind. She patted Rossana's shoulder.

'Come up to my room, we have things to discuss.'

Arriving from the kitchen with coffee, Lucy found Charlotte staring out of the front window across the black expanse of the barley field. She joined her, handing her a mug, and after a contemplative moment's silence turned her face towards her cousin.

'So when did it all start?'

'A couple of days before Christmas.' Charlotte exhaled loudly and took a sip of her coffee. 'He took me out to dinner and then he asked me to spend some time in London with him when he returned from Tuscany. That's where I've been most of this week.'

'Men are so bloody awful,' Lucy said, staring into her mug, 'You start a relationship, open your heart to them, and then find out everything they have told you has been a pack of lies.'

'Ethan?'

'Yes.' Lucy's expression hardened. 'He bowled me over, I honestly thought he loved me. That it was one of those glorious love-at-first-sight things. And why shouldn't I have believed? After all, he asked me to marry him, told me how happy we were going to be. Even decided how many kids we were going to have.'

'Would you feel better if we talked about it?'

'Hey, I'm supposed to be the one lending a shoulder for your problems, remember?'

The trace of a smile crossed Charlotte's face. 'Yes, I know you are but something tells me you've never actually opened up to anyone about what went on, have you?'

Lucy shook her head. 'Mum and Dad weren't interested. Their foolish daughter was back, that was all that mattered. And the scam, of course.'

Charlotte went over to sit by the fireplace, patting the empty seat beside her. 'Why not do it now? You know, the whole big confessional thing. To me.'

'Oh, Lottie, you're such a good human being, but you must stop putting other people before yourself.' Lucy came over to join her. 'We will talk about Ethan, I promise, but some other time. Right now I want to hear about you and Marco. Let this be your confessional. Get everything out of your system, and I mean *everything*.'

'Are you sure we have enough time for this?' Charlotte asked, turning to look at the mantle clock, whose hands were showing a little after eleven thirty.

'Yes, we have,' Lucy insisted. 'For something as important as this we have all the time in the world.'

The Little Court vehicles arrived at the manor around seven thirty. Charlotte was still angry with Marco and determined to get some answers from him, but joining the family for this dinner invitation she was putting her feelings on hold. She had come back especially from Devon to be there and her behaviour, she had told Lucy earlier, would be exemplary. Lucy had said that she thought her cousin was very brave, that she admired her and was not sure whether, given the same circumstances, she could have adopted such a lady-like stance. On the contrary, she would probably have been tempted to throw something over him.

They were greeted at the door by the manor's housekeeper, Madeline, who took coats and showed them through to the heavy-beamed ceiling drawing room with its mushroom-coloured carpet and expensive furniture. Following her mother and Rowan through into the vast room, Charlotte found herself face to face with Thérèse.

'Charlotte! Darling, you look wonderful,' Thérèse said, brushing

Charlotte's cheek with a welcoming kiss. 'So glad you could make it.'

Although Charlotte accepted the embrace with good grace she sensed duplicity in Thérèse's friendly welcome. However, she did not want to make assumptions about guilt until she had fully appraised the situation here. Marco and Rossana's arrival was required first. She would know by their body language if anything was going on. And so she made polite small-talk with her hostess for a few minutes before moving on into the room to accept a glass of wine from Madeline.

Glass in hand, Lucy joined her. Charlotte smiled, sensing a new and special bond building between them. A few moments later, Felica arrived, her face lighting up as she saw them both and walked over to join them. While the rest of the Little Court guests including CJ went off on a tour of the new ground floor extension, the three girls bagged a settee and chatted as they drank their wine.

Felica admired Charlotte's outfit. 'You look wonderful. Red for danger – it really suits you.'

'Thank you.' Charlotte accepted the compliment graciously.

Earlier, Lucy had insisted on taking her into Taunton to find something suitable for the evening. The stunning red V-neck, three-quarter sleeved dress they had decided upon fitted Charlotte beautifully, enhanced her colouring and accentuated her curves. To this, they had added a pair of high, black patent shoes and a small matching clutch bag. Returning home, Lucy had put the finishing touches to the outfit: the loan of some pieces of plain understated platinum jewellery from Ella's collection. The end result was exactly the statement her cousin was looking for – Charlotte looked fabulous.

'Is anything wrong? You seem upset,' Charlotte asked, seeing Felica's smile fade.

'I am. Very. It appears our guest of honour will not be here this evening. She decided she wanted Marco to take her to the cinema instead.'

'What! When we've all dropped everything to be here tonight?' Lucy snapped. 'Didn't your mother object?'

Felica shrugged. 'Not at all. It appears what Rossana wants Rossana gets. They are planning to eat out afterwards too, so I am not sure they will be back in time to meet everyone.'

'If it was simply me here,' Lucy continued crossly, 'I would be walking out right now.'

'But we're not, Luce,' Charlotte countered, a gentle hand on her arm. 'The whole family is here, and this is not Felica's fault. She's not the one to be angry with.' She sensed the possibility that Thérèse's reluctance to intervene meant she had had a hand in all this.

Lucy studied her cousin's face for a moment then turned to Felica. 'I am sorry, Lottie is right, it is not your fault.'

'I am afraid we are having a difficult time here at the moment,' Felica confided. 'Rossana is a very immature seventeen-year-old. She behaves like a small silly child with all her whims and crazy ideas. She has no idea about manners and social graces and I am not sure we will change her while she is with us. But let us not dwell on the subject.' She reached out to Charlotte, touching her arm lightly. 'Marco has confided in me about your relationship with him.'

'Relationship? Rather an ambitious word, Felica,' Charlotte said. 'We shared some time in London before and after Christmas, that was all. As I understand it he's with Rossana now.'

'What are you talking about? Marco is not *with* Rossana,' Felica's brows knitted together in a frown. '*You* are the woman in his life. In fact, he has asked me to take Rossana to Taunton on Wednesday so he can spend the day with you. He is not—'

'Felica, there's something you ought to know,' Lucy interrupted. 'We saw Marco and Rossana up in Hundred Acre this morning. They were leaning against a tree, they were kissing.'

'No! I cannot believe this of him.' She met both their nodding heads with a determined shake of her own. 'Not after how he said he felt about you. No, I know my brother, Charlotte. He never lies.'

Lucy cocked a dubious eyebrow. 'Perhaps you don't know him as well as you think.'

Felica opened her mouth to respond but the sound of voices beyond the door indicated the tour was at an end and everyone was returning.

'Well,' said Thérèse, entering the room, her benign gaze falling on the three young women, 'and what have you all been chatting about?'

'Oh, I have been telling them about my summer collection, Mother.' Felica replied, looking at her with an innocent smile.

'Yes, it's very exciting,' Lucy enthused. 'I can't wait to see it.'

'And there will be a show at Little Court in April, which is absolutely brilliant. We're all so looking forward to it,' Charlotte gushed, adding a snippet of information she had picked up from Ella.

With a benevolent smile Thérèse moved through the room with her usual graceful sway to talk to Madeline, who had arrived to announce dinner was ready.

'Leave things with me, Lottie,' Felica whispered. 'I will speak to Marco. Believe me, he is innocent, I know it.' She got up, straightening the skirt of her dress before joining her mother.

'Do you believe her after what we saw?' Lucy whispered curiously.

Charlotte's head swam in confusion. 'I don't know,' she said, 'I really don't know.'

As they took their places around the huge rectangular dining table, Thérèse slipped her napkin onto her lap and said, 'I apologise once more for the fact our guest of honour will not be with us tonight.' She glanced down the table, engaging each of her guests with a gracious smile. 'Marco has taken her out for the evening. In the short time Rossana has been here they have become very close. In fact, I feel he is quite smitten with her.' Her eyes landed on Charlotte, her smile full of self-satisfaction.

Charlotte digested Thérèse's words as she buttered bread on her side plate and concentrated on the soup placed in front of her. She had no idea who in this house was telling the truth. But after witnessing the scene in the wood there was, she realised, only one conclusion she could come to – that Marco *was* involved with Rossana, Thérèse was aiding and abetting him and, although she refused to accept it, like herself, Felica was being lied to.

TWENTY-EIGHT

Rossana sat opposite Marco in the small Italian restaurant in Abbotsbridge, picking at her cannelloni and feeling quite miserable that the new tactics Thérèse had suggested did not appear to be working. They had gone to the cinema to see *Romeo and Juliet*. It was a modern version with Leonardo DiCaprio which Thérèse had recommended. What Rossana had not bargained for was that the film, although set in modern day Verona, had a dialogue which was pure Shakespearian. It was all way above her head. Aware of Marco's much vocalised dislike for physical contact, she had sat quietly in her seat watching and wishing with all her heart he had the same passion for her as Leonardo had for his on-screen Juliet. Relief the film was finally over had washed over her when the credits rolled.

She had suggested a meal after the film and as it was Saturday, knew there was no way he would be able to use the excuse of having to be at home because of London and work the next day. Of course, as always, he had acted the complete gentleman, taking her coat, settling her in her seat and trying hard to make polite small talk. She had attempted to respond but even on the simplest of topics felt totally out of her depth. It was yet another disaster and the reasons were now glaringly obvious. Although she now had the looks and the clothes, she was simply boring and unworldly, a distinct disadvantage for anyone wanting to impress any man, much less a good-looking one like Marco D'Alesandro. The blame for this she placed fairly and squarely on her sheltered upbringing with Edoardo and Monica.

Quiet by nature and slow to make friends, she had gone from a life of an unwanted child shut away in private education in Switzerland to luxurious incarceration with her aging aunt and uncle. Her uncle had engaged tutors, she was driven everywhere, and for the most part cocooned against the outside world. There had been one brief moment of freedom when her outrageous godmother Zeta Ancona had taken her to one of Christian Rosetti's concerts; other than that, her life remained unfulfilled and dull. And so she had filled her loneliness with romantic novels, dreaming of a saviour who would rescue her: a strong, handsome man who would marry her, someone with whom she could live happily ever after.

The invitation to live with the D'Alesandros had come completely out of the blue. How her uncle had managed to persuade someone else to take her she did not know, but she welcomed it. To Rossana, escaping from her gilded cage into normal family life with young adults a little older than herself had been the answer to a prayer. Seeing Marco for the first time crossing the lawn that afternoon, it also appeared her dream had become reality. Now she knew that was not the case.

Dessert and coffee came and went and then Marco was calling for the bill, and after helping her into her coat, he followed her out of the restaurant to where his car was parked. All she wanted now was to reach the solitude of her room to be on her own, out of his impatient company. Twenty minutes later they turned into the gated entrance to the manor and the Porsche cruised through the parkland towards the house. As they pulled up outside she noticed a couple of vehicles parked a short distance away.

'Our dinner guests are still here,' Marco observed. 'I had better take you in and introduce you. After all, the purpose of inviting them here this evening was so they could all meet you.'

Rossana shivered under the sting of his disapproving words; he clearly thought her spoilt and ill-mannered wanting to go out this evening. If only he knew Thérèse had insisted she do this. She longed to tell him so he would think better of her, but it was impossible. To do so would make him aware of Thérèse's involvement, and she had been very insistent her support in the quest of her stepson should remain a secret.

As they reached the front porch the area was suddenly flooded with light and the door swung open. The guests, it appeared, were about to leave. Rossana did not know whether this was a good or bad thing but reasoned at least they would be introduced briefly before heading for their cars. The damage Marco believed her guilty of would be limited.

Thérèse appeared, her eyes lighting up as she saw them both. 'Well, well, what excellent timing!' she purred, stepping back. 'Our guests are about to depart. Did you have a good evening?' She beamed at Rossana then seeing her expression, stretched out to place a reassuring hand on her shoulder. 'Don't look so worried,' she said, smiling, 'everyone understands the reason you two wanted to be alone this evening.'

Rossana noticed the glare Marco gave his stepmother.

One by one the guests filtered out. Clinging to Marco's arm as if a storm were about to sweep her away, Rossana smiled and nodded as she was introduced, while imprisoned in her grip, he acknowledged them all as they passed. Then two young women emerged. One she recognised as Lucy, the other, dressed in scarlet, could easily have been her twin apart from the unusually brilliant blue eyes, eyes which scanned her face before glancing down to where her fingers tightly gripped Marco's upper arm.

'Charlotte!' Marco's dark eyes widened with surprise. 'What are you doing here? I thought you were spending the weekend in Devon with Beth.'

'Obviously.' The woman's frosted stare moved from his arm to his face, then without another word she hurried by to join Lucy as they began making their way towards the cars.

So that was Charlotte. What had Thérèse described her as? Ordinary? Plain? Merely a silly infatuation? A small niggle of apprehension wormed its way into Rossana's brain as she noticed the expression on Marco's face. Watching the beautiful sophisticated young woman depart, she saw only a deep painful longing in his dark eyes. No wonder he behaved the way he did – he was in love with her. Thérèse had lied! How could she be so cruel?

Untangling himself from Rossana's grip, Marco ran to catch up with the two women.

'Charlotte, please wait,' he called after her.

Standing in the wake of Matt's car accelerating away, she whirled round to face him.

'I am sorry, I honestly had no idea you would be here,' he said when he caught her up, automatically reaching for her hand. 'Thérèse told me you were planning to stay the weekend with Beth.'

Charlotte avoided his touch, her expression icy. 'Do you honestly believe I would have done that in preference to seeing you? I was deliberately left off the guest list tonight, Marco. Of course, when your plan to keep me away failed, I'm guessing it was Thérèse who arranged for you both to be absent tonight to avoid any embarrassing scenes in front of my family.'

'Plans? Embarrassing scenes?' He tilted his head back uneasily. 'I do not understand.'

'Don't play the innocent with me, please,' she said bitterly. 'I am not quite the gullible fool you think I am.'

As she turned to go, Marco took a step after her only to find Lucy blocking his path. She had the same cold appraising scowl as Charlotte; he wondered what the hell had happened.

'Hundred Acre Wood, this morning…' Lucy said frostily. 'Now do you understand what you've done? Leave Charlotte alone, she's had her fill of liars.'

'That was you watching? What have you told her?'

'We both saw you.'

He shook his head slowly. 'It wasn't what you thought. I can explain.'

'It's too late, the damage is done.'

'Get out of my way,' he bellowed, pushing Lucy aside and rushing after Charlotte. She had now reached CJ's car and was standing by the passenger door. As he approached she turned to face him.

'Charlotte, please listen. Nothing has changed. What you saw this morning I can explain. My feelings for you are…' His next words were lost as someone gripped his shoulder from behind. He swung round and found himself facing CJ.

'Get in the car, both of you,' CJ ordered, throwing the car keys to Lucy before turning his attention back to Marco. 'Keep away from my sister.' He waved a warning finger at him. 'I'm not a violent man but if I catch you bothering her again I won't be held responsible for my actions. Is that clear, you two-timing bastard?'

Marco nodded. The last thing he wanted to do was to make the situation any worse. Still glaring at him, CJ slid behind the wheel, the engine fired and the car left at speed, its tail lights soon lost in the distance. Slowly, he made his way back to the house.

Thérèse stood waiting for him on the porch. 'Marco,' she called, her voice laced with concerned innocence, 'what has been happening?'

'Don't play games with me, Thérèse.' He pushed past her and into the house. 'You know as well as I do you are responsible for all this. Stop throwing Rossana at me; I do not want her!'

Felica had thought it best to take Rossana up to her room away from the confrontation she saw brewing as she watched CJ striding purposefully after her brother. Returning to see what had happened, she reached the landing and nearly collided with Marco heading for his room. She reached out to stop his progress, searching his face for any sign of bruising amidst the look of fury.

'Did he hit you?'

'No, he merely warned me to keep away from Charlotte.'

'What will you do?'

'I do not know.' He ran a hand through his hair. 'Right now I am tired. I have suffered an evening of endless pointless chatter and all I want to do is sleep.' He moved towards the door of his room, pausing to look at her as his hand reached for the handle. 'But one thing I swear to you – whatever your mother has planned I will not let Charlotte go.'

The next morning there were questions around the breakfast table at Little Court. Matt had left for a round of golf and Jenny and Rowan were en route to a local plant wholesaler. Alone with the younger members of the family, Ella felt it was time they had a talk.

'Would somebody like to tell me what happened at the manor after we left last night?' she asked, looking across the table to where the three sat.

Lucy looked at CJ and then at Charlotte, wondering who should act as spokesperson. It was always best to come clean with her mother, she decided, and on this occasion even more so. Thérèse and Felica were in business with Little Court, there would be no room for atmospheres or bad feeling. Ella would have to know the details. Taking Charlotte's silence and CJ's nod as an indication she should speak first, she raised her eyes to look at her mother.

'Lottie has been seeing Marco.'

'I see.' Ella's eyes turned to her niece. 'Charlotte?'

'I've been seeing him for a few weeks,' she answered quietly. 'When he returned from Tuscany after Christmas, we spent some time in London together. He led me to believe we were in a relationship. But as you can see from last night, it appears we are not. He is with Rossana.'

'Last night after you left there was a slight incident,' CJ said uncomfortably.

'An incident?' Ella looked at each in turn. 'Then perhaps you had all better enlighten me. I have a meeting with Thérèse tomorrow and if she decides to raise the issue I need to have all the facts.'

Today, Charlotte thought as she stared out across Little Court's lawns, she should have been returning from Devon but instead here she was at home, kicking her heels. Lucy had left after breakfast yesterday to join Jay for her flight to Sydney; she was missing her already. She thought how lucky Lucy had been to find someone like Jay – strong and supportive in times when you needed them. But then, Lucy had always been the lucky one, always falling on her feet.

After breakfast, when all the others had left, she went to her room to call Beth and update her on what had happened over the weekend. Beth was very upset; clearly she set great store in her ability to recognise the good guys from the bad ones. Accepting Marco's fall from grace had been very difficult for her. As Charlotte finished her call she heard a car pull up outside. Looking out of her bedroom window, she saw Thérèse getting out of her Range Rover, briefcase in hand. The passenger door opened but instead of Felica it was Rossana who got out. *What was she doing here?*

Charlotte made her way quietly to the galleried landing above the great hall. As Helen let them in, Ella arrived, her eyes fixing on the girl with a look of surprise – obviously she was not expected. Too far away to hear all that was being said, she caught only slivers of conversation. The word *birthday* was mentioned several times. All through the conversation Ella's face was an impassive mask. Damn, Charlotte thought, she would not learn any more until dinner this evening. And then...

'Well, this is a surprise. A birthday and an engagement all in one party. What date are we looking at?' Ella's voice had risen in tone.

Thérèse smiled. 'The twenty-first of September. I think Little Court will make a grand setting for this double celebration. I want it to be a party to remember.'

'So where is your fiancé-to-be this morning?' Ella turned her attention to Rossana. 'I would have thought he would have been here too.'

Rossana did not answer, instead looking blankly at Thérèse.

'Oh, Marco is busy with work commitments,' Thérèse offered quickly. 'He was quite happy to leave all the arrangements to us, was he not, Rossana?'

The girl gave Thérèse a wide-eyed look then nodded.

Charlotte could stay no longer. Anger bubbled up within her. Why had he been trying to tell her nothing had changed when all the time it was clear Rossana had never been simply a house guest? His father had chosen her for his wife! Hurrying back to her room, she changed into her riding clothes, anxious to be away from the house, needing to find her own private space. Leaving through the back kitchen, she hurried to the stables and saddled Jet.

Within half an hour she was at Fox Cottage. She tied Jet to a nearby tree and then let herself in.

'What I do not understand,' Felica said as she let her horse pick its way carefully through a boggy area of Hundred Acre, 'is why Mother decided to take Rossana to Little Court this morning. Was it to show her the boutique, do you think? And if that was the case, why did she not want me along?'

'I am not sure I am bothered,' Marco offered, reigning in his mount as they reached the ridge which overlooked the valley. 'I am thankful I can spend the morning with you and not that aggravating girl.'

'It is not her fault really,' Felica reasoned. 'I know she has had a crush on you since she arrived, but I don't think how she is around you is the way she normally behaves. She is very introverted and naïve. I have a feeling Mother has put her up to this.'

'I am certain she has,' he said, as they came out of the wood and reached the track down to Fox Cottage. 'And in doing so has let loose an inexperienced young woman with no sense of proper behaviour. You are right, it is not her fault and in some ways I feel sorry for her, but I dare not show any weakness otherwise she will interpret it as an open invitation. Whatever I say I do not seem to be able to put her off. In fact, it makes her more determined.' He expelled a frustrated breath. 'Charlotte is furious with me, and after CJ's threats how will I ever get an opportunity to explain? It is hopeless.'

Felica looked at him and smiled. 'I think it is not as hopeless as you think, big brother. Look!' She pointed. 'Do you see what I see? Jet is tied up outside the cottage.'

Marco's face brightened. 'So he is.'

'Come along then, let us go and talk to her.'

Charlotte opened her eyes. The music had been soothing, a beautiful classical piece by Bach ideal for relaxing to. But now something else intruded into the melody – the sound of horses' hooves. Pushing herself up from the settee, she walked to the front window to look out. The lane was empty; she had missed whoever was passing. Turning back into the room with thoughts of returning to the music, she froze.

'What the hell are you doing here?' she demanded, seeing Marco dressed in riding gear standing in the kitchen doorway.

'I came to explain,' he said softly, 'about Saturday morning.'

'There is no need, I'm aware of what I saw.' She glared at him, feeling hot under his gaze.

'What you *thought* you saw.'

'Marco, I do not want you here,' she said, stepping over to the CD player and ejecting the disk. 'What we had is over, I—'

'No, Charlotte.' He closed the gap between them, his fingers closing around her upper arms. 'Please do not say that. You must believe me. I have no interest in Rossana, none at all. I had to go with her on Saturday evening, rude or not. That is what Rossana wanted and Thérèse was insistent I took her.'

Angry and reluctant to believe a word he was saying, Charlotte was all too aware of the familiar warmth of his hands triggering a prickle of heat through the whole of her body. He was too close, his physical presence unsettling. She lifted her eyes to look at his face, seeing only raw hurt lingering there. *He wears his feelings on his face*, Beth's voice came echoing into her brain...

'Let me go!' She pushed him away, knowing the potential those brown eyes had to confuse her thoughts. 'How can you stand there and lie? How can you say you want me when your stepmother has been at Little Court this morning giving Ella her requirements for Rossana's eighteenth birthday party. A party which will also celebrate your engagement? Tell me, Marco, how?' she screamed.

'Engagement party?'

She spun around. Felica was standing there with a look of bewilderment on her face. 'Marco, what is going on?'

'I honestly do not know.' Marco shook his head, his expression furious. 'But whatever it is, I am about to put a stop to it once and for all!' With a sharp intake of breath, he stalked from the room leaving Charlotte and Felica to stare at each other in stunned silence.

Thérèse left Little Court feeling very pleased with herself. The whole engagement issue was at a very tentative stage and there was a lot of work still to be done before Marco and Rossana were eventually together, but they would be. Charlotte was completely out of the picture now; her own anger coupled with her brother's threats would make sure Marco was an unwelcome visitor at Little Court or anywhere else in Charlotte's proximity.

She smiled at Rossana sitting quietly beside her. 'Happy now?'

'Yes, but I do not understand.' The girl shook her head. 'How can we be talking of an engagement on my birthday when Marco does not even like me?'

'Ah, but now Charlotte understands she is no longer in his life he will, *cara mia*, he will. I promise soon he will have eyes for no one but you.'

'But I saw the way he looked at her last night. How can I even dream he would want me when I can see how he feels about her?'

'I keep telling you, he is not in love with her. He is infatuated; it will pass.' Thérèse reached out and patted Rossana's hand. 'You are an innocent in this world, with little experience of love. Believe me, what has gone on between Charlotte and my son is like a firework display – something which burns brightly and will end quickly. Trust me, to fall in love properly it is best to go slowly. That is how we will proceed and in time he will be yours. Now, my dear, to celebrate let us make a day of it, shall we? Lunch, I think, and some shopping.'

'Yes, I would like that.' Rossana smiled, trying to hide her discomfort. She wanted Marco more than anything else in the world but she sensed perhaps Thérèse was being a little too confident about the situation. Maybe it was true Charlotte was no longer a problem, but the biggest obstacle had yet to be overcome – getting someone to fall in love with you when even a fool could see they didn't even like you very much.

Unsaddling her horse, Felica looked up to see Marco approaching the stable.

'Where have you been?' she asked, heaving the saddle onto a rack. 'Have you sorted things out with Mother?'

'Not yet. She called Madeline to say she was taking Rossana for lunch and then shopping. She will be gone a while.'

'I am glad your temper seems to have eased,' she said, noting his calm expression. 'Maybe it is better you are having the time to cool off before she gets back. It would be unfortunate if Rossana was caught up in all this.'

'Why do you always defend her when she is the cause of it all?' Marco demanded, leaning his shoulder against the stall.

'It is only that I sense if she were alone with her crush she would have accepted you do not want her by now, there would be no problem,' she said, concentrating on unbuckling the bridle. 'Instead, it is now clear Mother is very much the one who feeds the fire by giving approval to all she does and encouraging her with some ideas of her own. Might it not be better to deal with *her* rather than Rossana?'

'Do not worry, I have sorted everything.' Marco's handsome face broke into a broad smile. 'Soon everything will be back to normal.'

Felica turned to him curiously. 'Why, what have you done?'

'Wait and see.'

'Lucy, are you sure this is wise? I mean, do you honestly want to stay *here*?'

Jay gazed up at the exterior of the Sydney Park Hyatt with an uneasy feeling. He stared at the entrance, remembering the moment back in September when a young woman in a blue dress was being led out of the hotel by two plain clothed policemen. But now it was January, and alongside him Lucy was back to attend an identification parade and wearing a most determined expression on her face.

'Of course I do, that's why I booked it.' She stared at him as if she didn't understand what his problem was. 'The views are to die for. When I was here before I absolutely loved it.'

'Yes, Luce, but when you were here before—'

'Jay, be quiet.' She leaned across and kissed his cheek before pushing open the door of the taxi. 'Believe me, everything is going to be fine.'

Jay joined her on the pavement, taking charge of the luggage. Not quite sure what she was up to, he followed her into the hotel. In his book, revisiting a place where you'd had a bad experience was not exactly a very sensible thing to do. But then, since when could anything Lucy did be labelled sensible? At times she was one crazy woman, impetuous, even scatty, but heaven help him, he loved her even though she was not aware of his feelings or ever likely to be.

The manager, a red-headed, thick set forty-something, appeared and fussed around her as they registered at reception. Jay waited patiently, recognising him from when they had been there in September. It wasn't until they were in the lift he allowed himself to relax a little. They'd had a long flight, he was tired which, he thought, was probably to blame for the uneasy feeling he had. In the back of his mind he still had this niggling doubt something here would trigger the kind of sad memories she might have trouble coping with. He hoped he was wrong.

TWENTY-NINE

Thérèse pulled up outside the manor and killed the engine. She got out and went around to the rear of the vehicle and opened the tailgate. Rossana joined her, her faced filled with excitement. They had driven all the way to Bristol for their afternoon's shopping and the rear of the car was like an Aladdin's cave full of clothes and shoes. She had never had so many wonderful things in her life. The selection which Thérèse had purchased for her prior to her arrival in England had now been tripled. Her favourite item was a full-length leather coat in a beautiful light tan with a matching pair of high boots. She remembered the astonishment on the shop assistant's face when they purchased not one cashmere sweater, but several in different colours. Mrs D'Alesandro's American Express card appeared to have no credit limit and nothing, it seemed, was too expensive. If Rossana wanted it, she got it.

'Thank you again,' Rossana said, looping the bags over her arm. 'I am so excited. I think I now love shopping very much.'

'You can never have too many clothes,' Thérèse replied, slamming the tailgate closed. 'And we must have you looking your best for Marco, mustn't we?'

'Yes, of course.' With a nervous laugh, Rossana trailed behind the older woman to the front door. As they entered the hall a smiling Madeline walked across to intercept them.

'Mrs D'Alesandro, you have a visitor.'

Thérèse brow creased in puzzlement. 'A visitor? Who? I was not expecting anyone.'

'It is your husband.'

'Gianni? Come, Rossana, let us go and welcome him.'

Gianlucca was sitting in the drawing room, absently running his fingers over the keys of the grand piano which sat in front of the French doors. Feeling the smoothness beneath his fingers he remembered his youth when all his thoughts were of a musical career. But the death of his older brother had changed the direction of his life, propelling him into the role of heir to the D'Alesandro leisure empire. It had been hotels at the time; now under his careful guidance it encompassed health spas and restaurants as well. He looked up as his wife entered the room; immaculately groomed and looking as she always did: glamorous. Her mouth parted in a smile as she crossed towards him.

'Thérèse, darling.' Getting to his feet, he embraced her, kissed her forehead, then stood back and smiled at the quiet figure hesitating in the doorway. 'And Rossana, *cara mia*, come here. You look well. Have you been enjoying yourself?'

She dropped her shopping and hurried towards him. 'Oh yes, very much,' she said as he folded her into his warm embrace.

'Gianni, what brings you here?' Thérèse seated herself on one of the sofas as he fussed over Rossana. 'Do I gather you have at last found time to see the manor?'

Gianlucca broke away from Rossana. 'Yes, I would like to see what you have been doing, but it is not my only reason for being here.'

Thérèse cocked her head inquisitively.

'I have come to take Rossana and Felica away on a trip.' He looked down at his young charge and smiled widely.

'Honestly, Gianni, could this not wait until the end of the week when she flies home to Italy?'

'Sadly, no, it is already booked. We fly out early in the morning. I am planning to take them skiing.'

'Skiing? Have you lost your mind?' Thérèse's eyes flared. 'How can you be so insensitive?'

'I would like to go,' Rossana's bright, insistent voice joined, her face spiked with enthusiasm. 'I know what you are thinking, Mrs D'Alesandro, but my parents were killed in a helicopter crash, not on the ski slopes. Both were accomplished skiers. I would love to learn and hopefully someday be as good as they were.' She turned her beautiful smile on Gianlucca. 'And I will have Felica to keep me company. It will be fun.'

'And Marco, of course,' Thérèse added. 'He is a first class skier. It will be good for him to join you.'

Gianlucca walked over to the French windows, his hands in the pockets of his expensive slacks. Then he turned to face the two women. 'Sadly, I cannot spare Marco, I need him here.'

'But surely the restaurants will be fine for a week?' Thérèse protested. 'And if there is a problem he has a mobile and he can easily fly back.'

'We are not going for a week, Thérèse, we are going for a month.'

'A month!' she gasped. 'I do not understand.'

'I am taking the girls to Canada. We will spend some time skiing and then we will do all sorts of other things. Niagara Falls. City visits. We may even drop over the border into America, I am not sure yet. Part of the reason for my journey is to spend time visiting my Midnight Sun hotel chain, but I also feel the need to take my foot off the gas for a while.' He gave her a warm smile. 'You would be welcome to join us.'

Thérèse shook her head. 'It is impossible; I have too much to do.'

Her gaze floated across to Rossana, who was watching Gianlucca in awe. She could see the girl was completely sold on the idea. Her thoughts swirled for a moment, wondering if she could still persuade him to include Marco but soon realised nothing she could say would now sway him. He was too strong willed, damn him. But then a question bounced into her mind. Why now?

201

Rossana had only been here for three days, why couldn't he have left it until the weekend?

'Rossana,' she said softly, 'go and find Madeline and ask her to help you up to your room with the shopping, will you. I need to have a word with Gianni.'

Rossana left the room obediently, returning moments later with the housekeeper. They swiftly gathered up all the bags and then disappeared, Madeline closing the door behind them.

Thérèse turned on her husband. 'What is the meaning of this? Why couldn't you wait until the weekend? Why does it have to be now?'

Gianlucca seated himself on the piano stool once more, his fingers caressing the ivory keys. 'Why does it matter to you when I take them, Thérèse?' His eyes fixed on hers. 'Do you have plans or maybe schemes I appear to have interrupted?'

She stepped back uncomfortably. 'I do not know what you mean.'

'Oh, yes, you do – a birthday party which will also see her engaged to Marco. What nonsense have you been feeding the girl?'

'You have no idea, do you? You, the man of business, the man who always gets what he wants. Only you and I know she is here because you hope to make a favourable impression in order to persuade her to let you buy a stake in the Alba Dorata vineyards when she inherits them. Has it not occurred to you if we can get Rossana and Marco together, you don't even have to think about the purchase of a mere stake? You will have them automatically through marriage?'

'Have you gone mad?' He closed the piano lid and got to his feet. 'Whatever do you mean?'

'Unless you have forgotten, I have Edoardo's niece under my roof as a favour to him. She is an impressionable young woman I have sworn to look after and treat with respect. It appears you have taken a mere suggestion and decided to use her and my son in a rather stupid and, may I say, pointless plan. I keep telling you, it was merely something which cropped up in a conversation between two old friends concerning the *possibility* of investment, nothing more. You go too far.'

'Gianni, I have worked damned hard to—'

'Push my son together with a young woman he does not want.'

'How do you know he does not want her?'

'Because he told me, and because he is furious you have gone behind his back like this. It is bad enough you have set up this fiasco of a party, but you also give the girl expectations you have no hope of fulfilling. It is insane!'

'How did Marco know about the party? Ella Benedict was the only other person with me when this was discussed. If she told him, I'll have her head on a plate for breaching client confidentiality!'

'You do Mrs Benedict a disservice, my dear. What you should not have done in your eagerness to organise this folly is to have discussed it so publicly. It was Charlotte who overheard you.'

'Charlotte Kendrick...' Thérèse hissed through gritted teeth, 'I might have known!'

'Stop your mischief, Thérèse. Marco is a grown man. He knows his own mind and his heart. By deliberately pushing him into Rossana's path you do more harm than good. Leave him alone. Now, if you'll excuse me, I need to find the girls. We leave immediately.'

Thérèse watched the door close feeling as if she were about to explode. She would not be swayed from her goal: Marco and Rossana *would* be together, and Gianni, despite his protests, would get the vineyards she knew he secretly wanted. However, anger was not the way, but a steely determination to continue with her plans was. It was all about being patient and waiting for the right opportunity to present itself and the moment would come, of that she had no doubt.

As soon as Charlotte returned from Fox Cottage she went to her room and packed for London. She was not due to be there until tomorrow, but she had work to do and this was no longer a place where concentration was easy. After phoning Matt to say she intended staying in the city overnight and would be using the company's penthouse, she advised her mother and aunt of her intention and the reason behind it over lunch. Both were very quiet. She half expected Jenny to take her aside for some pearls of wisdom before her departure. Thankfully that had not happened.

Leaving a little after three o'clock, her mood seemed unwilling to lift as the motorway took her nearer her destination. She had always been a quiet individual, meeting her problems head on and overcoming them by working through the pain. And now she had her biggest challenge because she was hurting in a different way – she had never truly been in love before. Love, her inner self scoffed, a foolish wasted emotion, bearing in mind the man she thought she knew had, like Christian, been a consummate actor. Maybe, that same inner self reasoned, you are not angry through loss of love but rather, you have been made a fool of once again. Thinking about it, she was not sure which was true. Perhaps it was a little of both.

Evolution's apartment had been created on the top floor of their West London offices. Both Matt and his partner, Baz Young, had thought it useful to have somewhere to stay over when, as it often did, work took them well into the evening. Matt called it a crash pad but, Charlotte thought as she let herself in, that was rather a conservative term, given the luxury of its furnishings and fittings. Tired from her drive, she needed to relax her body as well as her mind, so the first thing she did was to run herself a bath before pulling a bottle of Chardonnay from the wine fridge. Pouring herself a generous glass, she took it through to the bathroom.

An hour later, having slipped into jog pants and a loose top, she retrieved the bottle from the fridge and settled down on one of the soft couches to go through the paperwork for tomorrow's meeting with Matt. With the accompanying strains of the Three Tenors in the background, she began her slow check of the figures she had compiled for his new shelter business plan. She was punching figures into her calculator when she thought she heard a door close in the hall. Lifting her paperwork off her lap and onto the couch, she went to investigate. As Matt had made no mention of calling in, she wondered whether it might be Baz. As she reached the living room door it swung open, and for the second time that day found herself facing Marco D'Alesandro.

'How the hell did you get in?' she demanded furiously. Besides the family, the keypad combination was known only to Baz and a few key staff.

'I have friends in high places,' he replied. She took this to mean that Matt had been the culprit.

'Charlotte, why did you run away from me?'

'I did not run away. I came up here because I have work to do.' She indicated the paperwork spread across the couch.

'But why here?'

She glared at him. 'You have to ask that after this morning? How could I have possibly concentrated on anything there after hearing about your engagement?'

'There is no engagement, Charlotte.' The calmness in his voice was at odds with the flare of exasperation which lit the depth of his eyes.

'And I'm expected to believe that, am I?'

'Why is it you do not? Why do you not believe me?'

'Because I have been subjected to one lie after another. How did you refer to her? Homely? Pleasant? She is beautiful! Since we parted company last week you've been deliberately avoiding me. What has happened over this weekend between you and her shows me quite clearly you've played me for a fool. Why couldn't you just have been honest and simply told me that your father intended her for you all along? Knowing that would not have made it any less painful but at least I'd have had some respect for you.' She shook her head, fighting back her tears. 'You are such a bloody coward, Marco.'

'Charlotte, I am telling you truth, if you will only listen,' he pleaded.

'Oh, for God's sake!' she threw at him, erecting a barrier of anger around her pain. 'Just go, will you. I can't bear to look at you a second longer.'

From somewhere deep in the soft leather depths of her tote her mobile came alive. Glad of the distraction, she moved across the room and extracted it. It was Felica.

'Charlotte, I'm sorry for leaving it so late to contact you but it has been a crazy day,' she said, her voice competing with the background echo of a public address system. 'I am calling from Heathrow.'

'What are you doing there?'

'I am with Father and Rossana. They are buying perfume in the airport shop at the moment so I need to be quick. I do not want Father thinking I am plotting like Mother by calling you; I am supposed to be impartial. Charlotte, you must listen. Marco has put everything right, as he said he would. When he left us he called Father. He flew in immediately to stop Mother's interference. He was very angry with her and is taking Rossana and me away to Canada on holiday for a month. This should give you enough time to make your peace with Marco. My father is a good man; he understands.' There was a pause and then Felica said, 'I must go, they are coming back. Let my brother back into your life. Please… He cares for you very much.'

Charlotte closed her phone and expelled a lung full of air. Felica's words left her head spinning. Turning back to speak to Marco, she found the room empty. Had she really expected him to be still standing there after she had demanded he leave? As if in answer, she heard a car engine fire below and looked out of the window to see the Porsche backing out into the road. Pulling on boots and grabbing her car keys and coat, she locked up and left.

Thirty minutes later she arrived at his apartment in time to see the electric garage door begin its slow descent. Quickly locking her car she ran, ducking under it before it closed. When she reached the lift, she could see it had already stopped at the second floor. Waiting for a few moments, she pushed the button to call it back down.

Taking a deep breath, she steeled herself for that first moment when he opened the door and saw her, and wondered what his reaction would be. And then the moment arrived and she was standing outside the pale ash front door of his apartment, her finger on the bell. This time the tables were turned – she was the one coming to explain and, of course, apologise. How would he react after having borne the brunt of her anger and scorn? Once more his words came back to her: *If we have no trust between us everything else is pointless.* Well, she had showed precious little faith in him, he would probably think…

As she heard the click of the catch, Charlotte braced herself. The door opened and there he stood, looking at her.

'Marco, I'm so sorry,' she began, feeling her eyes fill. 'I have been so foolish. I—'

'Shh…' Pressing a finger against her lips, he drew her inside and closed the door. Slipping her coat from her shoulders he let it drop to the floor. Then taking her in his arms, he brought his mouth to hers in a gentle kiss before releasing her.

'Felica phoned. I knew you would come,' he whispered into her hair.

'But aren't you angry with me?' she said, looking into his eyes and seeing only warmth in their brown depths.

'No. Your reaction was understandable. Thérèse has been very reckless and everyone has been caught up in the chaos she has created. You, me,

Rossana.'

'Rossana?'

He nodded. 'She is a young girl with a crush and for some reason Thérèse has decided to exploit the situation. I do not know the purpose behind the need to see me engaged to her.' He shrugged. 'But now it is at an end. She knows better than to go against my father's wishes.'

'So that means…?'

'We can return to how we were. It is time to celebrate.'

'Celebrate?' Charlotte echoed. 'How?'

'In the best way possible, of course,' he said, smiling as he took her hand and led her towards the stairs. 'In bed.'

Jay could not believe it was all over. He followed Lucy out of Sydney's City Central Police Station and into brilliant late afternoon sunshine. After a morning's sightseeing and a leisurely lunch they had arrived at Day Street to undertake the identity parade. Now the task was over he was amazed how calm she appeared to be. As he hailed a cab to return them to the hotel she reached out and laced her arm in his.

'Right,' she said, grinning broadly. 'Let's go celebrate, shall we?'

Once in the taxi she seemed to lose some of her sparkle, clutching her cream Lulu Guinness bag and silently watching the cityscape as the taxi motored back towards the hotel.

'Lucy?' Jay put a hand on the edge of her shoulder. 'You are okay, aren't you?'

'Yes, I'm fine, really I am.' She slotted her hand over his and patted it, looking across at him with the same smoky light brown eyes her father possessed. 'I know I wanted to do this but it was so strange, you know, seeing someone I once thought I was going to spend the rest of my life with.'

'You loved him, didn't you?'

'Yes, I did, but that was me then,' she said calmly, her eyes fixed firmly on him. 'The me now is an entirely different person. I realised when I saw him how shallow things had been back then. I let a handsome guy with a great body and a persuasive tongue sweep me off my feet simply because of those three things: his looks, which now leave me cold, his physique and his ability to bullshit. And bullshit it was. Empty, false gestures, merely a device to relieve me of a large amount of money, the sort of experience to make me wary of men and future relationships. But now I know differently. Now I realise falling in love is about the feelings you have for someone you know well, someone you really care for and who cares for you. I was very naïve; I'll never ever be that kind of girl again.'

'I'm pleased to hear it, Miss Benedict,' he said, slipping a comforting arm around her shoulder and pulling her tightly to him. 'And at least you've got most of your money back. I hope they are all going behind bars for a long time.'

'Oh, they are,' she smiled with satisfaction. 'They most certainly are.'

She had identified each and every one of them as they were lined up behind the one-sided mirror; something she had insisted on doing. Coming all this way, she wanted to face the flesh and blood versions of her last foolish action, but more than that – to take one last look at Ethan. All six, including the chauffeur Randall and Jack's secretary, stood in a silent row. Quiet and impassive, their blank gazes were fixed ahead, faces devoid of expression. She had no idea if they knew it was her standing there appraising them. In fact, it seemed they cared very little about anything.

When they entered the hotel, the red-headed manager intercepted Lucy with a smile and led her away to the far end of the lobby, stopping to have a quiet word out of earshot. He guessed Lucy was probably letting him know what had happened. They parted with reciprocal smiles and she walked over to join him once more and took his hand.

'Let's go up to my suite,' she said, leading him towards the lift.

'But I thought…?'

'What, that we'd have a drink in the bar? No, Jay, this celebration is important. Very important.'

Perplexed, he stood quietly as they rode up in the lift. His suite was on the floor below. The location suited him; it would have been very difficult to have spent last night in an adjacent room to her, although he had lain awake for some time, thinking about her alone in her bed, her black curly hair spread across the pillows, skin touched by the soft moonlight spilling through the window. Cursing himself for such foolish and hopeless thoughts, he followed her down the corridor to her suite.

A bottle of Dom Perignon nestled in a metal ice bucket on a table in one corner of the room.

'Would you like to do the honours?' she asked, as she disappeared into the bedroom, pulling off her jacket as she went.

Undoing the wire and tearing off the foil, he released the cork, capturing the golden foam in the first of two flutes placed next to the ice bucket. As he filled the other glass, she returned, having changed into a vest and sweat pants, her feet bare. She took the proffered glass with a smile. It was then he noticed the letter she was holding.

'It certainly is a day for celebrations,' she said excitedly, touching her glass with his. 'I brought this with me; it's the icing on the cake. Dad said I wasn't to open it until after I'd been to Day Street. This letter,' she waved it at him, delight in her eyes, 'means I can now move on. It's from my father to confirm that from the first of April I'm going to be working with Joss Livingstone.'

'Head of Media? But I thought—'

'I know. Dad said I had to do the hospitality thing for a year, but he's been so pleased with me he's letting me go early.'

Jay stared into his bubbling champagne glass. He was going to lose her. He knew it would have happened anyway but he had believed he still had another six months of her company. Now it appeared that was not to be. In helping Lucy it had enabled him to keep her close, but he now realised it had also given her the support she needed to learn the job much quicker. Although she came with a reputation of being work-shy, he had to admit she had tackled her responsibilities in a most determined way, and he couldn't begrudge her this moment of triumph, even though it meant she'd be gone and he'd probably not see her around very much once Joss took her under her wing. Raising his eyes to hers, he composed his face into a smile.

'Brilliant news, Luce. You deserve this promotion, you honestly do, and I know you'll do well.' He touched his glass against hers again. 'It won't be the same without you, though.'

'I'm not going anywhere, Jay,' she said softly. 'I'll still be here.'

'Of course you will. Maybe we can even grab lunch together sometime, eh?'

'Yes, I'd like that.'

Trying desperately to mask his feelings, Jay found a seat and sat listening while she chatted about the things she hoped to be doing in her new role, accepting a couple of top-ups, knowing there was no way he could escape immediately. He would simply have to dampen down his emotions until it was appropriate for him to leave.

Eventually, he set his glass down on the table and checked his watch before getting to his feet.

'I'll leave you to it, then. It's five thirty already and you'll no doubt be wanting some time to yourself before we go down to dinner. Eight o'clock in the bar okay?' He needed to get out of her room right now and flee to the tranquillity of his own where he could lie on his bed and indulge in his own private heartbreak. Tomorrow they would be returning home and once there, everything would be back to normal. He was due to fly to Amsterdam at the end of the week, to begin sorting out venues for a possible Northern European coast tour for one of Matt's other acts, something which would guarantee to keep him out of circulation for a couple of weeks. And as for tonight? Well, he would cope with her company over dinner, numbing his emotions with a healthy intake of wine.

He was at the door when he heard her calling him back. He turned to find her staring anxiously at him, biting her bottom lip.

'Jay, I'm so rubbish at this. I may have got this new very responsible job but at times I feel I'm still the same scatty, self-centred, pleasure-seeking air-head I used to be.'

He studied her with a bewildered shake of his head. 'Oh, Lucy, that is the last thing you are. It took real guts to go in and see Ethan in the flesh when you could simply have looked at mug shots. I thought you were very brave.'

'Actually, there was another reason why I wanted to come here to do it,' she said, lacing her hands in front of her. 'It was because of you.'

'Me?' He stared at her. 'I don't understand.'

'It was the only way I could get you on your own, away from everyone else.'

'Oh, I get it. You wanted me to be the first to know about your new job.'

'No, you idiot.' She crossed to where he stood and grabbed him by the shoulders. 'I wanted to tell you I love you!'

'You? Love me?'

She nodded, staring up at him from under her long lashes. 'You're like no one I've ever known, Jay. You're amazing, simply amazing, and I'm absolutely crazy about you.'

Jay's mind spun in confusion; this was the very last thing he had expected from her. He shook his head slowly, drawing his fingers through his mass of thick blond hair as he digested her words.

'Hell, Luce, I don't know what to say.'

'Oh God!' she groaned, stepping away from him, her hand grasping the back of her neck. 'I can see the embarrassment in your face. I've read you all wrong, haven't I? All you see me as is a best mate, isn't it?'

His laughter filled the room as he raised his eyes to the ceiling. 'Best mate? Oh, girl, how wrong you are. Come here.' He pulled her tightly against his body, happiness flooding deep into his soul as he wrapped his arms around her. 'Close your eyes.'

She frowned up at him curiously. 'Why?'

'Because I want to show you what I think of my best mate.'

Without any more protest, she obeyed. Jay smiled as he stared down into the face of the woman he had grown to love so much. His fingers gently brushed her cheek as he lowered his head, claiming the kiss he had dreamed of for so long.

THIRTY

Stuart Harper was serving a couple of regular customers when Marco D'Alesandro arrived. Josh Moon, the replacement cook for Kieren, had joined them just before Christmas. Both Stuart and Terri had never been involved with food – Kieren had been a real find; a self-starter who had slipped seamlessly into the Somerset Arms kitchen when they had first taken over the pub. Josh, a lanky twenty-something, although technically sound, needed some inspiration from an accredited source and Marco, growing up in the restaurant business, had agreed to come in and add a little sparkle to the menus.

Stuart poured Marco a glass of chilled white wine and placed it on the bar in front of him.

'Thanks, Stuart,' Marco said, surveying the bar and noticing the few drinkers there. 'You are quiet tonight.'

Stuart shrugged. 'January is always slow. People are all spent out after Christmas. I've had a two-for-one meal offer running which has brought some of the diners back. Now we're into February things should pick up. Of course, this cold weather's not helping and if we get snowed in, well—'

'Does that often happen?'

'Not for long. My father's snow plough usually clears the roads,' Kayte interjected, sliding against the bar to join them, her shoulder brushing deliberately against Marco's as she deposited a selection of dirty glasses onto the counter. 'If you do get snowed in I can get him to come over to the manor if you like,' she added, giving him one of her most enticing smiles.

'Can you clear those other glasses away please, Kayte?' Stuart nodded towards two tables in the corner. A group of walkers staying in Willowbrook Farm's cottages were about to leave, pulling on scarves and zipping up weatherproof jackets.

With a scowl on her face, she pushed herself away from the bar and headed for the table, her hips swaying.

'Let's get you out to the kitchen before the man-eater comes back,' Stuart said, sighing as he lifted the bar flap.

Marco slipped through and headed for the kitchen.

It was well past closing time before Marco finally reappeared. He'd had a good evening chatting to Josh in the kitchen. He'd looked at the two-for-one promotion and slightly changed the menu, giving the young cook a list of extra food to buy in. He had also left his business card so he could be contacted should Josh have any queries. The bar was now empty. Terri was hanging up the last of the clean glasses and Stuart about to cover the beer pumps with a cloth. Marco immediately noticed Kayte was missing.

'Where is she?' he asked, eyeing them both warily.

Stuart shook his head. 'No idea. I've only just come up from the cellar.'

'She left about fifteen minutes ago with Nikki,' Terri reassured him. 'She's long gone.'

'What, so easily?' The publican gave his wife a disbelieving look. 'Go upstairs and have a look out of the front bedroom window. My guess is she'll be out there hanging around Marco's car.'

Terri left the bar, returning moments later with a smile. 'Yep, she's there all right.'

'I've had enough of this,' Stuart growled. 'She's going to be looking for another job if she isn't careful. In fact, I've a good mind to fire her tonight.'

Terri put a calming hand on her husband's arm. 'Wait, she's a good barmaid. I'm reluctant to lose her.'

'So she might be, but she's a pain in the butt for Marco here.' He tugged at the young Italian's sleeve. 'Come on. If she wants a lift home, I'll take her.'

Kayte was leaning against the passenger door of Marco's Targa with her arms folded as both men crossed the car park towards her. Her face lit up when she saw him.

'Marco! I don't suppose you could give me a lift home, could you?'

'Sorry, Kayte, no,' Marco said, shaking his head. 'I am heading in a completely different direction tonight.'

'I'm taking you home,' Stuart said, placing himself between her and Marco.

'I don't want to go home with you,' she snapped. 'I'm sure Marco wouldn't mind a little detour, would you?'

Marco's expression hardened. 'Stuart is taking you home, Kayte. Please get off my car.'

Kayte pouted and refused to budge.

'All right,' Stuart said grimly, 'we can do it the easy way or the hard way. If you don't move I'll not only fire you on the spot, I will call Willowbrook and tell your parents exactly why I've had to do it.'

'You wouldn't!' Kayte glared at him as she reluctantly pushed herself away from the Porsche.

'You just try me.'

Kayte scowled at both men then grudgingly followed Stuart over to his Mondeo estate. With a last bristling glance towards Marco as he unlocked his car, she opened the door and slid into the passenger seat.

Marco watched the Mondeo leave, indicating a right turn out of the car park. Climbing into the Porsche, he followed, taking his car in the opposite direction, all the while thinking pushing her into the manure that day at the farm did not appear to have cooled her ardour. He usually managed to avoid her when he called in on Stuart, but this evening had made him realise she had not gone away. He wondered exactly what he could do to put a stop to it permanently. Maybe if he told her he was with Charlotte…? Fool, he scolded himself, if anything it would probably make her even more determined. He was rid of Rossana, now far away in Canada with his father and Felica, but now he was back to having trouble with Kayte. Was he never to have peace?

Stuart pulled up outside Willowbrook Farm and killed the engine.

'You can't keep doing this, Kayte,' he said, as she released her seat belt and reached for the door. 'What part of "not interested" don't you understand? For all our sakes leave him be, will you. You can't have everything you want, you know.'

Kayte didn't respond, she simply tossed her head and got out, slamming the door with considerable force. He watched her walk up the front path and then skirt around the side of the house. That girl's going to get herself into a whole lot of trouble, he thought, starting the car up again. Somebody's got to put a stop to her antics before someone really gets hurt.

Kayte leaned against the farmhouse wall, watching the rear lights of Stuart Harper's car disappear down the track to the main road. Damn his interference! And damn Marco for being so spineless! She slapped the wall with the flat of her hand, her breath coming in short angry spasms as fury built inside her. She wanted him, she *must* have him. Her temper exploded and she lost control, tearing at her hair and then her clothes. She banged her forehead across the pale stone of the wall as a scream of frustration tore from her throat. Her legs gave way and she sagged to the path with a sob.

'What was that?' Rachel O'Farrell sat up in bed and shook her husband.

Niall rolled over to stare at her, still groggy from sleep. He rubbed his eyes. 'I didn't hear anything.'

'I thought I heard a scream,' Rachel said, checking the bedside clock.

The sound came again.

'There it is. Oh my God!' She shoved the blankets back and grabbed her dressing gown. 'It's Caitlyn!'

'Rachel come back, I'll deal with it.' In an instant Niall was out of bed, taking a quick look out of the window before pulling on jeans and a thick sweater then racing down the stairs two a time. In the back lobby he pulled on boots and reached for his shotgun and a torch. Rachel, wrapped in her thick dressing gown, her feet encased in slippers, arrived behind him moments later. He threw open the back door and shone the torch out into the garden.

'Kayte!' he called. He heard sobbing coming from the side of the house. 'Here, hold the torch.' He handed it to Rachel as he cocked the gun ready to use it. Cautiously, they crept around the corner of the house, Rachel sweeping the beam from left to right.

'Oh my God! What's happened?' Seeing her daughter slumped against the house wall, hair dishevelled, her clothes torn and a large ugly graze across her forehead, Rachel rushed to her, knelt down and ran a gentle hand over the whimpering girl.

'Kayte?' Niall squatted down beside his daughter. 'Kayte, who did this?'

Kayte opened her eyes and stared into the horrified faces of her parents. 'Marco,' she gasped. 'He wouldn't...' The end of the sentence hung in the air, unfinished as she began to sob, fresh tears wetting her cheeks.

'Rachel, Call 999,' Niall ordered, as he lifted his distressed daughter into his arms. 'Police and ambulance. Quickly!'

Dawn was breaking as a lone police car passed through the gates of Higher Padbury Manor and cruised through the frost covered parkland towards the main house.

Roused by the bell, Madeline opened the heavy oak front door. One plain clothes officer and one uniformed man stood on the threshold, illuminated by the yellow glare of the porch light above them.

'Good morning. I'm Sergeant Martin Thomas.' The bearded plain clothes officer identified himself with his warrant card. 'Is Marco D'Alesandro at home?'

'I think you had better come in,' Madeline said, stepping back. As she closed the door behind the two men, Thérèse, securing a pale silk robe around her, appeared at the head of the stairs.

'Who is it, Madeline?'

'It's the police, Mrs D'Alesandro.' Madeline looked up anxiously as her employer descended towards them in a fluid movement reminiscent of her catwalk days.

'Officers?' Pushing her bed-tousled hair back from her face, she frowned at them as she reached the bottom of the stairs. 'What's happened? Has someone been hurt?'

Ignoring her questions, the plain clothes officer stared at her, his pale eyes expressionless. 'Does Marco D'Alesandro reside here, madam?'

'Yes, he does. Why?'

'We would like to see him please.'

'But it's five o'clock in the morning,' Thérèse argued, with an expression which indicated the request was totally preposterous. 'He's asleep.'

'Then, can you wake him?'

'Why, what's he done?'

'We need him to come to the station to help with our enquiries.'

Thérèse smiled. 'Well, I know his driving can be a little—'

Sergeant Thomas shook his head. 'It's nothing to do with driving. It's to do with an attempted rape. Now, please, I'd be grateful if you could wake him.'

* * *

Despite the fact milking was now a highly automated and mechanised affair, Niall had needed to keep himself occupied. Word had come via Rachel, who was at the police station with their daughter, confirming Kayte had not been raped, and he thanked God for that. It appeared her main injury had been to her forehead, which bore a heavy abrasion. Back from returning his herd to the south pasture, he entered through the front gate, skirting around the side of the house towards the back door, still trying to collect his thoughts. Marco D'Alesandro was the last person he would have imagined as a potential rapist. In fact, if the rumours were true, he spent most of his time trying to avoid Kayte's flirtatious manner with gossip of him being gay still continuing to drift around the village. Ringing from the station a second time, Rachel had told him their daughter was still quite traumatised and had not been able to give any real detail about the attack other than it was in Marco's car down on the main road and that she had managed to get away from him, falling and grazing her head in the process.

Niall hesitated for a moment, whistling up his two dogs lagging behind. As they caught him up, he glimpsed Stuart Harper's Mondeo in the distance, approaching up the track from the main road. After securing the dogs in the boot room, each with a bowl of dried food, he stepped back out into the cold February morning, wondering what Stuart wanted.

'Morning,' he greeted the publican, watching as he got out of his car and walked slowly towards him, the limp from the damaged knee which had seen his early retirement from the police force evident.

'Morning, Niall.' Stopping a few feet away, Stuart buried his hands in the pockets of his sheepskin, his expression serious. 'I thought I'd better come and tell you I'm on my way to Abbotsbridge Police Station.'

'To help Marco, I suspect,' Niall replied, keeping his tone even. 'Look, I know he's your friend but—'

'He didn't do it, Niall.'

'Stuart, I appreciate your loyalty but you should have seen my daughter. She was terrified. Her clothes were torn, her forehead badly grazed.' He shook his head. 'I don't think—'

'Niall, he didn't do it because *I* gave her a lift home, and I watched her walk around the side of this house.' He indicated the right side of the farmhouse. 'Marco left the pub car park at the same time I did. He drove off in the opposite direction, heading for Morden.'

'Are you sure?'

'Positive. And I think there's something else you ought to know.'

After Stuart left, Niall made his way back into the house. He kicked off his wellingtons by the back door and strode quickly into the hall to answer the phone. It was Rachel again, calling to let him know they were on their way home. His face set in a grim expression, he walked into the kitchen and turned on the kettle, trying to work out while he waited for it to boil exactly what he was going to say to his daughter when he saw her.

Marco felt he was in the middle of a bad dream, one that had to end soon. Pulled from his bed by Thérèse, he had hurriedly dressed and gone downstairs to confront the two policemen. Despite protesting his innocence, he had been ushered into a police car and driven to the station to be interviewed. Before he was taken away he'd had the presence of mind to ask her to contact Stuart. He couldn't imagine Stuart was responsible for the attack; there was only one sensible answer: he had been set up by Kayte. He remembered expressing his views to Charlotte months ago about how dangerous Kayte was. Those words had, it appeared, now come back to haunt him. Thoughts of Charlotte made him wish she were here with him now. However, he knew the last thing his stepmother would be doing was picking up a phone to let her know what was going on. He would have to ask Stuart to do that for him when he turned up.

Despite her mask of indifference, Marco was confident Thérèse harboured an intense dislike for Charlotte. Since Rossana's departure to Canada, she had been unable to stop their relationship developing and she was furious. Aware of the nights they spent together at Fox Cottage or his London apartment, he knew beneath his stepmother's unconcerned façade a great rage was building. A rage which, before long he would again need to call upon his father's assistance to deal with her. But for now she had been blown off course by this accusation hanging over him, something else which he could see might interfere with her plans and which she was probably seething about.

Huddled in the corner of a small bare cell while waiting to be interviewed, his thoughts turned back to his present situation. He had no idea how the British police worked. Kayte was clever, she could play the vulnerable innocent very well. As he hadn't touched her he felt quite confident they would find no forensic evidence to link him with any attack. But what if they decided to frame him? What if…? He damped down his panic, closing his eyes and praying Stuart would arrive soon.

Kayte was relieved she was home, pleased to have put distance between herself and that awful police station. Stepping out of the Volvo, she looked up at the farmhouse and shuddered. It had seemed so simple to blame Marco, to get some satisfaction out of paying him back for the way he had treated her. However, things had not gone quite the way she had imagined they would. She had arrived at the police station thinking she would merely be interviewed and allowed to go home. She had no idea her accusation would lead to the kind of treatment she had been subjected to; after all, wasn't she supposed to be the bloody victim? Her clothes taken for analysis, a medical examination, and swabs taken had not been at all what she had expected. The whole experience had been quite awful and made her wish she'd never accused him in the first place. Finally, she'd been interviewed by the woman police officer and a sympathetic-looking colleague and asked the most intimate of questions. Fearing she might trip herself up as she began to relate details of her fictitious attack, she brought the interrogation to a halt with a fresh wave of tears. The interview was postponed, with her agreeing to be interviewed when she felt stronger, and together with her mother, she was allowed to return home.

Now as she followed Rachel up the path she saw her father waiting at the open front door. She readied herself with her tears and a plan to fall into his arms and sob, but then she saw the expression on his face and heard her mother's voice.

'Niall, what's wrong?'

And as she looked into her father's face, she knew.

THIRTY-ONE

Scott stood at the foot of the ladder, staring up at Kayte busy restocking shelves. 'I came as soon as I could.'

Seeing him, she came down, taking each rung slowly before folding herself into his huge arms. She burrowed her face into his brown overalls that smelt of cow cake and disinfectant.

'Oh, Scott, it's been terrible,' she whispered tearfully.

He stroked her hair with one of his large hands. 'There, there. You're with me now.'

'I was so scared at the police station. They took my clothes away for examination and I had to do these tests.' Relaxing back in his arms she looked up into his face. As Scott's eyes bore down into hers, she could see the bubbling undercurrent of anger in their grey depths.

'Did he touch you, Kayte?'

'He…' She shook her head and buried it in his overalls again. 'It doesn't matter now. They've let him go,' she mumbled. 'Apparently, there's not enough evidence to prosecute.'

'The bastard!' His arms went around her again in a crushing bear hug. 'I'm going to sort him out,' he declared, burying his face in her hair. 'If the police won't do their job properly then I'll have to do it for them.'

Christian could not believe he was back here again. He honestly thought when he had been discovered with Talia and Leyna in that bedroom in Grand Cayman, Matt would sack him, if not for his behaviour then for the way he had used company money to fund the girls' stay and, of course, the drugs. Back then, before he had been discovered, he hadn't given a damn; as far as he was concerned the end of the album meant time to part company with Evolution and the two men he thought of as has-beens. However, on arriving back in the UK, Matt had sent him straight to rehab. It turned out he had been checking up on him and knew about his regular supply of pills, bought by the girls from a dealer on the island. Matt also knew about his excessive drinking. He had practically marinated in alcohol while making the album.

After having spent six weeks in Lakeside, an expensive clinic deep in the heart of leafy Surrey, he had left feeling a totally different man free of his addiction and able to face the world, his demons driven far away. But now the biggest test of all confronted him. Matt had invited him down to Little Court for the weekend. It had been last minute and unexpected but here he was coming back to a place where he had behaved badly when the monster inside him had taken control. He had a lot of apologising to do, and apologise he would. He owed everything to Matt and in some ways to Baz. No longer were they a source of contempt, he now viewed them with respect. He wasn't a meal ticket – he was a valuable part of their organisation. They regarded him as family.

As Matt's Mercedes turned in through the gates of Little Court, Christian's thoughts turned to Charlotte. He had no idea what his reception was going to be today. He had fouled up big time and hurt one of the most important people in his life. *After all he had put her through would she even want to speak to him?* he wondered. When the car came to a stop outside the front door of Little Court, Christian climbed slowly out and gazed up at its red brick walls before noticing the nearby car park was full of expensive vehicles.

'There's a wedding going on,' Matt said, looking at him across the car roof. 'Charlotte's been let off her function duties for the day. As you know, your visit was all very last minute, I'm afraid. We didn't think you'd be coming down for another couple of weeks, but when I phoned late last evening to tell Ella you had a free weekend she insisted I brought you back with me. Lottie was at Fox Cottage all night so she didn't know anything about you showing up today until she returned this morning.'

Christian felt uneasy. 'Is she happy to see me? I don't want to upset her with my sudden arrival. It's important I do this properly.'

Matt opened the boot and pulling out their bags. 'She's absolutely fine with it.'

Despite Matt's reassurance, he was still not totally at ease about what he was walking into. He took his overnight bag from Matt and followed him into the house.

She was waiting in the hall. Dressed in jeans and a loose white shirt, her black hair tied back off her face, Charlotte walked slowly towards him, regarding him closely as she closed the gap between them. Finally, she pulled him into a hug in the familiar sisterly way he remembered so well. He dropped his bag and held onto her tightly, not wanting to let go.

'I'm sorry, Lottie,' he whispered. 'I'm so very sorry.'

Nodding silently, she pulled back and they stood for a moment looking at each other. Then with a smile, she scooped up his case. 'Come on, let's get you settled in.'

'Welcome back, Christian.' It was Ella who spoke, unlocking herself from a welcoming embrace with her husband and walking over to Christian. She hugged him. 'We've all been looking forward to seeing you again.'

'I'll settle him in and then I thought we'd go to the Arms for a drink.' Charlotte looked at him and smiled.' We have a lot of talking to do.'

Ella nodded. 'Good idea. I wish I could join you but I'm afraid there's still a wedding to get through before I can put my feet up. I'll catch you both this evening at dinner.'

'I didn't expect this, Lottie,' Christian said, feeling totally humbled as they reached his room upstairs. 'Everyone has been so good, I don't feel I deserve it. I was well out of order, especially with you.'

'Matt told me about the amphetamines,' she said. 'He said they were the cause of your attitude problems and the reason why you were so paranoid with me.'

Christian gave a thoughtful nod as he swung his overnight bag onto the bed. 'Those two girls – Leyna and Talia – they got me onto them. I felt I needed some sort of lift and I didn't want to go anywhere near snorting cocaine or injecting heroin. It seemed so simple at first, popping a pill in my mouth to give me a buzz when my energy levels dropped. Then enjoyment started to become an addiction and by the time I'd reached that stage, I didn't realise how out of control I'd become. In the world I occupied I thought I was behaving quite normally.'

'And where did you meet Talia and Leyna?'

'In a club in London, about a year ago. At first, I thought they were a couple of rich little Sloanies out on the town. There were all the usual hallmarks. You know, shiny blonde hair, posh accents, expensive clothes. We seemed to click and I linked up with them whenever I could.' He gave a snort of amusement. 'So much for my assumptions; turns out they were actually a couple of highly paid escorts who liked to drop out of their usual routine with their rich clients and have fun once in a while. And it *was* fun until Grand Cayman.'

'Well, it's over now.' Charlotte ran an affectionate hand down his arm. 'We're simply glad to have the old you back.' She checked her watch. 'I'll leave you to unpack and freshen up and I'll meet you at, say, twelve thirty?'

'I'm good with that.' He smiled, his eyes meeting hers. 'Lottie, can I ask you something?'

'What?'

'Was there anything going on with you and the Italian?'

A smile lit her face. 'Not when I was with you, but yes, we've been seeing each other for a little while now. He's good for me. He makes me happy.'

'Good. I'm pleased.' He pulled her into his arms and kissed her forehead. 'Twelve thirty, then?'

'Twelve thirty,' Charlotte's voice echoed back as she left the room, closing the door behind her.

Finishing the magazine he was reading, Marco threw it onto the low table in time to see his stepmother enter the drawing room and take a seat opposite him. She reached for his discarded publication, flicking through the pages with an irritated expression on her face. This simmering displeasure had been her norm ever since his father took the girls off to Canada three weeks ago. However, the explosion he had felt coming had not materialised; maybe that was because she was wary of what his father might do if she stirred up any more trouble. He got to his feet slowly and stretched.

'Going to see Charlotte, are you?' Thérèse asked, peering at him over the top of her magazine.

'No, we are meeting later.'

'Ah, of course. She is busy with their weekend visitor this morning, isn't she?'

'Weekend visitor?' He frowned, wondering what she meant.

'Yes, Christian Rosetti. Ella told me yesterday. Matt's forgiven him and he's down for the weekend. Little Court, it appears, are killing the fatted calf and welcoming the prodigal back. I think you ought to know Ella also tells me he's keen to get back with Charlotte again.' She gave a sly smile. 'I can see by your expression you don't know about him being there. Strange Charlotte felt the need to keep it from you, don't you think? You don't suppose she's having second thoughts about you after those rape allegations, do you, and is planning to go back to—'

'Of course not,' he cut across her. Charlotte had hardly left his side since that horrific incident. She had insisted he stay over at Fox Cottage with her, where they now spent their nights together away from Thérèse and her spiteful tongue. He painted on a calm smile. 'It will not work, Thérèse. Charlotte does not want him.'

'Oh, Marco, you are so trusting...'

'And you are so transparent. Well, let me tell you – even if Charlotte and I were not together, the last woman I would want would be Rossana, is that clear?'

'Perfectly. I was merely looking after your best interests, as I always do.' She gave a placid smile and went back to her magazine.

'No, actually you were looking after your own, as you always do,' he corrected.

He left the room before she could say anything further. Damn Thérèse, stirring things up with her lies. On the stairs, his thoughts spun. No, she must be wrong; if Christian had been coming, Charlotte would definitely have told him. Maybe he should ride over and see her anyway. Anything to get out of the house and away from his stepmother's constant baiting.

THIRTY-TWO

'How did D'Alesandro get off, then?'

Leaning on the bar, Scott Elliott shot the question at Stuart, who was pulling a Saturday lunchtime pint for Roy Clarke, the village postman leaning on the bar next to him.

'He was innocent, that's why,' Stuart replied, taking the five-pound note from Roy's proffered hand and punching the transaction into the till.

'Innocent?' Scott's face creased into an angry frown. 'Kayte's clothes were torn. She had an injury to her face. Who was responsible then? Mr Bloody Nobody?'

'You'll need to ask her that,' Stuart replied, handing Roy back his change. 'All I know is Marco wasn't anywhere near Willowbrook that night.'

'You seem to know an awful lot about it.' Taking a mouthful of his beer Scott continued his badgering while standing just behind him, his two mirror-image workmates, Reece Walters and Patrick Hyde, continued drinking their beer in silence.

'That's because *I* took her home.'

Scott screwed up his face as he slammed his glass down on the counter. 'You what?'

'I dropped her home and watched her in,' Stuart replied calmly, wishing he'd never got involved in this conversation with a moron like Elliott. 'Scott, believe me, there was no way anyone could have had time to attack her.'

Scott took another mouthful of beer then gave a derisory snort. 'You would say that, wouldn't you? After all, he's your best mate, isn't he?' He drained his glass and set it on the bar. 'Well, maybe the police are reluctant to do anything about it but there are those around here who don't like rich boys getting away with things.'

'Is that a threat, Scott?'

'Nah, it's what you would call an observation, Mr Harper. Come on, boys,' he motioned to his two companions, 'time to get back to our wood clearing otherwise we'll have Farmer O'Farrell after us.'

Stuart watched as the three thick-set young men walked out of the pub. Scott's words made him feel uneasy. He only hoped after being found out and thoroughly chastised by her father, Kayte was not trying to take her spite out on Marco through Scott. Watching him and his cronies leave in the Willowbrook Land Rover, he pushed through the curtain to the back of the pub and picked up the phone.

Thérèse answered on the fourth ring.

'Stuart!' She sounded surprised to hear from him.

'Thérèse, sorry to bother you but could I speak to Marco?'

'I think he's gone out for a walk.'

'Would you get him to call me when he's back. It's quite urgent.'

'Of course. No problem, I hope?'

'A food query, that's all,' he lied. The last thing he wanted to do was alarm her.

Marco decided the quickest way to Little Court was through Hundred Acre which luckily bordered the manor parkland to the north. Reaching cover of the trees, he was soon lost in its depths, his mount's hooves kicking up the brown mulch of decaying leaves which covered the floor of the wood. As he rode, his thoughts centred on his stepmother's recent words. She was angry and, he supposed, this was the first opportunity she'd had for spiteful retaliation. He shook his head and smiled. Well tried, but she had no idea of the strength of feeling he and Charlotte had between them. Nothing could part them now.

As he reached a dense part of the west side of Hundred Acre he slowed his mount and lowered his head to avoid overhanging branches. Without warning a pheasant burst from the undergrowth. Startled, it screeched loudly, spooking his horse. He steadied the animal only to be aware of another sound, a rustle in the undergrowth immediately behind him. As he turned to see what it was something hit him in the back of the head. He felt himself falling then the world went black.

Scott Elliott stood eyeing the man tied to the chair in front of him. His captive sagged unconscious, his face a mass of purple bruising.

'Let's wake him up, shall we? Then we'll sort out what we need to do outside.' He grinned at Reece then nodded.

Holding the bucket of cold water he'd recently collected from the nearby stream, Reece Walters lifted it above Marco's head and tipped it over him.

Marco came to, spluttering and coughing as the water drenched him. He began to shiver as the icy wetness seeped into his skin. His wax jacket was gone, his heavy check shirt soaked. If they didn't finish him off, he thought, hypothermia would do the job for them. He opened his one good eye. He was in some sort of shack, tied to a chair, his arms bound tightly to the back of it, the ropes cutting into his wrists. The pain was intense; it throbbed and filled every part of him. Memories came floating back…

He remembered being hit from behind and falling from his horse. The next thing he knew, several pairs of hands were pulling at him, dragging him away as the animal galloped off into the woods. He was pushed roughly against a tree and as he regained his senses, found himself facing Scott Elliott, one of Niall's farmhands.

'Know why you're here, do you?' Elliot snarled, cold grey eyes glaring at him contemptuously.

He shook his head, still fuzzy from the blow.

Elliott came nearer, pushing his face up close. 'Attempted rape, rich boy. Putting your filthy paws on a young innocent girl.'

'I didn't do anything. I wasn't even near...' he began before Elliott punched him.

'Shut up! I don't want to hear your lies.'

He felt blood trickle from the corner of his mouth. Licking it away, he assessed his captor. Large, crew cut, piggy eyes, a bully who obviously enjoyed inflicting pain.

'What are you going to do with me?' he asked, although deep down he knew there was a beating coming.

'We're going to teach you not to mess with the girls around here, rich boy.'

Looking at the three of them, all thick set and threatening, he began to wonder whether he would get out of there alive.

'You plan to kill me?' It was more statement than question.

Scott shook his head. 'Nah, nothing as terrible as that. We want to teach you a very important lesson. Reece, Patrick, tie him up.'

And so they bound and dragged him through the undergrowth to this damp hovel where Patrick and Reece held him while Scott ripped the jacket from his back, throwing it to the floor. He was then pushed into a solitary chair set in the middle of the room. They secured him once more, pulling his arms tightly around the back of the chair so he was unable to move then all three stood glaring at him for a while. He guessed the purpose of this was to strike more fear into him as he waited for the first blow. Elliott was the first to hit him, followed by Reece while Patrick held the chair. The two men continued this relentlessly until in a sea of pain, he eventually lost consciousness...

Now as he gazed around the room, knowing there was precious little hope of escape, Marco wondered where they had gone and what they planned to do next.

Hearing footsteps outside the door, he decided to close his eyes and remain slumped with his head on his chest letting them think he was unconscious.

Scott entered, Reece behind him.

'Bugger, he's passed out again,' Reece hissed.

'No, he hasn't. Look he's shivering.' Scott's voice.

Marco opened his good eye again and peered at them. 'What are you going to do?'

Scott sneered unpleasantly. 'Give you your final punishment, rich boy. It will leave you with a constant reminder of what you did and thought you'd got away with. Patrick!' He jerked his head towards the door. 'Come outside. Before we can finish this there's something I need you to do for me.'

* * *

Replacing the phone, Stuart returned to bar. In the time it had taken to make his call to the manor he found Charlotte Kendrick standing there kitted out in jodhpurs and a wax jacket, a half of cider in her hand. Next to her, being handed his change by Terri, stood a tall man in a black leather jacket with a mass of curly dark hair skimming his shoulders. His features were slightly familiar.

Charlotte lowered her glass and smiled. 'Stuart, you're staring.'

Stuart tilted his head and frowned at the man. 'I'm trying to place you but I'm damned if I can.'

'Stu!' Terri elbowed him. 'What is he like?' She shot the pair an embarrassed smirk. 'This is Christian Rosetti... you know, the singer. Matt manages him.'

Stuart nodded. 'Ah, of course. Sorry. What brings you down here?'

'Weekend guest,' Christian replied, his dark eyes on Stuart as he lifted his glass to his lips. 'Charlotte thought it would be good if we dropped in for a drink.'

Stuart watched as Charlotte and Christian moved over to the fireplace, where a huge fire burned. She seated herself on a stool, Christian settled himself opposite her, their knees not quite touching. He bent his head, smiled and said something to her. She nodded, took another mouthful of her drink then smiled back.

'Wasn't he the one the trouble was all about?' Stuart eyed him curiously. 'Back in September, wasn't it?'

'Oh, the engagement that never was, yes.' Terri nodded. 'Seems Lottie's forgiven him, doesn't it?' She regarded them both. 'Well, it's not surprising, is it? He's gorgeous.' She turned to Stuart and smiled. 'But personally, I wouldn't trust him an inch, too much bad boy lurking there for my taste.'

Stuart sighed, wondering if Marco was aware Charlotte's ex-boyfriend was sharing a drink and cozying up to her. If he did, he was incredibly tolerant; if not, he was sure there would definitely be repercussions. He had a soft spot for Charlotte. She was well liked, a clever young woman who had far more depth to her than her fun-loving cousin Lucy. And she'd made a huge difference to the young Italian since she had been seeing him; it was as if she had unlocked a door, letting the sun spill into that serious workaholic world of his.

A couple of locals arrived, one with a border collie, settling themselves at the bar. They were followed shortly after by a group of half a dozen walkers wanting lunch. Leaving Terri to see to their drinks, he took the food order into the kitchen. As he returned he heard a commotion out in the bar. Pushing through the curtain, he came face to face with his wife.

'I think you'd better come,' she said. 'Something awful has happened.'

Leaning on the bar, Patrick Hyde was trying to get his breath back, his round face flushed from running.

'I came away... I couldn't do it,' he said in between heavy breaths. 'It's not right.'

'What's not right?' Stuart shook Patrick's shoulders, uncertain of what was coming next. 'Tell me?'

'It's Marco. Scott and Reece have got him up in the old woodcutter's cottage in Hundred Acre. They've beaten him up and now... well... they wanted me to get the bullwhip from Willowbrook. The one Niall brought back from his time in Australia.'

'Ring the police station at once. Speak to John Fowler,' Stuart instructed his wife. 'Then phone Niall. Tell both of them what's happened and to get up there straight away.' As he lifted the flap he saw Charlotte had left her seat and was coming towards him, her face full of concern.

'What's happened? Did I hear somebody mention Marco's name?'

'He's in trouble,' Stuart said. 'Scott and Reece are holding him up in the woodcutter's cottage.'

'But why would they do that?' Charlotte stared at him then Patrick in disbelief.

'To get even with D'Alesandro,' Patrick replied. 'Because he thinks he attacked Kayte.'

'I'm going up there,' Charlotte said in the kind of voice which challenged anyone to argue with her. As she searched her pocket for her car keys, she felt Christian's steadying hand on her arm.

'Please, Lottie, leave this to Stuart, eh? He's called the police, they'll deal with it. You'd only be putting yourself in danger...'

'But, Christian, what if—'

'No buts.' He placed himself between her and the publican. 'I'm sure between them Stuart, Niall and the law can handle it.'

'Christian's right, Charlotte.' Stuart gave a confident nod. 'Best you stay here.'

Reluctantly, Charlotte moved back to let the publican through.

Ten minutes later as Stuart's Mondeo bumped up the rough track towards Fox Cottage, he checked his rear view mirror, hoping to catch sight of John Fowler in the police Escort turning off the main road behind him, but was disappointed to find he was very much on his own.

Pulling up outside the cottage, he got out and stared for a moment, checking the road out of the village. It was empty. Knowing waiting was not an option, he began his trek up into the woods. The woodcutter's cottage, he estimated, was only five minutes away.

'Caitlyn!'

Kayte heard her father's bellow. The fact he was using her full name indicated he was not in a good mood. So what was new? Her return from the police station was supposed to have given her some respite from the endless questioning. Instead, it pitched her into the middle of another nightmare. He had not said a word, not even to her mother. He had waited until the door was closed before he had ushered them both into the front room and asked them to sit.

'What's wrong?' Rachel looked at him anxiously.

'Caitlyn,' he said, in a voice simmering with angry undercurrents, 'I would like you to tell me precisely what happened to you last night.'

She gave a careless shrug. 'You know what happened. Marco D'Alesandro tried to rape me.'

'Shall we try again?' He stood over her, his expression hardening.

She shook her head, defiant. 'I don't know what you mean.'

'Oh yes you do!'

'Niall, what are you doing?' Rachel's anxious eyes darted from him to their daughter.

'Stuart has been here this morning. He tells me he ran you home last night and Marco drove off from the Arms in the opposite direction.'

'Kayte?' Her mother frowned at her.

'He also tells me that ever since Marco arrived, you've been making a total nuisance of yourself whenever he comes into the pub. Is this true?'

'I...well...' Kayte scrabbled around in her brain for an answer but could find none.

'If you are found to be lying about this rape you're going to be in big trouble. Believe me, falsely accusing someone and wasting police time will incur harsh penalties.'

It was then she faltered, realising there was no option; she would have to own up. She had an idea her father would not betray her, convinced he only wanted to hear the truth for himself. She was sure he would protect her.

'I'm waiting,' he said, settling himself into the seat opposite her.

She nodded. 'All right.'

'And I want to know why.'

Afterwards, he simply sat shaking his head in total disbelief. Next to him, her mother brought her hand to her mouth.

'Oh my God, poor Marco,' she said.

'Caitlin!' Her father's voice came again and she turned to see him standing in the doorway, a furious expression on his face.

'Oh, Dad, no,' she groaned. 'What now?

'Come with me.'

'Where are we going?'

'To Hundred Acre.'

'Why?'

'You'll see.'

* * *

Stuart was following a boggy track through the east end of Hundred Acre. He was sure the woodcutter's cottage was around here somewhere, after all it was winter, the trees bare; it should be visible by now. He paused for a moment to get his breath back. Damn it, he was overweight and his knee injury was playing up, not exactly a good combination for facing two heavy yobs. He knew he should wait for police support to arrive, but the way Patrick Hyde was talking it sounded like Marco was in imminent danger. As if in answer to his thoughts an agonised cry carried through the wood.

'Shit!' he shouted, and summoning a reserve of strength he didn't know he possessed, forced himself onwards.

Scott handed Reece a dirty handkerchief from his pocket.

'Here, stuff this in his mouth. We don't want half the village up here before we start, do we?'

Reece walked round to Marco, who was now suspended from the overhanging branch of a large beech tree. 'You shouldn't have yanked him up so hard, he's losing consciousness again,' he grumbled, stuffing the material into Marco's mouth.

Scott scowled at Reece, annoyed at his criticism. 'Then go and get some more water. I want him fully awake for this. And where's that bastard Patrick? He should have been back by now.'

'Maybe he got caught,' Reece said, walking towards the cottage to get the bucket.

'Bugger! I needed that whip.' Scott thought for a moment. 'We'll just have to make do. I'll get the water, you go back to where we jumped him and try to find his riding crop, we'll have to use that instead.'

As Reece sloped off, Scott collected the bucket from the cottage and went to the stream to fill it.

THIRTY-THREE

Stuart stopped and listened again; there had been no more cries since the first one but he was sure they came from this direction. He could hear the rush of water, which meant he must be near the stream. The cottage couldn't be far now. He left the track and forged deeper into the wood. Coming to a massive grey outcrop of rock, he pushed round it and then froze. Below him, Scott Elliott was squatting at the water's edge, filling a bucket; to his left stood the cottage. Scott straightened up and made off around the side of the cottage. Cautiously Stuart followed.

Scott grinned as he threw the contents of the bucket over Marco. 'Wake up you bastard.'

Marco groaned but his head remained slumped on his chest. At the sound of running feet Scott spun round. Reece appeared from out of the undergrowth waving the crop at him. 'Found it,' he said, handing it over to him.

'Good. Now we can start.' Scott flexed the leather crop in his hands, a satisfied smile settling on his face. 'Get his shirt off.'

Stuart stepped cautiously round the cottage and stopped, horrified at what greeted him. Suspended from a tree by some sort of wooden yoke arrangement, his arms tied out at right angles, was Marco, Reece in the process of tearing the shirt off his captive's back. As Scott raised the crop, Stuart charged across the clearing, barrelling into him and knocking him to the ground. Fists flew but Stuart soon realised all he had done was to delay the inevitable as Reece grabbed him from behind, pinning his arms back while Scott hauled himself to his feet, his face filled with rage.

'You stupid sod,' he said, giving a contemptuous shake of his head. 'Come to rescue him, have you? A wasted effort, Mr Harvey. You should be pleased; after all, we're carrying out a public service.'

As Reece hauled Stuart back to the edge of the clearing and held him tightly, Scott picked up the crop and walked back to his victim.

'Now, rich boy, let's start again, shall we?' he said, slowly running the crop along the edge of Marco's jaw before stepping back to deliver the first heavy blow.

'Put the crop down!'

All heads turned to see Charlotte Kendrick standing on the edge of the clearing, feet apart, levelling a shotgun at Scott.

Scott shook his head and laughed. 'What do you think you're doing, you stupid cow?'

'Put the crop down *now*!'

He turned fully to face her. 'A woman with a gun? I'm so scared.' He took a step towards her, then another. 'I can disarm you in seconds.'

'I don't think so.' She eyed him coldly as she clicked off the safety catch. 'Drop the crop.'

'Oh, bugger off back to Little Court, you stupid woman!' Scott sneered then turned back towards Marco and raised his arm again.

A shot rang out, the rope broke and Marco's body sagged to the floor.

'You bloody bitch!' Scott turned on her, his face mottled with fury as he strode towards her brandishing the crop.

As Scott crossed the clearing towards Charlotte, constables John Fowler and Tim Matthews burst through the undergrowth. Flicking the safety catch back on, Charlotte grabbed the gun by its barrel and swung it like a club, catching Scott a hard blow to the face. He lunged past her and fell into the mud. Within seconds, John was handcuffing him. At the same time, Stuart elbowed Reece in the gut and Tim pounced. All three went down, Stuart pinning the huge lad to the floor while Tim slipped on the cuffs. Getting to his feet, Stuart walked over to where Charlotte had managed to untie Marco's hands and was now wrapping her wax jacket around his bare shoulders.

As she removed the gag from his mouth he raised his battered face to her. 'Charlotte, I...' he began.

'Shh... an ambulance is on its way,' she said gently, hugging his body against hers. 'It won't be long.' As the words left her mouth she felt his body fall heavily into hers and realised unconsciousness had claimed him.

'Take a good look at your handiwork! See what you've done!'

Everyone turned to see Niall O'Farrell pushing his daughter into the clearing, a livid expression on his face. As she took in all of those gathered there, her eyes settled on Marco cradled against Charlotte's shoulder.

'Oh no.' She shook her head before turning to face her father. 'You can't blame me for this. I didn't do this!' She wheeled around and pointed at Scott and Reece. 'They did.'

'Yes, Kayte, I did it.' Scott Elliott's voice broke the silence in the clearing, his words distorted by the swelling in his face from Charlotte's shotgun butt. 'It was no more than he deserved. I love you and I couldn't bear to think you'd wasted your time on a man like him, one who repaid your feelings by trying to rape you. I know he got off, but it was all down to his money and connections, wasn't it? He's guilty. Justice had to be served.'

'I think you've been duped by my daughter, Scott,' Niall said, shaking Kayte's shoulder. 'Tell him the truth, Caitlin. Tell him.'

'I...' Kayte chewed her bottom lip. 'I...'

'Tell him!' Niall bellowed.

'I... I made it up. I wanted to punish him because he didn't want me.' The words came out in a great gush. 'He didn't touch me. Stuart brought me home.'

'You mean to say I beat up an innocent man?' Scott's eyes widened with horror. 'What sort of woman are you?'

'I didn't ask you to do this.' Kayte shrugged uncaringly, watching as John and Tim pushed the two young men out of the clearing. 'This is not my fault,' she called after him.

As the two policemen disappeared with their prisoners, Kayte walked over to where Charlotte sat cradling Marco. She stood for a moment regarding them both with a detached expression on her face.

'If only he hadn't rejected me, none of this would have happened,' she said with an uncaring shrug. 'Not so pretty now, is he?'

Charlotte glared up at her then made eye contact with Niall. 'Get your daughter out of my sight,' she said calmly, 'before I take my shotgun to her as well.'

'I'll do better than that,' Niall said, cold eyes fixed on his daughter's back. 'I'm taking her to the police station. She's got some explaining to do.'

Kayte spun around angrily to face him. 'You wouldn't!'

'Whatever excuses you're making for yourself, young lady, you are responsible for this and you'll have to accept the consequences. Now, come on!'

With a final glare at Charlotte, Kayte left; father and daughter walking out of the clearing together, neither looking back.

Two green-clad paramedics carrying their equipment appeared from around the side of the cottage. Charlotte got to her feet, retrieved her jacket and stepped back, watching with Stuart as they took over.

'You were very brave,' Stuart said, taking her hand. 'You've saved him from a severe beating. Let's hope they can save his face, I think his jaw may be broken.'

Charlotte drew in a sharp breath and rubbed a tired hand down her cheek, her gaze fixing on the departing Kayte. 'What is it with her?' she said. 'Why doesn't she feel any remorse?'

'She's been giving him the come-on ever since he arrived and he's always politely avoided her. He has never given her any cause to think he had any interest in her but as we know, Kayte takes rejection very personally.'

'So what's the connection between her and Scott other than he works for Niall?'

'She's been playing him for a fool ever since he arrived.' Stuart shook his head wearily. 'She's a tease but sometimes she goes too far and most guys see her for what she is. But Scott? He doesn't have a lot upstairs. I genuinely think he believed he had a chance with her. You can see it all now, can't you? When he heard about the attempted rape his anger was as much directed at the fact he thought Kayte had been with Marco as it was about what he thought Marco had done.'

Marco was now being loaded onto a collapsible stretcher; Charlotte gazed down at his motionless form and shook her head. If this is what Kayte was capable of, she was dangerous. Very dangerous.

The paramedics passed them both, following the trail down through the wood towards the track where their ambulance stood.

'Go with him,' Stuart urged. 'Right now he needs you.'

Charlotte nodded and tucking her gun under her arm, walked out of the clearing. He fell in step behind her. When they reached the end of the track she held out the shotgun to him.

'Give this to Christian, will you, and ask him to take the Range Rover back to Little Court. I'll be back as soon as I can.' She thought for a moment. 'Can you ring Thérèse too and let her know what's happened.'

'Of course.' Stuart reached for the weapon then paused as he caught sight of movement along the main road. 'Actually, it looks as if someone already has.' He nodded in the direction of a black Range Rover travelling at speed towards them. They watched as it approached. Thérèse was behind the wheel, one of her grooms in the passenger seat. She slammed out of the vehicle her expression furious. Walking over to the paramedics, she stared down at the stretcher for a moment, her hands pressed against her lips, her features unreadable. Slowly, she reached out one hand and touched Marco then turned away, her eyes coming to rest on Charlotte. She marched over to her, a furious expression etched on her face.

'What the hell have you done?' she demanded.

'Me?' Charlotte frowned at her. 'Nothing.'

'Yes you have, you bitch.' Thérèse raised a hand to strike her but Stuart intercepted it.

He lowered her arm, his voice calm. 'Mrs D'Alesandro, I don't think you quite understand the situation. Charlotte saved Marco from a severe beating.'

'Saved him?' Thérèse hissed. 'I think it's you who don't understand. She caused all this. If Marco hadn't been so concerned about what she was up to with her ex-boyfriend, he wouldn't even have been here. And this whole horror would never have happened. Have you seen his face?' She turned her fury on Charlotte. 'Have you?'

'Mrs D'Alesandro, please...' Charlotte stepped closer to Stuart to avoid the chance of another angry slap. 'You are mistaken. Christian and I are not together. He is my aunt and uncle's weekend guest, not mine.'

'Then what is he doing here with you now? Why is he not at Little Court?' Thérèse demanded, pointing an accusing finger to where Christian stood leaning against the Land Rover, watching them. She tilted her chin with contempt when Charlotte did not reply. 'Hah! I thought as much. You can't answer me without incriminating yourself, can you, madam?'

Stuart stepped between the two women. 'Look, can we call a halt to this please? Right now the ambulance is about to leave. Someone needs to go with Marco. Charlotte was about to but—'

'Oh no! I don't want her anywhere near him. Not now or at any time in the future. Understand?' And turning on her heels, Thérèse headed towards the ambulance.

Charlotte let out a huge ragged breath and put a shaky hand to the base of her throat. 'Oh God, Stuart, this is a mess.'

'She doesn't know what she's saying, she's in shock,' Stuart replied, watching Thérèse's retreating back. 'I think it's probably best you keep away for the time being. Let me be your eyes and ears. I'll keep in touch with the manor and let you know what's going on. Don't worry, you'll be seeing him soon. Come on, let's go home.'

As the paramedics lifted Marco into the ambulance he regained consciousness. One of them, a dark-haired young woman, smiled down at him.

'We've given you something to ease your discomfort,' she said, her voice calm and reassuring. Marco nodded as the horrendous pain which seemed to have invaded all of his body was slowly numbing. He closed his eyes and wondered where Charlotte was. She had saved him. Out of nowhere she had come like an avenging angel. He couldn't wait to see her, to thank her and tell her how much he loved her.

As the paramedic stepped aside, he saw his stepmother climb in.

'Thérèse, what are you doing here?' he managed to say, unable to move his mouth much because of his stiff jaw.

'Rachel O'Farrell called. I came straight away. Oh my God, Marco, what have they done to you?'

'I will be fine,' he croaked. 'Please, I need to see Charlotte…'

She placed a gentling hand against his shoulder. 'Shh. Charlotte will not be coming.'

'Not coming? Why? Where is she?'

When she did not answer he managed to raise his head slightly and was able to get a view of the track. He saw a police car pulling away and Niall pushing Kayte towards a green Defender. Stuart was there too. Then he saw Charlotte. With the gun still tucked under her arm, she was talking to a tall, dark-haired man who slipped an arm around her shoulder and hugged her to him. As the ambulance doors closed, Marco saw the man glance in his direction before turning back to Charlotte and guiding her towards a nearby grey Range Rover. Christian Rosetti. She was with Christian Rosetti! Marco's head fell back onto the pillow, his eyes closing as every emotion he had ever felt for Charlotte Kendrick plunged and shattered.

Sitting behind him, Thérèse watched quietly and smiled.

Niall O'Farrell had been walking over to unlock his Land Rover when he caught sight of Charlotte and Stuart.

'Jim told me what you did,' he called out. 'Thank goodness you got here in time; he could have been badly injured.' He shot a reprimanding glare at his daughter leaning against the door of the vehicle with an unrepentant expression on her face.

Charlotte shook her head. 'It was nothing. I was in the right place at the right time, that was all.' She turned to Christian, who had walked over to join them. 'It's a good job I chose to ignore Mr Rosetti here,' she said with a half-smile and leaning her head into his shoulder.

'Yeah, well, I know what you're like when you get the bit between your teeth,' Christian said, looping his arm around her and giving her a hug. 'I was worried you might get hurt. I wanted to come with you, remember?'

She smiled up at him. 'I know you did. But the police were right behind me.'

'Come on, let's go home,' Christian said.

Opening the rear door of the Range Rover, she laid the shotgun carefully across the back seat, waved to Stuart walking back to his own car, then climbed in next to Christian as he started the engine.

Christian watched Niall and Kayte get into the Land Rover parked opposite. As he pulled away, he stared into the cab of Niall's car. Niall's head was bent towards the steering wheel as if he was searching for something on the floor. Kayte, however, was looking straight at him. The scowl which seemed a permanent feature ever since she arrived dissolved as their eyes met. She tilted her head defiantly and ran the tip of her tongue over her lips, giving him a clear unspoken message. He smiled back. He'd seen her arrive with her father earlier, her blonde hair spilling over her shoulders, jeans clinging to her hips and a top underneath her jacket which left very little to the imagination. It appeared she was central to all this trouble although she looked totally unconcerned and had secretly been giving him the eye as Niall and Charlotte had chatted. She was a hot little piece all right, and no doubt quite a handful for her father. But that was his sort of woman and they were fun, weren't they? He'd straightened himself out with the drugs and booze but women were still very firmly on the agenda. He smiled to himself, wondering whether he could swing a trip up to Willowbrook to make her acquaintance before he left.

The opportunity presented itself the next morning. Charlotte had to drive up to Willowbrook to discuss supplies for Lawns. This was normally Issy's responsibility but as she was away in Florida with Mick on a winter break, Ella thought it might be an opportunity for her niece to expand her responsibilities beyond the meet and greet role she currently had. Watching her ease out of the garage block, Christian crossed to intercept her.

'Where are you going?' he asked, as she lowered the window.

'Willowbrook. I won't be long.'

'Want some company?'

'You want to come to the farm?' She shot him an amused grin. 'Are you kidding me?'

'No, of course not.' His hand was on the door, his most appealing smile gracing his face. He knew she would not refuse him.

'Well, okay then. Hop in.'

The journey to Willowbrook took them less than ten minutes. He already knew the history of the farm from when he first visited the village and a sixteen-year-old Charlotte had taken him around. Now she was enlightening him about the new businesses Niall had set up; the farm shop selling not only Willowbrook meat and dairy produce but also food sourced from other local providers. Then there was the ice cream production company which had gained several prestigious awards and had a UK distribution network. Recently, land had also been set aside for a lavender farm project which was hoped to start next year. Niall was working on a business plan for this and had already visited Norfolk to view similar operations there.

'Diversification is the name of the game,' Charlotte said, as she swung the vehicle alongside Niall's Land Rover. 'Farmers have to be businessmen in order to survive these days and Niall is one of the best.'

The subject of their conversation appeared from around the side of the house as Charlotte climbed from the vehicle. Dressed in dungarees and wellingtons, his Barbour open to reveal a heavy fisherman's jumper beneath, he stopped and appraised them both.

'Morning. Ella told me to expect you,' he said with a friendly smile. 'Come on in.'

They followed him to the back door and into the boot room, where Niall prised off his muddy wellingtons and padded stocking-footed into a large warm kitchen filled with the wonderful smell of newly baked bread.

'Rachel's not here at the moment,' he said, moving over to the sink. 'She's gone up to see her mother at the home. Margaret had a fall the other week, no broken bones but it's unsettled her a bit. Drink?' He waved the kettle at them.

Minutes later, Charlotte and Christian were seated around the kitchen table with steaming mugs of coffee in front of them. Charlotte produced a list from her tote, spread it across the table and began talking Niall through her aunt's requirements for the coming fortnight. Christian finished his coffee and sat quietly watching them. He gave a sigh and stared at his feet, admiring his newly purchased boots. He was beginning to wish he had stayed home; there was no way he was going to be able to have a snoop around and track down Kayte now.

'You look bored, Christian.'

Christian raised his head and saw Niall looking at him.

'Why don't you have a walk around? Stretch your legs,' Niall continued. 'My foreman Sam is about somewhere. Ask him to give you the guided tour.'

Christian slid his chair back and got to his feet; his prayers had been answered. 'Thanks, Niall. I'll see you both later.' He gave Charlotte's shoulder a gentle pat before retracing his steps back through the boot room and out into the yard. He stood for a moment wondering how to avoid this Sam and then he saw him, a large broad-shouldered man with a shock of sandy hair about to climb into Niall's Land Rover. *Sorted!* He grinned and set off in the opposite direction.

The first place he looked for her was the trekking centre, but after a thorough check inside the building, found it empty. Leaning in the open doorway he stood, hands in the pockets of his leather jacket, surveying the other buildings set around the yard. And then he heard it – a woman singing. It was coming from the long, low white building to his right. He headed towards it.

'Nice to hear someone's happy in their work.'

'Christian!' Kayte wheeled around from the box labelling and stood open-mouthed.

'The one and only.' Smiling, he walked towards her, his arms open wide as if he were about to embrace her. She dropped the marker pen and leaned against the desk, waiting for him.

'So, how are things?' he asked, coming to a halt a few feet from her. 'I heard your father took you to the police station. I hope they didn't come down too hard on you.'

'A fine and a caution.' She shrugged as if it were no big deal. 'Dad said Mrs D'Alesandro might press charges, but apparently not. Well, I'm not sure how anything could be proved against me. After all, it was all Scott's fault, wasn't it?'

'Really.' Christian raised his eyebrows in surprise as he closed in on her, reaching out to take a sliver of blonde curl in his fingers, amazed at her lack of guilt.

'Yes, really. He's a lucky sod. He's got a record; he could have been put away.' Her lips parted in a perfect smile.

'And so are you, babe.' He released her hair with a teasing grin. 'I would hate to have seen you locked up somewhere.'

'Oh, no fear of that,' she said, turning back to her boxes. 'If you'll excuse me, I have to put these back in the cupboard. The staff will be in tomorrow and they'll be expecting them to be ready. It's an important order for one of the big hotels in Taunton.'

He nodded, stepping back as she lifted the marked boxes and disappeared into an adjacent room. Christian's gaze took in the room he stood in. It appeared to be the despatch office for the ice cream company: two desks covered in paperwork, two filing cabinets and a paper-covered bulletin board. He seated himself on the edge of one of the desks, folded his arms and waited for her return.

After a few moments Kayte reappeared, closing the door behind her and leaning against it. 'So…' She cocked her head and widened her eyes. 'What brings you all the way out here?'

'Oh, I wanted to have a look around the farm.' He tried to sound casual but knew he was failing miserably.

'Did you?' Her expression said she didn't believe a word he was saying. 'And how did you get here?'

'Charlotte brought me. She's with your father at the moment discussing orders for Little Court.'

'Boring stuff, then,' she said, stepping away from the door. 'Was that the reason you came to find me?'

'Yeah.' He grinned at her, pushing a wayward strand of his curly hair from his face. 'Your father suggested Sam might show me around but he left before I could catch him. So…' He put a thoughtful finger to his chin. 'I thought: who else might be able to give me a guided tour?'

'So, you're after my *services*?' she said ambiguously, raising an amused eyebrow and moving around the desk to place her palms against his chest.

'That's the general idea.' Her closeness was beginning to arouse him already but he fought it, drawing on a mask of calm indifference as he smiled into her face. He wasn't quite ready for her yet.

'I don't come cheap, you know,' she whispered, her mouth hovering near his.

'I never imagined you did.'

She pulled back, her head tilted to one side as she regarded him for a moment, then said, 'I've been reading up about you.'

'Have you now?' He wondered where she was going with this.

'Yes.' She wrinkled her nose and frowned. 'You have quite a reputation.'

'If you say so.'

'I like bad boys.' She licked her lips and let her hands snake around his neck. 'They are so much more fun than boring old good guys.'

His hands had now come to rest on her hips. 'I like to think so too.'

She smiled seductively as she brought her lips to within a fraction of his. 'Are you up for some fun, bad boy?' Her whispered words were hot against his mouth.

'Oh, I never say no to fun, Kayte.' He smiled, pulling her up against his hard chest and taking her in a punishing kiss.

THIRTY-FOUR

'Are you sure this is going to be all right?' Charlotte asked, as she crossed the car park of Musgrove Hospital in Taunton with Stuart. It had been forty-eight hours since the incident in Hundred Acre but she was still haunted not only by the accusations but also the hate she had witnessed in Thérèse D'Alesandro's eyes.

'Don't worry, it's fine. Thérèse seems a lot calmer now; she was quite happy for me to visit,' Stuart assured as they entered through the automatic doors and began walking down a long, glass-sided corridor.

Charlotte stopped him. 'Just a minute, Stuart. "Happy for *you* to visit?"'

'Yes.'

'But not me?'

'No.'

'So if she finds out I'm here, how do you think she's going to react?'

'Charlotte, I'm not a complete idiot. She's in London, I checked with Madeline this morning. We're quite safe.'

Charlotte shook her head; this was not going at all well.

Stuart's reassuring hand was on her arm. 'Relax, it will be fine, trust me.'

They took a lift up to the first floor, passed through several more sets of doors and another glass-sided corridor until they eventually arrived in the private wing. A young woman in a navy suit sat behind a reception counter, busily tapping at a computer keyboard. She looked up and smiled as they arrived.

'Good morning,' Stuart said with his usual well-mannered smile. 'We've come to see Marco D'Alesandro. I've been told he's receiving visitors.'

'Yes, he is.' She typed something, staring at the screen patiently. 'Can I have your names please?'

'I'm Stuart Harper and this is Charlotte Kendrick,' Stuart replied, trying but not succeeding to see what the receptionist was doing.

Charlotte could guess exactly what was coming – Thérèse had specified a list of authorised visitors and she knew her name was definitely not going to be there.

'Ah yes, Mr Harper.' The receptionist nodded then raised her eyes to Charlotte. 'But I'm sorry, it doesn't appear you are on the list, Miss Kendrick.'

Stuart's brow creased. 'There must be some mistake. Miss Kendrick is Mr D'Alesandro's girlfriend.'

'Sorry, but I'm afraid she's not on the list. However, I can ring Mrs D'Alesandro and arrange clearance; it won't take long.'

'No.' Charlotte took a step back. 'You go in and see him, Stuart, I'll grab something in the hospital coffee shop. Tell him I love him and let him know why I can't come in with you, will you.'

'Charlotte, no.' Stuart tried to pull her back but she broke away and left through the hiss of automatic doors.

The girl angled her head and looked at him. 'I'm sorry, I'm only doing my job. Mrs D'Alesandro was very specific about visitors.'

Stuart nodded his understanding. 'It's okay, I'll have a word with Mr D'Alesandro. He'll soon have Miss Kendrick added to the list, I'm sure.'

With an acknowledging smile, the receptionist walked over to a frosted glass door and punched into a keypad. The door slid open. 'It's the second on the right,' she said, before returning to her seat.

When Stuart entered the light and airy room, he found Marco propped up on fat pillows, his face still a multi-colour rainbow of bruising.

'Hi, how are you feeling?' he asked, closing the door and settling himself in the comfortable chair beside the bed.

'Better,' Marco said, attempting a smile. His voice was raspy and slow due to his still swollen face. 'I still look like a chipmunk. I have three broken ribs, a lot of bruising but luckily no broken jaw or internal damage. And as you can see, my right eye is now open.'

Stuart shook his head and stared at his hands, the horror of that morning revisiting him once more. 'I thought you were a goner. If it hadn't been for Charlotte...' He looked up to see Marco's eyes were concentrating on his blanket, rubbing a distracted thumb over the weave. 'What is it?'

'Do you know how they caught me?'

Stuart shook his head.

'I was riding to Little Court to see her and I took a short cut through the woods to save time. Thérèse said she had heard Christian was there. She said Ella had told her he had come down for the weekend and was going to persuade Charlotte to go back to him. Charlotte hadn't mentioned a word to me about his arrival but I was not worried. I did not believe she wanted him, not when we felt so strongly about each other. And then, when I was in the ambulance I saw them; he was holding her. I knew then Thérèse had told the truth. That Charlotte had made a fool of me.'

'No, Marco, you're wrong. She saved you. In fact, she's...' Stuart bit down on the temptation to tell him she had come to the hospital with him. What was the point? It was clear Marco had no intention of letting her anywhere near him any more than Thérèse did.

'What were you going to say?' asked Marco.

'It doesn't matter.'

'Saving me was the least she could do when she had caused all the trouble in the first place.' Marco turned his face away to the window, an unmistakable glint of tears in his eyes. 'I do not want to see her again. It is over. He is welcome to her.'

Stuart did not know what to say. It was true Charlotte had arrived in the pub with Christian Rosetti in tow, and he remembered the intimate way they had sat talking by the fire. Could there be any truth in what Marco said? Well, once his visit was over he was determined he would quiz Charlotte and get to the bottom of it. After staying a while longer he left, promising to return the next day.

Finding Charlotte sitting at a corner table in the hospital coffee shop, he joined her.

'How is he?' She looked at him eagerly as he eased himself into the seat opposite.

'Bruised, broken ribs, no internal damage. Physically on the mend but mentally, well, that's a different matter.'

'What do you mean?'

'Charlotte, why didn't you tell him Christian was staying the weekend?'

'Because the visit was a last minute thing.' She shrugged as if she didn't understand why he was asking. 'I stayed over with Marco at Fox Cottage on Friday night. Ella told me when I returned to Little Court on Saturday morning. That was the first I knew about it. Why are you asking me this?'

'So why was it arranged in such a rush and what made him want to see you in particular?' Stuart persisted, ignoring her question.

Charlotte drained her cup and took a deep breath. 'Christian was popping pills and marinating in alcohol,' she said quietly, looking around as if checking no one else was listening. 'This caused mood swings, weird behaviour both on and off stage, and a very scary possessive thing with me. Matt found out when they were in the Caymans and got him into rehab a few weeks before Christmas. He's clean now and I knew he planned to come down to see us all to apologise for his behaviour, especially to me – no doubt you heard about the engagement?'

Stuart nodded; the whole village had.

'Matt had been working with him well into Friday evening and they stayed overnight at the London apartment. As Christian was kicking his heels over the weekend my uncle thought that with all the other commitments he had lined up for him, it would be a good opportunity for him to visit. Matt said Christian was desperate for me to take him back as a friend.' She gave a pensive sigh. 'We go back a long way, eight years, in fact. He helped me through a very bad period when my father was ill, so even after what he'd put me through I felt it wouldn't be fair to shut him out of my life. I thought the pub would be a good place for us to talk things through. That's why we were there.' She gave him a knowing nod. 'Marco's upset, isn't he? Is that what this is all about? We were due to meet up that evening and I'd planned to tell him then. But no one outside Little Court knew about the visit so how—'

'Thérèse told him!'

'Thérèse!' Charlotte's cup clattered into her saucer. 'But how would *she* know?' She was silent for a moment, lost in thought, then raised her eyes to look at Stuart. 'Of course! I saw her leaving as I arrived back on Saturday morning. Ella must have told her. How pleased she must have been.'

'I don't understand...'

'She's trying to marry Marco off to their house guest Rossana Caravello.'

'That's crazy. She's a pretty girl but young and very immature, not his type at all.'

'That may well be, but it hasn't stopped her. It became so bad Marco contacted his father. He turned up and took Felica and Rossana away to Canada with him for a month. Because of this we were able to continue our relationship... until now, that is. This is all Thérèse's doing. She's been looking for an opportunity to part us again and now she's found it.' Charlotte let out a harsh laugh. 'She blamed me for the accident, but she was the one who put all those thoughts in his head. She was the reason he was riding through Hundred Acre.' Her eyebrows buffered together in a frown. 'But why did he believe her? Why didn't he realise? She's twisted it all to her own purpose, hasn't she? Made it look as if I was getting back together with Christian.'

'Yes, I think she has.'

'Oh God, what am I going to do?' She ran a hand through her thick black hair. 'I have to talk to him, Stuart. He has to know the truth.'

'I'm afraid that's impossible, Lottie. It's not only Thérèse who is stopping you visiting; he doesn't want to see you either.' Stuart reached across the table and took her hand. 'Look, I'm coming back tomorrow. When I see him, I'll tell him what you told me, I promise. Maybe once he's out of hospital I can arrange something, but for now I'm afraid there's not a lot I can do. Thérèse is firmly in control at the moment. But don't give up. I'll make it come right for both of you, I promise.'

The next day, Charlotte was sitting at her desk going through some figures when she heard the distinctive tone of her mobile. She pulled it out quickly from her tote and answered.

'Lottie, it's me, Stuart. Can you talk? '

Her heart soared. Stuart had news. She hoped he had managed to work the miracle he'd promised and she would soon be seeing Marco.

'You've seen Marco?'

'Actually, no,' came the sombre reply. 'Lottie, I'm here in Taunton. I came down to see him only to find he was discharged this morning.'

'Discharged? Well, that's brilliant news. He'll be back at the manor by now. When are you going over to see him?'

'I'm not.'

She hesitated. 'Stuart... what's happened?'

'He's gone, Lottie. He was collected from the hospital and taken straight to the airport. He's flown to Italy with Thérèse.'

'Italy?' She took a deep breath. 'When will he be back?'

'I honestly don't know. I called the manor and spoke to Madeline. Thérèse has flown to Milan for a fashion show and is due back on Tuesday but Marco's gone to convalesce at their house on Lake Como. She has no idea when he is expected to return.'

Thérèse stood gazing out across the water from the terrace of the D'Alesandros' pale pink villa a few kilometres from Bellano on the eastern edge of Lake Como. She breathed in the freshness of the air. It was early April with spring well on its way, the tender buds already bursting forth in the expansive seventeen acres of luxurious sculpted gardens and terraces which surrounded their beautiful lakeside home. As the water sparkled in the pale morning sunshine, she smiled. Everything was well in her world. More than well, in fact. Marco had made a complete recovery from the awful beating he had taken; bruises and broken bones had healed and his face had thankfully escaped any disfigurement.

It had been important to get him out of the hospital and away to a place where Charlotte could not reach him. She was aware she had tried, unsuccessfully, to visit with Stuart Harper and she could not allow it to happen again. She also knew that if her stepson had returned to the manor, he would have started to question the things she had told him. He would have needed to confront Charlotte, and the truth would have come out. But now, she reflected, everything was fine.

During Marco's convalescence she had been busy working with Rossana, redirecting her away from the boisterous puppy antics the girl had mistakenly thought would capture his heart. It was now a matter of her carefully guiding her towards their ultimate goal, and everything was progressing along nicely. In the month they had been in each other's company, Rossana's more reserved attitude towards him had won her his friendship – something unthinkable back in England, where he had been under Charlotte's spell and quite dismissive of their house guest. Now Rossana was sweet and attentive, something she felt sure would soon win Marco over completely.

Thérèse turned her head on hearing the sound of a car engine. They were back.

Marco killed the engine and opened the door of the silver Mercedes. He went around to the passenger door to help Rossana out. Taking his hand, she gave him one of her beautiful smiles.

'Well done,' he said encouragingly. 'Father will be pleased.'

Thérèse came down the steps towards them, her expression warm and happy. 'Ah, I see you have come with good news.'

'Yes, Rossana has passed her driving test.' Marco stretched a gentle hand across Rossana's shoulder and squeezed it gently. 'The examiner said she was fantastic.'

Thérèse stretched out her arms to the girl. 'Ah, *cara mia*, I cannot wait to tell Gianni,' she said, hugging her. 'I am going to ask him to buy you a car.'

'A car?' Rossana's gaze flew from hers to Marco. 'Oh, no, it is too much money. I am only a guest.'

'Even guests need their own transport,' Thérèse insisted. She reached to push a strand of hair back from the girl's pretty face. 'And it is important for you to practice now you have passed. Would you like one of these?' She nodded towards the sleek SLK.

Rossana shook her head, a worried expression on her face. 'I do not know. It is very powerful. I was thinking maybe—'

'Come along, try it,' Thérèse interrupted, her eyes glancing towards her stepson. 'Marco will take you out.'

Marco nodded and handed Rossana the car keys. 'Come,' he said, walking over to open the driver's door for her.

Thérèse watched the vehicle slowly leave then walked back to the house, secure in the knowledge that all thoughts of Charlotte Kendrick were evaporating from her stepson's mind. Soon, very soon, she told herself, Rossana will be the one foremost in his thoughts.

Marco sat belted into the passenger seat as Rossana pulled out between the electric gates. He had been amazed at the change in her a month in Canada had brought. He had not looked forward to her return, sensing in his weakened state she would use the opportunity to smother him in her touchy-feely way to the point he would want to scream. However, all her arrival at the villa had produced was an initial show of genuine tears at his battered state and a willingness to be there whenever he needed her. She was a gentle soul with a caring way, and now she had worked out that a more reserved manner was the order of the day, he actually found he was beginning to like her. He was not sure whether Felica had had a hand in this, but it appeared Rossana had grown up a lot and was now proving to be pleasant company. But he was still very suspicious of Thérèse, even though she was always quick to assure him she had merely used their house guest as a weapon to part him from someone she saw as most unsuitable company – something, he had now realised to his cost, was true.

At first, in those early days of recovery, he had ached for Charlotte, constantly feeling as if part of him were missing, and he was sure what he had felt with her he would never again experience with anyone else. Theirs had been a truly passionate relationship but, as the weeks had progressed, he saw things in a different light. Passion they may have had, but in the end she had played him false. Despite the intenseness of their relationship, and in spite of all her vows of commitment to him, she had returned to Christian.

He watched Rossana out of the corner of his eye. So far, she seemed to be handling the car competently. Her stay with them was certainly beginning to bring her out of her shell, and he felt pleased his father's philanthropic gesture was helping to bring this change about. The girl she was today was a far cry from the timid creature that had arrived during their Christmas holidays.

During the early days of his convalescence there were times when she had kept him company as he sat out on the terrace resting and watching the lake. Through their conversations he had learned about her life before she came to live with them. It had not been a happy one. He felt sad for the loss of her parents, for her lonely life and her missing out on the kind of growing up experiences most young women took for granted. His father had now hopefully remedied the situation, and Marco hoped by the time her eighteenth birthday arrived she would have turned into the young woman she should be: well groomed, confident, a little more experienced, and ready to meet the world.

The drive was without incident and on reaching a layby outside Dervio, he suggested she turn the car around and return to the villa. She found reverse gear a little more difficult to achieve, but with his gentle coaxing she was eventually there, and they began the homeward run passed clusters of houses and through open wooded hillsides. They were nearly at the villa when, rounding a left-hand bend, they came face to face with a car in the middle of the road. Rossana panicked, Marco grabbed the wheel and shouted to her to brake. Both cars passed within a hair's breadth of each other. The SLK skidded to a halt in a curtain of dust and spray of stones.

'Oh, Marco!' Rossana grabbed at his arm, burrowing her head into his shoulder.

He stroked her hair 'Shh... It is okay, these things happen.'

She looked up at him, her huge green eyes rimmed with tears as if looking for forgiveness. 'I am sorry, I should have been more careful.'

'You were not on the wrong side of the road, Rossana, the other driver was. It was his fault not yours.' Something in him bubbled to the surface, something warm and strong which wanted to protect this young, vulnerable girl. He bent his head to reassure her again and found her pretty mouth hovering inches from his own. He was close enough to kiss her but realising that was the last thing he should be doing, he was about to pull back when Rossana did the deed for him and brought her lips to his with gentle, chaste pressure. He remained where he was, letting the compression of her soft mouth do all the work. It was innocent and totally non-arousing, unlike his first kiss with Charlotte. Memories flooded into his mind... her fingers meshing in his hair, her softness pressing against him as his mouth claimed hers... He jerked away from Rossana as if burned.

'Oh, have I offended you?' Her expression was one of horrified surprise.

'Forgive me. I do not know what came over me.'

'It was shock, I expect,' he said, adding a smile to reassure her he was not annoyed. 'Do not look so upset. It was... pleasant.' He cleared his throat. 'Would you like me to drive the rest of the way home?'

'Yes, I think that would be a good idea.' Rossana said, unclipping her seat belt and getting out of the car.

Rossana smiled secretly to herself – she had kissed him and although he had not really responded, he had not pushed her away either. Mrs D'Alesandro was right: taking things slowly would bring results. She already had his friendship, and now a first kiss. Maybe given time there would be more. Much, much more.

THIRTY-FIVE

Charlotte headed for the stables, carrying her hat, her whip underarm. It was mid-April and beneath a blue sky filled with the huge puffball clouds associated with spring, daffodils were nodding their yellow heads in large clumps along the edge of Little Court's driveway. The warmth of the sun seeped through her thick sweater, making her wish its heat could wrap itself around her still cold heart.

It had been seven weeks since the incident in Hundred Acre; seven weeks with many more to come on the lonely journey without Marco that was now her life. As if the pain of separation was not enough, she hated the way he had been whisked away without her even being given the chance to defend herself. And now thanks to Thérèse, Marco lived in a world where his truth said she had been unfaithful, and there was absolutely nothing she could do about it. She had heard from Kieren that Marco was back in London. If he had returned to the manor at all, no one had seen him – even Stuart knew no more than she did. It appeared Thérèse had won.

She reached the stables and smiled her thanks to Jed, who appeared to have anticipated her need to ride this morning, handing her the reins of an already saddled Jet. Within twenty minutes she was sitting in her usual spot, surveying the valley. A horse's nicker alerted her to the arrival of another rider and she turned to see Felica approaching. She too had been absent from the manor, dividing her time between Italy and London, working on her new fashion collection.

'Lottie!' Felica reined in with a smile. 'I have not seen you for such a long time. How are you?'

'I'm fine, how are you?'

'Oh, busy.' She rolled her eyes. 'Even with Mother's help this collection is proving extremely hard work. But it will be well worth it in the end, I love what I am doing.'

Charlotte nodded, turning her attention back to the valley. She didn't want to ask Felica to leave but her presence was beginning to bring back painful reminders of her loss.

'Lottie, if you are not in a hurry could we talk?'

She swung around to look at Marco's sister. 'Talk?'

'Yes, I thought you might like to know how Marco is. You were very brave standing up to those thugs, and I think you still care for him.'

Charlotte gave a heavy sigh. 'It's pointless me having any feelings for him. I understand he is back in London now but I have not seen him. My guess is by now your mother's plans have come to fruition and he is with Rossana.'

'Not in the way you think. Come, let us talk…' Felica motioned towards the wood.

Finding a small glade, sunlight dappling through the fresh green leaves of the trees' budding canopy, they tethered the horses. A fallen oak served as a seat and they settled themselves, Felica leaning forward and clasping her hands between her knees.

'First, I am glad to be able to tell you he is totally recovered,' she said.

Charlotte gave a silent nod.

'Next, yes, he does have a different relationship with Rossana. She spent quite a lot of time with him at the Lake Como villa while he was recovering. She came back quite different from our time away in Canada. These days, she keeps her hands to herself and she tends to listen rather than drive everyone mad with her endless chatter. I think maybe my father might have had a hand in this. These were the two main issues Marco had with her, and since they have now been resolved he has settled into what I can only describe as a warm friendship, much like an older brother.'

Charlotte got to her feet; she should not have started this conversation. It was making things worse instead of better. Of course, she was glad he had not suffered any lasting effects and was fully recovered from the beating, but to know he had at last accepted Rossana and they had become friends was another matter. With this foundation laid no doubt Thérèse would be working out her strategy to move things on. It was like a knife in her heart. She walked over to Jet and untied his reins.

'Lottie, where are you going? I have not finished.'

She turned. Felica was still sitting on the tree trunk, looking at her with a puzzled expression.

'I'm sorry, I have to go.' She forced a smile. 'Thank you for letting me know how he is, you've put my mind at rest.'

'No, I have not; I can see it in your face.' Felica's eyes locked onto hers. 'Do you honestly think I brought you here simply to tell you about Marco?'

'What then? What else is there to say?'

'I spoke with Ella the other day. She tells me Christian's visit was a last minute arrangement. That you were only aware of it on the Saturday morning when you returned from Fox Cottage.'

'That is correct.' Charlotte shrugged, wondering where this was going.

'She also said part of the reason he came down here was to see you.'

'Yes, I've never denied that. But I don't understand why you are so interested.'

'Because I need to know the truth. What was the reason he needed to see you and why were you with him when you rescued Marco?'

'There's no point to any of this, Felica.' Charlotte slotted her foot into Jet's stirrup. 'Whatever I say to you today will make no difference. Marco will never believe what really happened, even if it comes from you. Thérèse has made his mind up for him and the evidence against me is overwhelming.'

'This is not for Marco, it is for me. I have concerns about my mother. She has never made any secret of the fact she wants Marco for Rossana, but it is her methods I am beginning to question. I am trying to put the pieces of the puzzle together to establish whether she had any involvement in Marco's beating.' Felica rose and walked over to Charlotte's horse. Holding on to the rein, she said calmly, 'You see, he told me she said Christian had returned and wanted you back. I have also learned from Ella that she was in her office at Little Court when Matt phoned, but at no time was anything mentioned about you getting back together with Christian. As you can imagine, when she told Marco what now appears to be false information, he was furious. He became suspicious as to why you had not told him about the visit, and in his anxiety to see you he took a short cut through the wood. So what is the truth of it, Lottie? Were you planning to return to Christian, or did my mother twist things to suit her own purpose?'

Charlotte looked down at her from Jet's back. 'Twist things for her own purpose?'

'I know my mother is no angel,' Felica said wisely, 'and from what Ella says of that day's events, it appears Mother has been very deceitful. I know she hates Marco. She feels he comes between her and my father. Seeing him married would get him out of the way and I think this is what is behind it all. Rossana comes from a very old wealthy Italian family, to my mother that is a match made in heaven. If I am right then I need to protect him. I do not want to have to look at his beaten face again because of what she has done.'

Thérèse! Stupid, scheming Thérèse had set everything up to discredit and get rid of her and it had backfired in the most horrific way. Oh, how easy it had been to pretend to be outraged, and who better to use as a whipping boy than herself? With Christian looking on it had been so simple to accuse and be believed.

Charlotte dismounted and took a deep breath. If she could never have Marco back at least helping Felica would keep him safe.

A week after her meeting with Felica in Hundred Acre, Charlotte was at her desk when she received a call from Kieren.

'I gather you and Marco are still worlds apart,' he said with a disconsolate sigh.

'Stuff happens,' she said, spinning her chair round to look out of the office window. 'You're not calling because of that, are you?'

'No. I thought you might like to have lunch with me today.'

'Today?'

'Yes, it's my birthday.'

Her hand flew to her face. How could she have forgotten? 'Oh no! Kieren, I'm so sorry.'

He gave a light-hearted chuckle. 'Say yes, and I'll forgive you.'

Charlotte turned back to her desk and checked her diary. 'Yes,' she said, staring down at the open page. 'I have to be back by three thirty, though.'

'Fine. I'll meet you at twelve forty-five.'

'Where?'

'San Raffaello's, of course.'

'No, Kieren, absolutely not!'

'He's not here, Lottie. He's away for the day. Besides, Vittorio and Florentine would love to see you. Oh, come on… it's as safe as houses.'

'I've heard that before. What about Thérèse? I do not want to run into that dragon.'

'She's in Italy at the moment, but even if she wasn't, you'd have three Saint Georges here to do battle on your behalf. Everyone feels you've been treated very shabbily.'

'Well, thank them for the support but tell them I've moved on,' she said in a voice more confident than she felt. 'Marco is yesterday's news.'

'Ah well, that's okay then.' Kieren's amused tone intimated he didn't believe a word she had said.

Taking a taxi into the centre of London, Charlotte got out and walked the last two blocks to the restaurant, stopping on the way to buy some expensive cologne and have it gift wrapped. Reaching San Raffaello's, she took a deep breath and climbed the steps to the door. Kieren was sitting at a window table and looked up with a smile when she entered.

Vittorio came forward to claim her raincoat. 'It's good to see you, Charlotte,' he said, giving her a wide welcoming smile.

'You look pretty hot today,' Kieren said as she joined him at the table.

'Trousers tucked into boots and a sweater, I don't think so.'

'Believe me, I know hot when I see it, even if I am gay.' His comment made her laugh.

'Doesn't she look great, Vittorio?' Kieren asked as the head waiter arrived with a large glass of wine and half a lager.

'Charlotte looks wonderful in everything she wears,' he said graciously with dark-eyed admiration, and left to take an order at another table.

Charlotte looked at the departing Vittorio. 'No menus?'

'I've already ordered,' Kieren said with a mischievous grin. 'Trust me, you'll love it.'

And she did. The meal was delicious: a selection of Italian bread pieces served with olive oil and balsamic vinegar, followed by prawn linguini and finishing with panna cotta, all washed down with a couple of glasses of Marco's best champagne. By two thirty the restaurant was empty, leaving staff clearing away while Vittorio joined Kieren and Charlotte to chat as she handed over his present.

His face lit up when he unwrapped it. 'Gee, thanks. I love this but it's mega expensive, I can't usually afford it.'

'I'm only sorry I forgot the big day.' She gave him a guilty look. 'I must remember...'

The words died in her throat as the restaurant door opened and Marco walked in, shaking rain from his hair. Taking one look at the small tableau, his brows drew together in an angry frown. Then he spied Charlotte and his face darkened.

'What the hell are you doing in my restaurant?' he demanded, storming to the table.

'It's my birthday and Charlotte is my guest,' Kieren said politely, standing up and squaring his shoulders ready to defend his stepsister.

He ignored Kieren, his anger still directed at her. 'I would like you to go.'

'It's okay, Kieren.' Charlotte got to her feet. The last thing she wanted was to get him into trouble and at this moment, the expression on Marco's normally placid face was murderous.

'No! This restaurant is open to the public, you're entitled to be here.' Kieren eyes flared at Marco. 'You have no right—'

'I have every right. This is *my* restaurant.' His words were forced through gritted teeth. 'And after what she has done she is not welcome here.'

'And what, exactly, has she done?' Kieren challenged. 'Saved your back from a beating, that's what, and has to suffer in silence while your stepmother has enjoyed publicly accusing her of something she is entirely innocent of. Go on, Lottie, tell him the truth about you and Christian.'

'Enough!' Marco slammed his hand down on the table, making the cutlery jump. 'Get out, now!' Glaring at Charlotte, he pointed a finger towards the door.

'Don't worry, I'm going.' Charlotte tried to control the way her body was visibly shaking. She had never been subjected to such raw anger, and coming from him it was doubly upsetting. Gathering up her bag and giving Kieren's shoulder a reassuring squeeze, she made her way towards the door, retrieved her raincoat, then left.

When the door shut, Vittorio shook his head, looking first at Kieren then at Marco. 'She did not deserve that,' he said.

'Keep out of my private life, both of you.' Marco scowled again before stalking off towards the rear of the restaurant and into his office. The door closed with a slam.

THIRTY-SIX

'You are joking, Lucy.' Charlotte took her eyes from her book and stared at her cousin, her head spinning with the implications of what she had just been told.

On a bright early May afternoon she had managed to find a quiet spot, tucking herself away in one of the sheltered areas of Little Court's extensive gardens. Settled and comfortable on one of the Lutyens benches, she had planned to spend the afternoon reading and enjoying her day off: a day simply for her, with nothing to think about... until now.

'No, I'm perfectly serious.' Coming straight from the stable after her daily ride, Lucy stood in front of her, holding her riding hat and whip, pale jodhpurs tucked into black riding boots encasing the slim hips and long legs Charlotte envied. 'When I saw Felica in the village this morning, she said we're an absolute must-have.'

'You and I? Models? Has she completely taken leave of her senses?'

'Actually,' Lucy grinned down at her cousin's dismayed face, 'I think we'd look pretty damn good. Apart from our eye colour we could almost be twins. Felica has designed these beautiful evening dresses. One is blue and one is green. She thinks we would be perfect models for them.'

'Twins?' Charlotte gave a heavy sigh, her eyes trailing down her cousin's slim frame. 'Oh yes, a bit like Swarzenegger and DiVito you mean?'

'Swarzenegger and DiVito? What are you talking about?'

'They were in the film *Twins*, remember? Well, that's exactly like you and me.'

'Of course it isn't!' Lucy gave a snort of exasperation, visualising both men. 'They are nothing like us. Stop it, Lottie, there is nothing wrong with you. If anything, I'm the one with the problem. I deliberately don't eat. Anorexia is my thing. I like being thin. Believe me, you are not fat. What size are you?' she demanded.

'Fourteen.'

'A size fourteen? Not exactly enormous, is it? You've got a bad body image, that's all.' Lucy shook her head disapprovingly. 'I can see I'm going to have my work cut out re-educating you.'

'What do you mean "re-educating"?'

'Making you happy in your skin. Most women would kill for a figure like yours.'

'Of course they would,' Charlotte bit out sarcastically.

'I'm serious. Do you know what most of your problem is? It's what you wear.'

'And what's wrong with what I wear?'

'Apart from the dress I persuaded you to buy in Taunton and that emerald green cashmere sweater CJ bought you for Christmas, everything in your wardrobe is pale. You have a good figure, great skin and fabulous hair. Colour! You need colour!' she said, waving a finger.

Charlotte glared at her for a moment, unable to answer. She had left her pre-university garb of black and Doc Martens at the door of Warwick University and moved into a more acceptable fashion phase – one of jeans and sweaters and pale colours. Her mother had accepted her Goth phase, calling her "an individual", "a free spirit". Her father, a proud man in his role of headmaster, had, she knew, suffered as a result. He was constantly aware both pupils and staff referred to her as Morticia, a character from the 1960s' American comedy about the ghoulish Addams Family. By retreating into pale insignificant clothes, had her actions been some form of atonement for that rebellious phase in her life? A phase which had left her with the fear she had been a contributory factor surrounding his eventual demise? Or maybe the difference between her and Lucy was down to their mothers. Ella was beautiful and glamorous, small wonder Lucy looked like a younger version. Her own, however, was a small, practical woman who rarely wore make-up and whose plain, functional, no-frills wardrobe was sensible and... dull.

She cast her mind back to the night in London when Marco had presented her with that beautiful midnight blue and silver dress with matching heels, telling her strong colour suited her. When she had stood in front of the bedroom mirror she had felt she was seeing her real self for the first time; totally stunned at the transformation. She had contemplated leaving her comfort zone, making the most of herself; the red dress and CJ's Christmas gift were to have been the start. However, events which lost her Marco had driven her back to her pale colour chart, wanting to blend into the background again.

Would she ever be free of him? she wondered. Nearly three months after the incident in the wood he still managed to surface intermittently in her thoughts, normally in the middle of the night when she lay awake unable to sleep. She had hoped when she had given Felica a detailed account of what had really happened that Saturday morning her words might have found their way to him; but after the incident in the restaurant when she had seen his violent reaction to her, she had given up hope. He loathed her, he'd made that obvious, and no matter what anyone said or did, nothing was ever going to change that. The moment she walked out of San Raffaello's front door she knew she had to move on.

'Lottie, you're with the fairies again.' Lucy's voice cut through her thoughts, bringing her back.

Charlotte squinted up at her. 'Sorry... Where were we?'

'Modelling for Felica?'

'Yes, okay, I'll do it,' Charlotte agreed. Five simple words spoken without any further need of persuasion from her cousin. It was time to put a painful past behind her and behave like an adult, not some lovelorn girl mooning over a man she could never have, a man who clearly no longer wanted her. Marco D'Alesandro did not deserve any more of her precious time and from now on he certainly was not going to get it.

'You will? Oh, thank you,' Lucy cried, jumping up and down. 'I'll go and phone her now, she will be *so* pleased.'

Later that evening, CJ arrived back from Dartmouth, where he had been staying for the last couple of days while he checked over the work being carried out on Gulls' Rest. Charlotte watched him across the dinner table. There was something different about him, something she could not quite put a finger on. After their evening meal, she suggested a walk in the floodlit gardens. She wanted him on his own, not simply for a progress report but to try to wheedle out what was going on.

They stood for a while where the lawn met the river's edge, watching the ancient willows trail their feathered branches in the current. After giving her a breakdown of how things were going on the house and how far Taylor Macayne had progressed with the extension build, CJ paused for a moment, his concentration fixed on the current. Charlotte was about to ask him what was wrong, when she noticed the corners of his mouth lift in a half smile as if he were in some secret place enjoying a memory.

Her eyes caught his with a questioning smile. 'What have you been up to?'

'Me? Why nothing.'

'Oh, come on. You're looking very guilty about something.'

'Am I?' He gave an amused grin.

A thought occurred to her. 'You haven't made any changes to my plans for Gulls' Rest, have you? I do hope not.' She gave a worried shake of her head. 'I know what you're like and if you have, well, you should have checked with—'

CJ placed firm hands on her shoulders, stilling her concern. 'Don't worry, I've made absolutely no changes to the house. It's nothing to do with work, more affairs of the heart.'

'You've a girlfriend?'

He nodded.

'About time,' she teased. 'Mum was beginning to despair of you. She thinks you're a workaholic, and that if you're not careful you'll end up burning yourself out like Dad.' The words came out before she could stop them. 'Sorry, wrong thing to say. But she worries about you. You need to balance your life, have some fun once in a while. But...,' she hesitated, 'but if you have at last found someone, I guess you'll be doing that, won't you?'

CJ nodded. 'I am, and I plan to bring her along to Felica's show next week so she can meet the family.'

She clutched his arm. 'This is very exciting, CJ. Where did you meet her? How old is she?'

'Question one – she's someone I met at work. Question two – shame on you, Charlotte, you should never ask a lady's age. We became friends first. I discovered we had a lot of interests in common, then everything... well, you know...' He gave an embarrassed shrug. 'And now I'm remarkably happy.'

'CJ!' she protested loudly. 'You're only giving me half the story.'

'I know,' he said in his irritatingly older brother way. 'And you'll get the other half when you meet her.'

Returning to the house, CJ made his excuses and headed for his room, saying he needed to check over a list of changes Thérèse had emailed him concerning work on the manor. They were virtually ready to submit a planning application for the next phase of external work there, and he wanted to familiarise himself with these before he returned to the office the next day.

Intrigued by this new woman in her brother's life, Charlotte went to find Lucy. She found her in her room, lying on her bed, listening to Urban Fox's debut album *Stolen from the Night*. As Charlotte entered, Lucy pulled off her headphones, swung her feet off the bed and looked at her expectantly.

'What is it?'

'I thought you ought to know CJ has a girlfriend.'

'You're joking!'

'Honest truth. He's just told me.'

'About time too.' Lucy rolled over excitedly and sat up. 'So... who is she? Come on, tell me. I want to know absolutely everything.'

'There is nothing to tell. He met her at work and she's under wraps until he brings her here to the show next week. Says we can meet her then.'

'Surely he must have given you some clues?'

Charlotte thought for a moment. 'Well, one thing did make me stop and think.' She paused and then continued, 'When I asked her age, he said it was rude to ask questions like that.'

'Her age,' Lucy repeated. 'Do you think...?'

'An older woman maybe?'

Lucy's mouth formed itself into a silent O.

'It makes sense in a way,' Charlotte reasoned. 'CJ's very quiet and quite mature for his age. I guess he would appeal to the older woman.'

'What, like *The Graduate*, you mean?' Lucy raised her eyes to the ceiling dreamily. 'Benjamin and Mrs Robinson. The older woman helping the younger man lose his virginity. I like it.'

Charlotte snorted with laughter. 'My brother's not a virgin, Luce. He had several girlfriends while he was at uni. Believe me, he's had experience with women.'

Lucy rolled her eyes. 'Sorry, airhead moment!'

Together, they laughed.

'Frustratingly for both of us,' Charlotte said, halting her hilarity, 'we'll have to wait until next week but, please, you must keep this a secret. He needs to tell Mum himself. I don't want her finding out through anyone else, otherwise he'll be really upset.'

'My lips are sealed.' Lucy ran an imaginary zip across her mouth. 'Oh, by the way, I forgot to mention... When I called Felica earlier, she asked whether we could go over to the manor for a fitting.'

'When?'

'This Saturday afternoon. Oh, and if you're worried about Marco—'

'Which I'm not,' Charlotte interrupted quickly.

'He's in Italy with Thérèse and Rossana until next week,' Lucy continued. 'So Felica thought we might like to stay over. They've had a new cinema room installed; she's having a Tom Cruise evening. Interested?'

Charlotte thought for a moment then nodded. 'Yes, why not. It'll be fun.'

The day of the show had at last arrived. Rays of spring sunshine danced through the windows of the great hall, while in Ella's office the Holy Trinity sat making final checks. Ella sat back with a smile as she gazed across her desk at Jenny and Issy.

'So, everything's in place. Food, drink, seating, stage, runway, flowers,' Ella counted off on her fingers. 'Matt's sorted out the technical stuff for Christian; one of the techs is due around eleven. Costumes and shoes are here, so are the dressers; models arriving at nine thirty with make-up and hairdressers. Gardens looking fabulous, as usual, Jen.' She waved a finger at her sister-in-law. 'Don't forget to let Rowan know what a fantastic job the lads have done, will you. And now...' She got to her feet and moved over to the small fridge located behind her desk. 'Although it's early, I think we ought to kick off proceedings with a toast.' With that, she pulled out a bottle of champagne. The pale bubbly liquid was soon poured and the three women stood and touched glasses. 'To Felica. May today be a fantastic success!'

Thérèse arrived, along with Felica, a little after ten, giving only a cool, polite nod to Lucy and Charlotte as she passed them in the entrance hall, Felica stopping to receive hugs before disappearing after her mother into the Blue Room, which had been turned into a dressing and make-up area for the models, an area soon awash with people.

By midday Little Court buzzed with activity. The show was due to kick off at two thirty and guests would soon begin arriving, their cars directed to the designated parking area behind the stable block.

Lucy and Charlotte were in a small side room having their styling options discussed, with Felica looking on. It was decided both should have their thick curly hair pinned up to accentuate what she termed their 'to die for' facial bone structure. Once their hair had been done and make-up colours finalised, they joined the other models for a run through. Still dressed in their own clothes but wearing the shoes chosen for their outfits, they followed each other slowly down the catwalk and back. This was not only to make sure the running order worked but also to get them used to their new footwear. When Charlotte and Lucy headed back to the side room, a tall figure was leaning in the doorway, his arms folded, a wide smile on his face.

'Christian!' Lucy give him a hug then stared at him. 'My God! Are you going to perform like *that*? No suit?'

'No suit,' Christian echoed, standing his ground, his dark eyes challenging. 'Do you have a problem, Miss Benedict? Because if you do, you'll have to argue with Felica. She's calling the shots on the dress code.'

After giving Christian a hug, Charlotte stepped back to take a better look at him. His jeans were black leather and tight, the white shirt Ralph Lauren, open-necked with sleeves rolled up to the elbow. Above his left wrist she noticed his familiar black panther tattoo and on his right, the newly acquired multi-coloured dragon which wrapped itself dramatically around his arm.

Lucy's face lit up. 'Actually, I think you look... incredibly sexy. I like it.'

'I'm also going to be barefoot, so ladies,' he glanced down to their high stiletto sandals, 'do be careful where you put your feet please.'

'You've had your hair cut,' Charlotte said, choosing the moment to step behind him to view what the scissors had done.

He ran a hand around the back of his neck. 'Only a tidy up.'

'We agreed it needed doing.'

Both girls turned at the sound of Felica's voice. She surveyed Christian with a calm smile and then sighed. 'You will be fabulous: a god-like figure between these two beautiful women. It will set the whole thing off perfectly.'

'Stop it, Felica,' Lucy scolded, winking at Charlotte. 'His ego is big enough already.'

'I do not care about his ego, in my eyes this man is wonderful. He has waived his fee today,' Felica said, her eyes wide with admiration. 'Can you believe he has done this thing for me?'

Charlotte studied him with a smile as he wrapped an arm around Felica and give her an affectionate hug. The old Christian was definitely back.

'Yes,' she said, 'I think I can.'

One thirty had seen a gradual drift in of fashion journalists to join the few who had been there for the run through, and from the curtained back of the catwalk Charlotte took the opportunity to watch as guests, clutching gold embossed programmes, were shown to their seats. Thérèse and Felica arrived, one wearing pale turquoise, the other in rose pink, both brushing cheeks with various elegant women and men.

Charlotte shrank back and returned to the dressing area where the first models were having finishing touches put to their make-up and hair. Thérèse came in and began issuing final instructions to everyone, and by two fifteen everyone was ready.

All the outfits were gorgeous, Charlotte thought as she admired the elegant, long-legged young women being given a last minute check over by the D'Alesandro women. There was a complete mixture in the clothes show today: pastels and strong block colours plus fabrics of all types, from silk and taffeta to light wool. She had no idea how much input Felica had had in the actual designs and choice of fabrics, but the finished collection was brilliant – sleek, stylish and very sexy.

The first models left to position themselves in readiness for their saunter from one end of the great hall to the other. A blast of music erupted from the speakers and Billy Joel's 'Uptown Girl' sent the first girl, a brunette, on her way, hips swaying. As they were to be the final two to go out, following Christian's performance, Charlotte and Lucy managed to find a quiet place in the darkness at the back end of the stage to watch. Judging by the expressions on faces in the audience, Charlotte thought everybody already seemed very impressed.

'I almost forgot,' Lucy hissed, after they had been observing for twenty minutes. 'Any sign of CJ?'

Charlotte peered out into the audience, searching for her tall fair-headed brother.

'No, no sign at all,' she said, her eyes unexpectedly landing on Marco. Wearing a light navy suit with a blue open-neck shirt, dark hair curling around his collar, he sat at the far end of the runway, and seated next to him was Rossana, her hand clasped in his.

'Do you think he was winding you up?' Lucy said, a few minutes later.

Charlotte tore her eyes away from Marco and turned back to her cousin. 'Why?'

'Well, you know what CJ's like.'

'One minute.' Charlotte peered again, scanning each row and eventually found him. She could not believe her eyes. She closed and opened them again. No, it must be her because he had his arm draped around her shoulder, his head close to hers.

'Found him?'

'Oh my goodness, yes, and he's sitting next to—' She turned back to Lucy.

'Your face! It's someone you know, isn't it?'

Charlotte nodded. 'It's Beth. He's with Beth! He said they met at work, which is kind of true. We stayed with her when we first went down to look at Gulls' Rest. He called it a friendship which progressed. They hit it off straight away, Luce. I thought they were simply good friends.' She put a palm to her forehead. 'I should have realised.'

'The age question had you fooled.'

'Yes. Had he said twenty-four, I might have rumbled him. Oh, I'm so pleased. I hope it works out, she's just right for him.'

'I'm looking forward to meeting her after our outstanding performance,' Lucy said, grinning. 'Talking of which, I think we'd better get back, we're due on soon.'

Felica was waiting for them in the Blue Room. After make-up and a final hair check, they were dressed, Lucy in emerald green and Charlotte in Mediterranean blue. Both wore one-shoulder full-length taffeta evening gowns, one split to the thigh on the right side, the other on the left. As they walked forward to the curtained entrance, Charlotte drew in a breath and smiled, her eyes fixed on the runway stretching out before them.

Christian finished to a tremendous applause, bowed to the audience and ran back to join them. Charlotte was disappointed they had missed his three song slot but knew his performance with them would more than make up for it. He reached the curtains and pushed through, pulling off his black t-shirt, his hair bouncing around his face. With a grin, he gave them both a peck on the cheek and growled, 'Go out and slay 'em girls,' before he disappeared back to the changing area.

Charlotte knew the plan off by heart, after all, they had both put a lot of time into rehearsals during the week. On cue, the curtains parted and they emerged onto the smooth white runway, and began their routine as an abbreviated version of Patti Smith's 'Because the Night' blasted from the sound system. At the circular end of the catwalk they stopped, twirled and stood, hands on hips, rocking to the pulse of the music. As they waited for Christian, Charlotte made the mistake of gazing down into the audience and found herself staring straight into deep brown eyes; eyes which looked up at her not with anger, but a different emotion altogether. Inhaling sharply, she met his gaze with a hard stare, trying to ignore the expression on his face and the way Rossana, who was also staring, clutched his hand even more possessively.

Tearing her eyes away, Charlotte concentrated instead on the task in hand, extending her arms out, palms up, towards the beginning of the runway in the same manner as her cousin. Silently summoned, Christian appeared, applause breaking out all around him. He walked towards them with his usual cat-like grace, hips swaying to the beat, a smile on his handsome face. His loose, white Ralph Lauren shirt was open to the waist, revealing a toned and muscular body Charlotte knew most women would die to get their hands on.

He took Lucy first, his arm encircling her waist loosely, moving around and around in a circle with her, smiling down into her face as they swayed to the beat for a while, then he released her with a graceful sweep of his arm and turned, catching Charlotte in his strong grip. She felt his fingers splayed across her hip as he pulled her close to him. Unlike with Lucy, he allowed no space between their bodies, instead moulding her intimately to him, his face so close to hers she could feel his breath in her hair. They moved in a slow deliberate circle, the edge of his hip pressed tightly against hers and she automatically responded. Mischief danced in his eyes as she rocked her pelvis against his. He leaned in and stroked her face, a slow and intimate gesture, and as the music came to a conclusion he bent his head, his mouth claiming hers. Then raising his head, he released her, gazing out into the audience with a smile as he punched the air. Enthusiastic applause and flash photography followed: the audience loved it. Charlotte knew his appearance here today would help Felica's launch as well as set many female pulses racing, which is exactly what his interpretation of their set piece had achieved. But she knew his actions had also intended to upset Marco, and staring down now at Rossana sitting there bewildered and alone, it looked as if he had succeeded.

THIRTY-SEVEN

The after-show party was in full swing. After changing out of her dress Charlotte's first task was to locate Beth and CJ. Accompanied by Lucy, she found them talking to Ella and Jenny.

CJ kissed her cheek and then Lucy's. 'You both looked fabulous.'

'Thank you,' Charlotte said. 'I had no idea Christian was going to do what he did, though.'

'Ah, the audience loved it,' Ella joined in. 'They all adore him, the man oozes sex. He's such a great showman. Where is he, by the way?'

Lucy glanced at Charlotte and shrugged. 'Mingling, I suspect.'

Charlotte turned to hug her friend. 'Beth, you dark horse. How did you manage to keep it such a secret? I mean, I know CJ plays everything close to his chest but, well... the times I was there with you both I had no idea.'

'It was pretty hard.' Beth glanced up at CJ, pushing her hand into his. 'We wanted our timing to be right, and today with this big party going on, it seemed an appropriate day to meet the family.'

'Well, we're all delighted,' Jenny said, as Charlotte introduced her to Lucy.

'Thank you, I've heard so much about you, Lucy.' Beth said, smiling as she hugged her. 'I had no idea the two of you were so similar. And Lottie, you looked fabulous. What do I keep telling you? Strong colours suit you, you should wear them more often.'

'That's exactly what I've been saying, haven't I?' Lucy interjected, her gaze going from Beth to Charlotte.

The two older women and CJ moved away, leaving the three girls alone.

'I guess this means there will be two of you ganging up on me now,' Charlotte said, accepting a glass of champagne from a tray which Lucy had managed to intercept.

'I told Lottie if she was a success at this show I'd take her shopping tomorrow,' Lucy explained.

Beth gave an amused grin. 'Great. Count me in.'

'Oh God, why do I get the feeling I'm being ganged up on?' Charlotte grimaced then laughed. 'Okay, you win, I'm up for it. Do your worst.'

Lucy raised her champagne glass. 'Here's to the new Lottie!'

Tilting her glass to her lips, Beth's eyes wandered around the reception area, eventually stopping when she spied Marco standing with a young woman whom, she guessed, must be Rossana. Pretty, she thought, but rather a little too animated, as if trying to impress. They were chatting to Ella, or rather, Rossana was while Marco stood there like a reluctant spectator. He looked troubled, his gaze continually drifting towards the window, making her think

259

there was something simmering below the surface, something angry which he was attempting to rein in. She felt she really ought to go over and say hello. She saw Ella lean in towards Marco and gesture towards the door. He nodded and she began to move away, Rossana following. Seizing the opportunity to catch him alone, Beth slipped between the guests, eventually reaching him.

'Hello, Marco.'

He swung around in surprise then smiled, wiping away the preoccupied expression he wore. 'Beth! It is good to see you.'

'You look well. How are things?'

'Oh, you know, busy. As always, the restaurants are demanding mistresses.'

'I gather that was Rossana,' she said, nodding in the direction of the two departing women.

'Ah yes. Ella is giving her a tour. She is particularly interested in the portraits. The manor does not have the history or magic of Little Court.'

'She's very pretty. I hope she will make you happy.'

Marco cast a puzzled frown. 'I'm not sure what you are implying. She is my father's guest; if anything, I treat her like a younger sister.' His face softened. 'She is very sweet and amusing but hardly the type of woman I would want. Felica and I are merely keeping her company and making sure she enjoys her time with us.'

Beth nodded and stared into her glass. 'I'm... I'm so sorry things didn't work out with you and Lottie.'

His troubled expression resurfaced once more. 'What is done is done. I thought once...' he shook his head, 'but it does not matter, does it? She has chosen Christian.'

'Christian! Is that what you think?' She was about to explain the reality of Charlotte's situation when she realised he was not listening; instead he was staring over her head across the room.

'If you'll excuse me,' he said politely, returning his attention to her. 'I think I need some fresh air.'

Eager to discover what had prompted his sudden exit, Beth switched her gaze and saw Christian making his way towards her. When she turned back to Marco she noticed he had reached the French doors and was letting himself out into the garden.

'Where's he going?'

She spun around to find Christian towering over her. 'To get away from you, I would think,' she said. 'Don't you think your performance this afternoon was enough? Rubbing salt in the wound is not a great idea.'

'Ah, so he does still have feelings for her. Good.'

As he made to move away, Beth reached out for his arm, pinning him with a suspicious stare. 'What are you playing at?'

His hand came down on her shoulder and his features softened. 'Relax. I simply want to try to talk some sense into the stupid sod, that's all. No one else appears to have convinced him Lottie's not some scarlet woman. Maybe he'll listen to me.'

'You think so? My guess is he'll probably want to punch you. Tell me, if you *are* so interested in convincing him of Lottie's innocence, why did you kiss her like that today, in front of everyone?'

'Because I wanted to make sure he still cared about her. The last thing I wanted to do was waste my time.'

'Oh, come on! Do you seriously think for one moment he'll believe the stunt you pulled was for his benefit?'

Christian shrugged. 'Whether he does or not, I've got to speak to him about Lottie. To tell him the truth. I won't have her blamed for what happened. It's so unfair.'

Before Beth could open her mouth to respond he had left her, pushing through the French doors and out into the garden, striding out across the lawn in the direction Marco had taken. Certain their confrontation would come to blows, she eased herself between the guests as she searched the room, frantically looking for Charlotte. She had to find her before it was too late and Felica's fashion launch spiralled into chaos.

'Marco!'

Marco looked up at the sound of an unfamiliar voice. Turning away from his contemplation of the river, he spotted Christian Rosetti walking towards him with the same animal grace he had exhibited on stage earlier and a determined expression set on his face. His walk was loose limbed and fluid and there was a definite aura of sexual predator about him, Marco thought, noticing the coal black eyes and sensuous curve to his mouth which no doubt drew women to him wherever he went. Little wonder Charlotte had fallen under his spell again.

'What do you want?' Marco kept his voice deliberately calm. Much as he felt a need to hit the man responsible for his misery, he knew he had to remain composed for Felica's sake.

'I came to talk to you.' Christian stopped a few feet away, eyeing him warily as if he expected him to lash out at any moment. 'I don't want a fight; I need you to listen.'

Marco gave a harsh laugh. 'And what makes you think there is anything I wish to hear? You have Charlotte, is that not enough? Go away.'

'Well, that's the thing...' Christian said, folding his arms across his chest and locking eyes with him. 'You see, I don't have Charlotte. She ceased to be mine when you came into her life.'

'I do not believe you. You are a man who takes what he wants. But I know you do not love her, she is merely a distraction, something you want to amuse yourself with.'

'Actually, you're wrong, I do love her,' Christian admitted. 'She's the type of woman it's difficult not to love. She's warm, funny, brave and loyal. Yes, loyal,' he said to Marco's disbelieving expression. 'But I made a mess of things. Because of what happened, I lost the right to her affection and I know we can never go back.' He stared at the ground for a moment before fixing his gaze back on Marco. 'Charlotte is one of the kindest human beings I have ever known and I'm grateful and honoured to still have her friendship.'

'Why were you with her that day in the woods?'

'Oh, you mean the day she saved your back from being beaten raw and didn't even receive a word of thanks?' Christian couldn't help the ring of sarcasm in his voice.

'She betrayed me,' Marco shot back, unrepentant.

'Betrayed you? Why aren't you listening to me, you idiot? Charlotte was totally faithful to you. She still is, although God knows why! From where I'm standing, you don't deserve it after the way you've treated her.'

'My stepmother said Charlotte was expecting you,' Marco insisted. 'That you were here to persuade her to go back to you.'

'After what I'd done I think I'm the last man she'd want to go back to,' Christian muttered. He rolled his eyes at Marco. 'Where the hell did she get that rubbish from?'

'Ella told her.'

'What! That is madness!'

'It is true.'

'You think so? Well, maybe your truth is just a wee bit flawed.' Christian moved closer to him. 'Allow me to enlighten you.'

Beth found Lucy and Charlotte chatting to Felica. Managing to coax Charlotte away, she gave her a quick résumé of what had taken place.

'You need to come now, Lottie,' she whispered urgently. 'Christian has gone to talk Marco but, well, I don't think he'll want to listen, and the last thing we want is a fight.'

'Where are they?'

'They were heading down towards the river.'

Charlotte made her apologies and left quickly with Beth. This was all she needed. If the two men did come to blows on a day which was so important for Felica, she knew Thérèse's temper would know no boundaries.

Hurrying across the lawn with Beth, Charlotte could see two indistinct figures facing each other beneath the overhang of willows at the water's edge. From their stance and body language they looked like two stags about to lock antlers. Nearing the river, Charlotte could hear their muffled conversation and saw Christian raise a hand to shove his mass of curly black hair back from his face. Then, with a shake of his head, he pushed through the curtain of willow fronds. He looked startled when he saw her standing there with Beth at her side.

'Beth thought you might come to blows,' she said, by way of explanation.

'I'm surprised we didn't; he's an awkward bastard,' he said, resting a gentle palm on her shoulder, 'but I think I've managed to get through to him. It's up to you now – if you want him back, that is.'

Charlotte reached out to stroke his face. 'Thank you.'

'Good luck,' Beth whispered, before turning and following Christian back towards the house.

In a silence broken only by the rush of the river, Marco stood quietly in those first moments after Christian's departure, digesting his words. He was stunned at the way someone he had viewed as a rival had opened up to him – about the drugs, the women and rehab, and the way Charlotte had ended their relationship. He had finished by explaining his reason behind the visit to Little Court that weekend: to build bridges with the family and ask for forgiveness from a woman he had wronged. Marco now saw their relationship in a completely different light and at the same time what he had, through his own foolishness, thrown away thanks to his interfering stepmother. The whole situation had been deliberately manipulated by Thérèse to push him together with Rossana.

Remembering Rossana's chaste kiss in the car on the day she had passed her driving test, he now guessed she was a victim in all this as much as he was. The only thing getting rid of Charlotte had enabled Rossana to do was allow her to continue her immature pursuit of him without any impediment. It had in no way advanced her cause, because he simply did not want her. He had never wanted her, nor was he likely to. No, this whole stupid chain of events was down to Thérèse and her schemes. He cursed her under his breath, but in the middle of this silent rant he realised he was not exactly an innocent in all this. If only he had had more faith in Charlotte and had made an attempt to contact her once he was back in the UK. If only he had taken the trouble to ask for her side of the story instead of throwing her out of San Raffaello's. It seemed to him today the world was full of *if only's*, but it was no use thinking of the past. It was now that mattered and knowing, like Christian, he had completely wrecked his chances, he could never hope to have her affection again.

'Oh, Charlotte...' he whispered, supporting himself against the trunk of the willow as he leaned towards the water. 'I have been such a fool.' He bowed his head and allowed the pain of his loss to flood through him.

A gossamer-light touch brushed his shoulder, like some water spirit hearing his breaking heart and deciding to give him comfort. Believing it must have been one of the willow fronds, he brushed it away with his hand, finding instead the warmth of fingers against his own. Startled, he turned. Eyes of incredible blue scanned his face.

'Charlotte?'

A soft smile filled her lips as she moved closer to him.

He pulled her against him, catching her familiar scent of lilies. This was not a dream; she was real. He took a step back to look at her, their faces only inches apart. Something pulsed between them in an invisible swirl of overpowering emotion. He leaned slowly forward to claim her mouth.

'Marco! Marco, where are you?' A young, girlish voice rang out on the afternoon air, instantly breaking the spell.

'Damn Rossana!' he hissed and drew away. Peering beyond the shelter of the willow, he could see her coming across the lawn, heading in their direction. 'I will have to go,' he said, turning back to Charlotte.

She nodded silently. Her expression gave nothing away but he sensed obvious disappointment. Leaning forward, he kissed her mouth gently.

'Meet me tomorrow afternoon. Three o'clock at Fox Cottage,' he whispered.

Another silent nod indicated her agreement. He took her hand in his, bending to tenderly kiss her open palm, then left her, emerging through the green curtain of willow tendrils to make his way across the grass at a leisurely pace to intercept Rossana.

Kayte O'Farrell had been in the trekking stable brushing up when she felt a strong pair of hands clamp around her waist. She shrieked and swung around, broom in hand, about to brain her would-be attacker, only to find herself facing Christian Rosetti. She stood robbed of speech for a moment. Wearing black leather trousers and a white t-shirt, she thought he looked incredibly sexy.

'You're lucky I didn't brain you with this,' she said, brandishing the broom at him when she eventually found her voice.

'You'd never have hit me, my reflexes are too good.' He grinned as he closed the gap between them. Taking the broom from her hands he threw it into the corner, grabbed her by the shoulders and took her mouth in a hard, demanding kiss. 'I've missed you,' he said, when he eventually released her.

'Oh yeah. Is that why I've not heard from you since February?' she asked cuttingly.

'Well, I'm here now, aren't I?' He shrugged as if his presence was sufficient to make up for his past absence.

'Ah, but you haven't come especially, have you? You've been at Felica's fashion show. Ella Benedict told Mum.'

'You didn't get an invite, then?'

She glared. 'Are you being funny?'

He leaned on the edge of the stall. 'No, merely asking.'

'Ella said Lucy and Charlotte were performing with you. Is that true?'

'Yes. Is there a problem?'

'Not with Lucy, but I hate Charlotte.'

He waved a finger at her. 'There's nothing wrong with Charlotte, she's one of the nicest people I know.'

'What is it with you? Why are you defending her?'

He could see she was bristling. 'My, are we jealous?'

'No. God knows what men see in her... what you see in her.'

'We go back a long way, she means a lot to me.'

'More than I do?' Her eyes widened questioningly as her indignant tone softened.

Christian smiled to himself. He loved Kayte this way, all angry and spitting one moment, seasoned seductress the next.

'You mean a lot to me too,' he said, concentrating on the clothes she wore and wondering how best to get her out of them. 'An awful lot', he added. 'In fact, I don't think I've met anyone quite like you, Kayte. You're quite unique.'

'Is that so? Well, I think it's time I put a little of my uniqueness into practice, don't you?' A satisfied smirk settled on her face as she slipped past him to close and lock the stable door. Returning, she took hold of his hand. 'Ever had sex in a hay loft?'

'Never.'

She pulled him towards a nearby wooden ladder. 'Well then, you're in for a treat.'

Marco made his way back to the house, Rossana keeping pace. She had reverted to incessant chatter, a habit, he noticed, which surfaced on occasions when she was excited about something. This time, it was the tour Ella had organised for her which she was now relating in great detail, although most of it was going straight over his head. All he could think about was Charlotte – that by some miracle he had her back. As they reached the terrace, Thérèse and Felica emerged through the French doors. The sight of them both hauled him back to reality.

'Ah, there you are, Marco.' Thérèse looked down at him, her brows drawn together in minor disapproval. 'Where have you been?'

'Down by the river, having a quiet moment to myself.'

'Poor Rossana was distraught. She couldn't find you.'

'Thérèse is exaggerating again, I think.' Dismissing the rebuke, he cast a glance at Rossana smiling sweetly back at him.

'I only wanted to tell him about my tour, Mrs D'Alesandro. It has been wonderful. There is so much history here. Did you know there is the ghost of a cavalier who sometimes walks in the west wing? He—'

'Yes, yes.' Thérèse flapped a warning hand at her. With a benevolent

265

smile, she turned back to Marco. 'Can you return Rossana to the manor? Take her riding or something.'

'Why now?' he quizzed, wondering if the girl was beginning to irritate his stepmother too with her excitable and enthusiastic outpourings.

'Because... Just do it, will you!' Thérèse demanded with an impatient frown.

'Of course.' He gave her an agreeable nod as he fished in his pocket for his car keys, masking the intense anger he felt when he looked at his stepmother. She was manipulative and cunning, but he now had the measure of her and there was no way he would ever allow her to get between him and Charlotte again.

THIRTY-EIGHT

'I'd better be getting back,' Christian said, pulling his t-shirt over his head. 'Someone is bound to have missed me.' He checked his watch. 'Shit! Is that the time?'

Kayte rolled over in the hay, admiring the body which had given her so much pleasure. 'So, when will I see you again?'

'Not sure.' He smiled down at her as he shrugged himself into his leather trousers. 'I'm about to go on tour.'

'You never mentioned it.' Her expression was a mix of panic and surprise. 'When?'

'Starts end of this month. I'm doing seventeen dates in the UK and Ireland first and then kick off my European tour in Geneva in June. Should be back early September.'

'September!' She grabbed his hand. 'Take me with you.'

'What? Are you mad?'

'Of course not.' She pouted, pulling herself up to stand beside him, pushing her nakedness against him in an attempt to seduce him into changing his mind. 'After all, you'll need someone to keep you company on all those lonely nights.'

'How can I, Kayte?' he argued, prising her hands from around his neck. 'I don't think you have any idea what touring entails. I'm surrounded by people, and on this trip Lucy is managing an on-tour photographic shoot. I'll be in the spotlight twenty-four/seven.' He shook his head. 'It would be impossible to sneak you in anywhere.'

'You could give me a job. I'd work hard,' she insisted, determined not to be put off.

'Matt Benedict does the hiring and firing. Besides, the team is made up of experienced people, everyone has a specific job, there's no casual labour. Sorry, you'll simply have to wait for me to return.'

'Until September. Are you having a laugh?'

'Listen, the last concert is on the tenth, in Madrid, then we fly home.' He kissed the top of her head. 'Think of it another way, babe – absence makes the heart grow fonder. And when I'm back I'll take you away to anywhere in the world. Choose where you want to go and I'll arrange it all.'

Kayte made a face, clearly unimpressed. 'I suppose it will have to do. But I'll be expecting a very expensive Christmas present as well, to make up for all this disappointment.'

'Oh, you'll have that, I promise.' He grinned at her wickedly and giving her a swift peck on the cheek, he grabbed the ladder and began his descent.

She stood at the top, looking down at him wondering how she could bear it.

He blew her a kiss. 'Till September then?'

There was the sound of the door being unlocked followed by his footfalls fading into the distance and then silence.

Searching around for her discarded clothes, Kayte began dressing. September! There was no way she was going to wait that long.

Charlotte sat waiting nervously in the front room at Fox Cottage. Once again she turned to look at the clock over the hearth. Ten minutes past three. She took a deep breath. He had definitely said three. He was not coming; she should have known this would happen. Oh yes, she had heard his words of remorse, his request for forgiveness but, as she knew from experience, twenty-four hours had the potential to change many things including, it now appeared, Marco's mind. Despondent and disappointed, she closed the front door after her, replaced the key in its digital key box and then left. Jet was tethered to the front gate. She mounted quickly, turning his head around and urging him up the track at a swift trot.

As she ducked under the branches of the first trees she found herself drawn into the cocooned shelter of the wood. Breathing deeply, she became immersed in its customary tranquillity. Her disappointment gradually dissipated, replaced instead by a gentle calmness and feeling of being one with nature. Hundred Acre always had this effect on her. May was one of her favourite months here. Trees were in full, fresh green leaf, and spread below was a mixed carpet of soft grass, ferns, and patches of wild garlic with their distinctive smell and, over towards Sedgewick Hill, she knew huge sprawls of bluebells were now in full flower.

She stopped for a while to enjoy the peacefulness watching strands of sunlight filter through the overhead canopy, listening to the birds and glimpsing the movement of a lone squirrel in the trees. The sound of water drew her on towards a small stream, where she dismounted and allowed Jet to drink. Seating herself against a nearby rock to wait, she tilted her face up towards a gap in the trees where sunlight pooled through, and closed her eyes.

Acutely aware of each and every movement within the clearing, she was alerted to the sudden sound of a horse's snort, the jingle of a bridle and soft footfalls. Opening her eyes, she swung round. Marco D'Alesandro was walking into the clearing, leading his horse. Dappled sunlight danced over his white open-neck shirt and the jodhpurs he wore tucked into high brown boots. Immediately, Charlotte was transported back to the very first time she had seen him on the terrace at Little Court. That undeniable surge of attraction, which had competed with her other, more hostile, emotions at the time, resurfaced as he tied his horse to a low branch and came towards her. Joining her, he sat with his legs bent, hands resting loosely over his knees.

'I thought you weren't coming,' she said softly. 'That you had changed your mind.'

'Unfortunately, I was delayed but luckily I saw you riding into the wood,' he said, reaching for her hand, holding it for a moment before turning it over and tracing his thumb gently across her palm and along each digit. 'I have missed you so much.'

'I have missed you too.' Charlotte rested her head against his shoulder, finding herself suddenly and inexplicably filled with a need for him to kiss her.

As if drawn by her silent summons, his dark eyes lingered on her for a moment and then he leaned over to press his lips against hers.

'Charlotte—' he began in a hushed whisper, but she touched her fingers against his mouth to stop him.

'No more talking, Marco,' she insisted, tracing a line along the contours of his face and down into the front of his shirt, liberating each button as she went. 'We can talk later.'

'Do you want to go back to the cottage?' he asked, mirroring her actions, placing a gentle kiss against her skin for each button of her cream shirt he freed.

She shook her head, pulling his shirt open, pressing her face into the warmth of his naked chest and inhaling the arousing mix of expensive body wash and his own familiar scent. 'No, I want you here, under the trees. Have you ever made love in the open?'

'Never. You?'

'No.'

'A first for both of us, then.' He gave one of his lazy smiles and easing her gently down into the grass, covered her mouth with his.

Something was going on. It was not blatantly obvious but rather an unsettling feeling Thérèse could not shake off. On the surface everything appeared quite normal. Marco was taking Rossana here and there, keeping her company in the evenings and seeming quite happy to do so. However, the whole plan of getting them together appeared to have come to a shuddering halt. They had regular trips to the theatre or cinema when Rossana was staying in the town house in London, and they ate out together at least twice a week. When staying at the manor, as she was now, she was never far from his side, and occasionally they went for rides up in Hundred Acre together in the evening. Thrown into each other's company so frequently something, she reasoned, should have happened by now. She had all but cured Rossana of her impulsive chatter and to look at her now, she felt she had created the near-perfect woman for her stepson. Certainly the girl was far more grown up and outgoing than when she first arrived. She could talk quite sensibly about many things and had a gloriously sunny nature, plus she now had the ability to make the most of her face and figure – she was quite a beauty. So what was the problem? Of course, there were still months ahead of them until Rossana was due to return to Edoardo. Plenty of time to get the two of them together. However, Rossana's recent reports that Marco continued to show her nothing more than a brotherly relationship made Thérèse realise something needed to be done.

Her stepson was now accustomed to regularly taking two afternoons a week off and disappearing mysteriously. When questioned, he would simply shrug and tell her he was setting time aside to spend with Stuart. This had been borne out when she had phoned the Arms with some frivolous request and dropped the question innocently into their conversation. Despite this reassurance she was still not convinced either was the telling truth.

Sitting in Ella's office, the thought intruded once more.

'Thérèse?'

She shook herself out of her preoccupation with this mystery to find a concerned Ella staring at her from the other side of her desk.

'Are you feeling all right?'

'Yes, sorry. Where were we?'

'We were talking about the outfits for the Morgan–Griffin wedding which are coming Thursday morning, remember? You're going to be in London when they arrive. Felica's giving a show in Birmingham and you were asking if we could take delivery for you.'

'Ah, yes. Forgive me for wandering away. Would you be happy to do that for me, or shall I get them to reschedule to another date?'

'No, no, Thursday morning will be fine,' Ella reassured her. 'If Jenny and I aren't around Lottie will be. Thursday is one of her days off.'

'Thank you, that will be so helpful.' Relaxing back in her seat, she eyed Ella Benedict thoughtfully. 'So, Lottie only works part time, does she?'

'Currently, it's only three days a week. She is home Wednesdays and Thursdays.' Ella gave an amused laugh. 'Although when I say "home", she's taken to spending a lot of time up at Fox Cottage these days.'

'I expect she likes to get away for some peace and quiet,' Thérèse said, aware those two days were the same ones Marco went missing. It was far too coincidental not to justify some extra investigation.

The following Wednesday she waited until Marco had left for the afternoon. Emerging from the stables astride his bay, she watched him urge the animal into a gallop across the parkland towards Hundred Acre. Waiting until he had disappeared from sight, she made her way to the stables and requested her own horse be saddled. Fifteen minutes later she entered the wood. Keeping within the tree line, she rode slowly along the perimeter of the barley field. Soon the silhouette of Fox Cottage could be seen low on the horizon.

She reined in at the top of the track leading past the cottage, using a small clump of young oaks to shelter her presence. Dismounting, she tied her horse to one of them and crept slowly through the undergrowth into the small orchard at the rear of the cottage. Marco's horse was tied by the back door, next to Charlotte's. She felt her fury building. No wonder he was not showing any interest in Rossana when this witch had pulled him back under her spell again! How had this happened? Incensed, her first reaction was to march in and confront them. However, she was aware this would only result in driving him even further into Charlotte's clutches. No, something a little more subtle had to be arranged – it was time to go home and plan. Somehow she had to get him as far away from Charlotte as possible. Still seething, she made her way quietly back to where her horse was tethered.

In the small front bedroom of Fox Cottage Marco lay on top of the bedclothes, his arm thrown lazily above his head, Charlotte nestling against him, her face pressed into his shoulder. Wrapped in each other's arms in a tangle of bodies and bedclothes, their skins glowed with perspiration after an afternoon of long and leisurely lovemaking.

'You are incredible,' he said, kissing the top of her head. 'I never thought I could ever feel like this with anyone.'

'Ah, but is it the illicit nature of what we do which makes it more enjoyable?' Charlotte tilted her head up to look at him curiously.

He looked affronted. 'Of course not. When Rossana has gone back to Italy I will still be here like this with you experiencing this wonderful thing we have together. Nothing will change. It is only at the moment our relationship has to be a secret; there is no other way, is there? If my stepmother discovers us she will think up some devious plan to part us again, and I cannot allow that to happen.'

Charlotte nodded. 'I understand.' He was right; currently they were tied into this subterfuge, Marco not wanting to involve his father again unless it was absolutely necessary. Soon Edoardo would be well enough to have his niece back. Soon. She smiled – there was light at the end of the tunnel, it was just a long way off at the moment.

'Did you know,' she said, her fingers teasing the damp hair on his chest, 'Beth once said when she saw you, she knew you were with me for the long haul?'

'She did? Beth is very perceptive and she is right; I am.' He lifted her chin with his finger and looked at her seriously. 'Charlotte, I have never said this to any other woman before but I know I am falling in love with you.'

'Marco, stop it.' She gave him a playful punch.

He gave her a wounded look. 'It is true. Do you not feel the same way?' His dark eyes searched hers in an obvious need for some response. 'Even a little?'

Charlotte thought for a moment. It was not a wise thing to reveal what went on in your heart when there was always a chance it could be broken.

This had happened to her with Christian, and Lucy had had the same experience with Ethan, but Luce had found the lovely golden, caring McShea and things were vastly different now. Could she dare hope for the same? Was Marco the special someone she had told Beth she hoped to find? Well, there was only one way to find out – she had to step out on that wire without a safety net and take a chance. She searched his beautiful trusting face – there was no guile there, none whatsoever. He had opened his heart to her and he deserved to have her do the same.

'Yes,' she replied tenderly, raising her eyes to his. 'I think I do, very much.'

His face radiated with an emotion she had never seen before, something so powerful it caused the smouldering still within her to flame again as he reached for her once more. He stroked her face then bent his head, taking her mouth in a warm, passionate kiss.

Rachel was unsaddling and checking through tack from the mounts of the last group of trekkers when Kayte stepped into the stable doorway,

'I thought I'd come and tell you I'd like to take a break from the farm over the summer,' she said, leaning against the door frame, her blonde hair spilling over her shoulders, 'to spend the summer doing bar work in Ibiza.'

Rachel looked up, brushing a stray lock of fair hair out of her eyes and seeing Kayte silhouetted against the early June sunshine. 'Ibiza? What, on your own?'

Kayte rolled her eyes. 'No, with friends. You've plenty of holiday help, I'm sure you can spare me.'

'Friends?' Rachel frowned. She had always regarded her daughter as a loner, spending most of her time chasing the opposite sex. Not exactly an occupation which endeared her to other women, particularly if the men belonged to them.

'Yes, Cassie and Laura. I see them regularly when I go into Abbotsbridge clubbing.'

'Oh, I see.' Again, this was news to her.

'It was Cassie's idea,' Kayte continued. 'We all thought it would be fun to get away and spend the summertime in the sun. Work will be a bonus and the extra money will make all the difference. Cassie has the contacts. She's found us work in this club in San Antonio and, well, we're planning to fly out from Gatwick next week.'

'Well, if that's what you really want to do...' Rachel nodded, glad her daughter appeared to have some female friends at last. 'Maybe your father could run you all to the airport.'

'No thanks, Mum.' Kayte raised her hands in protest. It was the last thing she wanted. 'I appreciate the offer but the last thing I want is a journey filled with his lectures. Honest, Mum, I've had enough of them.'

'He cares for you, Kayte, and he worries. You have to admit what's gone on in the recent past has given him good—'

'Please, Mum, no sermons! Even if Dad doesn't think so, I've learnt my lesson. Let's leave it at that, shall we?' Mellowing her defensive stance, she smiled at her mother. 'Look, I know I'm not currently flavour of the month where he's concerned but I promise you, one day I'll do something to make him change his mind about me.'

'I know you will.' Rachel's expression softened. The one thing she ached for was peace in the family. Perhaps this break from the farm might do Kayte some good and drive some of her devils out of her. 'I've finished here now,' she said, as she hung up the last bridle. 'Come on, I'll walk back with you.'

As they crossed the yard back to the farmhouse Kayte felt a glow of excitement inside. Her plan to go to Italy to find Christian was about to begin. She couldn't wait to see her father's face when she came back wearing his ring, the future wife of an A-list celebrity.

Thérèse was sitting in Marco's private booth in San Raffaello's inspecting the menu when Gianlucca entered the restaurant. He was in London for a series of business meetings and had suggested they meet for lunch. Vittorio greeted him enthusiastically then indicated the booth where she sat, picked up a menu and wine list and followed him to the table.

Gianlucca ordered a bottle of best champagne and settled himself down beside his wife with a smile and an affectionate kiss on the cheek.

'You are looking exquisite, as always, Thérèse,' he said, admiring her lilac Chanel suit and double string of vintage pearls.

'Thank you, Gianni. And you are looking very happy. Am I guessing your business meetings have gone to plan?'

'They have exceeded expectations. I have to say, I am in an exceptionally good mood today.'

One of young waiters arrived with the champagne, uncorked it and at Gianlucca's nodded instruction, poured out two glassfuls.

'Then we shall have an excellent lunch together,' Thérèse purred, taking the proffered glass and raising it to his.

Vittorio hovered expectantly but Gianlucca waved him away with a smile. It would be some time before they were ready to order, he told him.

'This restaurant is quite exceptional, you know,' Gianlucca said, gazing at the décor and the bustle of waiters serving food. 'It is the flagship of the D'Alesandro chain. It sets the standard for the others. Marco has done a splendid job. It is a shame he is not here today so I can tell him how much I appreciate his hard work.'

At first irritated by yet again having to listen to her husband praise his dead wife's son, Thérèse stilled her anger as her mind did a three-sixty

273

degree flip; she could have kissed him on both cheeks.

'And how, exactly, is this standard measured?' she asked, inclining her head towards him. 'Does Marco visit all the others regularly? I am not aware he does.'

Gianlucca looked taken aback. 'I think they run very well as they are, Thérèse. Marco receives monthly reports from each manager.'

'Ah, but figures can be manipulated, you and I both know that. Far be it for me to interfere, but would it not be a wise thing for Marco to spend some time away making sure everything is as the reports suggest? A precaution, you understand. Florentine and Vittorio are quite capable of holding the fort while he is not here.'

Gianlucca scratched his head. 'You may have a point. I would hate to think even one of my restaurants was not performing to the standard of the others. I will have a word with Marco in the morning.'

Thérèse took another sip of her champagne. 'Actually, there was something I planned to raise with Marco but as we are talking of the restaurants…'

Gianlucca looked at her expectantly 'What is it? What is wrong?'

'La Mariposa in Aberdeen. I happened to run into Eleyna Hanratty this morning.'

'Wife of the movie producer?'

Thérèse nodded. 'The very one. Hugo and Eleyna have recently returned from the Scottish Highlands where he's been filming some period piece, and she informed me while they were in Aberdeen they visited La Mariposa.'

'And you are about to tell me she was less than happy?'

'Oh, the food was excellent, she had absolutely no problems there, but she rather thought the service left a little to be desired.' Thérèse planted her twisted version of a recent conversation with the ease of a seasoned manipulator. 'So you see, Marco's visits would serve two purposes. It would make sure the accounts were in order and also the staff are providing the same excellent service we have here.'

Gianlucca twirled the stem of his champagne flute between his finger and thumb and stared thoughtfully into the pale effervescence.

'You need to make sure, Gianni.' Thérèse lowered her voice to a whisper. 'You cannot leave anything to chance. One bad review might send some Michelin inspector on a mission to check out your other restaurants, and that is the last thing you want, especially if La Mariposa is not the only problem.'

'Of course you are right,' Gianlucca said, releasing his grip on the glass to pull the bottle from its chiller to top up Thérèse's glass. 'I will arrange for Marco to leave as soon as possible. Now then, let's not keep Vittorio waiting. What would you like to eat?'

THIRTY-NINE

Christian stared open-mouthed at the sight in front of him. It was three in the morning and he had just returned from a late-night reception following his first performance at Milan's Siro Stadium, on the second week of his European tour. Tomorrow, he would be travelling with Jay to collect his brand new Lamborghini Diablo from the factory at Sant'Agata Bologenese. From there, he planned to drive south with him and meet up with the others in Verona, where he was scheduled to perform for three nights, so when he swiped into his suite his mind had been on one thing: falling into bed and sleeping like the dead for a few hours. That now looked as if it was not an option as he found himself staring at Kayte O'Farrell stretched across the sheets of his bed wearing nothing but a smile, her blonde hair spilling over her bare shoulders.

'Surprise!' She leapt from the bed and ran to him, her arms snaking around his neck as her mouth sought his.

'Kayte! What the hell are you doing here?' he said irritably, pulling himself out of her grasp.

She pouted. 'Well, don't look so pleased to see me. I couldn't wait until September so I got a flight here and a cheap room. I've been waiting for days. Then I saw on the news you'd arrived so I waited outside the stadium, but it was madness. I didn't have concert tickets and found all your shows were sold out anyway.' She gave a cunning smile and flicked her hair back off her face. 'I hung around for two nights hoping to see you. Then I had this brilliant idea. I found out you were staying here and blagged my way in. Well, you know, hotel staff can be *so* stupid.' She smirked. 'And here they seem to be more stupid than anywhere else. I simply told the maid I was Lucy Benedict's assistant and that she'd asked me to get something from your room.' She gave an amused shrug. 'And the stupid bitch let me in.'

He glared at her. 'You did what?'

'Well, how else was I to see you? If you're not with an army of security guards, you're surrounded by all those bloody women screaming and shouting. I couldn't get to you any other way.'

'I told you it would be difficult, didn't I? You shouldn't have come.' He ran his hand through his hair and let out a hiss of angry breath. 'Kayte, I'm dog tired. I've been working since early this morning and I really need to sleep.'

'Sleep then, baby.' She ran a finger down his cheek and traced it along his jawbone. 'You can have me later. I've always wanted to wake up with you, Christian,' she added with a giggle.

Christian sighed. It was no use, he'd have to let her stay otherwise he knew she would make one hell of a fuss. Besides alerting Jay and Lucy to what was going on, if it was that easy to evade security there could be paparazzi lurking and he had no wish to provide them with the kind of publicity capable of wrecking the tour. One thing was for certain, security needed tightening. He'd have to get someone to make sure this worrying gap was firmly plugged. But that was something for the morning. Grabbing a handful of bedding, he headed for the living area.

'Hey, where are you going?' she demanded as she watched him leave.

'To sleep on the couch.'

'Don't you want to sleep with me?'

'Yes, sleep! Kayte, be sensible; that's not going to happen if we're in the same bed, is it?' He shook his head and disappeared, shutting the door in her face.

Kayte glared at the door. How dare he give her the brush off when she'd come all this way to see him! She crawled onto the bed, pulling the remaining covers around her. Ah well, she was here and she certainly was not going back. He'd probably feel completely different about her in the morning.

Next morning, Christian ordered breakfast in his suite, pushing Kayte into the bathroom while it was being delivered. When he let her out he could see the fury in her face.

'Are you ashamed of me or something?' she questioned, clearly peeved, as he poured himself fresh orange juice.

'Sweetheart, let's have some sensible thinking here, shall we? I am on tour and this whole floor of the hotel has been given over to me and my support staff. That includes Lucy Benedict. If you are seen, someone will tell not only her but probably alert the tabloids as well. I can't have that sort of sordid publicity, and I'm sure you don't want it either.'

'But why is *she* on this floor with you?' Kayte exploded. 'Why is—'

'Lucy now has a job in media within her father's company,' Christian cut across her outburst, 'and her first major assignment has been to organise tour photographs and a video. She's brought professional photographers with her and, as she's calling the shots on this, I'm very much in her line of vision. So there is absolutely no way you can be here with me. Not only will there be trouble if Matt gets to hear about it, but Lucy will also make sure your parents know you are here, and they will most certainly demand you return home.'

'My parents have no control over me. I'm nearly twenty-one; I can do as I please. Besides, they think I'm in Ibiza doing bar work,' came Kayte's response. 'Christian, I have come all this way to be with you, and what do you do? You talk about sending me home. I don't mean anything to you, do I?'

'Babe, you know that's not true.' God, she was difficult to get through to. He sighed in exasperation, turning his attention to the food trolley. 'Hey, don't let's argue on an empty stomach, come and have some breakfast.'

He crossed the room and took her by the hand, intending to entice her over to the food and keep her quiet for a while. But as he reached her, she let go of the sheet she was wrapped in. As his hand went out to catch it, his fingers touched not cool cotton but firm, warm, round flesh instead.

Smiling, Kayte pushed herself provocatively against him, the palms of her hands pressing against his bare chest.

'Forget breakfast,' she said, as her mouth teased his and her hands moved over him, robbing him of the willpower to deal with her. Oh so easily she backed him into the bedroom, relieving him of his jeans as they went. They fell onto the bed together and she manoeuvred herself on top of him. Christian's last thoughts, as she rose above him with her golden skin and thick tumbling hair, was that Plan A was dead in the water. He'd have to go for Plan B instead, but at the moment he had no idea what the hell that was.

Arriving in the office a little after nine, Marco exhaled a sigh of relief. Today was Friday, and tomorrow he would have two days respite from this toing and froing along the M4 all in the cause of keeping Thérèse happy and Rossana company. The only thing currently keeping him sane was his secret afternoons with Charlotte – carried out under the pretext of spending time in the company of Stuart playing golf or other male bonding pursuits. Of course, in the beginning he knew his devious stepmother had phoned to check up on him, but Stuart had gently allayed her fears, and for some time now everything had gone quiet. Happily, they were far beyond the half-way stage of Rossana's stay. Edoardo had been out of hospital for a few weeks and, as far as he could gather from his father, his progress towards a full recovery was good. He knew Rossana's eighteenth birthday in September was likely to be when they would lose their house guest. Thérèse was already in the throes of organising a birthday party for her at Little Court, with invitations planned for at least one hundred and fifty guests. He imagined half of those invited would be there to impress rather than actually have a connection to Rossana. He looked forward to this magnificent send-off for it would mean a celebration for him too, marking the return to his normal life.

As he passed through his PA's office, she raised her dark head and looked up from her computer screen to give him her usual welcoming smile.

'Good morning, Marco. Your father is waiting to see you in your office.'

'Thank you, Lia. Would you organise coffee, please.'

'Already done.'

Entering his office, Marco dropped his briefcase on a nearby table and stood to face a man who was almost his mirror image, if somewhat older.

'Father!' He enveloped him in a hug. 'Thérèse said you were in London but I thought you had already returned to Milan.'

'My meetings have taken longer than originally planned. I return home soon.'

'Have things gone well? You do not look very pleased.'

'Things are fine with me. It is you I am concerned about, or rather the restaurant chain. We need to talk, Marco. There has been a complaint.'

Charlotte followed a well-worn path through Hundred Acre. Astride Jet, she relaxed the reins and let him pick his own way. She smiled to herself, knowing he was so agile he would probably be able to do it blindfolded. It was Thursday afternoon and usually at this time she would have been meeting Marco at Fox Cottage. But not today. Today he was flying to Aberdeen at his father's request. There had been a complaint about one of the restaurants and as a precaution, he had been asked to visit each of the twelve European and five English restaurants to make sure everything was in order, not only with the finances, but also the general operation. She understood how important this was because the D'Alesandros took great pride in everything they ran. It was when she had asked Marco how long he thought he would be away that the bottom dropped out of her world. Nearly a month! It was a painful reality she had yet to come to terms with. The only light in this darkness was that he had promised to call her every evening.

Reaching her favourite spot, she sat for a moment watching the activity in the valley below. To the east, Niall was bringing in the herd for the afternoon's milking, while on the hill opposite she could see a thin line of riders led by Rachel, astride her grey gelding, making their way back to the trekking centre. Moments later a train clattered through, disrupting the silence of the afternoon. She was about to turn Jet's head and make her way along the edge of the barley field when she heard the nicker of an approaching horse. Turning in her saddle, she saw a rider materialise from the depths of the wood – Thérèse. She kicked her heels into Jet's flanks, eager to be gone before her nemesis arrived, but Thérèse had already spotted her and urged her mount forward to intercept her.

She greeted her with a sugary smile. 'Charlotte, how fortunate.'

'For whom, Mrs D'Alesandro, you or me?' She kept her tone even. There was no way she would let this woman make her lose her temper and neither would she allow herself to be bullied.

'So formal, Charlotte. Call me Thérèse, please. I have been meaning to talk to you.'

'Have you? About what?'

'My stepson.' Charlotte noticed the formal way she referred to him, as if he were a stranger, someone she hardly knew.

Charlotte sat back in her saddle and waited. 'Well, I'm listening.'

'I want you to keep away from him.' The older woman's voice was calm but there was an undertone of menace backed by an icy expression in her eyes.

'Is there any particular reason?' Charlotte asked, trying hard to keep composed.

'I don't feel any need to justify my request, simply that you observe it.'

Charlotte's expression remained impassive. 'I think he is old enough to decide for himself, don't you?'

'He is under your spell, infatuated with you. It will not last. It will all end in tears.' Thérèse's horse moved restlessly and she tugged on the reins to still him.

'Why are you pushing him at Rossana?'

'That is my business.'

'If you think I am unsuitable for him then I assure you, she is too.'

'On the contrary, she has all the makings of a great wife. She is obedient, gentle and, of course, she comes from an excellent Italian family.'

'Those attributes may appeal to you but I doubt they would to Marco.' Charlotte still managed to keep her cool despite having the feeling the last description was a deliberate slur against her own parents.

'They will, in time. He will learn to appreciate her,' Thérèse said confidently. 'And he can only do this if you cease to interfere in his life.'

'Interfere in his life?' Charlotte's mouth turned up in a slight smile. 'I rather thought you were the one doing that.'

Thérèse brought her head up sharply. It was obvious she had not expected a challenge. She was a woman used to getting her own way with little or no resistance. 'I don't think you are listening to me.' She lowered her voice menacingly. 'Such a shame, because if you do not do as I ask, I have the potential to make things very difficult for the rest of your family.'

'And what, exactly, is that supposed to mean?' All at once Charlotte became aware their conversation was taking a less than pleasant turn.

'Ah, at last I have your attention.' There was a triumphant smile. 'Let me put it bluntly. If you refuse to leave Marco alone I may be forced to take my business elsewhere.'

'You would leave Lawns?'

Thérèse nodded. 'Precisely. And before you tell me Lawns could probably cope with my departure, remember it goes far deeper than that. Your aunt currently has the benefit of my international connections – already two European society weddings have been booked there. Don't you think people would be curious if I suddenly decided to sever connections with her?'

'You would end up in court,' Charlotte threw back, outraged her family's business was being used as a lever to get this awful woman what she wanted.

'Oh, I don't have to open my mouth. In fact, I wouldn't dream of it. People would wonder and gossip would start. Of course,' she gave a malicious shrug, 'I wouldn't be averse to giving such gossip a helpful nudge.'

'You would ruin my family just to make sure Rossana and Marco end up together?'

'I would kill to do it.' Thérèse bared her teeth in a feral snarl as she wheeled her horse's head around. 'So think long and hard, Charlotte. Make sure when Marco returns your decision is the right one. I want you out of his life permanently or I will make sure your family suffers. Is that clear?'

'Perfectly.' Charlotte replied angrily as she watched Thérèse D'Alesandro dig her heels into her horse and ride off into the wood.

'God, it's a beaut; a great black beast of a car. Am I allowed to drive it?'

'Not on your life!' Christian grinned at Jay as he lounged in the driver's seat of his new Lamborghini. 'This is my baby. She's been on order for ages. I wanted to pick her up from the factory at Sant'Agata Bolognese and now I have, I'm the only one who is going to be getting behind the wheel.'

Jay shrugged uncaringly. 'Oh well, I guess being a passenger is awesome enough for me.'

'Ah…' Christian shifted in his seat uncomfortably. 'Slight change of plan, mate. I've decided I'd prefer this journey to be solo, if you don't mind.'

'Solo?' The disappointment was clear in Jay's voice. 'But I thought—'

'I need time to myself, man. You know, deep thoughts. No distractions. First nights always freak me out. I need to feel completely settled. Another time maybe?'

Jay realised arguing was not an option. Christian dominated on tour; he was the star and he always got his own way even if the person he was upsetting right now was one of his oldest friends. He stood watching as, with a final wave and a grin of triumph, Christian accelerated away out of the car park.

Turning back to the hotel, he saw Lucy coming down the steps towards him, one of her cameramen following behind.

'Too late,' he said, shaking his head. 'You've just missed him.'

'But I thought… weren't you supposed to be going with him?'

'Change of plan. Apparently, I'd upset the deep vibes he needs before his first show in Verona.' He saw her disbelieving face and lifted his shoulders in a helpless gesture. 'I know, Luce, but what could I do?'

'Damn! He agreed we could do a photo shoot around the city this afternoon.' Lucy cursed under her breath. 'What the hell is he playing at? He's not back on the pills again, is he?'

'Definitely not. But you're right, there is something going on with him, I know it, although at the moment I can't figure out exactly what.'

'Bloody hell!' Lucy swore as she turned to her cameraman and instructed him to return to the hotel. 'What a complete waste of an afternoon.'

'Hardly a waste, Miss Benedict.' Jay smiled, winding a leisurely finger around one of her loose black curls. 'I can think of one really good way to use this free time we both appear have.' He bent his head and kissed her soft mouth. 'Your suite or mine?'

A few miles down the road Christian pulled up to the kerb outside a small café. A figure emerged from its shaded interior. Wearing tight jeans and a plunging sleeveless top, her appearance caused a stir among a group of men working on a building site opposite. Ignoring their cat calls and whistles, she slid into the passenger seat, dumping her holdall on the floor. Leaning across, Christian kissed her hungrily.

'Ready for Verona, babe?'

'You bet,' she answered enthusiastically, her gaze wandering over the dashboard. 'Great car. I thought you were joking when you said we'd be driving there in one of these.'

'This is my new baby. Picked her up yesterday from the factory.'

'No kidding! Have you ever had sex in one of these?' she asked, as he pulled away.

'Are you serious?' He stifled a laugh. Kayte seemed obsessed with different places in which to indulge in carnal delights.

'Of course I am, I like a challenge. How far is Verona?'

'About ninety miles.'

'We could stop halfway there. I'm sure by then you'll need to stretch your legs... and other important parts of your anatomy.' She smiled at him suggestively.

He grinned back. 'You're dreadful, Kayte. Simply dreadful.'

'Ah,' she said, running a long pink nail down his arm, 'but you wouldn't have me any other way, now would you?'

When Lucy called to suggest she fly out to Verona to join the tour, Charlotte could not have been happier. She missed Marco and, although they kept in regular touch, time seemed to be dragging. This unexpected invitation was exactly what she needed – time away from home in a totally unfamiliar environment where, despite being among familiar faces, everything would be strange, new and distracting. Clearing the airport, her case in tow, she did not have long to wait before she heard the blare of a car horn as Lucy pulled up in a red BMW convertible.

'You like?' she said, getting out and commandeering Charlotte's luggage to stow in the boot. 'I do. In fact, I absolutely adore this car and I plan to get one when I get home. Talking of which, how is everyone?'

'Fine. Little Court is, of course, extremely busy,' Charlotte replied as she slipped into the passenger seat. 'They've had three new wedding bookings this week.'

'Three? That's brilliant!' Lucy settled herself back behind the wheel. 'And what about you?'

'Oh, you know… missing Marco like crazy.'

'Well, prepare yourself for an enjoyable few days of fun and distraction,' Lucy said, grinning as she put the car in drive and pulled away.

Charlotte smiled back. 'Just what I could do with; I've been going stir crazy at home. How's the tour going so far?'

'It's an absolute blast. I so love what I'm doing here,' Lucy enthused. 'And, of course, I've got Jay with me to keep me sane when Christian decides to be difficult.'

'Are you having trouble with him again? I thought all that was over.'

'So did we, but over the past couple of days there's been some pretty weird stuff going on with him.'

'What sort of weird stuff?'

'Well, he took delivery of a new Lambo and insisted on driving alone to Verona, when all along he'd promised Jay could go with him. And then last night, he said he was going down to the venue to check on how everything was coming along and ended up staying out until the early hours. He wouldn't say where he'd been. In fact, he got quite stroppy when Jay quizzed him. It's completely out of character and very worrying given his history.'

'And you say it started a few days ago?'

'Yes. The day following his first Milan gig. He decided to take breakfast in his room, which isn't like him at all. Up until then he'd always joined us. Jay went up to see if he was okay but he wouldn't let him in, said he had an upset stomach. The day after was the same and then came this thing with the driving. Could you possibly have a gentle word with him? I'm sure it's nothing serious, but I know he'll open up to you. If he has any issues, we need to know about them. We're a team – here to help and support him. But to do that we have to know what's behind all this.'

'Leave it with me,' Charlotte said, as Lucy pulled away from a set of traffic lights. There was no question of her not helping. In order to bring her and Marco back together again, Christian had sacrificed a huge amount by exposing every element of his private life to him that day at Felica's fashion launch. It was now time to repay that debt.

FORTY

'I have to go, babe,' Christian said, trying to extract himself from Kayte's arms. 'I have rehearsals after lunch. It's my first performance in Verona tomorrow and I want it to be the best.'

Kayte groaned and rolled away from him. 'You know I hate it when you go. I want to be with you.'

'And so you will,' he said, leaning over to kiss her cheek as he pulled on his jeans. 'I'll be back later.'

'Later when?'

'Not sure. I'll give you a call.'

'So how am I expected to pass the time in this crummy hotel?' she threw at him angrily. 'And please don't say watch TV, because I can't understand a bloody word on any of the channels.'

'Kayte, try to be patient.' He raised pacifying hands at her. 'Hell, what do you expect me to do, eh? I can't have you in my hotel room. There are too many people about and, as I've already warned you, if Lucy or Jay catch sight of you I'll be in big trouble. And so will you.'

'You don't want me here, do you?' She screwed up her face, choosing to ignore everything he had said. 'Be honest, you don't care about me at all.'

'Baby, of course I do.' Now fully dressed, he crawled across the bed towards her. It was a mistake. As soon as he put his arms around her, she grabbed at his jeans and tried to get them off him again. He resisted and rested back on his haunches, his expression painful. 'I'm sorry, but I really do have to go. Kayte, you must understand people have paid an awful lot of money to come and see me. I have to be ready to perform and I can't be if I'm with you.'

'Why couldn't I have a ticket to see you?' she whined miserably.

'Because they were sold out way before I got here. It's a full house on all three nights.'

'What about a backstage pass?'

'Impossible! Jay and Lucy will be there. Why won't you listen?' He hauled himself out of her clutches and off the bed. 'I'm not being difficult, but you must understand there are some things I cannot do. You will simply have to be patient.' He closed his eyes; she was relentless in her demands, turning everything he said around to make him feel as if he was being unreasonable. He was beginning to wish he had put her on the next plane home to the UK when she'd arrived instead of letting her stay. He checked his watch. It was no good; he had to leave now otherwise he wouldn't make the Verona Arena on time. He had a feeling Jay and Lucy were already aware something wasn't quite right with him, and the last thing he wanted was to draw any more attention to himself.

'Right, I'm off!' he said, heading for the door. As he closed it, he heard something heavy hit the other side. He shook his head and ran down the corridor, hoping she would be in a better mood by the time he returned later that evening.

The concert over, Christian bowed to his audience. The roar was deafening and, as he straightened, he could see everyone in the theatre was standing. He wiped the sweat away from his forehead with his wrist band and, waving the radio mic in salute, turned and ran back down the tunnel. His first night at the Verona Arena, the Roman amphitheatre Matt had booked for his three performances there, had been spectacularly impressive. As nightfall had descended on the city, the audience had lit candles and joined in with some of his slower numbers, the flickering lights accompanying their owners' voices in a fluid, atmospheric mass of sound and movement in the darkness.

Backstage, Jay's grin nearly split his face. 'Bloody brilliant!' he said, giving Christian bear hug. 'What an evening. And as if that wasn't exciting enough, come with me. There's someone here to meet you.'

'Who?' Christian pulled himself out of his friend's brotherly embrace. His chest still heaving from the exertion of the performance, he frowned, praying Kayte had not managed to wheedle her way in with some cock-and-bull story.

Lucy appeared with a wave and a grin matching Jay's. She had her arm looped through Charlotte's – a beautiful Charlotte dressed in an aquatic blue dress and matching earrings. God, what had she done to herself? It was like seeing Cinderella after the fairy godmother had waved her wand.

'Surprise! Brilliant show, Christian.'

'Lottie!' He kissed her cheek, holding her appreciatively at arm's length. 'What a sight for sore eyes you are! God, you look amazing.'

'Good to see you, Christian, you were quite amazing yourself.' She smiled up at him; her eyes a more beautiful blue than the dress could ever be. 'They asked me to come as a surprise and I'm glad I did. You were fabulous!'

'Thank you.' He smiled down at her and he knew he meant it. Charlotte was here. His rock. His sensible Lottie. She would know what to do. But then a second thought struck him – how could he even begin to explain what was happening? It was far too dangerous when there was a chance her sensible attitude would be persuading him to involve Jay and Lucy. And he could not let that happen.

'I'm about to shower and change,' he said, moving off down the corridor.

'Want some company?' Charlotte offered, shooting Lucy a covert glance.

'Well…' Christian hesitated.

'It's the only time you two will get alone tonight. Don't forget, there's a party to go to and people to meet,' Jay reminded him.

'You're right. It will be manic, won't it? This way then, Miss Kendrick.' Christian indicated the direction with a wave of his hand.

Slipping past Evolution staff and security guards, Charlotte followed him down a narrow tunnel to a door on the right. He tapped a finger proudly against the plaque bearing his name.

'My dressing room.'

Opening the door, he stepped back to let her in then followed, closing it behind him.

From the shadows only feet away, Kayte O'Farrell stepped into the corridor, crept to the door and placed her ear against it. She heard the sound of laughter and muffled conversation. Anger curdled up inside her. After all the effort she had made to get here, all the groping she'd had to suffer from a revolting fat security guard, and now this! No wonder he didn't want her here, not when he was expecting someone else. And Charlotte Kendrick of all people! What had she got that was so special? She wasn't even attractive.

More laughter came from within. Kayte closed her eyes, imagining what must be going on behind the door, and hating every minute of it. Bloody Charlotte Kendrick! The one who had been instrumental in her father taking her to the police. The one who had been involved with Marco and now appeared to have her claws in Christian. Kayte gritted her teeth angrily wondering what she could do about it.

Watching was the thing to do, she decided. Watching and waiting for the right opportunity to teach that cow a lesson. Christian was hers, and there was no way she was going to let anyone else have him. Least of all *her*!

The next morning, Charlotte, Lucy, Jay and Christian arrived for breakfast on the roof terrace of the five-star Due Torri Hotel. Christian, looking surprisingly fresh, seated himself next to Charlotte and their heads bent together in quiet discussion. Lucy watched carefully, wondering whether her cousin had been able to get to the bottom of his strange behaviour. She had checked with reception on her way up to the roof terrace – Christian, it appeared, had returned to the hotel around four a.m. When she relayed this to Jay he had shaken his head uncomfortably.

'We've got to find out why this is happening. Have a word with Charlotte after breakfast. See whether she's found anything out.'

Lucy smiled as she continued to watch them certain, judging by their close discussion, Lottie would have something to tell her. She would be patient and wait.

By ten thirty, Jay and Christian were on their way to the Verona Arena to meet up with the rest of the Rosetti tour team, leaving only Lucy and Charlotte at the hotel. Lucy made her way along the corridor and knocked on her cousin's door.

'Any news?' she asked, as Charlotte stepped back to let her in.

'Not exactly.'

'What's that supposed to mean?'

'Well, I asked him how things were going on the tour and he said fine, he felt totally energised. Then I mentioned about the driving, not involving anything you had said, of course. He told me what he'd told you. Said he finds driving more relaxing than being cooped up in the tour bus, and better if he's alone because it's easier to run through his schedule in his mind and work out any changes for discussion at rehearsal. He's keen to make every performance a little bit different and a little bit better.'

'What about the late nights? Did you know he got back here at four this morning?'

Charlotte shrugged. 'He's having fun with the boys and girls.'

'The roadies?'

'Roadies, musicians, singers, technicians... anyone who's in the team. Says he's made a few good friends,' she confirmed, with a look which said she didn't feel there was anything to worry about. 'Apparently, he feels when he had his drug problem he treated support staff badly and very much played the big star. He's keen to make this tour the best he's ever done and, although he has you two to support him, he wants the feel of the whole operation to be like a family thing. He thinks it is the way to get the best out of people.'

'Do you believe him?'

'Why not? Look, Luce, I can understand you being suspicious about his behaviour, but we're dealing with a very different Christian now. And let's face it, none of this is affecting his performance, is it?'

'No, he's absolutely sensational,' Lucy agreed as she ran agitated fingers through her hair. There had to be more than this. Although the excuse *was* plausible, something still niggled at her.

Charlotte reached out and squeezed her cousin's arm affectionately. 'You could do with a break, you know. Since I've been here you've not stopped.'

'This is my first assignment and it is very important it's a success. Dad's put a lot of trust in me.'

'I know he has, but I'm sure no one would mind if you bunked off for a few hours relaxation. I plan to have a wander around Verona this morning. I've brought my camera. Why don't you join me?'

There was a moment's temptation but she managed to resist and shook her head. 'I'd love to but I can't. I have to get down to the Arena with my cameramen to get some more rehearsal shots. Are you sure you're going to be okay on your own?'

'Of course. I'm good with my own company – plenty of practice.'

'Thanks for helping.' Lucy smiled as she got up to leave. 'At least we know what we're dealing with now.' When she reached the door, she stopped and turned back to look at Charlotte. 'Just a thought... before you go sightseeing why don't you join us at the Arena, take your own shots of the rehearsal. Joe and Ray are great cameramen but it would be nice to get something from a different perspective.'

'Hey, I'm hardly a pro,' Charlotte protested, laughing.

'Yeah, but you'd enjoy the fun, I know you would. I don't like to think of you wandering around on your own for most of the day, it doesn't seem fair.'

'Okay, you're on.' Charlotte nodded her head in agreement. 'But don't expect Lord Litchfield stuff, will you. I'm a plain old Box Brownie girl.'

'With a Leica? I don't think so.' Lucy grinned and left.

After her cousin had gone, Charlotte sank onto the bed, her thoughts focussed on Christian. Although she had relayed to Lucy exactly what he had told her, what she had omitted to say was that she had a strong feeling he was lying. He seemed worried, edgy even, and there were times he was reluctant to make eye contact with her. Something was going on and she was determined to get to the bottom of it.

Finding her mobile, she called Safekeeping and asked if she could extend her absence in order to stay with the tour for a while longer. There was no way she was going home without getting the truth out of him.

Following a great morning and lunch with Christian, Jay, Lucy and the crew, Charlotte, dressed in white Capri pants and a French blue t-shirt, slipped out of the Arena. Dropping her camera in her tote, she checked the street map the hotel had given her. She was glad Lucy had invited her along because she had never seen rehearsals for a concert before and she was soon caught up in the energy and teamwork that went to make the final show slick and seamless. She was amazed there were so many people involved in the support of Christian on this tour. Merchandising, Lucy told her, brought in a huge amount of money at each gig: t-shirts, sweatshirts, mugs, badges, signed photos and, of course, CDs.

Then there was the technical team: the sound engineers and technicians who cared for the instruments, tuned them and did the sound-checking as well as doing any restringing of the guitars for both the band and Christian's on-stage rack. He also had a dresser and a hairdresser, but his PA wasn't there – she was back home in hospital, recovering from a bad RTA. Lucy had volunteered to step into the role, keen to have experience of the tour from another aspect. There were musicians too: a small orchestra of predominantly guitars, strings and backing singers. And last but not least, the catering to feed all these people when they were working.

Charlotte now understood the logistics of not only getting all these people together, but also from place to place must be enormous, and suddenly found herself having the greatest respect for Jay and his organisational skills. Not only was he responsible for all of this but he also liaised, prior to the commencement of the tour, with all the media for each country Christian was appearing in, to make sure Matt's star got maximum coverage for every gig. And then there was Christian himself. Even in jeans and a t-shirt he exuded the most astounding power on stage, his performance a mixture of formidable vocals, incredible sexual energy and fluid animal-like grace: a beautiful tattooed rock warrior.

Staying in the shelter of the Verona Arena's outer walls she headed northeast, her first stop being Juliette's Balcony and house. Getting caught behind a group of American tourists, she followed them through an archway into a small enclosed courtyard where, above and to the right, was a small carved-stone balcony at first floor level. Within the courtyard stood a bronze statue of Juliette. One of the Americans, a large man wearing a navy New York Yankees baseball cap, climbed onto the statue and clasped Juliette's right breast. Charlotte stared at the man, not knowing whether to laugh or be embarrassed.

'It's supposed to be good luck, honey, for those seeking true love,' the woman standing next to her said, waving a tourist guide at her. 'At least, that's what this says. And inside the house there are scraps of paper pinned to the wall. According to the book here, it means the people who have done that will stay together for the rest of their lives.' She gave a dreamy sigh. 'Italy is so romantic, don't you think?'

Charlotte nodded, wondering whether to scribble down hers and Marco's name and pin it to the wall, then decided against it. Instead, she pulled out her camera to take some shots of the balcony and the statue, once the man climbed down. She moved into the house, noticing the paper strips the woman had referred to, intrigued by the furniture and day-to-day items from fourteenth-century living.

Trailing behind the Americans and their guide, she moved northwest towards the river, where she left them all discussing the best place to stop for refreshments. Following the narrow road which bordered the river, she passed cafés and parked scooters, cars and the general bustle and smells of Italian life. One of the roadies had mentioned that Verona Cathedral, St Maria Matricolare, would provide a good photo opportunity. She checked her map again and, realising it wasn't too far away, stopped to buy a bottle of water before continuing. A short while later, she halted her walk to sit on the river wall as she got her bearings once more and to finish off the water. Studying the map, she saw she could shorten her journey if she took a short-cut along the small road directly opposite.

Waiting for a speeding scooter to pass, she crossed the road into the one-way street peppered with parked cars. Three-storey houses with dark shutters and a mixture of ornate stone and metal balconies faced each other silently in the afternoon heat, bordered by a froth of flower boxes. Up ahead, she could see the cathedral dominating the other buildings. Unlooping her tote from her shoulder, she pulled out her camera. As she passed a house with a high marble entrance step, its darkened doorway open to the street, she stopped to focus the camera ready for a shot of the dome. Out of the corner of her eye she became aware of a blur of movement before someone shoved her hard in the back. She screamed and dropped the camera, her hands flying out in front of her as she was thrown towards the rough stone of the wall. Intense pain followed before her whole world dissolved into darkness.

FORTY-ONE

Charlotte came to in a strange room with shades pulled low against the brightness outside. She was lying fully dressed on top of a large bed. Groaning, she put her hand to her temple as she tried to focus, her fingers coming into contact with a large gauze pad. On a shelf at the end of the room she could see an array of toys including a wooden train and two teddy bears. She twisted her head slowly to the side, blinking to clear her vision. As it returned she was aware of two people by her bedside. One, an attractive slim woman in her late forties with thick, straight, dark shoulder-length hair and even darker eyes gathered into an anxious frown was sitting by the bed. The other, a striking older man with greying hair, stood slightly behind her.

The anxiety faded from the woman's face, replaced by a relieved smile.

'Ah, you are awake at last.'

'How are you feeling?' the man asked in heavily accented English, leaning over to touch her face.

'My head aches. Who are you?' Charlotte squinted at them and winced, her fingers returning to the pad. 'What's happened? Why am I here?'

'My name is Gina Lombardi,' the woman replied, 'and this is my husband Alberto. I heard a scream and Alberto went out to investigate and found you unconscious in the street below. Did you fall?'

Charlotte tried to remember, the fog in her mind slowly clearing. 'No! I think I've been mugged. Someone jumped out of a doorway and pushed me against the wall as I was about to take a photo. My bag...' She looked around anxiously. 'Have you seen my bag?'

'Do not worry, it is downstairs,' Gina reassured her. 'We checked it to see who you were – Charlotte? There is no camera and I am afraid there is no money in your purse either.' The dark eyes became serious. 'You are right, you have been mugged. You need to report this to the police as soon as possible, *cara mia*. Would you like me to phone them? I am quite happy for you to see them here.'

'No, no thank you. I will call them as soon as I get back to my hotel,' Charlotte insisted, pushing herself up on her elbows. The movement made her head hurt, forcing her to grit her teeth. 'How long have I been here?'

'About twenty minutes,' the man replied. 'I am a doctor. Thankfully, you have no broken bones, only a nasty bump on your head which needed a dressing.'

'This is my godson's room,' Gina said, seeing Charlotte staring around the room. 'I am expecting him later but I am sure he will not mind you borrowing it for now.'

'I'm indebted to you both for what you have done, but I do need to get back to my hotel. I'm with friends and they will be worried.'

'Are you sure you are well enough?' Alberto's hand rested gently on Charlotte's shoulder. 'There may still be some dizziness.'

'No, honestly, I feel much better,' she replied, swinging her legs over the edge of the bed and getting to her feet. The headache she had woken up with was slowly fading to leave a dull ache in her temple. She stood still for a moment, trying to retrieve the memory of those last few moments before she had been attacked. She had glimpsed someone. Dark glasses, their head covered.

Gina rose from her chair. Tall and elegant in a red shirt and black trousers, a thick plain gold rope at her throat and matching studs in her ears, she was exceptionally beautiful, with the kind of Italian glamour that reminded Charlotte a little of Sophia Loren.

'Alberto?' Gina looked at her husband questioningly. 'Are you happy to let Charlotte leave?'

He gave a consenting nod. 'I think she will be fine. But,' he waved a serious finger at her, 'I insist on personally taking you back to your hotel. Where are you staying?'

'The Due Torri.'

'Ah, not far away. Here, let me help you, the stairs are quite steep.' Gina smiled and offered her arm to Charlotte while Alberto went ahead of them to fetch his car.

Ten minutes later Alberto dropped her off outside the hotel, leaving her with his phone number and strict instructions to contact him immediately if she should feel unwell. Walking through the glass doors and into the hotel foyer, she spotted Lucy, Jay and Christian in the lounge. They were chatting, an open bottle of wine in front of them. Jay saw her first and said something to Lucy, who turned round to look at her. Frowning, she got to her feet and rushed over to meet her.

'Lottie, your head. What's happened?' She slid a supportive arm around her. 'Are you okay?'

'I was mugged,' Charlotte replied.

'Lottie, my love.' Christian had come over to join them. Lucy stepped back, allowing him to wrap his arms around her cousin. 'Shouldn't we take you to the hospital? Get you looked at?'

'No need,' Charlotte said, smiling up at him. 'This kind woman took me in. Her husband's a doctor. He checked me over and when I'd recovered enough, he ran me back here.'

'Have you reported the incident to the police?' Lucy asked anxiously.

'Not yet.'

'Come and sit down.' Christian guided her over and helped her gently into one of the seats by Jay, settling himself beside her. 'We need to contact the police,' he said to Jay, who was on his feet immediately, pulling his mobile from his jacket and walking off somewhere quieter to make the call.

'If you're not up to making the concert again tonight, babe, I'll understand.' Christian patted her hand. 'There's always tomorrow.'

'I so wanted to be there,' Charlotte mumbled, her hand going to her temple, 'but I have to say I still feel a bit fuzzy.'

'Luce will put you to bed and we'll get the hotel to make regular checks to make sure you're okay.'

'No, I'll stay with her,' Lucy offered. 'I don't mind missing the concert. I can set Joe up so he knows exactly what I want.'

'No, no. You must go,' Charlotte insisted. 'It's your job and it's important, remember?'

'Well, if you're sure you're going to be all right.'

'I'll be fine.'

Around five thirty, the police arrived and took a statement and shortly afterwards, the team left for their evening at the Arena. Alone in her suite, Charlotte slept for a while and woke around seven, deciding a warm bath might be a good idea. There was satellite TV and a movie channel she could tap in to. To complete her chill-out evening, she phoned down for room service to send up a bottle of white wine and a light supper at half past eight. Replacing the gauze pad with a large plaster, which Lucy had appropriated from hotel reception, she undressed and slipped on one of the hotel's robes. Minutes later, as she was running the bath, she heard a knock at the door.

'Damn!' She turned off the taps. Although she had specified the delivery for eight thirty, it looked as if everything had arrived an hour early. Padding across the room, she heard the tap came again followed by a muffled 'Room Service'.

'Come in.' She smiled at the waiter, stepping back as he entered pushing a small trolley containing an ice bucket, champagne and two glasses. She stared at the bottle for a moment then at him. 'I'm sorry, you must have the wrong room,' she said, laughing. 'I didn't order champagne.'

'No, I did.'

Looking back towards the doorway, she saw Marco standing there. Tipping the waiter on his way out, he stepped into the room and closed the door.

Charlotte stood shaking her head, still unable to believe her eyes.

'I think I must be dreaming,' she said breathlessly, her eyes drinking in all six feet of her beautiful Italian.

He smiled and, crossing the room swiftly, captured her in his arms. 'Well, you are most certainly not.' He kissed her gently. 'I am very, very real.'

'But I don't understand. How did you know I was here?'

'Gina Lombardi is my godmother.'

Charlotte looked at him, stunned.

'It is her birthday tomorrow,' Marco continued. 'I called in to deliver presents from the family. She told me what had happened. How is your head?' He touched the plaster gently with the tip of his finger. 'Does it still hurt?'

'No, it's fine. Much better, thank you. How are the restaurant visits going?'

'Thankfully the checks in the UK are now complete,' he replied, his thumb grazing her cheek gently. 'And I am glad to say all of them are performing well, including Aberdeen where the problem was.' He kissed the corner of her mouth then stepped back to regard her with a curious tilt of his head. 'Tomorrow I begin my European visits, but tonight I intend to celebrate my luck in finding you.'

His smile sent a tremor of expectation through her, realising tonight she would have this glorious man in her bed once more.

'What has brought you to Verona of all places?' he asked.

'Christian is here on tour; this is his second night at the Arena. Lucy invited me over for a few days. She thought it might help me feel a little less adrift with you gone.' She looked up, finding herself once again ensnared in his deep brown gaze.

'You are missing me?' He looked pleased as he moved away to shrug off his jacket and drape it over a nearby chair.

'Of course I am, and I'm glad we will be back together soon.' She reached out to capture him in her arms as he returned to her.

'How long are you staying?'

'Another week. I'm having a fantastic time. I know...' she hesitated as a thought occurred to her. 'As you're here, why don't you come to tomorrow evening's concert with me? Everyone would love to see you again. And I can tell you, Christian is something to behold on stage.'

Marco laughed. 'I am sure he is and I would love to see him, but unfortunately my schedule means I need to be in Capri tomorrow.' He stroked her face gently. 'All we have is tonight.'

'Oh, Marco.' Charlotte gave a disappointed groan and buried her head in his shoulder. 'No sooner you are here than you're gone.'

He shook his head sadly. 'I know. But I promise when we are together again, I will take you to San Raffaello's and we will have a wonderful celebration.'

She shook her head, trying to hide her panic. 'But we can't. What if Thérèse finds out?' The thought of compromising Little Court in any way was the one thing which genuinely frightened her.

'Relax, it will not be a problem,' he said confidently. 'Come and sit and I will tell you why.'

When she joined him on the edge of the bed he took her hand and squeezed it tightly. 'My father called this afternoon. He tells me he is planning to take Thérèse to America for a coast-to-coast tour for her next birthday, and Rossana and Felica are going with them.' He raised her hand and kissed it. 'So for a whole month I will be free and at your command, my lady.'

'Time to celebrate, then.' Her smile resurfaced and she pulled him from the bed towards the unopened bottle of champagne still nestling in its cooler. Several uninterrupted weeks together – she could not believe it.

'Ah, no. No, Charlotte.' He resisted, spinning her around so that her back fell easily against his chest. 'The champagne can wait; I cannot,' he whispered huskily in her ear as his hands released the ties of the robe and reached into its folds to cup her breasts. 'I have been without you for far too long,' he continued as his warm persuasive hands teased her responsive flesh, 'and I refuse to wait a moment longer.'

Marco opened his eyes. Beyond the curtains, light was beginning to seep through, signalling the arrival of morning. Raising himself up on one elbow, he turned to gaze at Charlotte, peaceful in sleep, her hair spread over the pillow, one arm thrown out towards the edge of the bed. Gently, and without disturbing her, he eased himself away from her, rose to his feet and began to dress. As he bent to retrieve his shirt from the floor, where she had thrown it in her eagerness to relieve him of his clothes, he heard her sleepy voice.

'Marco, where are you going?'

'I have to leave,' he said quietly, slipping his feet into his shoes. 'My flight goes at ten thirty and I need to get back to Gina's house to shower and change.' Walking back over to the bed he leaned over with the intention of dropping a kiss on her cheek but instead, her arms reached up, capturing him for a passionate kiss.

'I will keep in touch,' he promised. 'As soon as I have news of Thérèse's birthday arrangements, I will let you know. But I will see you before then when my work in Europe is finished.'

'Have you any idea when that will be?'

'Only a couple of weeks more, but again, I will let you know. We will be together very soon, I promise.' He stood back to study her for a while, his lips parting, wanting to say more, then changed his mind. He gave her a farewell kiss on the forehead. 'Get some sleep,' he whispered then left the bedroom.

Hearing the door to her suite close Charlotte buried her head in her pillow, overwhelmed with sadness at the silence left by Marco's departure.

An hour later she still lay in bed. Sleep had not come but the sadness had passed, leaving her with warm memories. She reached out and touched the cold sheets where not long ago he had rested beside her. She thought of their night together, of the many times he had taken her in passion and in love. Their time together had been so precious, little of it had been wasted on sleep. She took herself back to those moments, feeling once more the magic of his exploring fingers and the sensation of his mouth as it covered her own. How easy it was to evoke the warmth and smell of his skin and the exquisite feel of his hard male body moving against hers in a rhythm as old as time. She stretched and rolled over, closing her eyes tightly, determined to lovingly hold all of this in her memory until they were together once more.

Thinking of their night together caused her to push her hand against her mouth in sudden alarm, remembering, with the attack yesterday, she had forgotten to take her contraceptive pill. Quickly, she slipped out of bed and crossed the carpeted floor to find her tote; she would take one now and another later this evening.

When a first search failed to locate the tablets, she turned out all the bag's contents onto the bed and searched through every individual item but was still unable find them. She gave a disbelieving shake of her head. They had been zipped into one of the inside pockets of the tote, a silly place, she reprimanded herself, knowing she should have taken them out and left them in the bathroom when she arrived. Finding both pockets empty, she realised there was only one reason they could be missing. They had been stolen along with the camera and her money. Perhaps the thief thought they were drugs. She could not think of any other explanation as to why they would have been taken. She took a deep breath and tried to think logically about her situation. Noticing the neat card lying among the contents of her bag, she picked it up. Dr Lombardi would know what to do.

FORTY-TWO

Thérèse D'Alesandro sat holding the phone to her ear whilst gazing out over the manor's parkland from the window seat of her bedroom. She had just picked up a call from Gina Lombardi, ringing to thank her and Gianlucca for her birthday gifts. After gushing overtures concerning the jewellery, which caused Thérèse to roll her eyes and thank heaven the woman was one of Gianlucca's friends and not hers, Gina asked, 'How are things with you Thérèse? Still keeping busy with your designing?'

'Yes, very much,' Thérèse replied, pleased she could now take over the conversation. 'I am showing my new collection of evening wear in Milan in September. I hope you and Alberto will be there.'

'Of course we will. And what of Felica? How is her new project coming along?'

'Exceedingly well. She launched her new young collection a month ago and demand is high. I am very excited for her.'

'That is such good news. You and Gianni are lucky to have such successful children.'

Child, Thérèse thought irritably. Had she forgotten Marco was not hers?

'Marco flew out to Capri this morning,' Gina continued. 'I was sorry to see him go. He is a credit to you both.'

Thérèse gritted her teeth again.

'And you will never guess what happened while he was here. A young woman was mugged outside the house yesterday afternoon. She turned out to be someone he knew.'

Thérèse was suddenly alert. 'Oh, who was that?'

'Her name was Charlotte Kendrick. She was staying in Verona with friends. Such a coincidence.'

'So Marco met up with her, did he?' Thérèse deliberately lightened her voice in an effort to dampen down the heated frustration welling up inside her.

'Yes, he went to her hotel last evening to see her.'

Thérèse gritted her teeth yet again. 'Really.'

'You know her, I take it?'

'Oh yes, very well.'

'She was such a striking young woman, with unusual blue eyes and so grateful for our help. Well, it is wonderful to talk to you, Thérèse, but Emilio Lucarelli has arrived to take us away for a few days. You remember him, don't you? Alberto's childhood friend. He breeds horses and has a luxury villa in Sardinia which is where we will be staying.' She laughed. 'Gianni always said Emilio reminded him of Marcello Mastroianni.'

'Didn't he die last year?'

'I hope not, he is due here in half an hour.'

'I mean Marcello Mastroianni.' Thérèse huffed irritably.

'Oh yes, yes, he did. Such a handsome man, was he not?'

Making her excuses, Thérèse ended the call and began pacing the room. Not only had Gina irritated her – yet another fan of Marco's – despite all her efforts, Charlotte had still managed to cross his path. She tried not to imagine what had taken place in that hotel room last night. She simply must get rid of her before he fell under her spell again. But how? She thought she had held the wretched girl at bay with her threats to ruin Little Court. However, Thérèse knew it was only that: a threat. There was no way she would pull out of her deal with Ella Benedict. It was far too lucrative. Had Charlotte known that? Is that why she had met with Marco? She drew in a deep breath and paused to think for a moment, trying to work out what best to do next. And then it came to her.

Returning to the window seat, she lodged herself against the wooden shutters and began punching a number into the phone.

Charlotte was going home at last. She had stayed on with the tour longer than planned as it worked its way from Italy to Austria and then into the Czech Republic. In the three weeks she had been with them she had thoroughly enjoyed herself and rediscovered the old and priceless friendship she had enjoyed with Christian during his Rosetti band days. But Marco had called her last night to tell her he was at last on his way home, which meant she would be leaving. Despite spending a huge amount of time in Christian's company and trying to engage him in conversation which might unearth some clue, she was no nearer to finding out what he was up to. His absences from his bed continued with plausible excuses, but she had the feeling someone among the roadies was covering for him, probably with the benefit of a hefty financial inducement. The performances he delivered were totally awe-inspiring and as his work was not affected, Jay had decided, with Charlotte's need to be home, it was best to accept what was happening and to stop worrying.

But even if they weren't worrying any longer, she was. She had been able to access a prescription through Alberto Lombardi, but it had been a Sunday – pharmacies were closed – so she was unable to gain access to the tablets until Monday. When she had returned to the Lombardi house to see if he could advise on what to do, she found he and his wife had left for a few days away in Sardinia. And so she missed two pills and now her period, due a week ago, had not arrived. She tried not to panic. Her periods were light anyway, and it was not the first occasion this had happened while she had been in a relationship. No, she would be fine, she assured herself. Worrying was silly and pointless. There was no baby. There couldn't be.

Her plane landed a few minutes after midday. Marco's flight from

Amsterdam had arrived earlier that morning. As she waited at Prague airport he had phoned to confirm he would be at Heathrow to meet her. The rest of the D'Alesandro family were leaving for the States that day, he told her, which meant they would be able to spend time in London, with the promised celebratory meal at San Raffaello's that evening. Charlotte could not believe she would have uninterrupted time with Marco, that they could go where they wanted without fear of being seen. The light was indeed at the end of the tunnel, blazing brightly.

Retrieving her luggage, she cleared customs and emerged into the arrivals hall. Her gaze scanned the people waiting to collect friends and loved ones, but he was not among them. Maybe he had been caught in traffic, she thought as she found a seat and waited. Fifteen minutes later when he still had not materialised, she called him on her mobile. The call tripped straight into his answerphone and she left a quick message. After another ten minutes with still no sign of him, she called San Raffaello's. Vittorio answered immediately.

'Ah, Charlotte, it is good to hear from you. You are well?'

'Yes, yes, I am, thank you. Is Marco there?'

'Marco? Why, no. He left earlier for the airport.'

Charlotte gave a thankful sigh, reprimanding herself for being so stupid.

'That's great news; he'll be on his way, then.'

'Yes, he will,' Vittorio replied. 'The flight left just before lunch. He is spending a whole month in America with the family for Thérèse's birthday.'

'What!' A cold, sick feeling seeped through her. 'When was this arranged?'

'Oh, only this morning. He had no idea. Thérèse and his father were both here when he arrived back. His father told him he deserved a break after all the time he has spent checking the restaurants, and what better way than with all the family. Apparently, Mrs D'Alesandro suggested it. Very thoughtful of her, was it not?'

Thanking him, Charlotte ended the call. She bunched her fingers into fists, feeling a great need to hit something or scream. Thérèse had done it again! Somehow she had found out about their meeting in Verona. What else could have prompted her to organise this?

A month, she thought depressingly, as she slid the telescopic handle from her case and began wheeling it towards the exit in order to find a taxi. Four whole weeks for Thérèse to make both their lives a misery. Of course, from the start she realised the woman had never liked her, but why was she so hell bent on pushing him into the arms of someone as young as Rossana? They were like oil and water, totally incompatible. There had to be something beyond the simple fact she did not approve of their relationship and wanted an end to it. She thought back to that morning in the woods when Thérèse had confronted her, remembered how she had said she would kill to get them together. Yes, this was definitely not about playing cupid – there had to be a hidden agenda. Maybe Rossana Caravello needed a little more investigation.

When the cab driver asked her for her destination, she thought for a moment then requested he take her to the Safekeeping offices. Her computer was there; she hoped the internet might throw up some interesting answers.

Marco rested his head against the back of his seat. The plane had now levelled out; he was leaving England and the woman he loved far behind. His mind was in turmoil, his emotional control resting precariously on the edge of a very explosive temper. He was there because Gina had told Thérèse about Verona. She did not have to say a thing – he knew that was the reason. Now she sat like a cat who had grabbed herself a very large bowl of cream, her pink-tipped fingers wrapped around her champagne glass as she chatted and laughed with his father at the far end of the cabin.

Across the aisle of their private jet, Felica stared out of the window, her face pulled into a tight frown. She had been surprised to see him when he arrived at Heathrow, and as infuriated as he was when he told her the reason for his unexpected inclusion in their party.

'Have you been able to get a message to Lottie?' she had whispered, aware her mother hovered only a few feet away as they waited to board.

Of course he had not, and his frustration in regard to that did nothing to quell his frustration and anger.

'She will probably ring the restaurant,' he answered. 'Vittorio will let her know.' He could imagine how the news would affect her. 'Thérèse has punished me, but I intend to punish her too. I will not play this game with her. I will make her see she has wasted her time forcing me to come on this wretched holiday. I will be charming to Rossana; after all, none of this is her fault. But when we return I will be with Charlotte again. Nothing will have changed.'

Raising his glass, he drank his champagne back in one gulp. As he handed the empty flute back to the steward for a refill, intending to numb himself with alcohol before they landed, he felt a small warm hand cover his. Rossana was sitting next to him; in his preoccupation with his situation he had forgotten she was there.

'Marco.' Her voice was low and urgent. 'Is it me you are angry with?'

He looked into her green eyes. 'No, it is nothing to do with you. It is Thérèse.'

'She only wants what is best for you and me.'

'Does she?' His gaze drifted down the plane towards his stepmother, where the steward was now refilling her glass. 'I think not, Rossana. Be warned, she is only ever involved in things which are for her own benefit. This is not about you and me; it is something deeper. Much deeper.'

'Oh, but you are wrong, it is. She knows how I feel about you,' Rossana insisted, her hand squeezing his. 'She also knows real affection takes time to grow. And now we have a month together maybe I can make you change your mind about me. I know you think you are in love with Charlotte, but it is only infatuation.' Her words held a confident ring. 'Mrs D'Alesandro told me and I truly believe it. It is you and I who are destined to be together.'

Marco closed his eyes; once again he felt incredibly sorry for this young innocent woman sitting beside him. He had to admit his stepmother had done an excellent job – Rossana's naivety with the world at large meant she was not equipped to recognise benevolence from evil intent. It must have been incredibly easy to manipulate her into this confident belief about her destiny. He only hoped Thérèse was as good at damage limitation because, on their return, he planned to ask Charlotte to marry him.

Leaving her luggage in reception, Charlotte took the lift up to the office she shared with Olivia Manning. Opening the door, she greeted her with a smile and a hello.

'Welcome back.' Livvy sat back in her chair watching Charlotte as she settled behind her desk and fired up her computer. Then, as quickly as it had appeared, her smile morphed into a curious frown. 'Am I missing something? I thought you weren't due in until next week?'

'I wasn't but, well....' Charlotte shrugged and made a face before proceeding to tell her everything that had happened.

When she had finished, Livvy shook her head. 'The woman's totally crazy. Why does she persist when it's obvious Marco does not want the girl?'

'I'm about to find out,' Charlotte replied, tapping Rossana's name into her computer's search engine.

'What is it?' Olivia asked when she saw the satisfied expression growing on Charlotte's face.

'I think I know what Thérèse is up to.' Charlotte looked up and smiled. 'Come and have a look at this.'

Arriving at Little Court by early evening, Charlotte went straight to her room and unpacked. Her scan of the internet had revealed some interesting details: Rossana Caravello's parents had been killed in a helicopter crash eight years ago and she was poised to inherit the family vineyards in Tuscany on her eighteenth birthday in September. Charlotte was not sure whether Marco was aware of this fact, he had never mentioned it in all their conversations. It seemed he merely viewed her arrival as something his father had arranged to help out an old friend. It was anything but. It was all about business, about gaining control of one of the premier producers of Chianti in Italy. Settling herself on the bed, she decided to leave Marco a text message confirming all she had discovered.

* * *

Marco was in the shower when his mobile rang. They had arrived in New York and had spent the afternoon settling into their luxury five-bedroom suite at the Waldorf Towers. He had left his mobile on the bed and the noise of the shower meant he was completely unaware of the incoming call, but the phone's distinctive ring drew Thérèse from the lounge. She entered his room and picked it up. Noticing it was a text message, she thought little of it until she saw the identity of the caller.

She opened the message, drawing an angry breath as she realised how this could completely wreck her plans. Quickly, she texted back a short message from Marco, thanking her for the information and telling her he was aware of the situation and not to worry. Pressing *Send* she hesitated, hearing the shower stop. She watched the screen, waiting for the message to successfully reach its destination, then deleted all traces of both communications, then quickly left the room.

'Good journey?' Beth reached up to kiss CJ as he walked into her hall, overnight bag in hand. She looked forward to these stopovers, which had become a regular weekly occurrence. It was nearly the end of August and it appeared the work at Gulls' Rest still required a weekly site meeting between himself and all parties working there. She smiled, wondering if any of his other projects were so well overseen, and knowing they most certainly were not.

'Yeah, traffic wasn't as bad as I expected,' he said when he broke away from her. 'I did stop at the services for a coffee, though, and picked this up on the way out.' He handed her a copy of *Celebrity Watch*.

She frowned as she took it from him. 'Something special in here?'

'Yes, and I'm hoping to God Lottie doesn't see it,' he said, moving past her and heading for the stairs. 'Check it out while I dump my things, you'll find it about halfway through.'

In the kitchen, Beth switched on the kettle and set the mugs out for coffee before placing the magazine on the worktop and starting to thumb through it.

'Found it?' CJ said when he returned, his arms slipping around her waist, his face nuzzling the back of her neck.

'Yes. This is awful. Do you think there's any truth in it?'

'Who knows, but if there is, I'll make him wish he'd never been born. Of course, this isn't something Lottie would read, but I'm seriously hoping she doesn't accidentally stumble upon a copy. She'll be devastated.'

'They look very cosy.' Beth turned her head, catching CJ's profile. 'They appear to be doing everything short of snogging. However, despite the famous saying, the camera does have a habit of lying.'

The kettle came to the boil and CJ moved over to make the coffee, leaving her free to continue her scrutiny of the article.

'*Marco D'Alesandro and his girlfriend Rossana Caravello enjoying their stay in LA,'* she read, stopping to re-examine the first photograph of them shopping together on Rodeo Drive. She bent her head closer, studying the other incriminating photos: Marco and Rossana in a swimming pool, his arms reaching up to support her as she slid into the pool wearing a small scrap of bikini revealing more than it covered; another of them dining out, both smiling into the camera.

Beth took a step back, frowning. 'Who do you think took these?' she asked, tapping the page with her finger as CJ placed a steaming mug of coffee in front of her.

He shrugged, tilting his head as he stared over her shoulder. 'Some photographer with a telephoto lens, I guess.'

'I don't think so… They look more like family shots to me. Photos taken from a distance are more covert, they don't have the posed look I'm seeing in these. In fact, if you take a good look at them, they don't look at all professional.' Beth shook her head slowly as she sipped her coffee. 'If you ask me, I think Thérèse is behind this. She took him off to America with the express purpose of getting him and Rossana together and now she wants to show Lottie she's succeeded. She's an absolute monster.' Beth looked up at him, her face full of despair. 'Oh, CJ, when will it all end?'

FORTY-THREE

Charlotte sat gazing out of her office window towards the leafy square below where late August sunshine danced across the pavement. Marco's messaging had picked up again once they left New York, and now after visiting the Eastern Seaboard, flying south to Florida and across to New Orleans, Dallas and Denver, they were spending their final week in LA and San Francisco. Each of his daily messages gave a brief note of where they were, how much he missed her, and it was only Felica's company which was making the whole trip bearable for him. Of Rossana there was no mention. Just as well, she thought, not even wanting to think about the ways in which Thérèse might be scheming. Only a few more days, she thought, and then he'll be home and things will be back to normal. She had survived the past twenty-four days, another three she could easily cope with. Their reunion would more than make up for this forced absence. The sound of the phone on her desk brought her back from her thoughts.

'Lottie?' It was Lucy.

'Luce, how are things?'

'Not good.'

'Oh.'

'It's Christian. I'm not sure what's going on but he's beginning to look unwell, and last night he was sick when he came off stage. He's refused to talk to Jay. In fact, he slammed his hotel room door in Jay's face. Jay is furious and threatening to call my father, but before that happens I wondered—'

'I'll come straight away. Where are you?'

'We're about to leave Bordeaux. The last three dates are in Barcelona, but we're resting up in Perpignan for two days. Oh, Lottie, it's such a mess...' Lucy's words were lost as she began to sob. 'None of us knows what to do.'

'At least you have a two-day breathing space. Please try to keep everything as calm as you can. And whatever you do, don't phone your father yet. We may be able to sort this.'

'I hope so, Lottie, I do hope so.'

'I'll book my flight and text you the details. Can you get someone to pick me up from the airport?'

'Of course. I'll get Jay to meet you.'

The next afternoon, Jay was waiting for Charlotte on her arrival at Riversaltes Airport, his face tight with worry, lack of sleep evident in the dark smudges under his eyes. He drove her to their luxury hotel, a beautiful chateau two kilometres east of the town. Normally, he would have been full of banter and joking, but today his conversation centred on what had been

303

going on since her departure a few weeks ago.

'It was extremely scary when he threw up last night,' he said as they pulled up into the hotel car park. 'The worst thing was he wouldn't let me help him. After all the years we've been together and he simply shouted and pushed me away. He made me feel like a stranger, as if I had no business trying to help.' He killed the engine and rubbed a tired hand over his face. 'We need to sort this, Lottie.' He turned to look at her, his expression grim. 'He's got three nights in Barcelona coming up and right now, I doubt he'd even survive one whole evening on stage.'

'Is he here?' She scanned the car park for the Lamborghini.

'No. He left just before I came to pick you up.'

'No indication of where he was going?'

Jay shook his head. 'None at all. Luce did ask him but he simply brushed past her.' He retrieved the ignition key and pushed open the door of the car. 'Come on, let's get you booked in then we can have a proper talk.'

By seven thirty when the three of them came down to dinner, Christian still had not put in an appearance. Their meal progressed without him as they continued their debate on what to do. Charlotte insisted the best plan was for her to try to talk to him on his own.

'You'll need an element of surprise,' Lucy confirmed, as the coffee arrived, 'otherwise he'll simply walk away. He refuses to listen to anyone.'

'Well, as you've managed to book me in the suite next to his, I don't see a problem.'

'When?' Jay reached for the sugar bowl, added two spoonfuls to his latte, and stirred energetically.

'Tomorrow morning. I'm guessing he still joins you for breakfast?'

'Yes, it's about the only normal thing he does,' Lucy said. 'We meet around nine.'

'I'll be waiting from eight, then.'

The next morning, Charlotte stood in the open doorway to her room. Hearing the sound of the door to the adjacent room opening, she turned to close her own. Dressed in a black t-shirt and combat trousers, at first glance Christian appeared his usual fit and healthy self. However, as he drew nearer, she could see not only the dark circles under his eyes but gauntness in his face which had not been there before. She stepped out to intercept him.

He widened his eyes in surprise and then his face lightened in a smile.

'Lottie! What are you doing here?'

'Thought I'd come back and join you guys again,' she said with a nonchalant smile. 'Marco is overseas again and it's been extremely boring at home.'

'Yes, I heard what happened.' He stroked her shoulder. 'But he's due back soon, isn't he?'

'Yes, this weekend.' Her face took on an air of seriousness. 'Christian, I'm sorry to be blunt, but you don't look at all well. How much sleep have you had?'

He gave a casual shrug. 'Two, three hours maybe. Look, it's not a problem, I'm fine. Honestly I am.'

'No, you are not fine. You look ill,' she argued, her hand on his arm to stop him as he attempted to move away. 'Please tell me what's going on.'

Christian took a deep breath, then crumpled against the wall. Thinking he might be about to faint, she pulled him into her arms, letting his head rest against her shoulder.

'It's all right,' she said softly. 'Whatever it is, you don't need to face it alone. I'm here with you. But you need to tell me. I have to know.'

He pulled away from her and she could see the glint of tears in the darkness of his eyes. Reaching up, she brushed the moisture away and gave him a reassuring smile.

'It's Kayte O'Farrell. She's here,' he gushed out in one breath.

'Here?' Charlotte released him, shocked. 'What do you mean "here"?'

'She's been following the tour since Milan, staying in cheap hotels. I've been driving her between venues. Her parents think she's in Ibiza doing bar work.'

'But why is she with *you*? You don't know her.' She closed her eyes, reality dawning. 'Oh no, Christian! How?'

'It was the morning I came with you to the farm, that's when I first met her. I'd seen her up in the woods with her father the day before.' He gave a painful smile. 'I knew she was trouble, but you know what I'm like. The temptation was too great.'

'So you started a relationship with her?'

'I saw her a couple of times, if you can call that a relationship. But, as usual, I began to get bored. The tours were coming up and I thought it might be a way to lose her. She seemed fine about the UK tour but when she realised I'd be away in Europe for a few months, she got upset. I told her there was no way she could come, even tried to discourage her by telling her Lucy was going to be with me. I thought I'd succeeded, but then she turned up in my room on our first night in Milan. I couldn't help it, as soon as she touched me all I wanted to do was let her stay. Taking delivery of the car was a blessing; it meant I could keep her out of the way.' He put his hands to his head. 'But everything has changed, Lottie. She's in my face all the time, making demands, and now she's starting to threaten me.'

'Threaten you? How?'

'By telling me if I won't marry her, she'll ruin my career. Go to the press with stories about me. I'm trying to put the whole thing into perspective. I mean, she wouldn't, would she? Tell me she's behaving like a spoilt brat because she can't get her own way.'

Charlotte blew out her cheeks. 'Christian, you idiot! Did you not realise how dangerous she is? You saw what she did to Marco.'

'I didn't think,' he said, his face paling. 'Do you think she will go through with this threat?'

'Probably. She's the kind of girl who will move heaven and earth to get her own way. And she's so blinded by what she wants she never sees the consequences of her actions. However, now you've made me aware of the situation perhaps we can get her off your back.'

'We?'

'Yes. Jay and Lucy will have to know about this. It needs to be a team effort.'

'Oh God, Jay will freak out.' He ran a hand across his face. 'He'll think I've been a complete prick.'

'Well, you are,' she said gently. 'But if we all get together and discuss the situation I'm sure we can find a solution. Look,' she placed her hands on his chest, 'let's have breakfast first, shall we? Then we'll all sit down and work out what to do.'

'I can't do it, Lottie, I honestly can't.'

'Christian, you have no other choice. Let us help. Jay and Lucy will understand—'

'Lottie's right, we do.' Jay pushed past Christian and planted himself between them.

Christian backed away, glaring first at Charlotte then at Jay, his face filled with suspicion. 'How long have you been there?'

'Long enough. And you're wrong, I don't think you're a complete prick.' He reached out and wrapped his arms around him, hugging him tightly. 'You're a bloody good mate; one who needs help, and that's what I'm here for. Come on,' he gestured towards his suite. 'I'll order up some breakfast, we need to sort this out once and for all.'

By nine thirty a plan of action had been agreed. At the start of their discussions, Lucy was all for abandoning Kayte in Perpignan, but Charlotte was forceful in her disagreement.

'She will carry out her threat and go to the press. She is incredibly spiteful, and by the time you arrive in Barcelona whatever she has to say will be all over the foreign press. Do you honestly want to be greeted by something like that?'

'So what do we do?'

'I think we should let things stay as they are and—'

'What?' Lucy rounded on her. 'Well, that's very helpful, Lottie.' She rolled her eyes. 'Very helpful indeed. Thank you!'

'Will you let me finish, please?' Charlotte raised her finger calmly, much to Jay's amusement. 'Listen. We let Kayte accompany Christian as far as

Barcelona. He will tell her he's made arrangements for her to stay with him at the Hotel Arts during the three nights and anything else he feels he needs to, short of agreeing to marry her, in order to keep her sweet. By the time they arrive at the hotel, Niall will be there waiting to take her home and it will all be over. Christian will be free.'

Lucy frowned. 'But what if she decides to run to the press once she's back in the UK? If she's as vindictive as you say she is, won't that be the first thing she does?'

Charlotte shook her head confidently. 'Not once she's been reminded about her own history and how it might come bouncing back at her should she try to do Christian any damage. Remember, she's already been in trouble for falsely accusing Marco of raping her. Matt's lawyers would hang her out to dry, and the press would then have a field day exposing her for what she is.' She looked at Lucy and Jay. 'Please give it some real thought. I believe it can work and, to be honest, I can't see any other way we can do this.'

Christian, who had been sitting quietly with his hands clasped between his knees listening to the debate, raised his head and looked at them.

'I think Lottie is right,' he said. 'It's a simple plan, and if a couple more hours with her means she's off my back for good, then it's not a problem for me. I'll do it.'

Jay and Lucy eyed each other silently, as if still trying to absorb Charlotte's words.

Eventually, Jay got to his feet and stretched. 'Right, let's get to it, then, folks. First thing to do is give Niall a call.'

307

FORTY-FOUR

When Christian left Perpignan the next morning, Kayte was not at the agreed pick-up point at ten thirty and he found himself delayed by thirty minutes before she eventually turned up, a thunderous expression on her face.

'Bloody hotel manager!' she cursed as she stumbled into the car, tossing her ruck sack onto the floor. 'He accused me of damaging a window and demanded payment for the broken glass. I told him to go to hell!'

'Never mind, you're here now, babe.' Christian gave her a reassuring smile, keen to nip her bad mood in the bud and make his final journey with her as peaceful as possible.

'You don't care really, do you, about me?' She glared at him from under her thick fringe. 'You've got your fantastic life and this bloody car, that's all that interests you.'

'Not true,' he countered. 'I do care about you. In fact, I care about you so much I've arranged for you to stay in my hotel in Barcelona. I want you in my bed for the last three nights of the tour '

'Oh, Christian!' Her dark mood fled immediately and she squealed, throwing her arms around him. 'That's absolutely brilliant!'

'Hey, settle down or you'll have us both off the road.' He struggled to keep the car in a straight line as she covered his face in kisses.

'Sorry.' She rested back in her seat. 'But I'm so excited.'

'Yes, well, I suggest you get some shut eye between here and Barcelona. If you remember, neither of us got much sleep last night.'

She giggled. 'No, we didn't, did we?'

'I need you fresh for this evening, babe. I'm told our room has silk sheets,' he continued, keen to prolong her good mood. 'Silk turns me on and you turn me on even more. It's going to be a lethal combination.' He grinned at her, reaching across to stroke her face.

Kayte grinned back. The next three days were going to be awesome and maybe, just maybe, with a little more leverage she could persuade him to put that ring on her finger before they left for home. She stared out of the window for a while then, closing her eyes, gradually drifted off to sleep. Waking an hour later, Perpignan was far behind and ahead of them a wide band of smooth road which twisted around the edge of a range of steep wood-covered hills.

'Where are we?' she asked sleepily.

'Not far from Gerona.'

She stifled a yawn and frowned. 'Where exactly is that?'

'About an hour away from Barcelona.'

As the car rounded a bend, she sat bolt upright and shrieked, 'Stop!'

Christian applied the brakes immediately, wondering whatever was wrong.

Rummaging in her holdall, she pulled out a camera, got out of the car and raced across the road. Christian could see a few hundred yards away in a small valley a scattered group of horses were grazing. Kayte stood for a few moments taking photos, then returned to the car.

'Brilliant!' She flopped into the seat with a breathless smile, the camera in her lap. 'Did you see that beautiful bay? Gorgeous, wasn't he?'

'I didn't know you had a camera,' he said, as he started the car and accelerated away.

'Oh, didn't you? I've had it ages.' She eyed him as if expecting him to challenge her. He didn't, choosing instead to concentrate on the road, his foot on the accelerator, picking up speed.

'I guess you get photographed a lot,' she said, tracing her fingers around the edge of the camera.

'Yes, I do. There are two professional photographers on the tour with me at the moment.'

'Yes, you told me. I bet they're not as good as I am.' She raised her camera and adjusted the focus to capture a profile shot of him.

'No, they probably aren't,' he replied, laughing.

She took another shot and then, undoing her seatbelt, skewed herself around so her back rested between the door and the dashboard. Christian took his eyes from the road to stare into the lens, keeping her amused by making silly faces.

'Don't do that, I like you serious,' she said, positioning the camera again. He looked at her, his brow creasing.

'What's the matter?' she asked, taking her eye away from the viewfinder.

'How does someone like you afford a Leica, Kayte?'

'Is that what it is?' She turned it over her hand.

'You didn't buy it?'

She smiled slyly. 'No... I acquired it.'

'You stole, it you mean?'

'I wanted it so I took it. Anyway, she's got plenty of money.'

'Who?'

'Charlotte bloody Kendrick.'

He flicked her a sideways glance before turning his eyes back quickly to the road. 'Christ, Kayte, what have you done? Were you the one who attacked her?'

Kayte's face hardened 'She had it coming. She's taken everything from me so why shouldn't I take from her?'

'Whatever do you mean?'

'Marco. I wanted him but she took him for herself. And she's had her hooks in you too, hasn't she?'

'That's crazy talk. I've got you, what makes you think I want her?'

'Because I was in the Arena's corridor the day she arrived and shut herself in your dressing room with you. I heard you laughing behind the door.'

'Kayte, nothing went on in my dressing room, I assure you. Lottie is not with me.'

'I took her contraceptive pills too, at the same time I took the camera,' she said, eyes glittering with malicious triumph. 'I thought at least that would stop you having sex with her.'

'I haven't seen Lottie for weeks now and I never had sex with her while she was here, and that's the honest truth.' He decided to try to appeal to her softer side, hoping to find it under all those layers of anger. 'Kayte, how can you accuse me of such things when they're simply not true? It's you I want.'

'Liar,' she screamed, grabbing the camera and smashing it into the side of his head. 'I knew exactly what you were up to. I saw her come out afterwards with that smile of hers.' Her face twisted with pain. 'Do you know what I had to let that bloody awful security guard do to me so I could get to you? It should have been me in your dressing room, not her, you bastard,' she yelled, aiming the camera at him.

'Stop it!' he shouted, feeling a numbness in his face and a warm trickle of blood dribbling down his cheek. 'I've told you, there is nothing going on between me and Charlotte.'

'You're a lying shit!' she snarled, as she hit him again.

'For God's sake, will you stop!' He grabbed the camera from her and threw it out of the window. She launched herself at him, punching him and pulling at his hair.

Christian fought to control the car but was finding it difficult to drive one-handed while at the same time trying to fend off the screeching hysterical woman beside him. He rounded a bend in the road, searching frantically for a layby or somewhere to pull in so he could put a stop to all this, but it seemed he was fated to be trapped on a highway with a high, grey rise of shrub-covered mountain on one side of the road and a sheer drop on the other.

They came up behind a white Mondeo estate. Christian swung the Lamborghini out, missing the other car by a fraction as he overtook. Still she pulled at his hair. 'Liar, liar, liar!' Unable to cope with the pain any longer, he took his left hand off the steering wheel and brought his elbow crashing into the side of her head. Kayte went limp, her fingers losing their grip as she slumped against the door.

Rounding the next bend, he could see a small pull-in up ahead on the right. He sent up a prayer in thanks and eased the car over to the crown of the road, but as he turned the wheel to the right, without warning Kayte came to, and, with an unearthly scream, grabbed at his hair with both hands, tugging viciously. Letting go of the wheel, he tried to elbow her again, slamming his foot hard on the brake pedal at the same time, but in the ensuing struggle his foot slipped back onto the accelerator. The engine screaming in protest, the car shot forward across the road and collided forcefully with the metal crash barrier. The intensity and angle of the impact carried the car along the barrier with a raw squeal of metal on metal until it reached a row of concrete blocks. Ploughing through, the car hung precariously out into the void for a moment before plunging down into the valley below.

An imposing forty-four storeys of glass and metal overlooking the sea, the Hotel Arts had been built in time for the 1992 Barcelona Olympics. Dominating the city's Barceloneta boardwalk, it was luxury personified and the reason Matt had chosen it to house his superstar and support team for the last three sell-out performances of Christian's European tour. Lucy, Charlotte and Jay checked in and were shown to their top floor suites and left to unpack. Of Christian, there had been no word.

After a shared shower, some leisurely lovemaking on their enormous bed and a quick lunch, Jay left for the Palau Sant Jordi stadium to meet up with the crew, leaving Lucy to join Charlotte in the lounge to await Christian's arrival. They settled themselves on comfortable couches with a chilled glass of white wine each.

'Has Marco been in touch?' Lucy asked curiously, as she savoured her first mouthful of wine.

'Yes, I got a text last night.'

'Where are they now?'

'Munich.'

'Germany? I thought they were all in America.'

'They were, but Marco's father decided to fly out a couple of days early and roped him into discussions about the possibility of purchasing a small boutique hotel chain in the Black Forest.'

'When is he due back?'

'The day after tomorrow. He's promised to meet me at Heathrow, so sadly, I'll be leaving the tour before the final evening.'

'That's a shame...' Lucy thought for a moment then smiled. 'Why don't you ask him to fly out here and join the end of tour party? I'm sure he'd enjoy it and you have that huge suite begging to be shared. Oh, go on, ask him,' she badgered.

'I'd love to, but he says he's taking me out to dinner at San Raffaello's and there's something important he wants to ask me.'

'He's going to propose, isn't he?' Lucy put her hand to her mouth to stifle a cry of excitement. 'Oh, Lottie, I'm so happy for you,'

Charlotte smiled at her cousin's uncontrolled enthusiasm. 'Lucy, I'm not jumping to any conclusions, it might be something entirely different.'

'But it won't be.' Lucy reached out and gave her cousin's hand a soft squeeze. 'I know it won't and so do you.'

Ten minutes later, and with a second glass of wine in front of them, Lucy checked her watch yet again and gave an impatient sigh.

'I think I'll give Christian a call, he should be here by now,' she said, rummaging in her bag for her mobile.

Charlotte sat patiently watching her cousin key in Christian's number on speed dial and wait for the call to connect.

'Come on, come on,' Lucy tutted impatiently then, smiling, said, 'Christian, hi, it's Lucy. We've arrived, where are you?'

'Hola!' a male Spanish voice responded. 'Hola!'

'Hello! Christian?'

The voice became muffled, there was interference on the line followed by conversation slightly out of earshot and then she heard another male voice, this time English.

'Who is this?' she demanded, wondering if his mobile might have been stolen.

'My name is William Townsend.' The well-educated voice sounded hesitant. 'Whom...whom am I speaking to?'

'Lucy Benedict. Who are you and how have you come by this phone?' It belongs to Christian Rosetti. Is he there?'

'Ah, is that his name?' the voice said slowly. 'Well... yes.'

'I need to speak to him. Could you let him have his phone back.'

'I'm afraid, my dear, that's not going to be possible.' She heard a heavy rasp of breath on the other end of the phone.

Lucy stood up, closing her eyes and running a hand through her hair. Oh God, what was going on? She drew in a sharp breath. 'Exactly what do you mean?' she snapped, looking down and catching the concerned curiosity in Charlotte's face.

'Miss Benedict, my wife and I are tourists on a fly drive holiday—'

'I'm not sure this is relevant, Mr Townsend,' Lucy interrupted. 'I need to speak to Christian. Can you hand the phone back to him?'

'My dear, will you please bear with me and listen for a moment?' William Townsend's calm but insistent voice responded. 'As I said, my wife and I are tourists. We were driving towards Gerona when your friend's car passed us being driven erratically and at considerable speed. About a mile later, we could see there had been some sort of recent accident, tyre marks on the road and black paint all over the damaged safety barrier. So we got out to investigate. The car...' he hesitated, 'well... it...'

'For goodness' sake!' Lucy shouted her frustration into the phone. 'What about the car?'

'The car appeared to have hit the barrier and... and... it was at the bottom of a ravine. We phoned immediately for the emergency services. They are here now. One of the fire crew picked up your friend's phone. It must have been thrown clear during the accident.'

Lucy's legs collapsed under her and she fell back onto the couch. She felt the pressure of Lottie's hand on her arm and saw her mouth the words 'What's wrong?' Taking a deep breath, Lucy made a calming gesture towards her before forcing herself to ask the next question into the phone.

'How is Christian?'

'I don't know. He was unconscious when they reached him. They are still trying to cut him out of the car. They won't let anyone near. Paramedics are there as well. He's in good hands, my dear. There was a girl with him.'

'Yes... Kayte. Her name is Kayte.'

'I'm sorry, my dear, I'm afraid she didn't make it.'

Lucy dropped the phone, her hand covering her mouth, tamping down the sickness rising in her throat. Jay! She must get hold of Jay. He would know what to do. Swallowing hard, she bent down to retrieve her phone from the floor.

'Phone Jay,' she said to Lottie. 'Tell him to get back here quickly. We have an emergency.'

'What's happened?' Lottie asked, pulling her bag onto her lap to retrieve her mobile.

'I'll tell you when I've finished my call.'

'Something awful has happened, hasn't it?'

Lucy nodded, her eyes blurring with tears. 'Lottie, please get hold of Jay as quickly as you can.'

Keeping her voice as even as she could, Lucy requested more information from William Townsend. As she wrote down the location of the accident he gave her, she glanced towards the hotel entrance where a taxi was dropping off a fare. It pulled away and she watched as Niall O'Farrell stood for a moment staring up at the hotel. The nightmare had just got worse.

Marco returned to his room, pulled off his tie and turned on the television. After a day of intense discussions it looked as if the hotel deal was done. Gianlucca had haggled, Herr Vogel and his legal representative had resisted, but gradually the two parties had met somewhere in the middle. A knock at the door brought his father into the room.

'Well, another successful business deal concluded, son. Now you can join Charlotte in Barcelona.'

'Yes,' Marco replied, picking up the remote and turning down the volume on the television. 'I cannot wait to be with her again.' He frowned, noticing his father appeared to have fixed his gaze on the television. He turned to see what he was looking at.

Marco's mouth fell open as he watched the tangled wreck of a black Lamborghini being recovered from a Spanish ravine by crane, and read at the bottom of the screen the slow measured line of text announcing rock star Christian Rosetti and his young woman passenger were dead.

313

FORTY-FIVE

Marco's flight from Munich landed in Barcelona late the next morning. He was so relieved to be told Charlotte had not been Christian's female passenger. During the fifteen-minute drive from the airport to the Arts Hotel, he hardly noticed anything going on outside the cab, so immersed were his thoughts about what he would find when he reached his destination.

As the taxi pulled up outside the hotel he noticed half the world's media were camped outside, making him realise this was not merely a tragic accident, but the death of an international icon. The reality of the situation hit him for the first time, and his need to get to Charlotte and protect her from all this surfaced with a vengeance.

Entering the hotel, he saw Lucy sitting with Jay in the lounge area, their heads close together in conversation. Lucy looked up; her hair was scraped into a severe ponytail, her face pale. Seeing him, she got to her feet and walked over to meet him.

'Marco, thank you for coming.' She hugged him tightly then stood back, tracing her hands gently down his arms as if trying to convince herself he was real. Her eyes were unnaturally bright, tears still threatening. Looking across at Jay, Marco could see the accident had left the same emotional imprint on him. 'Dad's with Niall at the moment at the mortuary,' she added.

'Where is Charlotte?' he asked, noticing her absence.

'In her room. She's still very upset. A doctor has seen her and has given her a sedative. We've booked you a room. Come and say hello to Jay first, then we'll collect your key and I'll take you to see her.' She gave a sad smile, 'I'm hoping your arrival will help pull her out of this.'

'Nikki is with her at the moment,' she said, as she punched the button in the lift for the top floor. 'She's one of the merchandisers. She brought a pile of magazines for Lottie.' She looked up at him, the tiredness evident in her eyes. 'I'm afraid the medication has made her listless and she doesn't seem to want to do anything other than stare out of the window. But I guess it's better than the way she reacted when they confirmed Christian was dead. And she is eating, although not a great deal, I have to say.'

Marco listened as Lucy briefly outlined the events leading to Christian's death. Charlotte, it appeared, blamed herself for the accident because the plan to get Kayte away from Christian had been her idea. Lucy explained it had been a joint decision, and that if the finger of blame was to be pointed anywhere then Jay and she were as culpable. The words spilled out of her and Marco realised she obviously needed to fill the space with noise as a distraction. Silence, he knew, would only bring back the raw remembrance of yesterday's catastrophic events, and with it more tears.

Reaching the top floor, the doors opened to reveal an athletic blonde in navy shorts and a red t-shirt waiting. Stepping out of the lift, Lucy hugged her.

'How is she, Nikki?'

'Oh, up and down.' As the blonde shook her head, Marco could see a glimmer of moisture behind her eyes. 'She did thank me for the magazines and I stayed for a bit. Difficult to know what to talk about, though, isn't it? I felt I was treading on eggshells. You know, one wrong word and she'd be in tears again.'

'Well, Marco is here now. He and Lottie are very close, I'm sure his arrival will make all the difference.'

Nikki nodded, fixing her eyes on him, a curious expression on her face.

He tilted his head curiously. 'Is something wrong?'

'No, forget it. You looked kind of familiar, that's all. Well, I'd better go.' She squeezed Lucy's shoulder. 'Sophie and I are catching the afternoon flight back to Heathrow. Take care, Hun, I'll see you soon.' She brushed cheeks with Lucy before stepping into the lift.

'Stay here for a moment, I'll go in first,' Lucy whispered, swiping into Charlotte's room.

Marco did as requested. From where he stood he could see Charlotte staring out of the window, her chin resting on the back of one of the settees. She was clutching a magazine tightly in her hand while several others were strewn haphazardly across the floor.

'Lottie, you have a visitor,' Lucy announced quietly as she approached her.

'A visitor?' came the tired reply.

'Yes, Marco's here.'

He noticed at the mention of his name, Charlotte's grip tightened on the magazine. He stepped into the room and closed the door.

'Tell him to go. I don't want to see him.'

'But he's come all this way. He—'

'Keep him away from me!' The voice was insistent.

'Lottie, what's wrong?' Lucy was now at her side. As if sensing her closeness, Charlotte leaned back into the room to face her, her face blotchy from crying.

'Oh, Lottie, whatever's happened?'

'Everything has happened. My whole world been destroyed,' she said, shaking her head as she looked up at her cousin. 'Christian is gone and now this... this despicable betrayal...' She raised her eyes and saw Marco hovering in the doorway, and threw the magazine to the floor. 'All the time I was with you, when you held me, when we were in bed together, you... how could you, you lying bastard!' she shouted, before burying her head in Lucy's shoulder and sobbing.

Marco took a step towards them but Lucy waved him back.

'Come and lie down for a while,' she said, gently coaxing Charlotte off the couch and helping her through to the bedroom.

Feeling totally confused, he remained where he was, trying to work out the reason for her violent reaction to him. He could hear Lucy's gentling tones as she settled Charlotte into bed. Only yesterday, her texts spoke of looking forward to meeting him at Barcelona. Could the accident have caused her to have some sort of breakdown? His gaze went to the floor and the magazines scattered there. He bent down to retrieve the one Charlotte had tossed aside. *Celebrity Watch* – not exactly the sort of thing she would normally find an entertaining read, he thought, flicking through the pages. Celebrity gossip and photographs, not something he or his family ever... He stared at the open pages, then closed his eyes and expelled a hiss of anger.

'What's wrong?'

He had not heard the click of the bedroom door closing or Lucy arriving by his side; the first he knew of her arrival was her hand on his arm.

'Oh my God!' Her eyes flew from the magazine to rest on him accusingly. 'No wonder Lottie's so upset. How could you?'

'I did not do this,' he said through gritted teeth. He began sifting through the pile and pulled out a later copy. 'Let us see if there is any more of this trash.'

There was. In two more editions, each filled with more pictures of the D'Alesandro family enjoying their American holiday, there were more photographs of him and Rossana, the accompanying text indicating a romantic attachment.

'Did you have a photographer travel with you?' Lucy demanded. 'Because that's what it looks like.'

'Oh yes, we had a photographer,' he answered, barely able to control the anger he felt. 'Thérèse! Her camera took these.' He thrust the pile back into Lucy's hands. 'They were supposed to be sent to Rossana's uncle, to show him how much she was enjoying herself.'

'Oh! What are you going to do?'

'I will stay until tomorrow,' he said, his voice a little calmer, 'and hope Charlotte will see me so we can sort out this terrible thing that now sits between us. And then I am going home. My stepmother will be punished for this. It is a totally wicked thing to have done.' He wrapped an arm around Lucy's shoulder and kissed her forehead. 'I will leave you in peace. I have brought some work with me and will spend the rest of the day in my room. I will see you all at dinner this evening.'

Ella, Issy and Thérèse sat in Ella's office waiting for Jenny to return from taking a call from Spain.

'She is anxious for news of Charlotte and for some indication of when she would be returning to the UK,' Ella offered by way of explanation.

316

In Jenny's absence, they continued their discussions about Rossana's birthday party, due to take place in little over a week. It was purely a catch-up meeting to make sure all Thérèse's requirements were in place. Although some guests were staying at the manor, extra rooms had been made available at Little Court. Ella knew this was a very important event: a milestone birthday which came with an extensive VIP guest list.

Eventually, Jenny returned. Thérèse thought she looked quite pasty; understandable, of course, with the events of the past few days.

'Jen? Is everything okay?' Ella asked, as Jenny settled herself.

'Yes, of course.' Jenny then shook her head vigorously, her teeth snagging her bottom lip. 'Actually, no. No, it isn't. Not at all.'

'Is something wrong with Lottie?'

'Not exactly wrong...' She shot a glance at Thérèse, who got to her feet immediately.

'I understand, Jenny.' Thérèse gave a gracious nod and made to leave the room. 'This is a family matter which you wish to discuss in private. I can busy myself in the boutique for a while.'

'No, Thérèse. Please, you're more than a friend to all of us. I'm sure Jenny won't mind you hearing what she has to say.' Ella shot a glance at her sister-in-law, who looked up and nodded her agreement.

Thérèse settled herself in her seat once more, curious to learn what had been responsible for unsettling Jenny.

'I'm not quite sure how to tell you all,' Jenny began, looking at everyone hesitantly as she played nervously with her fingers, 'but it appears Lottie's going to have a baby.'

Ella's eyes widened in surprise. 'A baby?'

'Yes. She's just told me.'

'When?' Issy asked, 'and more importantly, who is the father?'

'From what Lottie says, the baby was conceived in mid-July, so sometime in early April.' Jenny looked at them all with an expression which said she was still trying to come to terms with the news. 'And as for the father, she refused to say.'

All eyes turned to Thérèse.

'Oh, it cannot be Marco, if that is what you are thinking.' Thérèse gave an innocent shrug. 'I believe he has not seen Charlotte since the end of May. And if she is refusing to name the father, is there not every possibility it could be Christian's?'

'Christian?' Ella stared at her. 'Why do you think she's having Christian's baby?'

'Well, if Marco is not the father, who else could it be?' Thérèse fixed Jenny with a compassionate smile and an outstretched hand. 'It is heart-breaking that Christian is no longer with us, but to think he may live on in a child... well, is that not a wonderful thing to come out of all this unhappiness?'

Behind the false veneer of sympathy, Thérèse felt triumph. This news, relayed in an appropriate manner to her stepson, would achieve what a month in America had failed do to – free him from Charlotte's influence for ever. She could not wait to return home.

Lucy was seated in the VIP lounge at Barcelona Airport, waiting to be called through to board the Evolution jet. Beside her, Jay was engaging Charlotte in some harmless small talk, trying to cheer her up. What a mess, she thought. First the magazine thing with Marco and now the added bombshell of being three months' pregnant. Worse still was Lottie's refusal to name the baby's father. Well... it had to be Marco, didn't it? Surely the baby couldn't be Christian's?

She had said goodbye to Marco earlier that morning when he left for his flight back to London. He looked tense; frustrated and unhappy because he had been unable to make his peace with Charlotte. There had been no change from her original stance; she simply would not see him. Lucy had also glimpsed a glimmer of Charlotte's old feistiness surface when she expressly forbade her to tell anyone about the baby. She would, she said, tell everyone in her own time.

Lucy reflected on the changes which had taken place during the last forty-eight hours. The whole world appeared to be in mourning. The loss of Christian Rosetti had touched so many. There were those who loved him for his music; those who loved him because he encompassed looks, charisma and sexual energy; and those who loved him for both. Kayte O'Farrell's name had only received a brief mention in the press. The accident would, of course, need to be investigated but it appeared, given the road conditions and the report from the Townsends of Christian's erratic driving, excessive speed had been the cause.

The arrival of Matt and his entourage at the hotel, within hours of the tragedy, had seen Evolution's skilled machine take over, liaising with the authorities and smoothing out the process of returning the bodies to the UK. Alongside them, their PR department went into overdrive, describing Kayte as a Benedict family friend, an innocent girl who had been in the wrong place at the wrong time.

Matt, meanwhile, had devoted a big part of his time to Niall. The man was in pieces. The daughter he thought had been spending the summer in Ibiza doing bar work had not been there at all. Instead, she had been trailing around Europe after Christian Rosetti. Neither he nor Rachel had had any idea of this latest obsession – an obsession which had, in the end, killed her. Matt accompanied him to identify the body and from there onto the private flight home, while he remained in Spain making arrangements to return Kayte to the UK.

Lucy looked up to see they were being called to the boarding gate. Picking up her bag, she fell in step behind Jay and Charlotte, wondering, not for the first time, what the future held in store for all three of them.

Marco was picked up by the D'Alesandro limo from Heathrow. Dropping in to San Raffaello's first, he then went on to his apartment, where he showered, changed and collected the Porsche, ready for his drive to Somerset and the confrontation with his stepmother.

Arriving at the manor, he found Thérèse in the drawing room. She was sitting by the window, browsing through the latest copy of *Brides*, a glass of champagne in her hand.

'Marco!' Setting down her glass and casually tossing the magazine onto a nearby table, she crossed the room, arms outstretched to greet him in her normal tactile way. He stood in the doorway watching her approach, his expression stony.

She tilted her head questioningly, dropping her hands to her side as she reached him. 'What has happened?'

'Thérèse, why did you send photos to that trashy magazine?'

'Oh, *Celebrity Watch*, you mean?' she said airily. 'Well, it was a special birthday and some of my friends were keen to see how I was enjoying our month away.'

He turned away, smiling. When he spun round to look at her again there was no mirth in his expression. 'Is that so? I would have expected the sort of friends you have to read *Hello*, or *OK* at the very least. But of course, they don't accept photographs from amateurs, do they? No doubt *Celebrity Watch* was overjoyed when you made contact. Have you any idea of the damage you have done?'

'Damage? To whom, Marco? The faithless creature you call a girlfriend?' She fixed him with an unrepentant stare.

'Do not speak of her like that!' His eyes blazed angrily. 'You do not know her.'

'And neither, it seems, do you.' It pleased her to see a flicker of uncertainty in his expression.

'What do you mean?'

'I have been at Little Court this morning. While I was there, Jenny Miller left to take a call from Spain. When she returned, she was quite upset. Charlotte had called to tell her she was pregnant.'

'Pregnant! She is having my baby?'

Thérèse watched him carefully, seeing his surprised expression change to a smile. With a raise of her elegant eyebrows she feigned surprise. 'Yours? How, Marco? I had no idea you were still seeing her.'

'I saw her when I was in Verona visiting Gina. I spent the night with her,' he added, matter-of-factly. 'She was there with the tour.'

'With Christian,' she redefined his sentence. 'I am sorry, Marco, but if what you say is true, it cannot be you.' She brushed her heavy hair back from her face and stood looking at him, casting her expression somewhere between concern and resignation. 'According to Jenny, the baby is due in May. Charlotte is only two months pregnant. Actually...' She paused to tap her forehead. 'Yes, I remember Jenny mentioning she decided to continue with tour after Verona, although she didn't seem to know the reason. But now I guess we know, don't we?' She watched the swirl of emotions in his dark eyes; a seed of doubt had been planted and was slowly beginning to take root. 'Oh, Marco, you think I interfere,' she said quickly, switching on her concerned face. 'You have been so blinded by her. She was never able to let go of Christian and, well, he was quite handsome and totally irresistible to women, was he not? They had been lovers once so, in all honesty, who could blame her?'

Marco looked at her grimly. All this was too much to cope with. First Charlotte's belief that he had betrayed her and now a complete reversal of their roles with the news she was pregnant by her ex-lover. With his thoughts very much in turmoil, he stood there, unsure of how to deal with this dreadful situation. He was aware of Thérèse walking slowly around him, her hand trailing gently over his back.

'My beautiful boy, you deserve better,' she crooned. 'Much, much better.' She stopped in front of him, stroking the lapels of his jacket.

Marco pushed her away, his eyes flaring. 'If this is another attempt to force Rossana on me, it will not work. I have had enough of your schemes, so hear me well. Until she goes home I will be living in London, and I will not be available to chaperone her any longer. Is that clear? And if you choose to complain to my father, I will tell him *exactly* what has been going on.'

Turning his back on her, he left, slamming the door behind him.

'Marco, come back!' he heard her anxious voice calling, accompanied by rapid footfalls as she came after him.

'Go away, Thérèse,' he shouted back, not bothering to stop. 'Leave me alone!'

Thérèse stood at the window, cursing under her breath as she watched the Porsche leave. She had hoped twisting the truth about the identity of Charlotte's baby's father would finally sever her stepson's ties with the wretched girl. And whilst she may have planted sufficient doubt in his mind, in doing so it appeared she had also succeeded in alienating him. She had to get him back; she had to dispel his fears about her motives. There was a little over a week left before Rossana's eighteenth birthday and her return to Italy; one week to gain access to the vineyards for her husband.

Meeting Madeline in the hall, she informed her: 'I am leaving for London. If anyone wants me, I'll be there until next Thursday evening.'

FORTY-SIX

Jenny pushed through the French doors and went out onto the terrace. September had brought with it an Indian summer and the evening was unusually warm for the time of year. After returning with Matt earlier that afternoon, Charlotte had gone straight to her room. Knowing the best thing to do was to wait until she decided to reappear, Jenny was pleased to see her sitting at the table, reading a book.

'There you are,' she said gently, settling herself in the chair opposite. 'I'm glad to see you up and about.' She noticed the dark smudges still evident beneath her daughter's eyes, her face pale.

'I couldn't stay in my room any longer. In Spain it was different; the room made me feel safe, it kept me away from all the horror that had happened. But here,' she gazed out with the briefest of smiles to the lengthening shadows across the lawn, 'the open spaces are calming.'

Jenny nodded; the gardens did look especially beautiful this evening. 'Have you thought about what you're going to do?'

'About the baby, you mean?'

'Yes.'

'What is there to do? I'm going to have it, of course.'

'Will you tell Marco?'

'Why should he have to know anything? He chose Rossana, not me. That means I don't want him anywhere near this baby. It's mine.'

'But he is the biological father. He has rights. Or—'

'Or what, Mother?' Charlotte cocked her head defiantly.

'There is a rumour it might be Christian's.'

She shook her head firmly. 'Well, it isn't. We didn't have that kind of relationship any longer. Please, can we talk about something else? Or maybe not at all.' She lowered her eyes to her book and Jenny realised the mention of his name had brought painful memories to the surface again. She sat in silence as Charlotte resumed her reading.

'I'll leave you, then. If there's anything you need, give me a shout.' Jenny rose and with a final concerned look, left.

Charlotte watched her go. The numbness inside from the loss of Christian was still there, and she knew the funeral next week would bring it all crashing back again. However, she now had a bigger challenge to face – her pregnancy. She was determined not to lie about anything. If people thought it was Christian's there was no way she would hide behind that to keep Marco at bay. Nevertheless, she meant what she said – she did not want him anywhere near this baby. The magazine photos had been quite revealing, in complete contrast to his texts saying how bored it all was and how he was

321

missing her. They told an entirely different story. In every one he was either laughing or smiling and touching Rossana; their relationship quite obviously an intimate one. She shook her head. There was no way she could have him anywhere near her ever again. But then, would he want to be? He'd made his decision. In fact, it had not taken him long to forget about her. His visit to Barcelona to see her had probably only been in order to save face until she was feeling well enough for him to tell her the truth. Yes, she decided, I can see everything now. How little he really cared, despite his claims he was falling in love with me. Maybe, she reflected, that was the worst part of it. If only he had not uttered those lies, and if only she had not been foolish enough to believe him. She stared out into the garden, noticing the sun was about to disappear behind the run of hills in the distance. She turned her thoughts once more to Tuesday and the funeral.

Marco reached his London apartment a little after six thirty. Throughout his journey he had been trying to shoot holes through Thérèse's claim about the identity of the father of Charlotte's baby. She was playing her spiteful games again. It *had* to be his; there was no way Charlotte would have slept with Christian although, much to his frustration, he was currently not in a position to verify this. Charlotte would have arrived at Little Court by now, he thought, but it was far too early to make an attempt to see her again. He knew if he did, it would only make matters worse. But see her he must; he needed to know the truth. But the thought she may have slept with the rock star only served to cause him renewed pain.

The maddening constraints of his situation ate away at him while he showered and changed. Returning to his living room, he poured out a whisky and crossed to his window, his gaze fixed on the wide flow of the Thames below. The whisky fired his insides; he had hoped it would help numb the pain, but it failed miserably. He checked his watch, deciding to drop into the restaurant and spend the evening there with all the noise and distraction a Friday night brought through its doors. If he stayed here, all he would do is become more depressed and get drunk. Tonight, he wanted people about him. Noise and company a diversion to blot out all this confusion. Finishing his drink, he pulled out his mobile and called for a taxi.

San Raffaello's was busy, most of the tables taken. Vittorio, dark and dignified, was there to greet him with his usual serene smile, guiding him to the back of the restaurant and the booth which was exclusively his.

He ordered a bottle of wine and was scanning the menu when he heard voices. One was Vittorio's, the other a woman's. Sliding from the booth, he walked out into the main dining area.

'But I do have a reservation,' she was insisting. 'A table for two at eight o'clock. My fiancé booked it ages ago. It will be in his name I expect. Stephen Richards?'

Marco watched as Vittorio scanned the booking sheet, clearing his throat uncomfortably as he looked at the woman again. 'It appears your reservation has been cancelled, madam,' Vittorio informed her.

'Cancelled? I don't understand.' There was confusion written on her face as she stared at him. Her mobile rang, halting their conversation. She pulled it from her bag and, from her words, clearly having a conversation with her partner.

'He's stuck in Edinburgh Airport... Fog.' She gave Vittorio a wistful smile as she ended the call. 'Says he cancelled earlier and called to tell me but couldn't get an answer. So he left a message.' She shook her head ruefully. 'Guess I was so busy getting ready I forgot to check my phone. I could have saved myself a journey. Ah well, it's back to my apartment for a bottle of wine, a takeaway and an evening on the couch with a video.' She gazed around the restaurant. 'A pity, I was so looking forward to eating here tonight.'

'And you still can.' When Marco appeared at Vittorio's side, the girl's eyes widened in surprise. 'I am Marco D'Alesandro. I am the owner, and I too am on my own this evening. Please, won't you join me?'

She was smiling at him, a wide friendly open smile. 'Thank you, I'd love to. I'm Abby McQueen, by the way.'

'This way, Abby.' He guided her through towards the back of the restaurant, his eyes drawn to the sway of her hips and the glossy brown hair falling in waves down her back.

Lucy was waiting for Jay to pick her up. With her father taking Charlotte back to Little Court, Jay had persuaded her to stay overnight in London with him after their flight back from Spain. For the last three hours she had been getting ready. Hair, nails, skin – the works. A special evening, he said, after all the emotional upheaval of the last couple of days. She wondered whether this meant a meal or an upmarket club full of A-listers. Whatever he had planned, she simply had to look her best. Returning to the Evolution flat, she went about dressing her newly pampered body. Eventually, she stood in front of the large full-length mirror in her room and nodded, pleased with the end result: a dark silver top under a three-quarter white jacket and skin-tight shiny black trousers which finished at the ankle. And to complete the outfit, a wonderful pair of black lace Jimmy Choos, not to mention, of course, the fabulous Chanel clutch she had found when shopping in Milan. The buzzer went as she was finishing fixing diamond studs in her ears. She pushed the door release button, and moments later a smiling Jay entered the room.

'Wow, look at you!' he said, before taking her by the shoulders and planting a chaste kiss on her cheek.

'You remembered,' she said, laughing as she stepped back to admire the new navy Hugo Boss jacket he wore.

'I certainly did.' He waved a finger at her. 'Don't smudge the lipstick. As always, I'll save your mouth till later.' He lifted her chin with his finger, his eyes dancing with mischief. 'And what a delicious mouth you have, Miss Benedict, if I may say so.'

'Come on, tell me… where are you taking me this evening?' she badgered again, as they were driven through into central London. 'Celebrity party maybe?' She had been pestering him ever since she got in the taxi, trying to find out where they were going, but he had remained tight lipped.

He shook his head. 'Sorry, there's no party. You want to know what's happening? Okay, I'm taking you out to eat and then we're going dancing.'

'Where are we eating? Ah, I know. San Raffaello's.' She clapped her hands together with excitement.

'Where else? A man needs an exceptional restaurant if he's going give the woman in his life a special evening.'

'Special?' She eyed him curiously. 'Why is it special?'

'Wait and see,' he teased, fixing his gaze out of the window at the passing traffic.

'Another drink?' Marco offered, pulling his wallet from his pocket.

Abby smiled across the table. 'I think you're trying to get me drunk, Mr D'Alesandro.'

'It's, Marco,' he said, waving her protest away, 'and the night is young.'

'Where did you find this place?' she asked, gazing around the smoky atmosphere of the South Bank Blues Club. 'I had no idea it existed. I must remember to bring Steve here.'

'Ah, Abby, do not spoil the evening by talking of other men. Tonight it is all about you and me.'

'He's my fiancé, Marco,' Abby reminded him with a laugh. 'He is the love of my life and we're getting married in a month's time.'

'You are very lucky to have such happiness.' His mood suddenly became sombre. 'At the moment I do not know what the future holds for me.'

'I know and I'm sorry.' She stretched a hand across the table towards him, thinking how sad it was that someone as charming as him was in such a bad place at the moment. 'But as I told you before, you need to sleep on things. Tonight you are hurting; you have so much uncertainty in your life. Tomorrow, you will see everything very differently. I know you will.'

'I wish I had your faith. At the moment I can see no way out of my misery.' He gave her a lopsided grin which she assumed was triggered more by the whisky he'd been drinking than any humorous thought.

'Until you talk to Charlotte you will never know the truth. And from what you tell me about her, I cannot believe she would have got herself into this situation with another man. I think this baby is yours, only all this second-hand information floating around about the dates has confused everything.

Honestly, you need to hear what she has to say.'

'And if it is his?' His dark eyes grew mournful. 'I could not bear it, Abby. I honestly could not.'

'Trust me, it won't be,' she said, collecting her handbag and getting to her feet. 'Now I do have to go. I need my beauty sleep.'

'Wait, let me call a cab for you?' He pulled his mobile from his back pocket.

Moments later they were standing outside the club, the glare of its brightly lit neon sign reflecting off the wet pavement under their feet from the light rain falling around them. Marco pulled up his jacket collar against the damp evening and sheltered under Abby's umbrella until the cab arrived. She kissed him goodbye – a light, sisterly peck on the cheek – before climbing in then leaning forward to wind down the window.

'Thank you for a brilliant evening, Marco,' she said, treating him to another of her affectionate smiles. 'And please, please promise me you'll go home and sleep. You aren't doing yourself any favours staying here. You'll only get drunk and injure yourself or end up getting mugged.'

He watched the tail lights of the cab disappear up the road and suddenly he felt terribly alone. Abby had been a godsend; someone kind who had listened all through their dinner together while he told her of his situation. She had taken in everything, sympathised, and offered him sound advice. He had brought her to the club, wanting to prolong their evening together, needing to feel her continuing emotional support. But now she had gone, and an inner beguiling voice was urging him to ignore everything she had said. Go home? Well, yes he would, but not yet. Returning into the club, he found a seat at the bar and ordered himself another drink.

Lucy's evening was full of surprises. Never in a million years had she guessed what Jay had planned. It all happened over the dessert and she knew with a sure certainty Florentine and Vittorio had both been in on it. Prompted by the head waiter, she had ordered one of the specials: a mini Baked Alaska.

'Florentine said he would be most honoured if you tried this,' Vittorio had encouraged when he came to take the order. Staring around the restaurant, Lucy studied the other diners' plates, trying to identify someone who was eating this particular pudding, in order for her to see exactly what it was like. Unfortunately, she could not find anyone.

'Go on, give it a go,' Jay urged, opting for the panna cotta.

And so it came, a mountain of meringue which supposedly hid not only ice cream but Morello cherries marinated in Kirsch. Vittorio placed the creation before her and stood back to admire it. She stared at her plate then at Jay.

'Come on,' he grinned, waving his spoon at her, 'eat up.'

She knew there was something wrong as soon as her spoon broke through the meringue and the whole thing collapsed in on itself. There was no ice cream or fruit, only a small green box sheltering under the debris.

'What's this, Jay?' She frowned as she extracted the box and stared at it.

'Open it and see.' Watching her from across the table, his eyes were gleaming with pleasure.

She did, and gasped. There, nestled in the black velvet, was a ring. A huge antique-cut emerald surrounded by diamonds.

Jay's blue eyes gazed into hers as he stretched across the table and covered her right hand with his. 'Marry me, Lucy? Christian's death has made me realise life is far too short to waste. I want to enjoy every moment with you beside me as my wife.'

Before she could stop them, tears began to trickle down her cheeks. Leaning across the table, Jay reached out to intercept the wetness with his fingers. As he did, Vittorio appeared holding a clean white handkerchief.

She looked at both men as she took the handkerchief. 'I don't know what to say.'

Vittorio beamed broadly. 'It is usual to say yes.'

'Well... yes!' The tears were instantly replaced by her smile as Jay slipped the ring onto her finger and applause broke out in the restaurant from diners who had been watching events unfold.

'How did you know my ring size?' she asked, when the applause had died down and the restaurant returned to normal.

'Matt.'

'He knows?' She laughed, glad he had involved her father and that he'd obviously approved.

'Yes, he knows. And he's extremely happy for both of us.'

The meal over, they left the restaurant, stepping out into a cold, wet September evening. Lucy was glad of the coat Jay had persuaded her to bring with her.

'Where to now?' she asked, as he hailed an approaching taxi.

'Wait and see.'

South of the river, the taxi pulled up outside a red-bricked building. At first floor level a blue neon arrow flashed, pointing towards a metal staircase which led to the building's basement. A matching South Bank Blues Club sign sat just above it.

'Is this for real?' Lucy frowned at Jay uncertainly as the taxi pulled away. 'It looks like something out of a gangster movie.'

'Oh, it's definitely for real; in fact, it's an absolute gem,' he said, ushering her forwards. 'Mind how you go, the steps are wet, they may be slippery.'

Carefully negotiating the staircase, Lucy reached the bottom and waited for Jay to join her. Pushing open the half-glass door, Lucy entered and gasped in amazement at the small, crowded basement club.

'I love it already.' She kissed his cheek. 'Thank you. When you said "club" I thought you meant, you know, laser light show, pulsating music. But this is... fabulous!'

Through the smoky haze, Lucy observed a glamorous coffee-skinned woman, her black hair cascading over her shoulders. As she walked up to the microphone on a low stage, a small support group emerged behind her picking up their instruments. The woman smiled as the spotlight caught her, running her hands down the molten red of her tight dress, swaying her body from side to side as the music started and she began to sing 'I've Got You Under My Skin'.

While Jay ordered drinks, Lucy watched, fascinated. They found a table and sat, mesmerised by their surroundings: the intimate atmosphere, the shadowy dancers and the sensuality of the singer and her husky voice.

'She's brilliant,' Lucy said, clapping enthusiastically when the song came to an end. Couples left the dance floor and returned to their seats or headed for the bar.

'It's a great place,' Jay smiled, enjoying his lager as he watched a couple, looking more than a little drunk, leave unsteadily. 'See, everyone's happy.'

With her eyes still fixed on the stage, they sat through the singer's next offering: Ella Fitzgerald's 'Every Time We Say Goodbye', which had Lucy in raptures.

When they returned to the table a little while later, having smooched to several numbers, Jay reached for her glass. 'Another drink?'

'Please.' Watching him head off to the bar, she took the opportunity to find her mobile and call her mother, to check on how Lottie was. As she was about to punch in the number she noticed a figure slumped at the end of the bar. Pushing himself up from the counter, he turned and slipped off the stool he was perched on, landing heavily on the floor. People gathered around him; someone hauled him to his feet. Jay returned to the table, looking back at the scene.

'Looks as if someone's overdone it on the booze,' he said, laughing as they watched two hefty men lift the drunk between them, dancers parting as they manhandled him towards the door.

Lucy's eyes widened with surprise. 'Jay, it's Marco!'

'Surely not? He went back to the manor, didn't he?'

'I know, but it's him. I'm sure of it.' She pushed back her stool and was about to follow when Jay's hand shot out and caught her wrist. 'No, Luce, leave it. Don't interfere.'

'It is Marco,' she insisted, 'I know it is.'

His grip tightened. 'It's too dangerous for you to go out there.'

'No!' She pulled away from him and got to her feet, tipping the stool over. Then she was gone, walking briskly towards the exit.

'Damn!' Jay sprang to his feet and headed after her.

Lucy met the two men in the corridor.

327

'What have you done with him?' she demanded, blocking their path.

The first man, heavily muscled, the fluorescent lighting reflecting off his bald head, smiled down at her, his teeth uneven. 'He's outside, cooling off. Don't worry, we haven't hurt him. We have instructions to remove drunks from the club in case things turn nasty. It's the rules.' He shrugged and then nodded his head in acknowledgement of someone behind her.

She felt Jay's hand slide protectively around her shoulder.

'Everything okay?' Jay asked.

'Yes, we've put him on a bench outside to sober up,' the bald-headed bouncer informed him.

Jay stepped back, letting the two men through. He squeezed Lucy's shoulder. 'Come on, then, let's see if you were right.'

Marco was slumped on a metal seat at the bottom of the stairs to the club, his jacket already wet from the falling rain. Jay stared down at him.

'How come he's here? He was supposed to have gone home.'

Lucy shrugged. 'Who knows, but in his current condition I don't think we're going to get much sense out of him, do you?'

'What do we do, then? We can't leave him here.'

'We'll have to get him home and put him to bed,' Lucy said, looking for her mobile. 'I'll call a taxi.'

'Marco, what's your keypad number?'

Marco forced opened his eyes to see two indistinct faces peering at him. He was propped against a wall, and as he shook his head his vision cleared enough to see he was outside his apartment.

'Who are you?' he slurred. 'What do you want?' He waved his arms about erratically, trying to push them away. The taller of the indistinct figures stood in front of him, pushing his arms back down to his side. He heard a loud voice in his ear saying, 'It's Jay. I'm here with Lucy.'

Marco shook his head, trying to clear the fog which had settled in his brain. 'What are you doing here? Are we still in Spain?'

'No.' A female voice this time. 'We found you in a club, Marco. You were drunk.'

'Abby. Where's Abby?' He shook his head, disappointed, 'Ah yes... gone home, back to Steve.'

'Marco.' Someone was shaking him again. 'What's your keypad number? You're very drunk and we need to put you to bed.'

He squinted, trying to wade through the cotton wool clinging so resolutely to the inside his head. 'Four-nine-three-six.' He felt himself lapsing into unconsciousness as, supported by his arms, he was helped through an open door and then unsteadily up a flight of stairs.

'Find his room, Luce, will you,' he heard a voice say, then his arm sagged on one side as, without warning, the support disappeared.

'It's in here.'

'God, he's a heavyweight. Give me a hand.'

He was gently lowered into softness. 'Thank you, whoever you are,' he said, closing his eyes and drifting away.

Jay looked down at the sleeping form. 'We'd better undress him.'

'What do you mean *we*?' Lucy looked alarmed. 'There's no way I'm taking his clothes off. He's all yours.' And with that she left the bedroom, closing the door behind her.

'Come on then, Marco, old son,' Jay said, grinning as he pulled off Marco's shoes. 'Let's get you into bed.'

A little while later Jay emerged from the bedroom and walked down the wide staircase. He could see Lucy sitting in the lounge reading a magazine.

'Ready?' he called to her.

Returning the mag to the coffee table, she joined him. 'While you were putting him to bed I decided to call San Raffaello's,' she said, as he opened the front door. 'I asked them to let Thérèse know. If she's not here in London then I'm sure she can send someone round to check on him.'

'Good thinking.' Jay stroked her shoulder. 'And now, my wife-to-be, let's get you home and put *you* to bed, eh?'

FORTY-SEVEN

After taking Vittorio's call, Madeline rang the D'Alesandro's London home. Hannah, the housekeeper there, went straight to Thérèse working late in her office making final checks for the Milan Fashion show in three weeks' time. Once Hannah withdrew, Thérèse sat contemplating the situation, tapping her pen thoughtfully on the open paperwork in front of her. She had been planning to stay away from Marco this evening and visit in the morning when he was calmer. Now she had been told he was sleeping off a night of alcoholic over-indulgence. So... Lucy had suggested to Vittorio that someone might want to go and check on him. What if Rossana...? Was it worth a chance? Could it work? Well, there was only one way to find out.

Leaving her office, she went straight to the girl's bedroom and knocked. As she entered, Rossana sat up in bed, trying to focus eyes bleary from sleep.

'Mrs D'Alesandro? Is everything all right?'

'Yes, *cara mia.*' Thérèse settled herself on the bed. 'I need to know something. Do you really love my son?'

'Of course.' The girl nodded, her green eyes huge, hair spilling untidily around her heart-shaped face. 'And he likes me, I know he does. It's just that it's not enough, I—'

'Shh,' Thérèse interrupted, placing a calming finger to Rossana's lips. 'Would you do absolutely anything to have him? To make him yours.'

'Well... yes. Yes, of course I would. It is my greatest wish for us to be together.'

'Good, then listen. It will not be easy but I have a plan.'

Half an hour later Rossana found herself in the back of the D'Alesandro limo, Thérèse sitting next to her as the streets of London passed by outside the window.

'Now you understand what you have to do?' Thérèse's voice was gentle, her hand reaching to reassure. 'As I said, it may not be easy for you, but it will guarantee Marco will be yours.'

She nodded, watching as the car turned off the main road and followed the river until it reached an expensive-looking apartment block. The driver pulled up and killed the engine.

'We may be some time, Paulo,' Thérèse instructed. The driver nodded his understanding and pulled a paperback from the glove compartment.

Rossana followed the older woman through a doorway and into a lift which took them up to the second floor. As the doors opened, she found herself in a small lobby facing another door. Thérèse punched numbers into the keypad on the right, and they entered. She looked around in awe. It was beautiful; the colours bold, the furnishings plain but expensive. She banished the feeling of jealousy stirring within her. This might have been the place where he spent time with Charlotte, but it no longer mattered because after tonight, things would be very different.

Thérèse reached the stairs and motioned for her to follow. At the top was a wide landing punctuated with six doors and a scatter of pale rugs on the floor. Indicating she should wait, Thérèse opened the first door on the left and disappeared inside. She reappeared seconds later and beckoned. Rossana stepped cautiously forward.

Inside the room, Marco lay sprawled on his side across the bed in a tangle of sheets. The regular rise and fall of his chest indicated he was deeply asleep. Thérèse nodded encouragingly. Slowly, and with shaking hands, Rossana began to take off her clothes.

The next morning Marco awoke with the king of all headaches. He lifted his hand to his forehead to try to ease the throbbing but as he did so, his elbow came into contact with warm flesh. With a start he sat up in bed, his head swimming and the pounding inside increasing tenfold. Abby? No, he'd put her in a taxi, hadn't he? Looking down, he gasped in horror. Beside him, Rossana lay stretched out sleeping peacefully.

'What the hell!' He sat there open-mouthed.

At the sound of his voice she came to, her first vision a man's naked torso covered with a mat of fine dark hair. She screamed and grabbed the sheet, launching herself across the room and into a nearby chair.

'What are you doing in my bed?' Marco shouted at her. 'How did you get here?'

'I... I...' She pulled the sheet tighter around her, shaking like a leaf.

'Well?' he thundered, unravelling himself from the remaining covers and getting out of bed, a hand going to his head to still the throbbing his voice had triggered.

Rossana gaped at him, her eyes running over his broad-shouldered muscular body. Caught between curiosity and awe, her gaze then settled on what sat at the apex of his thighs. She slapped her hands over her eyes, colour rushing into her cheeks.

It occurred to him then that this was probably the first time she had ever seen a naked man. As he grabbed his robe from the back of the door to cover himself, he heard his name being called. Thérèse! What the hell was she doing here? He groaned, aware any explanation he gave would not be believed. The door to his room opened; he turned to see his stepmother and Felica standing there, horror in their faces as they took in the scene.

'Oh my God, Marco, what have you done?' Thérèse exclaimed, throwing her hand to her mouth. 'No! Please don't tell me...' She walked quickly to the bed and pulled back the sheet. Bright red spots of blood showed clearly against the stark whiteness of the cotton. Walking over to him, she gave his face a vicious slap. 'You hypocrite,' she growled. 'You make it clear to the poor girl you do not want her and then this is how I find you!' She pointed to the bed. 'Put on some clothes on and come with me.'

'I did not touch her,' Marco shouted, but staring at the bed, he knew that was not what had happened.

'Shut up and get dressed,' Thérèse snapped, picking up a pile of neatly folded clothes from a chair and shoving them at him. Then, hurrying across to Rossana, she adjusted the sheet around her and hugged her tightly, whispering comforting words. She kissed Rossana's forehead as she let her go, then beckoned to Felica.

'Take care of Rossana, please, Felica. Get her dressed and take her back to the town house. She will need a bath and some breakfast. We will talk later.' She turned her attention back to Rossana, stroking her hair gently back off her face. 'It will be all right, *cara mia.*'

Marco dressed in fresh clothes, all the while trying to recall what happened last night, and drew a blank from the point he remembered saying goodnight to Abby. Pulling on his jacket, he followed his stepmother out of the apartment and down to the basement garage.

'We will take your car,' she said, with a commanding wave of her hand towards his Porsche. 'I will let Paulo know he needs to stay to pick up Felica and Rossana.'

They drove silently through the city. It was still early, traffic only just beginning to pick up. Marco's concentration was half on his driving, half on what would happen once they reached the house. His mind was still in a fog over what had happened last night, but part of it said a skilful trap had been set for him; one which, given the evidence, he knew he had little hope of escaping.

Eventually, he turned left into the street beside his parents' town house and swung the car off into the small underground car park. Inside the house, he followed Thérèse upstairs and into Gianlucca's study, seating himself quietly in one of the comfortable leather chairs, waiting as she closed the door.

'I should tell your father of this.' Her voice was quiet as she stared at the floor.

'Tell him what? I have done nothing,' he answered, deciding to challenge. 'It is you, you who have colluded with Rossana to put me in this situation. I was drunk. Very drunk. Too drunk to be in any position to do what I have been accused of.'

'I think the sheets tell a different story,' she replied, her tone measured and calm. 'Be honest, Marco, you had drunk yourself silly over that worthless Kendrick girl and you took advantage of Rossana's affection for you when she came to see if you were all right.'

'Came to see me?' He frowned, trying to clutch some memory out of the stupor which still filled his brain. 'Why would she do that?'

'Lucy and Jay took you back to your apartment last night. They found you drunk in a club. Lucy phoned to let me know. I had arrived in London late and had gone straight to bed. Hannah took the call, and was about to wake me when she found Rossana in the kitchen and told her. She insisted on coming; she was worried about you and thought I should not be disturbed. She said she could deal with it.' She gave a heavy sigh. 'When I woke early this morning and discovered what had happened and that she was missing, I came straight over. I did not know what I would find, but...' she shut her eyes for a moment, opening them again to glare at him, 'I had no idea it would be the mess we have.' Her tone softened. 'She is still an impressionable girl, Marco, did you not understand that?'

He put his head in his hands and groaned. 'I do not know what happened... I... I simply do not remember.'

'But it did happen, there was blood.'

'Blood is not enough. We could ask a doctor to examine her; that way we would know for sure. If I'm guilty, I will do the honourable thing. I—'

'There will be no examination,' she cut across him. 'I will not have the poor child subjected to prodding and pulling about. You could see how traumatised she was this morning.'

'Traumatised? Are you suggesting rape?' Memories of Kayte O'Farrell's accusations came flooding back together with all the associated horrors.

'Of course not.' She cast a weary glance in his direction. 'Part of this is her fault, of course. She has been besotted ever since she first set eyes on you. And she probably went to you quite willingly, but now the deed has been done, understandably she is afraid.'

'So where do we go from here?' He rubbed his face, the fog still swirling. 'What happens now?'

'I think there is only one thing that can be done. You ask her to marry you and we announce the engagement on Saturday at the party. And...' she paused, 'as there is a possibility your actions have resulted in pregnancy, the wedding will follow at Christmas.'

'Thérèse, I cannot do this.'

'But what other choice is there, Marco?' She shook her head as she drifted over to the window and peered out. 'No other man will want her now you have breached her; she has lost her value.'

He eyed her disdainfully. 'That is an archaic view; we *are* living in the twentieth century now. My sister is not a virgin – it will not stop her chances of a good marriage when the time comes.'

'It is not the same. The D'Alesandros do not have the aristocratic pedigree of the Caravellos and, unlike Rossana, Felica is a worldly young woman. Why do you think Edoardo has kept her so well protected all this time?' Sadness filled her face. 'You have no idea of the damage that has been done. You must do the honourable thing by her.'

'And what if I still say I do not want to?'

'Then you leave me no choice – I will have to tell your father.'

Marco's hands returned to his head. His father would never forgive him. He would see what had happened as an act of total betrayal. And, of course, the outcome would be the same: he would still have to marry Rossana. To have any chance of clearing his name she would need to agree to a medical examination. And, of course, this was not going to happen. Thérèse had advised against it and even if she had agreed, Rossana, he knew, would most certainly refuse, particularly if marriage to him was now a possibility. After all, wouldn't that be her dream come true? The pain of his situation cut through him – Charlotte out of reach, with the questions he wanted to ask her forever to remain unanswered, and his future neatly set in front of him. A future chained to a woman he did not love and a marriage he did not want.

'Marco?'

He looked up to see Thérèse standing over him, felt her hand resting gently on his shoulder.

'All right, all right.' He got to his feet. 'I will ask her this evening after dinner.' He gave a harsh laugh. 'I hope you are pleased, Thérèse. Not only has Rossana's wish come true, but yours also.'

'Please do not think so badly of me, Marco,' she said calmly, as he headed for the door. 'Yes, I had hopes for you both but I did not want it this way. If you want to direct your anger anywhere then do so at the faithless creature who betrayed you. It is her actions which have put you in this situation. I am truly sorry, I really am.'

Thérèse stood watching him leave. As the door clicked shut she relaxed, a smile of satisfaction lighting her face.

Felica closed the door, leaving Rossana to her own devices. The girl appeared to have calmed herself very quickly since returning home, she thought, and she could hear the distinct sounds of humming coming from the other side of the door. She frowned. There was something odd about all of this, something which had been sparked by the last remnants of conversation before she left the bathroom.

'Why did you go there, Rossana?' she had asked her curiously. 'Why did you not wake my mother?'

'I did not want her to be disturbed. I wanted to do this. I care for Marco very much,' Rossana had answered in a voice full of emotion. 'I love him and I wanted to be the one to see he was all right. I felt it was my duty.'

Felica had thought the girl sounded a little too dramatic. 'So when you arrived, why did you not take Paulo in with you? What made you think you could cope with an intoxicated man alone? Did my brother rape you?'

Rossana's huge green eyes had stared up at her in horror. 'Oh no, Marco would never hurt me. I knew he would eventually come to love me. He was lying in the bed; he looked so beautiful. I sat there and spoke to him and stroked his face. He woke up. He looked so sad... because of what Charlotte has done to him, I suppose. He put his arms around me and kissed me. And, well, I wanted to show him how much I loved him. I would do anything for him, so I let him...' Her voice had trailed away.

'Rossana, did you go to the apartment with the intention of getting Marco to do what he did to you?'

The girl had thought for several moments, dipping the sponge into the bathwater and squeezing out the liquid a few times before looking up and smiling. 'Of course not, but I am glad he did.' Her innocent eyes were filled with bright expectancy when they had fixed on her once more. 'I guess after what has happened we will be married now.'

'That is for my mother to discuss with you,' Felica had replied, knowing the outcome and that it was exactly what Rossana wanted.

Oh yes, she thought as she made her way to her room, there was collusion here all right and Thérèse was in the thick of it. Proving it, however, was something else. She would ask Lucy Benedict, she decided, maybe she might be able to shed some light on all of this.

FORTY-EIGHT

Charlotte emerged from St Sepulchre without Newgate into a bright afternoon of early autumn sunshine, Jay and Lucy by her side. The funeral service had been quite beautiful, attended by many other artists and celebrities, the coffin carried in by Jay and the other former members of Rosetti. The eulogy was delivered by her uncle, the man who had discovered Christian and developed his talent. There were times when she could see he struggled with his words, the poignancy of the occasion overwhelming him.

Black limos were now lined up against the pavement, ready to whisk the mourners away, while behind them, Christian's coffin, still draped with a profusion of floral tributes, was being loaded into the back of the hearse. The barriers surrounding the church, adorned with all sorts of memorabilia, held back waiting crowds of fans, many of whom were clearly distressed. As expected, the fans' reaction had been one of total distress and grief for the loss of such a star.

Waiting for their own vehicle to arrive, Charlotte knew, despite her own misery in losing him, the service had changed her perspective. During his eulogy, Matt had spoken about Christian being a man who embraced life and enjoyed it to the full. The words had stayed in her mind. His star had ascended and fallen in such a short time, but she was still here and had a life and a future to think about.

'Lottie.' She felt Lucy's hand slip into hers. 'Are you okay?'

'Yes, I'm fine. Your father said some beautiful things about Christian and his zest for life.' She turned to her cousin and smiled. 'It made me realise he would not want me to spend my life grieving, he would want me to make the most of what I have. So tomorrow I'm going down to Gulls' Rest. Everything's in store ready so I'm going to get the place furnished and stay a while. I'm sure Beth would enjoy the company.'

Lucy nodded. 'That's a good idea. After all this I think it would be quite sensible for you to get away from Little Court for a while anyway.'

Charlotte knew Lucy was referring not only to the funeral, but also to this coming Saturday and Rossana Caravello's eighteenth birthday. She was right; she did not want to be there, not now Thérèse had told everyone Marco was due to announce his engagement to Rossana on the night of the party. The news had shocked her, but it was obvious to her that with his parents, he had been part of the vineyard scheme all along.

As the limo pulled up to the kerb, Jay opened the door and stood back to let them get in. Charlotte tucked herself into the back seat, thoughts of Marco's ultimate betrayal pushed to the back of her mind as she prepared herself for the crematorium.

* * *

'Lucy, there's someone in reception to see you,' Magda's husky voice announced.

'Who is it?' Lucy frowned, checking through her diary and finding nothing until later that afternoon. It was the day after the funeral and she had kept it deliberately empty, needing to catch up on her work.

'It's a Felica D'Alesandro. She says you know her.'

'Yes. Yes I do. Send her up, will you.' She was curious to know what Felica wanted.

She emerged from the lift dressed in an expensive charcoal pants suit. With her understated chic, as always, she looked immaculate. She smiled, but Lucy caught the tenseness in her face.

'Come through, take a seat.' Lucy ushered her into her office, indicating the leather chair in front of her desk. 'Can I get you some coffee?'

'Please.' She waited while Lucy buzzed through to Magda before continuing. 'I am not sure coming here is going to make any difference, but I had to speak to someone.'

'About Marco?'

'Yes. No doubt you are aware of his coming engagement?'

Lucy nodded. 'He didn't waste any time, did he, after losing Lottie.'

'What do you mean?'

'Some of my family feel Marco was less than honest with my cousin. That perhaps he had been two-timing her.'

Felica shook her head vigorously. 'Never. I have spoken to him only this morning. He holds much pain in his heart concerning Lottie. A lot has happened that you do not know about and which I am not sure I can reveal. All I can say is that the situation is not of his making. He has been forced into this. It has all come about as a result of that evening you put him to bed in the apartment, and it is one of the reasons I came to see you. I wanted to talk to you about it. Lucy, would you tell me exactly what happened?'

Magda arrived with two cups of coffee, setting them down on the desk, Lucy nodding her thanks as she left.

Lucy picked up her cup and took a sip. 'We found him in the South Bank Club, extremely drunk.' She took another sip. 'He fell off the bar stool and was taken outside to sober up, so we called a taxi and got him back to the apartment. We couldn't get a lot of sense out of him; it took ages for him to even let us have the keypad number.' She smiled, remembering. 'Then we got him inside and up the stairs, where Jay undressed him and put him to bed.'

'So Marco was very drunk?' Felica's interest was evident as she returned her cup to its saucer.

'Extremely. He kept passing out. That's why I phoned the restaurant. I thought it best to let someone know so they could come round and check on him.'

'Lucy, forgive me, but I have not much personal experience with drunks.'

'And you think I'm the expert?' Lucy gave an amused grin. 'What sort of company do you think I keep?'

Felica smiled back. 'Sorry, I did not mean to offend. I only wanted to know... well... do you think someone in his condition would be capable of... how can I put this... of having sex?'

'Hardly!' There was an accompanying snort of laughter. 'He was completely out of it. Why are you asking?'

Felica sighed. 'I am sorry, I cannot tell you more.'

Lucy brought her cup and saucer together and narrowed her eyes in thought. 'So... he's had sex with someone, has he?' When Felica didn't respond, she said, 'It's Rossana, isn't it? Ah... the sudden engagement; now I understand.'

Felica nodded uncomfortably. 'I think he has been tricked. I do not think it happened.'

Lucy sat forward, resting her elbows on the blotter. 'Do you know something – neither do I. Maybe you should tell me everything. If I can, I would like to help.'

'Oh my, this looks absolutely fabulous!' Beth stood back, her gaze scanning the room. 'I sense a definite flare for interior design here, Lottie. If you were to go into business down here, they'd be queuing up to employ you.'

'No way, Beth!' Charlotte held up her hands in protest. 'This is for me and me only. I'm definitely sticking with accountancy, it's far simpler.'

'I brought some bubbly.' Beth revealed the bottle she had been holding behind her back. 'Although in your condition—'

'Oh, I doubt one drink will do too much damage,' Charlotte interrupted, not wanting to be seen as a party pooper. 'I'll go and get some glasses.'

As she came out of the living room CJ was coming down the stairs, returning from his inspection of the bedrooms.

'It's brilliant, sis. I love absolutely everything you've done,' he said, wrapping his arms around her. 'I hope you'll be happy here.' He placed an affectionate kiss on the top of her head.

She smiled, delighted he liked what she'd done to the place. 'I hope so too. Why don't you join Beth? I'm off to get some glasses to celebrate with the champagne you brought.'

'I'd better not drink too much; we're travelling back to Little Court this evening ready for the big day tomorrow.'

'Oh yes, I forgot. The party.' She gave him a thin smile. 'I received an invitation last week.'

'What! My God, the woman is a complete bitch, isn't she?'

'Don't worry, she can't touch me down here and anyway, I'm over Marco. Rossana is welcome to him.'

'Lottie.' CJ's broad hands settled on her shoulders. 'You're carrying his baby.'

'Everyone seems to believe it's Christian's.'

'So you are going to pass it off as his – is that sensible?'

'No. But I'm not planning to admit who is the real father either. I'm leaving everyone to speculate.'

'If the press get wind of this…' He raised his eyes skywards. 'If they believe this child has anything to do with Christian, you realise you'll have no peace?'

'Of course I do. That's why I'm here. I plan to stay in Devon and keep a low profile until the baby is born. You worry too much.' She waved a confident hand at him. 'At the moment, the press have their hands full with all the women who are coming forward to tell the world Christian Rosetti fathered their child. And with his reputation, that will keep them occupied for a good while.'

'And what of the real father?'

She gave an indifferent shrug. 'Well, he won't be here, will he? He'll be back in Italy with his bride and the family's newly acquired vineyards.'

'Vineyards?'

Her hand went quickly to her mouth 'Oh, of course… you don't know, do you? In fact, no one knows except Livvy at Safekeeping. I checked on the internet at work and I believe I've discovered the reason why Thérèse was so keen to get the two of them together. It's all about the acquisition of some very profitable vineyards. In fact, I texted Marco about it when he was in America, but he said he already knew and not to worry. With hindsight, it appears to me he used our relationship as a smokescreen to make his initial resistance to Rossana seem more plausible. After all, it wouldn't have looked good to the outside world if he had been swearing undying love to such a naïve little heiress from the start, would it? He had to play hard to get otherwise her uncle would have definitely smelt a rat. Believe me, CJ, the D'Alesandros are all in it up to their necks.'

'Rossana's an heiress?' CJ looked at her with an excited glint in his eye. 'How interesting… Do tell me more.'

Gianlucca arrived at the manor late on Friday evening. Thérèse was there to greet him at the door, immaculate as ever in a new burgundy dress from her autumn range.

'You're looking very happy, Thérèse.' He smiled, noting the expression on her face as he kissed her cheek before motioning for Giulio, his valet, to bring in his cases.

'Of course I am. We have a very special party this weekend and are expecting a house full of guests.' Her eyes danced with excitement. 'I love this, Gianni. We should do it more often. Come, Giulio.' She indicated the stairs with a sweep of her hand. 'I will show you to Signor D'Alesandro's dressing room and then to your own accommodation.'

When Thérèse returned from escorting the valet to his quarters, she took both her husband's hands in hers and smiled.

'I have some splendid news for you, Gianni. Since our return from America, Marco has proposed to Rossana. They will announce their engagement at the party tomorrow evening.'

Gianlucca snatched his hands away. 'What! How has this come about, Thérèse? What have you been up to?'

'Up to? Why, nothing.' She took a step away from him, her innocent expression hiding the discomfort she felt at his violent reaction to her news. 'I thought you would be pleased.'

'I would be if I felt the match was appropriate, but I do not.' The severity of his tone was reflected in his dark eyes. 'I was with Marco in Germany only last week. All he talked of was Charlotte. In fact, he flew to be with her as soon as he heard of the crash which killed Christian Rosetti.'

'Ah!' She gave him a satisfied smile. 'Well, there is another story. She turned him away, she would not see him. And do you know why? Because she is having a baby and Christian is the father.'

'What?'

'Yes, it is true,' she said smugly. 'I tried to tell your son, to turn him from his foolishness, but he would not listen. And now look what has happened. His heart has been broken.'

'I do not believe this, Thérèse, I really do not. Are you sure Christian is the father?'

'Of course. I was at Little Court for a meeting when her mother came in and told us the news. Of course, they all thought it was Marco's, but she confirmed it was definitely Christian.'

'And at this news he very conveniently falls into the open arms of young and impressionable Rossana and proposes? I do not believe it. You forget I spent a month in America with both of them. Marco treated her in the same way as he does Felica. There was no spark, no attraction there. Oh, I know Rossana has some immature crush on him, but for Marco there was no such emotion present. Something tells me he has not done this of his free will. Has he been coerced into this at all?'

'Coerced? Of course not. Do you not think maybe losing Charlotte made him see the truth of his feelings for her?'

'Oh, Thérèse, please... Do you think I am a fool?'

'Of course not, but why do you not accept things for what they are? Love is only a very small issue here. There is far more at stake here than the engagement.'

'There is?'

'Yes. Marco will have the vineyards. Isn't that what you want?'

Gianlucca's eyes darkened angrily. 'No, it is not! Edoardo's discussion with me regarding buying into the vineyards was merely that: a discussion. It was never definite and it was about investing, not owning. I have already told you all this. And I expressly asked that you leave Marco alone.'

'Marco!' she shouted at him hatefully. 'Always it is Marco. The most important thing in your life – Marco, Marco. Not me or the baby I lost.'

'That is a foolish thing to say. You know I mourned the loss of our unborn son.' His eyes misted. 'You have no idea of my feelings, learning your fall meant not only the end of one life, but that we would not have the opportunity for any more children.' He stepped towards her, intending to comfort her, but she backed away, avoiding him.

'No, Gianni. All you have ever cared about is Marco. Many times during our marriage I have tried so hard to please you, but it seems you do not notice this. And then when I get you the one thing you want so badly – and yes, do not deny you do want the vineyards – when I try to be the supportive wife, you throw it back in my face yet again, as if it means nothing. Yet for even the smallest of achievements, you sing his praises.'

'How many more times do I need to tell you? I do *not* want the vineyards,' Gianlucca ground out. 'It was small talk over dinner and you have turned it into a nightmare for Marco.'

She tossed back her head. 'Hah! There we go again. Your precious son. Well, even if he has caught her on the rebound, it is not so bad for him, is it?' She rounded on him. 'He is a man and, as we all know, you men usually do exactly as you please. No doubt he will eventually find she is not enough for him and leave her in Tuscany. He can return to London. Even take a mistress if he so wishes. No one will care as long as he manages to get Rossana pregnant with at least one male child.' She waved a dismissive hand. 'Anyway, the deed is done. Edoardo arrived in London this afternoon. I have given him news of the engagement and he is extremely pleased for both of them. It has his blessing.'

'I am not happy about this. I told you before, your interference could blow back on you badly. Well, I want no part of it and I insist on seeing Marco. I cannot believe he has done this willingly. There is something I am not being told.' He moved towards the door.

'It does not matter what you believe,' she said, putting a restraining hand on his arm. 'Edoardo is very happy with this match. In fact, he is overjoyed. Should you attempt to interfere in any way you may lose his friendship. And be warned, the upset may well trigger more health problems. Remember, he is not yet out of the woods after heart surgery. Do you want that?'

He glared at her as he shook off her grip. 'Do not threaten me, Thérèse.'

'I am only asking you accept what has happened,' she replied softly.

A sudden creak of the door caused them both to turn. Thérèse noticed it stood slightly ajar. She frowned; she was sure she had closed it upon her return. Quickly, she crossed the room and peered out into the corridor, finding it empty. Breathing a sigh of relief, she turned back to her husband.

'Just a draft, nothing to worry about. Gianni, you are tired after your long journey. I suggest you have a bath and get some rest. We have a long day ahead of us tomorrow. I'm sure after a good night's sleep you will see everything in a different light.'

'I doubt that very much,' Gianlucca replied as she left the room.

It was Saturday morning, and at Little Court the organisation for Rossana's party was well under way. Issy had arrived and the kitchen had become a hive of hectic activity. Eager to escape from all the frenetic bustle, Matt had taken refuge in his study, leaving newly arrived CJ and Beth with Lucy and Jay to finish their breakfast.

'How's, Lottie?' Lucy asked, slipping the last corner of her toast into her mouth.

'Fine,' CJ said with a grin, 'and absolutely in her element.'

'The house is fabulous,' Beth added, looking at Lucy and Jay as she poured herself another coffee. 'No doubt you'll both get an invite soon.'

'How is she in herself though?' Lucy pushed her empty plate away. 'You know, bearing in mind what's happening this evening.'

'Oh, she could have been here.' CJ's voice was edged with sarcasm. 'The wretched woman sent her an invitation.'

Lucy bristled. 'You are joking. Hell, what is the matter with her?'

'For some reason she's always disliked Lottie,' CJ said. 'We had quite a talk before we came away, didn't we, Beth?'

Beth nodded. 'Yes, some interesting things came to light. Would you like us to share them with you?'

'Is it anything that will help free Marco?' Lucy asked.

CJ frowned at his cousin. 'Who says he wants to be freed?'

'Felica does.'

'Well, my gullible little cousin, Lottie now thinks her and Marco's relationship was a front to stop anyone guessing what the family were really up to.'

'And exactly what was that?' Jay leaned forward, curious.

'They were after the Alba Dorata vineyards in Tuscany. Since Rossana's parents died, they've been held in trust until her eighteenth birthday. As of today they are legally hers and soon they will be Marco's by marriage. Lottie thinks the whole family are in on it.'

'No!'

All four heads turned towards the doorway, where Felica stood staring at them a horrified expression on her face. Lucy got to her feet and drew her into the room, closing the door.

'Here, sit down,' she urged, pushing her towards a spare chair.

'Lucy, you realise you may be bringing a spy into our midst,' CJ said, his eyes fixed on the new arrival as she sat down at the table.

'Oh, don't be so stupid, CJ,' Lucy snapped.

Felica shook her head vigorously. 'I am not a spy; I am as innocent as all of you. My parents? Yes. But Marco? No, he is not part of this, I swear he is—'

'Is Thérèse here with you?' CJ interrupted.

'Of course not. I left her at the house. She is fussing over Rossana, as usual. Lucy and I have been in regular touch over this whole issue of Lottie and Marco. I came here to give her the latest news.' She drew a tight breath. 'Not that it is good. Rossana's uncle arrived in London yesterday. My mother was quick to tell him of the engagement. It has his blessing.' She looked across the table at Lucy. 'I do not think there is anything more that can be done.'

'So you're convinced Marco's not involved in any of this?' CJ looked at Lucy in confusion. 'Are you sure?'

'Positive. Felica told me what led up to the engagement. Believe me,' Lucy looked at all of them, 'he has been well and truly deceived although, sadly, we cannot prove a thing.'

FORTY-NINE

Rossana stood at her bedroom window looking out over the manor's parkland. Today was her eighteenth birthday, a day which should be full of happiness and celebration. Presents had been arriving since yesterday; beautiful elegantly wrapped gifts all to be opened this evening at the party. Until last evening she had been filled with a sense of euphoria, looking forward to a milestone birthday, claiming her inheritance, her independence and the man of her dreams. Dreams, she realised, which had now turned into an unbelievable nightmare.

Signorina D'Alesandro plan had been quite simple. Marco, she told her, had discovered Charlotte was pregnant. The baby was Christian Rosetti's and, understandably, Marco had been extremely upset. He had returned to London and spent the evening drinking himself into a stupor. Luckily, someone had found him and returned him to his apartment where, she understood, he was now in bed sleeping off his night of excess. She could not bear to see him so distraught over such a worthless young woman, she said. It was therefore time to take control, to force his hand and make him see it was she, Rossana, who indeed loved him and should be with him. She told her she had a plan, one which she assured, if successful, would ensure Marco would be hers. It was not straightforward, but all they had to do was keep cool heads. During the drive to his apartment, she had found her mood fluctuating between the joy of at last having him and the concern that this plan, however well-conceived, might go terribly wrong.

When they had arrived at his apartment they found him deeply asleep. He looked so beautiful lying there, the moonlight spilling across the bed, black hair in a riot about his face, his smooth bare back exposed above the crumpled sheets. Suddenly, she didn't care that they were tricking him – the desire to have this exquisite man totally blotted out the pang of conscience which had plagued her during the car journey. Under the watchful eye of Signorina D'Alesandro, she had undressed and then waited while her mentor produced and uncapped a small glass tube from her bag. Pulling the sheets back carefully, she had dripped some of its contents onto the bed before instructing her to climb in beside him.

'This,' Signorina D'Alesandro had whispered as she'd watched, 'will make him think he has made love to you. It will guarantee he will be yours.'

And so she had overlooked the horror on his face when he awoke the next morning to find her there beside him; had ignored the protests of innocence when Signorina D'Alesandro and Felica arrived. Then came the apology for his shameful behaviour as he came to her that evening, eyes full of pain and distress. The fact he said he could remember nothing, she brushed aside, concentrating instead on accepting his apology with grace and his proposal with quiet acceptance. To have showed the real joy she felt might have revealed her part in his entrapment, and that was the last thing she wanted. No, to play the victim, as Signorina D'Alesandro had suggested, would bring her all she sought, and more. And so she did, and it seemed everything had fallen into place wonderfully well: her engagement to be announced at the party this evening, followed by a Christmas wedding. Everything she had hoped and dreamed of was about to happen.

Of course, she had not meant to eavesdrop. Once again she had been unable to sleep, and was returning to her room from the kitchen with a glass of warm milk when Signorina D'Alesandro's loud, angry voice had brought her to a halt outside a slightly open door. There were things she knew she should not have heard; private family things. Embarrassed, she was about to move on when she heard the vineyards mentioned. She could not leave then; she had to know exactly what they were talking about. And now she knew.

All the time she thought Signorina D'Alesandro had been helping her gain Marco's affections, she had been doing nothing of the sort. Marco had once told her his stepmother only ever did anything for her own benefit. And now she understood the truth of his words – this was all about gaining possession of the vineyards for her husband, Gianlucca. A great irony, it seemed, when he made a point of telling her he had not wanted them, that it had been merely a conversation he had had over dinner with her uncle. She knew he loved his son, he could not believe what had happened. He had demanded to see Marco, but Signorina D'Alesandro had prevented him with a threat about her uncle's health should he try to disrupt her plans. And once she had finished with her husband, Signorina D'Alesandro had turned her venom on her.

Like a house of cards caught by a gust of wind, both the engagement and her belief that she had everything she had ever dreamed of collapsed before her eyes. Hearing the Signorina say Marco could simply dump her in Tuscany after the wedding and go back to his life in London if he chose – that no one would care if he took a mistress as long as he did his duty and got her pregnant – was more than she could bear. That had been when she saw how evil Thérèse D'Alesandro was, and for an instant wondered whether Marco had been part of all this too. But no, the shock on his face that morning had been very real. And now, with the rose tinted glasses removed, she saw things as they really were. He had been used in exactly the same way she had. He did not actually want her – Thérèse had used her naïve vulnerability to gain something she wanted. It meant if the engagement went ahead, they would be tied into a life together based on lies and deceit. She knew that now this callous and calculating woman had achieved her goal she would not hesitate to abandon her to bear the brunt of Marco's anger once he discovered the truth on their wedding night.

Rossana turned away from the window, her mind made up she must do something to bring this madness to an end.

Thérèse had arrived two hours before the start of the party, keen to make sure the arrangements were in place. What she found exceeded her expectations: Little Court looked magnificent, the whole function suite was ready for a sparkling evening, and Issy Taylor had done an excellent job with the catering. Rossana had asked for blue, her favourite colour, to form the main theme for the party; Thérèse wondered how Ella had managed to find so many different shades to incorporate into the décor of the room and the set of the tables. The ice sculptures were something to behold too, and she made a mental note to ask Issy where she had found the company for this, they were quite exceptional. She clasped her hands together, picturing Rossana at the top table cutting her cake, the applause and then Marco's announcement.

Walking back out onto the terrace, she caught sight of the marquee that had been erected on the lower lawn where Matt's technical crew were nearly finished setting up the music for the evening. There would be a laser show too lighting up the sky over Little Court, and fireworks as the party ended. Another smile of satisfaction lit her face as she noticed the torches which had been positioned around the garden. Oh yes, everything was perfect.

Felica smoothed down her pale cinnamon silk dress and stood admiring herself in front of the full-length mirror. In an hour's time they would be departing for Little Court and the party. Inside, her rage still burned from what she had learned this morning. Marco had been betrayed by both their parents; forced into a marriage of convenience to secure something her father wanted. She was appalled to think he, a man she had adored since childhood, a man well known for his honesty and fairness, could resort to such underhand tactics. Of course, it had taken two, and no doubt her mother had relished the opportunity to take charge of the planning of all this deception. She had a reputation for devious schemes, causing trouble among her friends, what few there were left. Checking her make-up for the final time, she picked up her evening bag and left the room.

As she made her way down the corridor towards the stairs she met her father coming the other way. His concentration was so fixed on adjusting his cufflinks he did not see her until the last moment. He stopped, his face lighting up with pleasure when he saw her.

'Ah, Felica! You look absolutely beautiful. I guarantee every man in the room this evening will fall in love with you.' He stepped forward, intending to plant a kiss on her forehead but she stepped to one side to avoid him, and eyed him angrily.

'Am I the next sacrifice then, father? Have you someone lined up this evening whose wealth you covet? Well, I will tell you... you will not find it as easy to trick me as you have Marco.'

'Whatever are you talking about?' He looked at her in total confusion.

'I know about the Alba Dorata vineyards.'

Again he frowned. 'What do you know?'

'Everything! That he is the sacrificial lamb. Mother did a good job coaxing Rossana into his bed in order to force him to marry her. You should be proud.'

'Rossana in his bed?' She felt his hand seize her arm. 'Felica, what are you talking about?'

'Let go of me. You know exactly what I mean.' She shook his hand off and made to pass but he stepped in front of her, gripping her arm again. Seeing the fury in his dark eyes, she felt suddenly afraid. 'What are you going to do?'

'I am returning you to your room,' he said, propelling her back along the corridor.

'I see. You are going to lock me in to ensure I do not cause a fuss this evening.' She struggled against the iron grip on her elbow. 'Is that what you plan?'

'No,' he replied, opening the door and pushing her inside. As he closed the door, he indicated a chair by the window. 'Sit down!'

Obeying his demand, she sank into it, realising she was in dangerous waters. Her father's brows were drawn together like heavy grey thunderclouds as he stood over her.

'Now then,' he said, his voice calmer, 'I would be grateful if you would please explain to me exactly what has been going on.'

Gianlucca listened whilst she relayed the events which had taken place in Marco's apartment, her temper at boiling point as she accused him of being part of a greedy conspiracy with her mother.

'I had no part in this, I swear to you I did not.' Gianlucca paced the floor, running a tired hand over his grim face. 'And now matters are worse than I thought.' He paced down the room again, then turning, said, 'Does Marco know of your suspicions?'

Felica shook her head. 'No. Are you going to tell him?'

'I cannot, *cara mia*, without causing total chaos and bringing the whole family into disrepute.' His expression was bleak. 'The party will go ahead as will the engagement, but tomorrow I will have your mother's head for this.'

By eleven thirty Rossana's party was in full swing; Thérèse moved among the guests in the huge marquee, chatting and smiling. The music was loud, people were dancing, others drinking and chatting. Everyone appeared to be enjoying themselves and she had to admit Lawns had delivered an exceptional party for Rossana. Marco seemed to have become resigned to his fate, searching out his fiancée-to-be to start the dancing, although she could see his smiles were few. Oh yes, it was all going very well. She checked her watch. Another forty minutes and the cake would be set up in the banqueting suite ready for Rossana to cut, and after that – she took a deep breath – the engagement would be announced.

Rossana looked absolutely fabulous in the two-tone blue silk off-the-shoulder creation especially designed for her by Felica. Her thick hair fell loosely over her shoulders and her skin glowed. Heads had turned as she entered the banqueting suite earlier to take her place of honour. Seeing the girl moving among the crowd, greeting people as she arrived, the thought struck Thérèse that she looked a little pale. Her concern, however, was soon dismissed; she was worrying too much, of course. It was, after all, only to be expected. Being centre stage with over a hundred and fifty guests must be a little overwhelming for the girl. Marco too had looked incredibly handsome as he mingled. Seeing them as they chatted to different guests, she knew they would produce the most beautiful children. She sighed and drained her champagne glass as thoughts of branching out into children's designer clothing settled in her mind. Consigning her empty glass to a passing waitress and taking a fresh one, she saw Issy Taylor skirting around the edge of the dance floor.

'Thérèse! Just checking everything is fine.'

'Fabulous, Issy. I could not have wished for a better evening. Thank you so much.' She reached out and captured Issy's arm with red-tipped fingers, feeling quite emotional now everything she had worked for was about to come to fruition against the backdrop of this wonderful party.

'We have the cake set up ready.'

'So soon? There's another forty minutes yet.'

'I'm always an early bird, I never leave anything to chance,' came Issy's parting remark as she excused herself and moved on, waving out as she saw Ella.

'Very wise,' Thérèse called after her, and decided maybe she should think about rounding up Rossana and Marco. Now, where had they got to?

Marco wondered what he was doing allowing himself to be dragged away from the party by Rossana. She had been most insistent she wanted to talk to him, no doubt, he thought, to give him last minute reminders from his stepmother on the overblown theatrical scene she had dreamt up for their engagement announcement. He had lost count of how many glasses of champagne he had consumed but it appeared even alcohol was unable to dull the depressing ache within him. To the outside world he appeared his normal relaxed, good mannered self. Inside, however, he felt nothing but pain; his life was over, robbed from him by his own stupidity. He still could remember nothing of that fateful night but it must have happened; the evidence was there, droplets of red in the bed bright and condemning. In one drunken night he had taken Rossana's innocence and now there was a possibility she could be carrying his child. He guessed Edoardo probably felt he was a little older than the bridegroom he had envisaged for his niece, but this was more than balanced out by his long-term friendship with Gianlucca – a trusted friend – which was why he had whole-heartedly approved of the union.

He followed Rossana out of the marquee and across the lawn towards the river. *What was she playing at?* he wondered. Tugging on his arm, she seemed anxious to distance herself from the noise of the party. Reaching the pathway which skirted the high red brick wall of the kitchen garden, he realised where they were going.

She stopped as they reached the river garden. Had things been different, he would have admired the rebirth of this neglected area by Jenny Miller and her husband. Its neatly edged pathway, rich mixture of plants and ornate glass wind chimes in the surrounding trees were a fitting backdrop to the decorative wrought-iron bench set against the wall. The whole area was softly lit, and he could imagine in happier circumstances, it would be an ideal place for lovers. But the woman with him was far from that and he now stood facing her, waiting for her to speak.

'I do not know how to begin this,' she said quietly, clasping her hands nervously in front of her, 'but I have... I have decided to break the engagement.'

'Break the engagement,' he echoed back, both surprised and furious at her statement. 'What kind of stupid game are you playing now?'

'It is not a game.' She crossed to where he stood, resting her hand on his arm, her big green eyes never leaving his. 'This is the only way I can make things right.'

'I do not understand. I am bound by honour to marry you. You may be pregnant and it is my fault. Do you not realise what will happen if we break this off and your uncle finds you are having a baby? There are more people involved in this than you and me; the damage to them would be far worse than the damage to us. I forbid you to do this.'

Sucking in a deep breath, she shook her head. 'Marco, I am not pregnant.' A small sob erupted from her throat.

'You have seen a doctor?'

'No.'

'Then you cannot possibly know.' It was his turn to grip her arm. 'Rossana, even if you are not, you are no longer a virgin. The engagement *has* to go ahead.'

She looked at him, the glimmer of tears in her eyes. 'Marco, you are such a wonderful, decent man, but you are not the one for me. Oh, I love you, I really do, but I realise now to find real love, a love which lasts, it has to be returned. Even if you could grow to love me, I would always have to live with the awful lies and the things I have done to you out of my own selfishness, and I cannot do that.'

'Lies?' What lies? What are you talking about?'

'I am still a virgin. You did not touch me.'

'But the evidence was there... the blood.' He let go of her and took a step back. When he next spoke he could hear the cold anger in his voice. 'What have you done?'

Rossana teetered on the brink of tears. 'It was Thérèse. She...' Heavy sobs halted her explanation. 'I am sorry, I am so sorry.'

Pulling a handkerchief from his pocket, Marco offered it to her. 'Come,' he said, softening his voice and leading her to the bench, where he settled her down. 'Now, please dry your eyes, take your time, and tell me everything.'

Thérèse was becoming anxious. With thirty minutes left until the cake was due to be cut she still had not been able to find either Rossana or Marco. It was important they were ready in time, and so she could do a last minute run through with them. She came across Edoardo in a jolly mood sipping champagne as he sat with a couple of elderly Italian matrons.

'Ah, the love birds.' He smiled in answer to her question. 'Yes, I saw them crossing the lawn together several minutes ago, going in that direction.' He pointed to the pathway that led to the river garden.

Thanking him, she hurried to catch them.

She could hear voices quite clearly above the rush of water as she came around the corner of the high wall bordering the river. Then she saw them up ahead, sitting on a bench, Rossana dabbing at her eyes with a handkerchief.

'Rossana?' She stopped in front of them, frowning as her gaze went from one to the other. 'Rossana, are you all right?'

Marco got to his feet and, when his eyes met hers, she saw fury simmering there.

'What is going on?' she demanded. 'Rossana, why are you crying?'

'I...' Rossana hesitated, clutching Marco's handkerchief to her mouth, her eyes riveted on the older woman's face and her obvious displeasure.

'She has just told me the truth.' Marco's voice was icy.

'The truth. What are you talking about?' Thérèse snorted disdainfully. 'Rossana. Explain, please.'

'I do not want to marry him,' Rossana blurted out, finding her voice at last. 'I thought I could live with the lies, but I cannot. I have told him the truth that I did not sleep with him. That it was you who planted the blood in the bed.' She looked up at Thérèse, her eyes fearful but defiant. 'I thought you did this to help me, but I now realise it was to help yourself to the Alba Dorata vineyards.'

'The vineyards? What nonsense is this? I know nothing of the vineyards.' Thérèse's soft laugh held a hint of embarrassment as she turned to her stepson. 'I am sorry, Marco, she is obviously having last minute nerves. I don't know what she has told you, but please ignore it. Come, both of you.'

She waved an imperious finger before hooking her hand under Rossana's elbow and hauling her to her feet. 'We need to do a final run through before the cake cutting,' she said, flipping over her wrist to look at her watch, 'which takes place in less than fifteen minutes.'

Rossana tugged against her. 'No. I overheard you talking to Signor D'Alesandro last night.'

'Such rubbish, you silly girl! Your uncle will be most displeased with you,' Thérèse scolded. 'Do you want that? He and Gianni go back a long way; you will be upsetting him too you know.'

'Leave her!' Marco's calm but chilling voice drew Thérèse to a halt. 'Let her go.'

'I most certainly will not. What have you said to her, Marco?' She stared at him suspiciously. 'Have you bullied her into this false confession? Are you the one to blame for this?'

'I rather think it is *you* who are to blame, Thérèse.' Gianlucca stepped out from the shadows, two dark-suited men at his side. 'Marco, take Rossana back to the party, please. I will return in a moment; this will not take long.'

'You foolish man.' Thérèse tried to push past him. 'Have you forgotten? The engagement is to be announced shortly. Whatever issues you have with me will have to wait until afterwards. Right now—'

'There will be no engagement,' Gianlucca said firmly, placing a tight grip on her arm before turning to his son. 'Go, Marco, please. Thérèse and I have things to settle between us. We will catch you up.'

As midnight struck, Rossana cut the cake and everyone serenaded her with an energetic version of 'Happy Birthday'. Luckily, Edoardo, singing along with everyone else, was so inebriated he did not even notice the engagement announcement had not been made.

Issy's waitresses were moving among the guests, handing out slivers of cake on elegant porcelain plates by the time Gianlucca returned. Thérèse was not with him. Deciding to leave Edoardo to get over his intoxicated state before talking to him, he walked over to join Marco.

'Have you settled everything?' Marco asked, watching as Rossana chatted animatedly to a group of guests.

'Yes,' his father replied. 'I think I have made Thérèse see the error of her ways.' He heaved a heavy sigh. 'However, I am unable to tolerate this any longer; the damage she has done this time it is too much.'

'Where is she now?' Felica asked, joining them and looking around the room as if she expected her mother to materialise at any moment.

'She is being accompanied to the airport as we speak,' Gianlucca said, his voice sad and troubled. 'I am flying her back to Italy tonight. I will deal with her on my return tomorrow.' He gave both his children a resigned look. 'I am afraid our marriage is over; I can accept no more of this behaviour from her. I am therefore taking steps to legally separate. And, children, it is not so bad.

After all, we have lived independent lives for many years now, and I have been under no illusion that she chose to remain with me only for my connections and the lifestyle it gave her.'

'But are you not afraid she will take some sort of revenge on all of us for this?' Felica asked anxiously.

Gianlucca shook his head. 'I do not think so, *cara mia*. Rossana will prove a most effective deterrent. I have told Thérèse that Edoardo has powerful friends in certain places and if he ever got to hear what she has been responsible for, there would be nowhere for her to hide.' He smiled briefly. 'No, I am sure she will embrace her new found freedom with great energy and leave us all in peace.' He turned to his son. 'So, Marco, what are your plans? Will you now seek out Charlotte?'

'No, Father, it is finished. Charlotte lied to me. It appears while we were together she was still seeing Christian Rosetti.' He shook his head sadly. 'And now she is having his child, so there is no more to be said.'

'But you do not know that for certain,' his sister argued, dearly wanting him to give Charlotte a chance. 'You should at least talk to her before you leave.'

Marco touched his sister's shoulder gently. 'No, Felica. I know you mean well, but it is best I return to Italy. I am sure Father can find me something to do there.'

Gianlucca smiled. 'As a matter of fact, I have just the project for you.'

FIFTY

Marco stared across the lake, a half-empty glass of wine in front of him. Seated beneath the shade of a large beige parasol outside a bar near the ferry terminal at Bardolino, he was taking time out after a busy morning of meetings. He was here on behalf of his father to undertake negotiations for the purchase of several luxury apartment blocks around Lake Garda. Gianlucca was moving into the upmarket rental business, looking to attract well-heeled professional couples with a blend of lavishly furnished accommodation and exclusive access to top eateries and leisure facilities. Marco had already made successful acquisitions in Riva and Garda, and Bardolino was his last port of call. He liked it here – the ferries coming and going taking on and dropping off passengers before turning back across the blue waters to resume their journey to other towns on the lake. There was colour too: the green of trees and shrubs, and flowers in abundance whether in municipal displays or private window boxes. There was a strange, laid back energy about the place coupled with the delicious smell of food and the accompanying pop of wine corks.

He watched a convoy of holiday cyclists peddle leisurely by heading in the direction of the park. Along the boarded walkway fronting the lake, he noticed a plump matron unsuccessfully supervising a small dark-haired boy who seemed determined to escape her clutches. Watching the woman and her charge as they disappeared into the flow of people along the pedestrian pathway caused him to think of Charlotte. Born in April, Christian Rosetti's son was now five months old, a permanent reminder of her callous betrayal. Turning his back on her, he had carved out a new life for himself here in Italy; one where women now occupied his bed, but not his heart. Love was a game for fools, he thought cynically, for dreamers so blinded by it, they had no idea of the pain it would inevitably bring them. Currently, however, all involvement with the opposite sex had been put on hold. His responsibilities in overseeing this new project meant that there was no place in his life at the moment for anything other than work.

Tonight he would be on a plane out of Verona bound for Milan and a reunion with his father. This was where his home was now, with no thought of returning to the UK, although he had to admit he missed San Raffaello's. It had been his concept, something he had nurtured from a basic Italian bistro into one of the best dining experiences in London, and he was proud it stood as the benchmark for all other D'Alesandro restaurants. Yes, that night just over a year ago had changed everything, and not only for his father and himself. Rossana, he recently heard, was engaged to a handsome young corporate lawyer with striking grey eyes and dark brown hair. He hoped in his heart of hearts she had at last found the one special man she had been so desperately searching for.

As for his stepmother, Thérèse's new-found freedom had opened a fresh door in her life too, as his father had predicted. Retiring from the fashion world, she currently enjoyed an independent and energetic social life in Rome. She was regularly featured in the celebrity magazines and gossip columns, photographed on the arm of an endless supply of handsome older men dining out or at the opera, while Felica, still living in the manor, had taken on the mantle of Lawns' new partner, the business continuing to thrive.

Finishing his wine, Marco was about to call for the bill when someone with a familiar smile settled in the seat opposite him.

'Matt!' His eyes widened in astonishment. 'What a surprise.'

'I wasn't sure it was you. Luckily, I have an eagle-eyed wife.' Matt Benedict grinned, brushing his collar-length hair back from his face and holding out his hand. 'What a small world.'

Marco reached across the table and shook Matt's hand. 'Yes, it is. What brings you to Bardolino?'

Marco watched as Ella, looking stunning in a short-sleeved blue silk shirt and white trousers, slid into the seat next to her husband. 'A bit of rest, actually,' she said, smiling widely. 'I've always wanted to visit the Italian lakes and as my husband is always keen to indulge me, here we are.'

Marco smiled at them, suddenly glad of company and some light-hearted social banter. 'Where are you both staying?'

'At the Lido Palace in Riva.' Matt slipped a hand over his wife's. 'We drove here today for a look around. And you?'

'Oh, business. My father's moving into luxury rentals and decided Garda, as the largest of the lakes, was the place to start. I've been heading the negotiations and, well, I'm pleased to say business has been successfully concluded. I'm flying back to Milan later but I've plenty of time. Would you stay and have a drink with me?' He looked around to catch the attention of a waiter.

'We'd love to. A glass of Prosecco, please,' Ella requested with a smile to the attentive young man arriving promptly at the table.

As the waiter left with their order, Ella's attention returned to Marco. 'So, you're living in Milan now, I gather?'

'Yes, my father has a large house there, plenty of room for me.'

'Will you ever come back to England?' Matt asked.

'I do not think so.' Marco shook his head, his expression guarded. 'Rossana's party was a bad night for all of us; I had to leave. I guess you think I am a coward, Mrs Benedict, but what my stepmother put me through was unforgiveable. I am afraid England holds only painful memories for me.'

'Is Lottie included in those bad memories?' Ella's grey eyes rested on him thoughtfully.

'Yes and no. We had some wonderful times together but—'

'She's been very badly hurt, but I know she still loves you,' Ella interrupted. 'There's been no one in her life since.'

He felt wounded by her remark. 'Charlotte has been hurt. And you think I have not? You think it is easy knowing the woman you love is carrying someone else's child?'

Matt gave a huff of annoyance as his eyes settled on Marco. 'The baby is not Christian's.'

'I know you are fond of Charlotte,' Marco said, trying to hold onto his temper, 'but the child is not mine. The timing... Thérèse told me when he was conceived. I was not there, but Christian? Oh, yes, he was.'

'Marco, for God's sake! I am not lying,' Matt bit out angrily. 'Christian wasn't able to have children. We had an arrangement.'

Marco eyed Matt hesitantly. 'What sort of arrangement?'

'Christian simply could not leave women alone,' Matt began to explain, pausing as the waiter arrived, placed their drinks in front of them, and departed. 'When he started a relationship with Lottie I thought he'd settled down. But gradually it became clear that wasn't the case. I could also see his appetites meant no matter how much he claimed he was in control of the situation, disaster would eventually strike. Someone would go to the tabloids with a claim and the floodgates would open, mostly with publicity-seeking opportunists. The last thing I wanted was to have to fund an expensive legal department sorting out paternity claims, bogus or otherwise. So, it was a case of leave the ladies alone or—'

'Have the snip,' Ella completed the sentence for her husband, a surprised look on her face. 'Well, well. I had no idea.'

'No one did,' Matt replied. 'Technically, it was reversible but he wasn't bothered. He maintained he'd never wanted children anyway.'

'So why was I not made aware of this a year ago?' Marco demanded, feeling as if someone had just kicked him in the gut.

Matt looked at him thoughtfully, glass poised at his lips. 'Probably because straight after Christian's funeral I flew to LA. Todd Graham, one of my old band mates who lives there, asked me onto his chat show with the rest of the group. I stayed on for a few days – old boys' reunion.' He grinned, remembering. 'By the time I got back, you were planning to marry Rossana. I was furious with you. I could not believe you'd walked away from Lottie and chosen someone else to spend the rest of your life with so quickly. Worse than that, you thought she was carrying someone else's child. So I told Lottie about Christian, said I planned to come and see you to tell you, but she stopped me. She said what was done was done and it would only bring more pain to more people.' Matt took a swift swallow of wine. 'Of course, at the time I had no idea about the circumstances behind your engagement. But once you were free again I was sure you would go and see her. Instead, you let what your stepmother did infect everything else in your life. You went back to Italy and, although I tried to contact you, you refused to take my calls. So I phoned your father to ask him to intervene, but even he couldn't convince you to talk to me.'

'No, he could not.' Marco sighed, recalling the phone call and how he had refused to listen, slamming the phone down on Gianlucca. 'I did not want to listen to anyone. As you say, Thérèse had poisoned my life; I wanted nothing more to do with women.'

'And do you intend to let that poison blight your life for ever?' Ella asked. 'Can you not find it in your heart to see Charlotte and the baby? She knows Thérèse tricked you. If she has any negative thoughts about you it is only that you chose to walk away instead of making the effort to see her.'

'Exactly! I did not bother, which means she either believes I do not care or that I am a coward.' His dark eyes held hers, feelings of both bitterness and sadness swirling around the situation he found himself in. 'It is too late for both of us. It is best we leave things as they are.'

Matt's mobile rang and he excused himself from the table to take the call.

'Marco, please.' He felt Ella's hand on his arm. 'You have a son,' she said gently, 'at least go and see him. She would want you to do that.'

Marco drew a deep breath and gazed out across the lake for a moment before turning back to look at her.

'I will think about it,' he said.

Two weeks later, Marco landed at Heathrow on a bright autumn day. Felica was waiting for him behind the wheel of his Porsche.

'I see you have been making good use of my car, little sister,' he teased as he got in and dumped his holdall at his feet.

'I love it, Marco,' she said, selecting first gear and pulling out of the car park. 'In fact, I find I have become quite addicted to driving it.'

He shrugged amicably. 'Have it if you want. It is not as if I am going to be here any longer to use it.'

'You are determined to stay in Italy, then?'

'Yes. I am enjoying the new challenge there.' He gave a relaxed smile. 'Now D'Alesandro Leisure is branching out into the specialist holiday market I am busier than ever.'

'I hear that Illario is being called back to Italy,' Felica said, easing off the accelerator as traffic ahead slowed, 'which means someone will be needed in London to look after the restaurant chain.'

'Yes, Father has offered it to me.'

'Ah, so there is a possibility—'

'No,' he interrupted. 'I am happy where I am. Of course, it would be rude to refuse outright so I have said I will consider it. However, it is merely delaying the inevitable. I shall not be returning to London.'

'I suppose I understand,' Felica empathised. 'Not only is it because of your work, I guess it is also that you are now with someone and you do not want to leave her behind in Italy.'

'No, that is not the reason. I do have girlfriends but there is no one special in my life.' He inclined his head thoughtfully. 'I have learned my lesson. After two bad experiences with women I do not intend to fall under anyone's spell again.'

'Your mathematics are rubbish,' she scolded, as they emerged from the Heathrow tunnel. 'You have had one bad experience, and Lottie was as much a victim as you.'

'Ah, so everything comes back to Charlotte. You are so predictable, my baby sister. Well, we can stop this attempt to match make before it goes any further.' His waved a finger at her. 'My visit is to see my son, that is all, and I have only agreed because both you and Ella have been quite relentless in your demands.'

'But Charlotte has made it clear she is happy to see you,' Felica said, determined not to let go of the subject. 'Does that not tell you something?'

'All it tells me is she has put the past behind her and has moved on, as I have.'

'Marco, you are so aggravating!'

'Let us not argue,' Marco said softly, eager to get away from this particular topic. 'What is my son called? I have no idea.'

'Luca Nicoli.'

'Luca after our grandfather?'

Felica nodded. 'Lottie asked me about family names before he was born and decided on Luca. Nicoli is for her own father, Nicholas. And if it had been a girl, she would have called her Isabetta, after your mother.'

Marco took a deep breath and looked out of the window; this was not the way he had envisaged things. He had only agreed to fly to the UK to see his son in order to placate his sister and Ella, who had been in touch regularly since their meeting in Italy. Knowing his son was named after his grandfather, he suddenly felt himself being drawn into something deeper; something that might see him losing control over the protective barrier he had so carefully built around his heart. And he knew how potentially dangerous that could be.

Finally arriving at the manor, Felica slipped from the driver's seat to allow him to continue his journey to Dartmouth.

He had booked into the Royal Castle Hotel, with the intention of arriving at Gulls' Rest at the agreed time of eleven the next morning to see Luca. Once his overnight bag was unpacked, he decided to call into the gallery and see Beth. It would be strictly a social call to say hello; he had no intention of becoming drawn into any more persuasive discussions regarding Charlotte. It was too late, neither of them could go back, but they could go forward, with a mutual love of their son to keep them in touch. After all this time, he realised, he still had affection for Charlotte, but that was it: affection. Anything beyond that was far too risky.

Beth was pleased to see him, full of excitement about her planned summer wedding to CJ. She made him coffee and they sat and chatted for a while. He thought about inviting her to dinner, aware he faced an evening alone in the hotel's dining room, but decided against tempting fate. It would be easy to drift into the wrong conversation, and it was important he approached his meeting with Charlotte clear-headed and free from any external female influence. Felica's comments had been quite enough.

At ten forty-five the next morning he found himself standing at Charlotte's front door. The house, as Beth had told him, was beautiful: white walls under a grey slate roof with large bay windows facing the road and an elegant landscaped garden. 'Wait until you see the back of the house, though,' she had said, 'it will take your breath away.' Those words echoed in his head and, unable to resist, he pulled his finger away from the doorbell and made his way around the side of the house instead. Beth was right; it was breath-taking, and he stood for a moment to take in the silver twist of river bordered by a riot of autumnal colour gracing its banks. The garden sloped down to the river in gentle tiers, a roped pathway to one side leading down to a small jetty, where a dinghy was moored.

The sound of a baby's cry coming from inside the house made him pull his gaze away from the river and back toward patio doors, which he saw were open. He stepped across the glass and chrome edged patio and when he reached the doors, he peered inside. He saw on the far side of the room a large wooden playpen, a dark head bobbing up and down within its confines. Cautiously, he stepped into the room, eager to make contact with the child he had come to see. Venturing deeper into the room, when he looked down into the playpen, he found dark eyes in a small face framed by black curls staring curiously up at him.

'Ah, Luca,' he said, reaching down and sweeping him up into his arms. The child relaxed into the crook of his arm then pushed a tiny fist into his mouth and sucked hard, brown eyes fixed on his. As Marco's hand splayed around to support the back of his son's head, he was filled with wonder that this small human being was actually part of him. Soft sound and a sudden movement to his right alerted him to the fact he was no longer alone in the room. He turned to find Charlotte standing in the doorway. Dressed in black trousers and a loose cream shirt, her dark hair tumbling around her shoulders, she looked relaxed and – his heart rocked – more beautiful than he remembered.

Charlotte had not heard his car arrive, but as she came down the stairs and paused to look out of the lower landing window, she caught sight of the red

Porsche parked outside. He was here at last; she felt a small stab of apprehension. Although she had made it clear she was willing to see him, now he was only seconds away she had no clue as to how they would be with each other after all this time. She felt she had made a huge concession allowing him to visit, especially, she thought, and not without a stab of bitterness, that it had taken Matt's words to bring him here. She was under no illusion that, had they not run into each other in Italy, this visit would not be happening. It was something that still sat heavily within her heart.

Waiting for a few moments, she anticipated the sound of the doorbell. When it did not come, she descended to the hall and threw open the front door. Finding no one there, she stepped back inside and made her way down the hall to the lounge at the rear. The sight as she entered the room made her stop and catch her breath. Marco, dressed casually in jeans and an all-weather jacket over a blue check shirt, was holding Luca, a rapt expression on his face. Aware of her presence, he turned and stared at her as if frozen to the spot. The moment soon passed, replaced with an expression of absolute joy wrapped around the wide smile he gave her.

'Charlotte, he is simply beautiful,' he said, as if the baby were the most miraculous thing in the world. 'Oh, I am sorry, this is very rude of me.' He shook his head, embarrassed, then kissing Luca's forehead, he bent over to return him gently back to the playpen. Straightening up, he came towards her. 'How are you?' He took her hands in his and held them for a moment, his dark eyes scanning hers.

'I am fine.' She smiled, feeling the warmth of his fingers. The forgotten magic his touch held pulsed through her, dancing its way down her spine, unexpectedly dredging up old memories and shaking the calm safety of the world she now inhabited.

'Can I get you a coffee or would you like something stronger?' she asked pulling from his grasp.

'Ah,' he said sighing, his face lighting up with the glorious smile she remembered so well. 'I would love a drink but as I am driving, coffee will be fine.'

'Come through to the kitchen.' She led the way, reprimanding herself; his effortless manner had so easily drawn her back to the way they had been with each other. Of course, he was still the same handsome man she had once loved, but their lives were separate now and, given the manner of their parting, it could be no other way.

'Are you happy here?' Marco looked at her over the rim of his coffee cup as they sat by the huge window looking out onto the river.

'Very. I can't say I miss London,' she answered truthfully. 'The pace is easy and I've made some good friends here. And, of course, there's Beth, although she'll be married to CJ soon and I doubt they'll be making their home here.' She gazed out of the window, thinking of the consequences.

Then she turned back to him, masking her sadness at the thought of losing a friend. 'Still, we can't expect things to stay the same, can we? And I'm truly happy for them. Is there anyone in your life at the moment?'

'Ah, you know, no one special; they come and go.' He heaved his shoulders and stared into his coffee cup. 'And what about you?'

She nodded, thoughts of Luca making her smile. 'Yes, one very important young man with dark eyes and black hair. He takes up a lot of my time but I love it. He makes me feel... fulfilled.'

'He is a good baby?'

'Always. He has your calm temperament.' She smiled again. 'I count myself very lucky.'

'Seeing him, I feel that way too.'

'Do you?'

'Of course. He is a beautiful child; a wonderful gift. Thank you.'

He reached for her hand, pulling it slowly towards his mouth, as he had so often before. The feel of his lips brushing her knuckles caused a ripple of unexpected emotion to flood through her body. It brought back memories of the warmth of his hands against her skin and the persuasive pressure of his mouth against her own.

'Would you like to see the house?' she asked, removing her hand, even more unsettled by the way his brown eyes were now fixing themselves on her.

'Yes, thank you.' Slowly getting to his feet, he paused to check his watch, 'And then I will have to think about leaving. I promised Felica I would spend some time with her this evening before I catch my flight back to Milan in the morning.'

'Of course.' Charlotte nodded, understanding. 'You must have a lot of catching up to do. This way.'

Marco's eyes were full of admiration as he stopped to make comments about the decoration and furnishing in each room.

'You have done a fantastic job,' he said, when she showed him into the master bedroom with its balcony. 'And so many rooms with such beautiful views. It must be wonderful to wake up here to this.' He walked out onto the balcony to look at the river. 'How I envy you.'

'Yes, it's beautiful,' Charlotte agreed, trying to push away the uninvited wish that he could be there beside her each morning. Seeing him again was bringing all those dormant feelings rushing back, the sensation building in her throat, making it difficult to swallow.

'You are miles away.'

She felt the gentle pressure of his hand on her arm.

'Sorry.' She turned to look at him, her automatic smile masking the emptiness she felt. 'The river does this to me sometimes; Beth is always telling me off.'

'Ah, but there is so much peace here. It is quite magical.' He gazed down at her with another of his heart-stopping smiles.

Charlotte looked away; she did not know how much longer she could bear this. But bear it she must, and would need to continue to do so in the future now he was part of Luca's life.

'Charlotte?' His fingers caught her chin and he turned her face towards his. 'I can see in your eyes there is much sorrow. Is it because I am here?'

She nodded, hoping maybe with this admission he would take her in his arms and comfort her the way he used to.

'Maybe it is time for me to go, then.' He turned back into the room and her hopes died. 'I never came with the intention of causing you unhappiness.'

He crossed to the door and she followed. At the bottom of the stairs, he turned and walked into the living room, where he retrieved Luca. Holding him closely for a while, he talked to his son quietly then, with a final kiss against his soft cheek, lowered him gently back into the playpen. Moving back into the hall, Charlotte reached the front door and swung it open. Marco stepped through and turned to look at her. His expression became serious, guarded, as if he was holding something back.

'I will let you know when I am in the UK again,' he said. 'Goodbye, and thank you for giving me something so precious.'

He bent his head towards her and Charlotte closed her eyes, lifting her face to him, anticipating, hoping. One kiss, one simple gentle pressure of his mouth against her own that might cause him to change his mind and make him realise the love they had was not over, but simply lost in all the chaos they had been caught up in. A love which currently sat like a tiny glow in the dark needing only his lips against her own for it to flame and burn again. The pressure of his mouth when it came, however, fell disappointingly on her forehead and then he was walking away.

She watched as his car reversed, turned and then with a final wave of farewell, he was gone. Slowly, she walked back into the house, closing the door behind her. Moments later, she emerged onto the rear patio and stared at the river. As a sudden flurry of wind sent a multi-colour swirl of red-gold leaves cascading out across the water, Charlotte hung her head and wept.

The jangle of the bell caused Beth to halt her picture hanging activities in the rear of the gallery. Stepping off the small ladder, she went to investigate. She found Marco sitting on one of her comfortable couches, his hands covering his face.

'Marco, what's wrong? Have you seen Lottie?'

'Yes.' His answer came muffled through his fingers.

'Have you argued or something?'

'No.'

Kneeling in front of him, Beth prised his fingers away from his face.

'Please tell me what is wrong?'

'Heaven help me, Beth, I still love her.' She could see the raw pain etched in his features as he looked at her.

'Have you told her this? Has she rejected you? Is that why you're so upset?'

'No, it is nothing like that.'

'What then?'

'When we were together there were times when all I wanted to do was hold her, but I was afraid. There was something in her face which made me feel she felt the same as I did but I was not sure, so I held back. It was only when I had driven away I realised I should have told her how I...' He sat up and rubbed a tired hand over his face. 'Once again it is too late.'

Beth got to her feet. 'No, Marco, no, it isn't. She called about ten minutes ago. She was tearful, said she had made the biggest mistake of her life in letting you go. It appears she loves you too.'

'What!' He sat back, his eyes filled with surprise.

Luca was now peacefully asleep. Pulling a jacket over her thick sweater and jeans, Charlotte headed down the pathway to the jetty where she now stood watching the autumn sunlight filtering through the trees on the far bank of the river. Despite her call to Beth, the sadness she felt at Marco's departure had not lifted. She hoped her friend's imminent arrival and a heart-to-heart over a large glass of wine would help numb the sorrow she was currently feeling. Footsteps on the boarded steps behind told her Beth had arrived.

'Okay, Beth, guilty as charged, I'm here day dreaming again,' she said, not bothering to turn around as she waited for her friend's usual teasing reprimand.

'So you are, Charlotte. It appears to be a habit you are very fond of.'

'Marco!' She swung around in surprise to see him standing a few steps above, hands pushed into his jacket, his dark eyes fixed on her thoughtfully. 'Did you leave something behind?'

'Yes, it seems I have misplaced an extremely valuable item.' He smiled as he descended the few steps, closing the gap between them and reaching out to capture her face in his hands, splaying his long fingers across her cheeks. He kissed her with a passion that left her breathless.

'It is you I left behind,' he said as he pulled away to look at her, his eyes tinged with moisture. 'I find I cannot live without you. In fact, I do not want to live without you.' He shook his head. 'Charlotte, I am so sorry. You did not deserve what happened... I am guilty of so much—'

'Marco, please,' she interrupted, her expression serious as she looked up into his face. 'We cannot change what has happened in the past. All we have is now and the future. I love you. Despite all that happened to us, I don't think I ever really stopped, and I don't care if I have to spend half my life in airport lounges as long as we can be—'

Marco placed a finger against her lips. 'Ah, but I will not be in Italy for much longer. My father has asked me to return to London to manage the restaurant chain again and, well, I have decided to accept.'

'You're coming back to work in the UK?'

'No.' He wrapped his arms around her, pressing his lips close to hers again. 'I am coming back to make a new life with my son and the woman I love.'

ABOUT THE AUTHOR

Born and raised in rural Wiltshire, Jo Lambert grew up with a love of books and a vivid imagination. As a child, she enjoyed creating her own adventure stories similar to Enid Blyton's *Famous Five*. Writing always stayed with her, but college, work and eventually marriage found it kept very much in the background as a hobby. In 2009 everything changed when she decided to self-publish a novel she had completed. After *When Tomorrow Comes,* three other books – *Love Lies and Promises, The Ghost of You and Me* and *Between Today and Yesterday* – followed. In 2013 she decided to give up full-time work to concentrate fully on her writing.

Jo is married and lives in a village on the eastern edge of Bath with one small grey feline called Mollie. She shares her husband with Bridget – a 48-year-old white MG Midget. 'She's his hobby car and keeps him occupied while I'm in front of the PC,' says Jo.

ALSO PUBLISHED BY THORNBERRY PUBLISHING

FICTION

A DRIFT OF DAISIES by Avis Randall

A KETTLE OF FISH by Ali Bacon

DIAMOND HEART by Tricia Jones

EVERY STEP OF THE WAY by Kit Domino

GHOST OF WIDDECOT MANOR by Hazel Eggleton

LIFE AFTER 6 TEQUILAS by Gina Rossi

MEGAN by Carole Llewellyn

MINI SKIRTS & LAUGHTER LINES by Carol E Wyer

POLAR NIGHTS by Simon Hacker

SO, YOU THINK YOU'RE A CELEBRITY… CHEF?
by Caroline James

SURFING IN STILETTOES by Carol E Wyer

TIME OUT OF MIND by Shirley Wright

TOUGH LUCK by Nina Milton

WATER'S EDGE by Jane Riddell

NON FICTION

JUSTINE'S JOURNEY by Justine Forrest

WORDS'WORTH: A FICTION WRITER'S GUIDE TO SERIOUS
EDITING
by Jane Riddell

YOGA FOR WRITERS by Tricia Jones

http:/www.thornberrypublishing.com

Lightning Source UK Ltd.
Milton Keynes UK
UKOW04f1334240914

239097UK00015B/677/P